THE NIGHTINGALE GIRLS

Three very different girls sign up as trainee nurses at a big London teaching hospital in 1934. **DORA** Leaves her overcrowded, squalid working-class home for a better life. But has she got what it takes to keep up with other, better-eduated girls? **HELEN** Born for the job, her brother is a doctor, her all-powerful mother a hospital trustee. But will Helen's secret misery be her downfall? **MILLIE** An aristocratic rebel, her carefree attitude will find her up in front of Matron again and again. Will she ever care enough to make a nurse? Or will she go back to the glamorous life she was born to?

THE NIGHTINGALE GIRLS

The Nightingale Girls

by

Donna Douglas

Magna Large Print Books
Long Preston, North Yorkshire,
BD23 4ND, England.

British Library Cataloguing in Publication Data.

Douglas, Donna
    The Nightingale girls.

    A catalogue record of this book is
    available from the British Library

    ISBN   978-0-7505-3633-2

First published in Great Britain in 2012 by Arrow Books

Copyright © Donna Douglas 2012

Cover illustration © Colin Thomas

Donna Douglas has asserted her right under the Copyright, Designs
and Patents Act, 1988 to be identified as the author of this work

A catalogue record for this book is available from the British Library

Published in Large Print 2013 by arrangement with
Random House Group Ltd.

Magna Large Print is an imprint of Library Magna Books Ltd.

Printed and bound in Great Britain by
T.J. (International) Ltd., Cornwall, PL28 8RW

Chapter One

'Tell me, Miss Doyle. What makes you think you could ever be a nurse here?'

After growing up in the slums of Bethnal Green, not much frightened Dora Doyle. But her stomach was fluttering with nerves as she faced the Matron of the Nightingale Teaching Hospital in her office on that warm September afternoon. She sat tall and upright behind a heavy mahogany desk, an imposing figure in black, her face framed by an elaborate white headdress, grey eyes fixed expectantly on Dora.

Dora wiped her damp palms on her skirt. She was sweating inside her coat, but she didn't dare take it off in case Matron noticed the frayed cuffs of her blouse.

'Well–' she began, then stopped. Why did she think she could ever be a nurse? Living on the other side of Victoria Park from the Nightingale, she had often seen the young women coming and going through the gates, dressed in their red-lined cloaks. For as long as she could remember she'd dreamed of being one of them.

But dreams like that didn't come true for the likes of Dora Doyle. Like any other East End girl, her destiny lay in the sweatshops or one of the factories that lined the overcrowded stretch of the Thames.

So she'd left school at fourteen to earn her living

at Gold's Garments, and tried to make the best of it. But the dream hadn't gone away. It grew bigger and bigger inside her, until four years later she had taken her courage in her hands and written a letter of application.

'What have you got to lose?' Mr Gold's daughter Esther had said. 'You'll never know if you don't try, *bubele*.' She'd even lent Dora her lucky necklace charm to wear for the interview. She could feel the warm metal sticking to her damp skin beneath her blouse.

'It's a hamsa,' Esther had explained as Dora admired the exquisite little silver hand on its delicate chain. 'My people believe it brings good fortune.'

Dora hoped the hamsa's powers weren't just extended to Jews. She needed all the help she could get.

'I'm keen and I'm very hard-working,' she found the words at last. 'And I'm a quick learner. I don't need telling twice.'

'So your reference says.' Matron looked down at the letter in front of her. 'This Miss Gold clearly thinks a lot of you.'

Dora blushed at the compliment. Esther had taken a real chance, writing that reference behind her father's back; old Jacob would go mad if he found out his daughter was helping one of his employees to find another job. 'Miss Esther reckons I'm one of her best girls on the machines. I've got the hands, she says.'

She saw Matron looking at her hands and quickly knotted them in her lap so the woman wouldn't see her bitten-down nails, or the calluses the size of mothballs that covered her fingers.

'Grafter's hands', her mother called them. But they didn't look like the right kind of hands to soothe a fevered brow.

'I have no doubt you're a hard worker, Miss Doyle,' Matron said. 'But then so is every girl who comes in here. And most of them are far better qualified than you.'

Dora's chin lifted. 'I've got my certificates. I went back to night school to get them.'

'So I see.' Matron's voice was soft, with an underlying note of steel. 'But, as you know, the Nightingale is one of the best teaching hospitals in London. We have girls from all over the country wanting to train here.' She met Dora's eyes steadily across the desk. 'So why should we accept you and not them? What makes *you* so special, Miss Doyle?'

Dora dropped her gaze to stare at the herringbone pattern of the polished parquet. She wanted to tell this woman how she took care of her younger brother and sisters, and had even helped bring the youngest, Little Alfie, into the world two years ago. She wanted to explain how she'd nursed Nanna Winnie through a bad bout of bronchitis last winter when everyone thought she'd had it for sure.

Most of all, she wanted to talk about Maggie, her beautiful sister, who'd died when Dora was twelve years old. She'd sat beside her bed for three days, watching her slip away. It was Maggie's death more than anything that had made her want to become a nurse and to stop other families suffering the way hers had.

But her mother didn't like them talking about

9

their personal business to anyone. And it probably wasn't the clever answer Matron was looking for anyway.

'Nothing,' she said, defeated. 'I'm nothing special.' Just plain Dora Doyle, the ginger-haired girl from Griffin Street.

She wasn't even special in her family. Peter was the eldest, Little Alfie the youngest. Josie was the prettiest and Bea the naughtiest. And then there was Dora, stuck in the middle.

'I see.' Matron paused. She seemed almost disappointed, Dora thought. 'Well, in that case, I don't think there's much more to say.' She began gathering up her notes. 'We will write to you and let you know our decision in due course. Thank you, Miss Doyle...'

Dora felt a surge of panic. She'd let herself down. She could feel the moment ebbing away, and with it all her hopes. She would never wear the red-lined cloak and walk with pride like those other girls. It would be back to the machines at Gold's Garments for her until her eyes went or her fingers became so bent with rheumatism she couldn't work any more.

Esther Gold's words came back to her. *What have you got to lose?*

'Give me a chance,' she blurted out.

Matron looked askance at her. 'I beg your pardon?'

Dora could feel her face flaming to the roots of her hair, but she had to speak up. 'I know I don't have as much proper schooling as the other girls, but I'll work really hard, I promise.' The words were falling over themselves as she tried to get

10

them out before she lost her nerve.

'Really, Miss Doyle, I hardly think–'

'You won't regret it, I swear. I'll be the best nurse this place has ever seen. Just give me the chance. Please?' she begged.

Matron's brows lifted towards the starched edge of her headdress. 'And if I don't?'

'I'll apply again, here or somewhere else. And I'll keep on applying until someone says yes,' Dora declared defiantly. 'I'll be a nurse one day. And I'll be a good one, too.'

Matron stared at her so hard Dora felt her heart sink to her borrowed shoes.

'Thank you, Miss Doyle,' she said. 'I think I've heard enough.'

Matron Kathleen Fox watched from the window as Dora Doyle hurried across the courtyard towards the gates, head down, hands thrust into her pockets. The poor girl couldn't get away fast enough.

'Well?' she asked Miss Hanley. 'What did you think?'

'I'm sure it's not my place to say, Matron.'

Kathleen smiled to herself. Her Assistant Matron's mouth was puckering with the effort of not voicing her opinion. Veronica Hanley was a tall, broad-shouldered woman, strong-featured, with sensibly short greying hair, large hands and a deep, booming voice. 'Manly Hanley' Kathleen had overheard some of the younger nurses calling her. She had just turned fifty, a good ten years older than Kathleen herself, and had been at the Nightingale since she was a pro. She struck terror into the hearts of all the nurses, including the sisters. Even Kathleen sometimes had to remind herself who was in charge.

'All the same, I would value your opinion,' she said.

'Her shoes were scuffed, there was a hole in her stocking and a button coming loose on her coat,' Miss Hanley said without hesitation.

'I'll admit she was hardly promising.'

'She could barely string two words together.'

'That's quite true.'

Matron was used to interviewing girls who couldn't wait to gush about their talents, their dedication to nursing and their admiration for Florence Nightingale. But Dora Doyle had just sat there, staring out from under that explosion of frizzy red hair like a trapped rabbit.

And yet there was something about her, a spark of determination in those green eyes, that made Matron think she had real potential.

'Perhaps she might be better applying to the Infirmary?' Miss Hanley suggested.

The City Infirmary was an old Poor Law hospital, a former workhouse just down the river in Poplar. It was small, badly funded and run by ill-trained staff and auxiliaries. It also had a shocking reputation among the locals, who referred to it as The Graveyard.

'After all, she's hardly Nightingale's material, is she?' Miss Hartley went on.

They were interrupted by the maid bringing in afternoon tea. They paused as she set the tray down on the console table just inside the door and arranged the bone china cups and saucers.

12

'What makes you say that, Miss Hartley?' Kathleen asked when the girl had gone.

'I would have thought that was obvious. We only accept girls with education and breeding.'

'Miss Doyle is adequately qualified.'

'From a night school!' Miss Hartley's lips curled over the words.

'Which surely shows determination and character, if nothing else.' Kathleen moved across to the table to pour the tea. 'I can't imagine it was easy for a young girl, working long hours in a garment factory then trooping off to study in the evening, can you?'

'That may be. But it takes more than that to be suitable for the Nightingale.'

It certainly does, Kathleen thought as she passed a cup to her.

As the Nightingale was a prestigious teaching hospital, it tended to attract girls of a certain background. Well-bred, well-spoken, middle-class girls who were looking for a respectable way to fill their time until they found themselves a young doctor to marry.

It was the same in most hospitals, she knew. But even more so at the Nightingale. Sometimes when she heard the young students talking among themselves, she wondered if she'd accidentally strayed into an exclusive finishing school.

Miss Hanley had even boasted that the previous Matron's sure-fire way of discovering if a girl was suitable for training was to ask if she belonged to a tennis club. Kathleen doubted if Dora Doyle had ever seen a tennis racquet, let alone picked one up. But she was passionate, determined, and

13

obviously no stranger to hard work. Which was more than could be said for many of the students who came through the Nightingale's doors. Most of them were totally unprepared for the rigours of nursing; many of them didn't make it through the twelve weeks of preliminary training.

'Obviously it's your decision, Matron,' Miss Hanley conceded stiffly. 'But I have to say, girls of that class seldom do well as nurses. They simply don't have the character for it.'

'Oh, I don't think Miss Doyle is short of character.' Kathleen lifted the teacup to conceal her smile.

She wondered what Miss Hanley would say if she knew that Kathleen was once just like Dora Doyle, a millworker's daughter from a small Lancashire town, who had dreamed of something beyond life in the blowing room of a cotton mill. She too had once sat across the desk from a forbidding-looking Matron and begged for the chance to show what she could do. And now look at her. Barely forty and already in charge of the nursing staff of one of the country's top teaching hospitals. Sometimes she had to pinch herself to believe it was true. Not everyone approved, of course. She knew there were some people at the Nightingale who thought that she and her newfangled ideas would lead to the ruination of the hospital's good name.

Change was a dirty word at the Nightingale. The hospital had been run the same way for the last thirty years, under the iron rule of its old Matron. And when she retired, many had believed Miss Hanley was the natural choice to carry on her good work – including Miss Hanley herself. But the Board of Trustees decided the Nightingale needed new blood, and so Kathleen had been appointed instead.

Now, after a month in the job, she still felt like the new girl. She could hear the whispers of the senior staff following her down the corridors as she did her morning rounds, everyone wondering what to make of the new Matron, who smiled too much and talked to the young nurses in the same friendly way she did to the senior consultants.

It didn't help that Miss Hanley didn't miss a chance to remind her: 'That really isn't the way we do things here at the Nightingale, Matron.'

She went to look out of the window. Beyond the gracious Georgian façade of its main building which fronted the road overlooking Victoria Park, the Nightingale Hospital was a sprawl of blocks, extensions and outbuildings arranged loosely around a central paved courtyard with a small cluster of plane trees at its centre. These housed the wards, the operating block and the dispensary. Beyond them lay more buildings, including the dining rooms, nurses' homes and the doctors' quarters.

Up until a few weeks ago her office had also been situated down there. But when she took over as Matron, Kathleen had insisted on moving into the main hospital building so she could be closer to the wards.

It had caused much consternation among the senior nursing staff. 'Why does she need to keep an eye on us?' the disgruntled sisters asked amongst themselves – stirred up, Kathleen

15

suspected, by Miss Hanley. But it was worth the trouble. She was now in the heart of the hospital, where she belonged. Not only was she closer at hand to deal with emergencies on the wards, but her new office gave her a good view over the courtyard, where she could see everyone going about their business.

The damp chill of early September had given way to a few glorious days of Indian summer. Patients basked in their wheelchairs under the shade of the plane trees, enjoying the autumn sunshine. As she watched, a young nurse emerged through the archway from the dining block, heading back across the courtyard to the wards, doing the brisk heel-toe walk that almost but didn't quite break the 'no running' rule.

As if she knew she was being watched, the girl suddenly caught Kathleen's eye. She ducked her head, but not before Kathleen saw the guilty flush on her cheeks.

She turned away, smiling to herself. 'So you don't think we should give Miss Doyle a chance?' she said.

'I don't believe she would fit in.'

I know how she feels, Kathleen thought.

Perhaps for once Miss Hanley had a point. If the new Matron couldn't even fit in, how would someone like Dora Doyle ever cope?

Chapter Two

Dora had managed to convince herself she didn't want to be a nurse by the time the letter came.

She was walking back to Griffin Street with her friend Ruby Pike on a drizzly October evening after their shift at Gold's when her little sister Beatrice came running up the street, boots undone, curls flying.

'All right, Bea? Where's the fire?' Dora laughed.

'Your letter from the hospital's come!' she panted. At eleven years old she looked like a miniature version of Dora, with her snub nose, ginger hair and freckled face. 'Nanna wanted to open it but Mum says we've got to wait for you. Come on!' She pulled at her sister's hand, dragging her along the street.

Dora looked at Ruby. 'This is it,' she said.

'Just think, this time next month you'll be out of that ruddy sweatshop!' Ruby grinned back.

'I doubt it.' Dora knew she'd made a proper fool of herself in the interview. She was surprised they'd even bothered to write.

''Course you will. They'd be daft not to take you on. Haven't we always said, you've got the brains and I've got the looks?'

Dora grinned. With her wavy blonde hair and buxom curves, Ruby looked more like a movie star than a machinist. But she could have been clever too, if she hadn't been too busy flirting

17

with the boys at school.

Ruby saw Dora's smile wobble and took her arm, propelling her down the street after Bea, who'd run on ahead to warn the rest of the family at number twenty-eight.

'Stop worrying, you'll get in,' she said. 'You're doing the right thing, I reckon. I wouldn't mind being a nurse myself, come to think of it. Think of all those handsome doctors. Not to mention all those rich old men with incurable diseases, just waiting to die and leave me all their worldly goods!'

'I think the idea is to keep them alive, Rube.'

They reached Dora's front doorstep. 'Go on.' Ruby gave her a little shove. 'You can't put it off forever, y'know.'

'I wish I could.' She dreaded seeing the disappointment on her mum's face. Dora might have given up on the idea, but it was all Rose Doyle talked about.

'Well, you can't. Now get in there before your nanna changes her mind and opens it for you. Let me know how you get on, won't you?' said Ruby as she let herself in next door.

'I won't need to,' Dora said. 'If I get in, you'll be able to hear my mum screaming all the way to Aldgate!'

The letter was on the kitchen mantelpiece, tucked behind the old clock. The rest of the family were ranged around the fireplace, doing anything but looking at it. Dora's mum Rose was mending shirts, while her younger sisters Josie and Bea played cards and Nanna Winnie peeled potatoes while sitting in her old rocking chair. The only one who genuinely paid no attention was Little Alfie, who played with his wooden train on the rug instead.

Her mother pushed the mending off her lap and shot to her feet as soon as Dora walked in. 'There you are, love,' she greeted her with a fixed smile. 'Had a good day? I'll put the kettle on, shall I?'

'Oh, for Gawd's sake!' Nanna Winnie rolled her eyes and dropped another potato in the pan of water at her feet. 'Dora, open that bleeding letter and put your mother out of her misery or we shall never get any peace in this house. She's been on pins all day.'

Dora pulled out the letter from behind the clock and stared down at the Nightingale's crest: the silhouette of a woman carrying a lamp. The thick cream envelope felt heavy. Her heart started to flutter in her chest.

'Can I read it on my own?' she asked her mother. She knew it would be bad news and she needed time to compose herself before she faced her family.

'No, you bleeding cannot!' Nanna Winnie snapped. 'We haven't sat here all afternoon so you can go and–'

'Of course you can, love.' Rose Doyle shot her mother a silencing look. 'You just take your time.'

'But don't be too long about it,' her grand-mother warned. 'I told you we should have steamed it open,' Dora heard Nanna Winnie saying as she let herself out of the back door. 'She would never have known if we was careful.'

Their narrow strip of back yard was sunless and damp, overshadowed by a high brick wall that separated it from the railway line high above. Dora took refuge in the privy at the end. The cold October wind whistled through the gaps in the old wooden door as she sat on the weathered pine seat and read her letter by the fading evening light.

Dear Miss Doyle,
The Board of Governors of the Nightingale's Teaching Hospital is pleased to inform you that you have been accepted in their three-year programme leading to State Registration. Please report to Sister Sutton at the Junior Nurses' Home on Tuesday, 6 November 1934 after 4 p.m. Enclosed is a list of equipment you must bring with you. You will also need to send us the following measurements for your uniform, which will be waiting for you when you arrive...

A train rumbled past, rattling the privy door and shaking the ground under her feet, while Dora read the words over and over again, right down to the signature: Kathleen Fox (Matron). Then she snatched up the envelope and checked the address, just to make sure it had come to the right person.

She lowered the letter and stared ahead of her at the yellowing squares of newspaper stuck on a rusty nail on the back of the door. From somewhere outside she could hear their neighbour June Riley singing tunelessly. The sound seemed to be coming from miles away. None of it felt real.

When she finally emerged she found her mother in the yard, sweeping the cracked paving slabs, her eyes fixed on the privy door. She froze when she saw Dora.

'Well?' she said.

Dora nodded, not trusting herself to speak. Rose Doyle gave a yelp of joy and dropped her birch broom with a clatter.

'You did it!' she cried, putting her arm around Dora. 'Oh, Dor, I'm so proud of you!'

The rest of the family, who had been gathered around the back door, came out of the house and suddenly Dora was lost in a clamour of jumping, cheering and hugs. Nanna Winnie looked on from the doorway, her arms folded across her chest.

'I don't know why she's bothering,' she grumbled. 'The glue factory was good enough for you and me, Rosie. Why does she have to be different?'

Next door, June Riley flung open the back door and stuck her head out, her thin face framed by a halo of spiky curlers. 'Hello, what's all the ruck about?'

'Our Dora's going to be a nurse,' Rose called back, loudly enough for the rest of the street to hear.

June rushed out into the back yard in her dressing gown and slippers and stepped over the section of fence where the slats had broken, into the Doyles' back yard.

'Fancy, our little Dora, a nurse!' Dora could smell the gin on June's breath as she was trapped in her bony embrace. 'Wait till I tell my Nick. He's a porter up at the hospital, he'll look after you.'

'We know all about your Nick,' Nanna Winnie muttered. 'You stay away from him, Dora. There's plenty of girls round here wish they'd done the same, the dirty little sod.'

'Nanna!' Dora hissed, as June moved over to

hug Rose.

'I speak as I find,' Nanna said primly. She looked at June and shook her head. 'Look at the state of her. I expect she's just got up. Down the pub till all hours, I daresay.'

Dora blushed, but luckily June hadn't heard Nanna. Drink made June Riley unpredictable, and she was as likely to go for Nanna Winnie with a poker as she was to laugh it off. They'd lived next door to the Rileys for the last ten years, ever since Dora's father had died and they'd moved back in with Nanna Winnie. Poor June had turned to drink four years ago when her husband ran off, leaving her to bring up her two sons alone.

The Turnbulls and the Prossers came out of the house they shared on the other side, to see what all the noise was about, and Rose recounted their news over and over again. It gave Dora a warm glow to see the pride on her mother's face; this was her moment of triumph as much as Dora's own.

'It's good news, then? What did I tell you?' Ruby stuck her head out of the upstairs window, alongside her mum Lettie's. She and June greeted each other with the curtest of nods. The Pikes lived upstairs from the Rileys, but the two women rarely saw eye to eye. 'What am I going to do without you, Dor? Gold's Garments won't be the same!'

'You'll have to find someone else to cover for you while you sneak outside for a fag!' Dora called up to her.

'I won't have anyone to have a laugh with, that's for sure. They're a miserable lot there. And as for that cow Esther–' Ruby rolled her eyes.

'She's all right,' Dora said, thinking of the

22

hamsa, still nestling under her blouse. She'd tried to return it, but Esther had insisted she keep it.

'Only 'cos you're her favourite.'

'You'd be her favourite too, if you put a bit of effort into your work and didn't give her so much cheek!'

'I put enough effort into that place just by turning up, thank you very much. I'm not killing myself to line that old Jew's pockets!'

'I hope you don't think you'll have it easy?' Lettie joined in. She worked as a ward maid at the Nightingale. Unlike her pretty, easy-going daughter, she was a thin-faced, sour little woman, always ready to look on the black side of life. 'I've seen the way they treat them up at that hospital. They work them into the ground, and keep them locked up in that home like nuns. It's do this, do that, all day long. And those young nurses are right stuck up, too. Very posh they are, don't give the likes of us the time of day.' She looked Dora up and down. 'Don't know as they'll take to you.'

'Gawd, Mum, do you have to be so bloody cheerful all the time?' Ruby rolled her eyes at Dora.

'I'm only telling the truth,' Lettie said huffily.

'Take no notice of her,' Nanna Winnie muttered as Lettie and Ruby went back inside and closed the window. 'She's always been a bitter old cow. Just because her daughter's a trollop.'

'Nanna! That's my best mate you're talking about.'

'That doesn't stop her being a trollop, does it? Like I said, I speak as I find.'

'They're not really going to lock you up, are they,

23

Dora?' her sister Josie asked. She was fourteen, and the only one of her sisters not to inherit their father's red curls and sturdy figure. Josie was dark, slender and pretty like their mother.

"Course they're not, Jose. But I will have to live at the nurses' home.'

'How long for?'

'Dunno. Forever, I s'pose.'

'You mean, you won't live here with us no more?' Josie's wide brown eyes filled with tears as she took in the news.

'I'll be able to come and visit,' Dora said. 'I'll keep an eye on you all, make sure you're keeping up with your schoolwork and Bea's behaving herself.'

'That'll be the day!'

'Then you'll just have to keep her in line, won't you?' Dora put her arm around her sister's skinny shoulders. 'You're the big sister now, Josie. It's your turn to show the little ones what's what.'

'I'll try,' Josie promised. 'I'll miss you, Dor,' she whispered.

'I'll miss you too.'

As she looked around the shabby back yard, it began to dawn on Dora what she was leaving. Griffin Street was far from fancy. The narrow terrace of cramped houses, overshadowed by looming railway arches, had seen better days. Brickwork cracked, roofs sagged, and damp seeped through the walls.

Dora's stepfather Alf had been all for renting them a better place when he and Rose got married. He was earning enough for them to move into one of those new blocks of flats the Corporation was building, with electricity, inside toilets, proper bathrooms and the rest of it. But Rose wouldn't go without her mum, and Winnie had no intention of leaving the only home she'd known for fifty years.

'I've lived here since I got married, and they'll have to carry me out in my box,' she'd declared. 'I don't want to live somewhere not a soul speaks to each other.'

And she was right. In spite of its faults, Griffin Street was a close-knit community of neighbours who laughed together, cried together, and saw each other through good times and bad. There was always someone to have a giggle with, a shoulder to cry on or to lend you a few bob when the rent man was due.

At least when Rose married Alf, they had been able to afford to take over the whole house, instead of making do all cramped together in a couple of rooms on the ground floor, as they had been.

It still wasn't grand. They did all their cooking on an ancient range in the kitchen, and washed at the sink in the tiny curtained-off scullery. But it was homely, and Rose kept it like a palace. The step was whitestoned every day, the windows shone, net curtains sparkled and the house always smelt of polish.

Dora knew she'd miss it. But there was one person she wouldn't miss.

'Aye-aye. What's all this, then?' As if on cue, Alf Doyle stood in the back doorway, smiling around at the scene. He was a big man, over six foot tall, with thick black hair, a broad face and bright blue eyes.

Bea ran to him, Little Alfie toddling behind her, and he scooped them up easily, one under each arm.

'We're celebrating.' Rose's face lit up at the sight of her husband. 'Dora's got a place to train as a nurse.'

'Is that right?' Alf turned to face her, the two children still wriggling under his arms. 'Aren't you the clever one?'

'But she's got to leave home and move away forever,' Josie put in.

'Has she now? I don't remember anyone asking me if that was all right,' he frowned.

'You can't stop me,' Dora's chin lifted defiantly.

'I can do what I like until you're twenty-one, my girl.' Their eyes met, clashing in mute challenge.

'He's only teasing,' her mother broke the tense silence. 'Your dad would never stop you bettering yourself.'

'He's not my dad.'

'I still say what goes.'

Not for much longer, Dora was about to say. Then she caught the pleading look in her mother's eyes and kept silent.

'We should celebrate,' Nanna suggested. 'I dunno about you, but I reckon a nice bottle of stout would go down a treat.'

'Good idea,' Rose said brightly. 'What do you say, Alf?'

All eyes turned to him. Still glaring at Dora, he lowered Bea and Little Alfie to the ground and dug into his pocket.

'Not seeing your miserable boat race around here would be a cause for celebration, I s'pose.'

26

He pulled out a handful of change. 'Josie, go to the chippie. Fish and chips all round, I reckon.'

'But I've made a stew!' Nanna Winnie protested.

Alf grimaced. 'All the more reason to get fish and chips, then.'

'Can I have a saveloy?' Bea asked.

'You can have anything you like, my darlin', as long as it keeps you quiet.'

Dora watched her mother as she followed him inside. At forty-two years old, Rose was still a beautiful woman. Her dark hair was threaded with grey but no one would ever have guessed her slim figure had brought six children into the world.

'I wish you wouldn't talk back to him like that,' Nanna said to Dora as they went back inside. 'Alf's not a bad bloke. And he makes your mum happy. She deserves that, after everything she's been through.'

Dora knew her mum hadn't had much to smile about over the years. Widowed at thirty-two with five children, she had struggled to bring up her family on her own. She'd had to work all hours, cleaning offices and taking in mending for the local laundry.

And then, when Dora was thirteen, Alf Doyle had come into their lives. He didn't look like anyone's idea of a knight in shining armour, with his big lumbering body and hands like ham hocks. But he had certainly rescued Rose Doyle and her kids.

A gentle giant, everyone called him. He worked as a van driver on the railways. Not the best-paid job in the world, but it was steady and at least he didn't have to line up with the other men at the dock gates every morning, looking for work.

Everyone said Rose was lucky. After all, it wasn't every man who would take on a widow and all those children. But Alf loved the kids as if they were his own. He took them all on outings to the coast and the countryside and the boating lake at Victoria Park, treated them to sweets and ice creams and all kinds of other delights.

Dora couldn't have hated him more if she'd tried.

By the time Josie returned with the food, they'd warmed the plates and were crowded around the table. The hot fried rock salmon and chips was a lot better than Nanna Winnie's notoriously inedible stew, especially when Dora was allowed the batter scraps soaked in salt and vinegar to celebrate her big achievement.

'Don't suppose they'll be feeding you like this in that nurses' home!' Rose said.

'It's hard work, from what I hear,' Alf mumbled through a mouthful of chips.

'I'm not afraid of hard work,' Dora said.

'A bit of hard work never hurt anyone.' Nanna Winnie took out her teeth and slipped them into her pocket.

'Mum!' Rose protested. 'Do you have to do that at the table?'

'Why not? I don't need 'em now I've finished eating. And they rub my gums raw.'

After tea, Dora and Josie cleared the plates away while Alf relaxed in his armchair beside the fire. Rose sat opposite with her mending, while Nanna Winnie half dozed in her rocking chair.

'You know what I'm going to do one day, Rosie?'

Alf said. 'Buy you a house. A proper modern house, out in Loughton near your sister Brenda's place. You'd like that, wouldn't you? Somewhere with a decent garden, not that stinking little back yard.'

'Oi, do you mind? That back yard's been good enough for me all these years,' Nanna said, opening one eye. But Alf wasn't listening.

'You can grow flowers, and I can grow fruit and veg, and keep chickens. And we'll have electricity in all the rooms.'

'I don't hold with electricity,' Nanna grumbled.

'That sounds nice.' Rose smiled down at her mending. She never stopped working, no matter what the occasion. King George himself could come round for his tea, and Rose would still be turning the collars on a couple of shirts.

'Nice? It'll be more than nice, love. And it's what you deserve.' Alf scratched his expanded belly and sighed with contentment. 'I'm the luckiest man in the world, do you know that? I've got a beautiful wife, lovely kids – what more could a man ask for, eh?'

'Listen to him go on, making all kinds of stupid promises he can't keep,' Dora whispered to Josie as they loaded plates into the sink in the scullery. 'I don't know how Mum puts up with it.'

'She doesn't mind.' Josie shrugged, stacking the dishes in the deep sink. 'She knows how Alf likes to talk.'

'All the same, I wish he'd shut up about the bloody house in Loughton. He's only a van driver, not Governor of the Bank of England.'

'Dora!' Josie laughed at her in surprise. 'I don't

know why you don't like him.'

Dora looked at her sister. Josie was very grown-up for her age. There were four years between them, but since their middle sister Maggie had died they'd become more like friends than sisters. They had once shared all kinds of secrets, tucked together in their big bed, whispering and laughing together under the covers so Bea couldn't hear.

But there were some secrets Dora couldn't share, not even with her sister.

'I just don't,' she mumbled, picking a plate off the draining board to dry. 'I won't miss him when I leave, that's for sure.'

'Don't talk about leaving, I don't like it,' Josie said, pulling a face. Then in the next breath she added, 'Do you think I could have your old bedroom when you go?'

'No!' She shouted it so forcefully Josie stared at her in surprise.

'Why not? It's no fun being stuck in a bed with Bea. She kicks me in the night, and she snores worse than Nanna. And she's so nosey too. She's always into my things.'

'All the same, you don't want to be in my old room. It's so cold and draughty, and – it's haunted.'

Josie's dark eyes widened. 'You've never said.'

'That's 'cos I've never wanted to frighten you. But there's a ghost all right.'

Just then Rose appeared in the scullery doorway, her cheeks flushed pink from the port and lemon she'd had.

'Everything all right?' she asked. 'I thought I heard our Dora shouting.'

'She says her bedroom's haunted,' Josie said.

Dora didn't meet her mother's eye, but she could feel her frown. 'Your sister's having you on,' she said briskly. 'The only thing haunts this place is your Nanna. And she'd be enough to scare any ghost off. Now Dora, stop filling Josie's head with nonsense.'

I wish it *was* nonsense, Dora thought.

After they'd washed up the dishes, Alf went to the pub, and for the first time in the evening, Dora felt herself relax. She played Snakes and Ladders with Josie and Bea while they listened to Henry Hall on the wireless. Nanna dozed by the warmth of the fire and her mother got on with the rest of her mending for the laundry.

Later, they all went to bed. Nanna Winnie complained loudly, claiming the fish and chips had made her ill.

'I'll probably die in my sleep,' she predicted gloomily, as she rose stiffly from her rocking chair.

'No one ever died of indigestion, Mum!' Rose laughed.

'That's what you reckon,' Nanna said darkly. 'You lot will be laughing the other side of your faces when you find my cold dead corpse in the morning.'

Dora and Josie stood side by side at the scullery sink, brushing their teeth.

'It's going to be lonely here without you,' Josie said.

Dora spat toothpaste down the plug hole. 'You'll have Bea and Little Alfie.'

'But I won't have you.'

'I told you, I'll come home for visits.'

'Promise?' Josie rinsed her mouth out and turned to face her sister, her dark eyes shining. 'Promise you won't forget me?'

'How could I forget you? I'm your big sister, ain't I?' Dora stroked her silky dark hair. 'I'll always look out for you, Jose.'

When they'd all gone to bed Dora lay in the darkness under the weight of her old eiderdown, listening to Nanna's snores through the thin wall. From next door, she could hear June Riley yelling at her sons.

Tired though she was, she didn't dare sleep until she heard the sound of Alf's key scraping in the lock.

Her stomach clenched in fear as she heard his heavy tread in the passageway. Please God, she prayed. Please don't let him come in. Not tonight.

His footsteps stopped outside the bedroom door. Dora held her breath as the knob began to turn, ever so slowly...

He moved quietly for a big man. Dora felt him standing over her as she lay still, her eyes tightly shut, pretending to be asleep.

But he wasn't fooled. 'I know you're awake.' He leaned closer to her, his hot breath fanning her face, stinking of beer and cigarettes. 'Waiting for me, are you?'

'Leave me alone,' she whispered into the darkness, her eyes still closed.

'Not until I get what I've come for.' He wrenched off the bedclothes, leaving her trembling and exposed. Dora curled up in fear, head down, knees pulled up to her chest, as if she could disappear inside her flannel nightdress. But it was no use. He had already pinned her to the bed with his knee as he fumbled with his trouser buttons.

'I'll tell Mum,' she threatened, twisting away from him. 'I'll scream and everyone will come running.'

'And then what?' Alf mocked her. 'What do you think will happen then? She might kick me out, but I'm telling you now, you won't be far behind. D'you really think she'd want to see your face again, knowing what you and me had done?' He was on top of her, his bulky body stifling her. His breathing was hard and ragged as his rough hands pawed under her nightdress. 'And what about the rest of the family? They'll be on the streets before you know it, without me to pay the rent. Is that what you want?'

'I want you to leave me alone.'

He grunted with laughter. 'No, you don't. You love it.' He grabbed her hand and plunged it into his trousers. She tried to pull away but he gripped her tightly, forcing her against him until she felt her arm would snap in two. 'You should count yourself lucky. Ugly little cow like you, no other man would ever look at you.'

He suddenly yanked her arms back, pinning them above her head as he thrust himself clumsily against her. All the fight gone out of her, Dora could do nothing but blank her mind. She turned her face to stare at the crack of dim lamplight between the faded rose print curtains, listened to the distant sound of June Riley's screeching voice, and told herself it would all be over soon.

Chapter Three

If things had gone as her grandmother had planned, Lady Amelia Charlotte Benedict should have been celebrating her engagement by her eighteenth birthday. The Dowager Countess of Rettingham had even taken the trouble to draw up a list of the most eligible prospects, starting with the son of a duke and ending with a minor baronet from Lincolnshire – not ideal, but better than nothing, as she'd pointed out.

And yet here Millie was, on a November morning six months after her nineteenth birthday, standing in Matron's office yet again. It was simply too tiresome.

Matron obviously felt the same. 'So, here you are once more, Benedict,' she said with a heavy sigh.

'I'm afraid so, Matron.'

'Do you realise you are the only one in your set to have failed Preliminary Training?'

Millie stared down at the parquet floor. 'Yes, Matron.'

'Do you know why you have failed, Benedict?'

'I think so, Matron. But it was an accident,' she added quickly. 'If that soap enema solution hadn't exploded in my hands–'

She saw Matron's forbidding expression and stopped. A student was not supposed to speak to her superiors unless spoken to. Even making eye contact with Matron was discouraged. Millie

34

knew some pros who hid in the sluice room during her ward rounds so they wouldn't have to be in her presence.

Which was a shame, really. Matron looked as if she might be rather fun, once you got to know her.

Not that there was much chance of a humble student ever doing that.

'The soap enema incident was ... unfortunate,' Millie could have sworn she saw Matron's mouth twitch, 'but it is not the only reason you failed PTS. According to your tutor Sister Parker, your general attitude leaves a lot to be desired.' She consulted her notes. 'She says you're easily distracted, you chatter in class, and you spend a great deal of time daydreaming. Sister Sutton also says you're untidy and you have a lax attitude to the rules of the nurses' home. I see you've been caught by the night porter on two occasions returning after ten o'clock, and without a late pass?'

'Actually, it was three times, Matron.' Millie could have bitten off her tongue as soon as she'd said it. Her grandmother always said honesty was one of her biggest character flaws, and she was right.

'Is that so?' Matron's brows rose. 'Are you trying to set some kind of record, Benedict?'

'Indeed not, Matron.'

'I'm very glad to hear it.' Matron regarded her steadily. 'Well, Benedict, I'm afraid all those late nights and gadding about have cost you dear. While the rest of your set are commencing their training on the wards, you are back to square one, having to repeat your twelve weeks' Preliminary Training...'

Millie gazed past Matron's shoulder and out of the window at the wintry grey sky, tinged yellow by smoke belching from the factories. Winter seemed much bleaker in London, where the creeping damp made your bones ache, and a thick, acid fog rolled up off the river, clogging your lungs and leaving a metallic taste in the back of your throat.

It wasn't at all like the winters in Kent, where the air was crisp and clean and refreshingly cold, smelling of nothing more than bonfires and damp earth and leaves. She loved to go out riding then with her father, galloping across the bare fields, shorn of their crops, the naked trees silhouetted dramatically against the vast, empty sky.

Most people assumed a girl wouldn't be interested in the land, but Millie knew every one of Billinghurst's five thousand-odd acres, and the tenants who farmed them.

Naturally her grandmother didn't approve.

'She is your daughter, not your son and heir!' Millie had overheard her scolding her son. 'Really, Henry, isn't it hard enough for the girl growing up without a mother to guide her, without you turning her into some kind of hoyden as well? Next thing we know she'll be wearing trousers and keeping the company of Bohemians like your sister Victoria. And who do you think will want to marry her then?'

'Benedict, are you listening to me?' Matron's voice snapped her back to reality.

'Yes, Matron. Sorry, Matron. You were saying?'

'I was saying, Benedict, that this is your last chance. If you fail PTS again, I will have no choice but to dismiss you from the Nightingale.'

'Yes, Matron. I understand.'

'Do you, Benedict? I wonder.'

'I do, Matron, honestly. I will try very hard indeed to get through PTS and become a credit to this hospital.'

She really had no choice. It was either that or return to Billinghurst with her tail between her legs and get married.

'In that case, you'd better get back to the nurses' home and prepare to start your training again.' Matron made a note in her file and closed it. 'Perhaps if you apply yourself rather more to your studies and less to your social life, you'll have better luck this time, Nurse Benedict.'

Dismissed, Millie headed out of the office where a trail of dejected-looking nurses were nervously waiting in the corridor for their turn to meet Matron's wrath, and went downstairs. She immediately headed round to the back of the nurses' block, to the narrow, overgrown strip of ground where the student nurses sneaked off for a cigarette away from the watchful eye of the Home Sister.

Glenda Pritchard, a girl from her set was already there, shivering with cold as she puffed on a Craven A. She started nervously as Millie rounded the corner of the building.

'Oh, it's you.' Glenda put her hand to her chest, sagging with relief. 'I thought it was Sister Sutton on the warpath.' She handed Millie her cigarette. 'How did it go with Matron?'

'Well, she didn't send me packing, which is something.' Millie took a long drag and blew the

37

smoke out in a steady stream. 'But I have to retake PTS.'

'Poor you!' Glenda looked sympathetic. She was what Millie's grandmother would have called an 'unfortunate-looking' girl, with glasses and buck teeth. 'But at least you don't have to go home.'

'True.' Millie hadn't been looking forward to seeing the triumph on her grandmother's face when she arrived back at Billinghurst. 'But I'm not looking forward to spending another twelve weeks with Sister Parker either. She hates me.' Millie took another drag on the cigarette and passed it back to Glenda.

'She doesn't hate you. She just thinks you're hopeless, that's all.'

'Thank you. That makes me feel so much better.' After three months on PTS with Glenda, Millie knew the other girl meant well, but she could be a bit tactless at times. 'I'm so envious of you lot. You'll all be starting work on the wards while I'm stuck with the new students.'

'Damp dusting the practice room every morning,' Glenda reminded her.

'Listening to all those lectures,' Millie sighed.

'And doing battle with Mrs Jones!'

'Don't remind me!' Mrs Jones was the dummy patient they used for practice sessions in PTS. Millie always seemed to end up wrestling with her. Once Mrs Jones' arm had come clean off in her hand. She'd thought Sister Parker was going to explode with rage.

'I wonder if you're really cut out to be a nurse, Benedict?' she would say to her almost every day, peering at her over the top of her pebble-thick

38

spectacles as if she were a specimen in one of the jars lined up on the shelves of the classroom.

Millie couldn't help being accident-prone. Objects just seemed to take on a troublesome life of their own in her hands.

Like that wretched enema solution. Heat rose in her face at the thought of it. For the past week she'd had nightmares about seeing the soapy water dripping off the examiner's chin...

Glenda Pritchard dropped the cigarette on the ground and stubbed it out with the heel of her stout shoe. 'A few of us are off to celebrate our last night before we start on the wards. Come with us, if you like?'

'No, thanks.' Much as Millie usually enjoyed a night out, the thought of listening to everyone chattering about their new ward allocations only made her feel worse. 'I think I'll stay in and study.'

'You, study? That'll be the day!' Glenda scoffed.

'I'm serious. I'm going to be a model student from now on.'

'If you say so.' Glenda grinned. 'But I give it a week.'

We'll see about that, Millie thought as she headed back through the double doors into the student nurses' home. The rambling Victorian building was once a grand mansion for a well-to-do family, but now the elegantly proportioned rooms and hallways were hidden under dull brown paint, and thick net curtains shrouded the bay windows, as if the sight of sunlight might lift the poor pros' spirits more than was good for them.

Around a hundred students lived in the house for the three years of their training, crammed three or four to a room, under the care – if that was the right word – of Sister Sutton, the Home Sister. She occupied three rooms on the ground floor, just inside the main entrance, from which she and her horrid little dog Sparky kept a watchful eye on her charges. She was supposed to be like a mother to them, but her bad temper and the heavy ring of keys jingling at her belt made her seem more like a gaoler.

Millie trod carefully past her door, holding her breath as she went. She had almost reached the stairs up to her room when she heard a tell-tale heavy tread from the landing above her. Next moment Sister Sutton's broad, squat figure filled the space at the top of the stairs, blocking out the feeble light from the landing window. Sparky, a small brown-and-white Jack Russell terrier, pranced around her own feet, yapping.

'Benedict!' Millie cringed at the sound of her own name. 'Why are you creeping about here at this time of the day?' Sister Sutton demanded.

'I've just been to see Matron, Sister.' Millie held out her hand to pat Sparky. He let out a low growl and retreated behind Sister Sutton's voluminous grey skirt. Nasty, bad-tempered thing, Millie thought. Nothing like Nero, her father's beloved Labrador.

'Hmm. Why am I not surprised to hear that?' Sister Sutton glared at her. Her eyes were like tiny black raisins, almost lost in the doughy folds of her fat face. 'I hope she's given you your marching orders?'

'No, Sister. I'm to retake Preliminary Training.'

'And what a waste of time that will be for

everyone!' Sister Sutton tutted impatiently. 'Poor Sister Parker, her patience must be stretched to breaking point already, with all you useless girls. But I suppose Matron must know what she's doing,' she murmured under her breath.

'Yes, Sister.'

'Well, don't just stand there, girl. Go to your room at once!'

As Millie went to move past her, Sister Sutton's hand shot out and fixed on her arm, holding her back.

'Have you been smoking?' Her tiny eyes narrowed even further.

'No, Sister,' Millie lied guiltily.

Sister Sutton thrust her face close to hers, so close Millie could see the wiry grey hairs sprouting from her chin. 'You know I can't abide smoking. It's a filthy, detestable habit.'

'Yes, Sister.' As Sister Sutton stared beadily into her face, Millie suddenly caught a familiar whiff. 'Is that Guerlain perfume you're wearing, Sister?'

Sister Sutton released her abruptly, her cheeks flushing 'What an impertinent question!' she spluttered. 'As if I have time for such fripperies. Go on with you, girl. Get up to your room. I shall come up there in a minute and inspect it. I dare say it's a terrible mess as usual?'

Still blustering, she stomped off down the stairs, Sparky trotting behind her.

Millie watched her go, smiling to herself. Smoking might be a nasty, detestable habit. But it wasn't nearly as bad as rifling through other people's drawers and stealing their perfume.

Chapter Four

Dora's first impression of the Home Sister was that she had never seen anyone so fat in her life. Sister Sutton was about five foot tall and almost as wide. She filled the doorway of the nurses' home, her grey uniform stretched to bursting over a formidable shelf of a bosom. Her head seemed to be connected to her body by a cascade of quivering chins. Even her ankles were fat, spilling over her stout black shoes.

'You there!' She waddled towards Dora at surprising speed, trundling as if she were on wheels. Grey wisps of hair escaped from her starched cap. Behind her scampered a yapping terrier.

'I saw you,' she accused, pointing a fat finger straight between Dora's eyes. 'Canoodling with that porter.'

'I wasn't canoodling with anyone!'

'Don't lie to me, girl, I saw you with my own eyes. Quiet, Sparky!' she roared at the dog, who was circling Dora's legs, his lips drawn back to show yellow teeth. 'I was watching you from my office. You are a disgrace. I have a good mind to send you straight home and inform Matron of your conduct. This is not what we expect of our student nurses here at the Nightingale.'

Blimey, Dora thought. It's my first day, I haven't even set foot in the place and I'm already in trouble.

'I was only asking him for directions,' she protested.

'Do you think I'm a simpleton, girl?'

'No, but–'

'And please address me as "Sister" when you speak to me.'

'No, Sister.'

'What?'

'I mean, no, I don't think you're a simpleton. Sister.'

'I'm glad to hear it. I wish I could say the same about you. What is your name?'

'Dora Doyle, Miss. I mean, Sister.'

'Are you Irish?'

'No, Sister.' Sparky lunged at her ankle. Dora sidestepped his snapping jaws and fought the urge to kick the wretched thing.

'I'm glad to hear it. Irish girls are always far too much trouble. Man-mad the lot of them.' She considered Dora for a moment. 'I hope I'm not going to have any trouble with you?'

'No, Sister.'

'You see I don't, or you will be straight to Matron's office. I don't put up with any nonsense from young nurses.' She suddenly turned on her heel and trundled back towards the nurses' home. Dora guessed she was supposed to go with her, so she picked up her battered suitcase and followed, being careful to keep a safe distance between herself and the bad-tempered dog.

The gleaming lino floors squeaked under Dora's feet as she followed Sister Sutton through the warren of corridors, all painted a drab brown. The whole building was eerily silent, and full of gloomy shadows.

The Home Sister led the way up to the top of the house, where the staircase became so narrow she could hardly squeeze her ample body up it. Dora puffed along behind, not daring to stop to draw breath.

As Sister Sutton went, she recited a litany of rules and regulations.

'Lights out is at ten o'clock sharp, and you are expected to be back in the nurses' home by then unless you have a late pass. Although why any respectable girl would want to be out after that time I have no idea,' she said. 'Laundry day is Monday; in the morning you must strip off your bed and put your sheets and towels in the bags at the end of the corridor. Personal items are to be put in your own laundry bag and left out for collection on Tuesdays and Thursdays. While a probationer, you must not leave the hospital grounds in uniform. And while in uniform you will behave with the decorum that befits the good name of this hospital. Which means no make-up or jewellery, no laughing, no speaking loudly, and strictly no talking to men. Is that understood?'

Dora nodded, but she was beginning to wonder if she would ever remember all the rules of the nurses' home, let alone take in any medical knowledge.

Sister Sutton stopped so suddenly Dora almost collided with her, and threw open a door to reveal a long attic room with three beds tucked into the eaves. A small dormer window cast a dim patch of wintry light on to the bare polished floorboards.

A nurse sat on the bed at the far end of the

44

room, her stockinged feet up. As Sister Sutton barged in, she shot to her feet so quickly she nearly hit her head on the sloping ceiling.

'What are you doing here, Tremayne?' Sister Sutton demanded.

'Please, Sister. I'm off duty until five.'

'So why are you skulking about up here?' Sister Sutton sniffed the air. 'You weren't smoking, were you?'

'No, Sister.' The girl towered over Sister Sutton, as tall and slender as the Home Sister was short and wide. Her dark hair was coiled in a smooth bun at the nape of her long, elegant neck. Dora tucked a frizzy curl behind her ear and wondered if she would ever get her hair to look that neat.

'You know I do not allow smoking in the rooms. If you must smoke, do it downstairs in the library or outside like everyone else.'

'Yes, Sister.' Sparky jumped up at the girl's legs, clawing at her black woollen stockings, but she didn't flinch.

Dora could feel her tension as Sister Sutton inspected the room through narrowed eyes. 'And what's this?' She pointed to the far corner. 'Why is this bed in such a mess?'

Dora looked at the immaculately made bed with its perfectly turned down sheet and neat corners, and wondered if she was seeing things.

'Where is Nurse Benedict?' Sister Sutton asked.

The tall girl cleared her throat. 'It's her day off, Sister.'

'Disgraceful! You nurses get far too much time off.' Sister Sutton went over to the bed, tore off the bedclothes and, with a great effort, upended

45

the mattress on to the floor. Dora looked at the dark girl, but her gaze remained fixed on the worn rug at her feet.

Sister Sutton stood back, breathing heavily. 'Tell Benedict if I ever find her bed a mess again, I will send her straight to Matron. Is that clear?' she said.

'Yes, Sister.'

'And you,' Dora jumped as Sister Sutton swung her attention back to her. 'Let this be a lesson to you. I will not tolerate slovenliness in nurses. If you can't keep yourselves neat and tidy, how on earth do you expect to care for patients?' Once again, Dora felt the full force of her gaze, raking up and down, looking for faults. 'Well?'

'I – I don't know, Sister,' Dora stammered.

Sister Sutton tutted and shook her head. 'This is Doyle,' she said to the other nurse. 'Please help her settle in.' She turned back to Dora. 'Get changed and go down to supper at eight. Your training will begin at nine o'clock sharp tomorrow morning. Tremayne will show you where to go. Come, Sparky.' She left, slamming the door behind her.

Dora stared at it. 'Blimey, is she always like that?'

'Sometimes she's worse.' The girl picked her way across the room. 'Here, help me sort out this bed.'

'I'm Dora, by the way,' she introduced herself as they hauled the heavy horse-hair mattress back on to the bed.

'Helen. But we're not supposed to use Christian names on the wards, only surnames.' She pushed the mattress into place and stood back, smoothing down her blue-striped dress. 'There, that'll do. Benedict can do the rest when she gets in. You can put your things in that chest of drawers.' She nodded towards the corner of the room.

'I'll unpack later.' She didn't want Helen Tremayne to see her few poor belongings. She sounded so posh, Dora was sure she would look down her nose at her.

'Suit yourself, but you'll have to have everything folded and put away before supper, or Sister Sutton won't be pleased. And you'd best get changed, too.'

Dora watched Helen as she rolled down the sleeves of her dress and deftly fastened them at the wrist with neat starched cuffs. She wondered if all nurses were as cool and brisk as her. If they were, Dora didn't stand a chance.

She warily eyed the neatly folded pile of clothes on the bed – three blue-striped dresses, several white aprons and bibs, collars, cuffs and a laundry bag. On top of it all sat a square of white fabric starched like cardboard, which she had no idea what to do with.

Dora carefully unfolded the dress and shook it out. It was so freshly laundered, she wanted to hold it up to her face and breathe in the clean, starchy smell. But with Helen Tremayne watching, she could only hurry to get it on.

It was easier said than done. The dress was thick and heavy, lined with calico, and reached almost to her ankles. The room was chilly, but by the time she'd put on her dress and black woollen stockings she was sweltering.

'What do you do when it's hot?' she asked.

Helen shrugged. 'You just put up with it, same as you do everything else.'

Dora struggled to fasten up her cuffs. The studs were small and fiddly, and her hands became clammy with panic.

'Do you want any help?' Helen offered.

'Thanks.' Dora studied the other girl as she fastened the studs. Even her severe uniform couldn't disguise her striking beauty. Her face was a smooth, perfect oval, with huge dark eyes framed by thick lashes.

She would be even more beautiful if she smiled, Dora thought.

She wasn't the easiest person to talk to, either. Dora tried again to make conversation with her. 'How long have you been here?'

'I'm in my second year as a student.'

'What about Benedict?'

'She's still a pro – a probationer, I mean. That's what we call students in their first year. Pass me your collar.'

Dora handed it to her and lifted her chin so she could fasten it. 'Thanks – ow! That hurts!'

'Nothing I can do about that, you just have to get used to it. Putting Vaseline on your neck helps if it rubs too much... There, that's done.' She paused. 'What's this around your neck?'

'It's a hamsa. A kind of lucky charm. A friend gave it to me.'

'It won't be very lucky for you if Sister Sutton catches you wearing it,' Helen warned. 'You'd best take it off and keep it somewhere safe.'

Dora removed the chain from around her neck, wrapped it in a handkerchief and placed it in the empty drawer that had been allocated to her. Meanwhile, Helen deftly fashioned the mysterious square of starched fabric into a neat cap.

'I'll never get the hang of that!' Dora sighed as she watched her.

'Of course you will. Everyone does.' She placed the cap on Dora's frizzy hair. 'Have you brought any pins with you? It doesn't matter, I've got some spares. Although you might have to do something about your hair.' She frowned. 'It's supposed to be hidden at all times, and you'll never get it all under your cap.'

'I'll have to shave my head to do that,' Dora said mournfully.

Helen Tremayne's mouth curved slightly, the first hint of a smile Dora had seen. 'I don't suppose it will come to that.' She jabbed a pin into the cap, narrowly missing Dora's left ear. 'There, that's the best I can do, I'm afraid.'

Dora checked her reflection in the scrap of mirror over the chest of drawers, and a bubble of excitement started to rise inside her. She could scarcely believe the transformation. In her smart striped dress, with her collar fastened tightly under her chin, and her hair almost hidden under her cap, she looked almost like a real nurse.

'I'd best go, I'm due back on the ward in ten minutes.' Helen's voice broke into her daydream. She was on the other side of the room, ramming her feet back into her shoes. 'Make sure you're in the dining room for eight o'clock.' She threw her cloak over her shoulders and hurried for the door. 'It's block three, this side of the courtyard. Out of the main doors, then turn right. And whatever you do, don't be late.'

Chapter Five

When Helen had gone, Dora quickly unpacked her belongings, shoving them into the empty drawer. She didn't have much, just underwear and a couple of dresses, plus all the things she had been told to bring for training – black stockings and stout black shoes, blunt-ended scissors, pens and pencils and a watch.

She suppressed a shudder as she placed the watch carefully in the drawer. Alf had made a big song and dance about buying it for her. He'd presented it to her in front of all the family, and she'd had to pretend to be grateful and let him put his arms around her and listen to everyone say what a good, generous man he was.

It doesn't matter, she told herself. You're safe now. He can't hurt you any more.

At eight o'clock prompt, she made her way to block three as Helen Tremayne had directed. She followed the sound of clattering crockery and excited chatter down the corridor, and found herself in the brightly lit, noisy dining room, reeking of overcooked cabbage and disinfectant. It was the size of a gymnasium, and laid out with several long tables. At the far end of the room, steam belched from a serving hatch where a large woman in a white overall was doling out loaves of bread, bowls and huge enamel jugs of cocoa.

Each of the long tables was crowded with young

women in a different-coloured uniform – some royal blue, some striped, some purple. Over by the window, away from the hustle and bustle, a group of women in grey uniforms ate their meal in dignified silence, served by a maid.

Dora's stomach rumbled in anticipation; she had been too nervous to eat the sausage sandwich her mum had made her at lunchtime.

Sister Sutton was waiting by the door. 'You're late,' she greeted her. 'And your cap is crooked. Go over there and sit with the other probationers.'

As she made her way across the room, Dora noticed Helen Tremayne sitting at a table with a group of other nurses in striped uniforms – second years, she guessed. Dora waved but Helen stared straight through her and went on eating.

Dora found a seat at the end of the probationers' table, where a dozen or so nervous-looking girls sat casting sidelong glances around them. Unlike the other pros at the table, they all wore blue armbands, denoting they were in Preliminary Training and not yet let loose on the wards.

As she sat down, an excited-looking pro came back from the hatch bearing a bottle of Daddies Sauce, like a trophy.

'Look what I've got,' she grinned.

'Quick, before the seniors get hold of it!' The girls at the far end of the table passed it around eagerly, watched in bewilderment by Dora and the other new students.

'The senior students get first dibs on everything,' the girl opposite her explained. 'The pros have to make do with whatever's left. And being new, we're right at the bottom of the pile.'

'How do you know that?' the girl beside Dora asked.

'My sisters trained here. One of them is a staff nurse on the Male Orthopaedic ward now.' The girl was plump and dark-haired, with a sweet, round face and a lilting Irish accent. Dora wondered what Sister Sutton had made of her.

Their food arrived in front of them. The girl next to Dora poked squeamishly at the contents of the bowl. 'What is this horrible stuff, anyway?'

'Dripping,' the Irish girl said, digging her knife in and ladling a dollop on to her bread. 'Try it, it's delicious.' She sank her teeth into the crust, her eyes closed in bliss.

'It looks disgusting.' The girl grimaced. 'I'm sure my mother would just die if she knew I was eating such awful food.'

'You'll get used to it,' the Irish girl mumbled, her mouth full. 'My sister reckons you get so hungry you end up eating whatever they put in front of you.' She filled her cup with cocoa and offered the jug to the student next to her, a timid-looking girl with spectacles.

Before she could move to take it, the girl beside Dora reached out and grabbed it, then filled her own cup. 'Ugh, this is revolting too.'

'We wouldn't know. We haven't had a chance to find out.' Dora sent her a sideways glance. The girl was pretty, with neatly plaited shiny chestnut-brown hair and a disdainful expression. Her small nose pointed towards the ceiling, as if permanently turned up at the world and all it had to offer.

'Sorry, did you want this?' The girl offered her the jug. Dora took it and handed it back to the

52

timid-looking girl, who smiled shyly across the table at her.

Over supper, the new students chatted amongst themselves, swapping stories of their schools, their families, and how they had come to be at the Nightingale. Dora found out the Irish girl was called Katie O'Hara. She had come over from a tiny village in Ireland to train at the same hospital as her three sisters. 'It was either that or become a nun!' she laughed.

She also found out the girl with the turned-up nose was called Lucy Lane. She was an only child, her father had made a fortune manufacturing light bulbs, her mother did charity work, and she was simply the best at everything. Dora felt her eyelids begin to droop as Lucy listed the prizes she had won at her school, from needlework to Most Polite Pupil. If they'd given a prize for talking the hind legs off a donkey, she would have won that too.

'Everyone expected me to go on to university after school, but I decided I wanted to be a nurse,' she announced. 'It's such a worthwhile profession, isn't it? And of course, once I'd decided on nursing, I had to come to the Nightingale. Everyone knows it's the best teaching hospital in the country. Only the best will do for me, Daddy says.'

Dora stayed quiet. Apart from Katie O'Hara, who was very down to earth, the other girls seemed so posh, talking about their schools and their ponies and what their fathers did for a living. She felt out of place already.

She glanced across at Helen Tremayne who looked out of place too. She was surrounded by chattering nurses, but no one seemed to be speaking to her as she sat in silence, shredding a crust of bread between her fingers.

It seemed as if they'd barely started eating before the serving hatches clanged shut and the sisters rose to their feet. Instantly the room fell silent. Dora sneaked a look at the grey-uniformed women as they filed out of the dining room. Tall, short, thin, plump, they seemed a forbidding bunch, not a smile among them.

'They look terrifying, don't they?' Katie whispered across the table. 'Thank the Lord we don't have to meet them for another three months. I hope I've managed to get some nursing knowledge in my brain by then!'

The silence held until the last sister had left. Then there was a stampede of nurses towards the doors.

Dora immediately began collecting up the dishes.

'What are you doing?' Lucy Lane said.

'Tidying up – what does it look like?' Dora scraped one of the plates and added it to the stack.

The other girls looked at each other and giggled. Except for Katie O'Hara, who whispered kindly, 'They have maids to clear the tables here.'

Dora glanced around in confusion. Sure enough, women in overalls were gathering up the mugs and plates on to huge metal trays.

Embarrassment washed over her. 'I thought we had to do it ourselves,' she mumbled.

'Someone clearly isn't used to having staff,' she heard Lucy Lane say to another of the girls as they walked off.

54

So what if I'm not? Dora wanted to shout after her. There was nothing wrong with getting your hands dirty.

After supper, they made their way back to the nurses' home. The timid girl, whose name was Jennifer Bradley, went straight up to her room. Dora was tempted to turn in too, but she forced herself to join the others in the living room. After all, they were going to be together day and night for the next three years, so she should make an effort to make friends. Even if things hadn't got off to a promising start.

The living room was big and high-ceilinged, with the kind of ornate plasterwork Dora had only ever seen in a church before, and a bay window shrouded in drab net curtains. Her mum would have those down and soaking in a bucket of Reckitt's Blue in no time, she thought with a smile.

The room was filled with a haphazard arrangement of sagging settees and chairs that had seen better days. On either side of the empty fireplace were shelves filled with a random selection of tattered old books and boardgames.

'Ludo?' Lucy Lane said incredulously, pulling a battered old box off the shelf. 'Do they think we're five years old?'

Dora said nothing. After her embarrassment in the dining room, she didn't want to admit that she often enjoyed playing boardgames with her sisters.

There were a few older students already in the living room, listening to the wireless and laughing together in one corner. Dora and the other new students gathered in the opposite corner, where once again, Lucy held court.

Dora wondered if any of the other girls were as bored listening to her as she was. But they all seemed very impressed, listening with rapt attention as Lane held forth in her clipped voice about everything, including the state of her room.

'It's just appalling,' she declared. 'It's so cold, and the bed is like something you'd find in a prison. My mother would simply die if she knew about it.'

Katie O'Hara caught Dora's gaze across the room and rolled her eyes just a fraction towards the ceiling. Dora guessed she was one of the unfortunate ones sharing Lucy's prison cell.

'And it's so small,' Lucy went on. 'Three people, sharing a room that tiny? It's inhuman.'

Dora thought about the old days in Griffin Street, when she had shared a big double bed with Josie and Bea, but said nothing.

Then Lucy turned her attention to the other girls in their set. 'Did you see that girl who was sitting across the table from me? The one with the glasses? What a funny little thing she was. Didn't say a word all through supper.'

'Probably because she couldn't get a word in edgeways.' Dora hadn't realised she'd spoken aloud until she caught the venomous look Lucy gave her.

'I beg your pardon?' she said in her clipped voice.

The other girls were looking at Dora expectantly, so she felt she had to say something. 'I don't know what they taught you at that posh school of yours, but where I come from it's not considered polite to talk about people behind their backs,' she said bravely.

Lucy's simpering smile didn't meet her eyes. 'I'm sure I don't need a lesson in manners.' Especially not from the likes of you, her glacial look said.

The other girls giggled, but Dora and Lucy regarded each other across the room. Dora had the bad feeling she'd made a nasty enemy.

Opposite them, one of the older girls was twiddling the wireless knobs, trying to tune it in.

'Wretched thing hasn't worked properly since Gordon dropped it,' she muttered.

'Give up and put a record on instead,' another suggested. They pulled a box out from behind the sofa and rifled through it while another wound up the gramophone. After much bickering, they finally decided on one. A moment later the crackly sounds of 'You Are My Lucky Star' filled the room. The girls all began twirling around the room with imaginary partners, laughing and swooning over Eddy Duchin.

But the laughter stopped abruptly when Sister Sutton burst in and turned off the gramophone, scratching the needle carelessly across the record.

'Lights out at ten,' she reminded them briskly, as Sparky rushed around their feet, rounding them up. 'You should be studying, not being frivolous. You have exams to pass, if you want to be nurses.'

'Who says we want to be nurses any more?' One of the girls, a slim blonde, made a face at the door as it closed, while another mournfully examined the record for scratches.

'Look at it. It's ruined. She did that deliberately.' One of the older girls caught up with Dora as they made their way up to their rooms.

'I'm Amy Hollins,' she introduced herself.

'Dora Doyle.'

'I suppose this must all seem very strange to you? I know I was scared at first. But you'll get used to it.'

'I hope so.'

'Just stay on the right side of Sister Sutton, at least until you've got to know the ropes a bit better.'

'Thanks.' Dora smiled back uncertainly. It was a relief to meet a friendly face at last.

As they headed towards the stairs, Amy said, 'Who are you sharing with?'

'Helen Tremayne and a girl called Benedict. I haven't met her yet, but–' Her voice trailed off as she saw Amy's expression change. 'Is something wrong?'

'You're sharing a room with Tremayne?' Amy Hollins gave a hard laugh. 'Good luck to you, then. You'll need it.'

Dora shrugged. 'She seems all right.'

'You reckon?' Amy smirked. 'Maybe you'll change your mind when you've got to know her better.' She leaned towards Dora confidingly. 'A word of advice. Don't trust her an inch.'

'Why not?'

'Because she'll be watching you. And every word you tell her will get reported back to her mother. You do know Constance Tremayne is on the Board of Trustees, don't you?'

'The Board of what?'

'Trustees. They're the ones in charge of the hospital. That's why Tremayne thinks she's so

58

much better than the rest of us. She's always running to her, telling tales about the rest of us. She'll stab you in the back as soon as look at you. Trust me, I know,' Amy said. 'Why do you think none of the other girls speak to her? If I were you, I'd steer clear of her.'

Dora frowned, trying to take in what she was hearing. Helen was a bit quiet and stand-offish, but she didn't strike Dora as the untrustworthy type.

'I'll choose my own mates, thanks very much,' she said.

Amy Hollins shrugged. 'Please yourself. I'm only warning you, that's all,' she said huffily. 'But you really don't want it to get around to the others that you're a friend of Helen Tremayne's or they might start thinking you can't be trusted either.'

Back in the room, Helen was sitting up in bed, writing. She looked quite different in her flower-sprigged nightgown, her hair falling in a dark, silky curtain around her face.

Dora stepped carefully over the tumble of sheets and blankets on the floor. 'Still no sign of Benedict?'

'She won't get in until after lights out. She never does.'

'Won't Sister Sutton mind?'

'Probably. But she'll have to catch her first.'

She went back to her writing. Dora got changed quickly into her nightgown, shivering in the chill of the room. Back in Griffin Street there would be a fire blazing in her bedroom on a cold night like this.

'What are you writing?' she asked.

'Just a letter.'

'To your boyfriend?'

'I don't have a boyfriend.'

'A friend, then?'

'If you must know, I'm writing to my mother. And I want to finish it before lights out, so if you don't mind?'

'Sorry.' Dora watched her scribbling, her hand moving quickly over the page. Amy Hollins' words came back to her. Was she telling her mother about her new room-mate? Dora wondered.

She slipped into bed and pulled the covers up to her chin. The mattress was hard and lumpy, and the starched sheets felt cold and stiff against her skin. But it wasn't just the bed that didn't feel right. She missed brushing her teeth at the kitchen sink with Josie, whispering and laughing as they got ready for bed, with Bea hanging around, straining her ears to hear their secrets. She missed her mother singing Little Alfie to sleep. She even missed Nanna's snoring.

The only one she didn't miss was Alf Doyle. She shivered under the sheets, relieved that for once she didn't have to sleep with one eye open and a chair wedged up against the door. A few minutes later there was the sound of creaking floorboards from below them, and Sister Sutton's voice rang out.

'Ten o'clock. Lights out, Nurses.'

Helen put away her letter and pattered across the room to turn off the lights, then hopped back into bed.

''Night,' Dora said.

'Goodnight.'

Within a few moments, soft breathing from the other side of the room told her Helen was fast asleep. Dora lay on her back, staring into the darkness. The silence seemed to close in on her.

She had never been away from home before, not even for a single night. She felt a sudden, sharp pang of longing to see her mum again.

But slowly, gradually, the weariness of the day took over. As she fell into a fitful sleep, Alf Doyle crept into her dreams just as he had on so many nights, his bulky body looming over her, big clumsy hands groping for her in the dark...

She opened her eyes, saw the shadowy shape at the end of her bed, and let out a scream.

Immediately a hand was clamped over her mouth, pinning her against the pillows.

'Shut up, for God's sake, before you bring everyone running!' a female voice hissed.

But there were already footsteps and voices in the corridor as the other girls gathered outside.

'What's going on?' someone called out.

'Nothing. Just the new girl having a nightmare.' Helen's voice was sleepy in the darkness.

'It sounded like someone was being murdered,' one of the students grumbled.

'She will be murdered if she wakes me up again,' muttered another.

No one inside the room moved as the footsteps shuffled away. Then the weight rolled off Dora's chest and sat up. In the gloom, she could just about make out a figure at the end of her bed.

'That was a bit close for comfort,' the other girl said, taking off her beret and fluffing up her hair.

'I don't know why you can't just get in on time

61

like everyone else,' Helen grumbled, turning over and pulling the covers up around her ears.

'Where's the fun in that?' The newcomer looked down at Dora. 'Sorry, did I give you a frightful shock? You mustn't mind me, I'm always doing it.' She peeled off a glove and held out her hand. 'How do you do, by the way? I'm Millie Benedict. We're going to be sharing a room, won't that be fun?'

Chapter Six

Millie broke into a brisk trot down the empty corridor. She knew she would be in trouble if she were caught running – nurses were allowed to run only in case of fire or haemorrhages – but she would be in worse trouble from Sister Parker if she were late on her first day back in preliminary training.

The new students were already busy cleaning when she slipped in to the classroom. Every morning after breakfast and before they started lectures, the PTS students had to clean every inch of the classroom and practical area. They damp dusted, high dusted, cleaned out the cupboards, washed bedpans and bottles, and washed and powdered the rubber mackintosh sheets that were used to protect the mattresses on the wards.

Millie tried to slink off to the sluice before she was seen, but naturally the eagle eye of Sister Parker, the Sister Tutor, sought her out straight away.

'Oh, Benedict, it's you again.' Sister Parker may have seemed like a harmless old dear with her white hair, bright blue eyes behind round pebble spectacles and soft Scottish accent. But Millie knew from bitter experience that she had a sting like a scorpion. Her standards were extremely high, and she could reduce a pro to tears over a badly made bed. 'I do hope your lack of punctuality this morning is not going to be a sign of things to come?'

'No, Sister.'

She could feel Sister Parker's eyes on her, searching for faults. Finally, to Millie's relief, she said, 'Well, don't just stand there looking decorative, girl. Those lockers need cleaning out.'

Do they? Millie thought ten minutes later, as she got down on her hands and knees to scrub out the corners of a locker with Lysol and hot water. No one ever used the lockers in the practice area. It was set out like a ward, with beds, screens, trolleys and all the usual equipment, but no patient ever saw these things. And yet every morning they had to scrub every inch of them.

Millie knew better than to ask why. Once, at the very beginning of her training, she had had the temerity to pose the question. She wished she hadn't. Sister Parker had ranted for ten minutes about the importance of a regular hygiene routine – 'Not just when you feel it warrants it, Benedict' – and then made her copy out the whole lecture on basic asepsis, word for word. She had also made it very clear that a student nurse's job was to answer questions, not ask them.

Millie had never spoken up in class since.

She sat back on her heels and examined the painful cracks between her fingers. The disinfectant made her chilblains sting so much she wanted to cry.

At times like this, she wondered why she had ever given up her old life. As the only child of the 7th Earl of Rettingham, she was accustomed to a world of privilege and ease. She mixed in grand society and was waited on by a retinue of faithful servants. Before she came to the Nightingale, she had never had to cook, clean or even dress herself, since she had a lady's maid to do it for her.

She smiled to think what Polly, her maid, would make of her mistress now, on her hands and knees, scrubbing out cupboards. Even she had never had to face such drudgery – her most arduous trial was persuading Millie out of her riding clothes and into a dress occasionally.

'Daydreaming again, Benedict?' Sister Parker was standing behind her.

'No, Sister.'

'I'm pleased to hear it. Make sure you get into those corners.'

'Yes, Sister.' Millie picked up her scrubbing brush again.

And yet, hard as her new life was, she wouldn't go back to her old one. She loved her father, and Billinghurst, and growing up in the Kent countryside. She would have loved nothing more than to become mistress of the house herself one day. But as she grew older, her grandmother had made it clear that her future lay elsewhere.

'Billinghurst will never be yours,' she had told Millie bluntly. 'Under the terms of your great-grandfather's will, the estate is entailed so that only a male heir can inherit.'

Which meant that unless Millie married and had a son before her father died, her beloved Billinghurst and the thousands of acres of prime Kent farming land around it would pass to an obscure cousin in Northumberland.

The Dowager Countess had put all her considerable energies into making certain such a disaster did not befall them. For the last two years, Millie had been groomed and paraded like a show pony before any number of eligible men, culminating in the biggest horse market of them all – the Season.

Millie had been looking forward to it. She loved parties and having fun, and hoped to make new friends. But the reality was very different; she had never known a more humiliating and tedious experience. Being chaperoned around endless dinners and dances, changing her clothes three times a day, making small talk with exactly the same people everywhere she went. And always under the critical eye of her grandmother, urging her to be more vivacious and charming to the biggest bores.

And as for making friends ... Millie had found most of the other girls to be even more tedious than the men. Far from having fun, they were constantly caught up in petty squabbles and bitter rivalries, all of them as desperate as their ambitious mothers to be seen in the right places and to snare the right husband. It was all too pointless for words.

Millie had come out of the Season, not only

unmarried and with no prospect of an engagement in sight, but with a conviction that she wanted to do something more worthwhile with her life than organising a household of servants and deciding what to wear for dinner.

Her grandmother was appalled when she first suggested going into nursing.

'And how do you propose to meet a suitable husband in a hospital?' she had demanded.

Thankfully, Millie's doting father had overruled his mother's objections. Although Millie suspected that both of them were expecting her to give up and come home as soon as she had her first taste of hard work.

Which was why she was so determined to see it through. If only to prove to her grandmother that becoming a nurse wasn't just another fad, like her ballet or tennis lessons.

Once cleaning was over and all the mops, brooms and brushes had been put away, it was time for lectures in the classroom.

Millie felt like an old hand as she joined the new students who had gathered in the cramped wooden desks, nervously fiddling with pencils and notebooks. She spotted her new room mate at the back of the class and went to sit next to her.

'Hello again.'

'Hello.' The red-haired girl barely looked at her. Millie knew she hadn't got off to the best start, waking her up in the night like that. It was entirely her fault; she hadn't even remembered they were getting a new room mate until the poor girl started screaming.

She had tried to apologise that morning as they

queued up for the bathroom, but the girl had barely spoken to her. Millie hoped it was just first-day nerves, and she wouldn't turn out to be as unfriendly as Helen Tremayne. They had shared a room for three months and the only time they spoke was when Helen was taking Millie to task for her untidiness.

The door opened and they all rose to their feet as Sister Parker entered the room and made her way to the raised dais at the front of the classroom. The class skeleton, christened Algernon, dangled limply beside the blackboard behind her.

'Good morning, Nurses,' she greeted them. 'Welcome to the Nightingale Preliminary Training School. As your Sister Tutor, I will be teaching you basic nursing skills and preparing you for life on the wards during your first three months of training. Should you be fortunate enough to pass your preliminary examination,' she fixed Millie with a meaningful look over the top of her glasses, 'you will be returning here for weekly lectures for the next three years. These will be fitted in with your nursing duties on the wards, until you pass your hospital and state examinations and become nurses at the Nightingale.'

A ripple of excitement ran through the classroom. Sister Parker clapped her hands, demanding silence.

'Really, Nurses, if you're going to chatter like monkeys every time I say something, we shall never get anywhere.' Once everyone had calmed down, she continued, 'Usually at this time we will be having lectures on anatomy, physiology, nutrition, first aid and so on. But as it is the first day in PTS for most of you–' again she glanced at Millie '–we will commence by getting to know each other. You will go around the class and each tell me your names and where you come from. Then later in the morning, we will have a visit from the bookseller and you will be able to purchase some textbooks. I will advise you on what you need. Now,' she swung round to face the bespectacled pro on the far end of the row, who looked as if she was about to burst into tears, 'we will start with you. Name?'

'J-Jennifer Bradley, Miss. I mean, S-Sister.'

'Do speak up, Bradley. You're not a mouse.'

A couple of the girls in the front row sniggered unkindly as poor Jennifer Bradley turned puce with shame. Sister Parker rounded on them.

'Since you seem so sure of yourselves, perhaps we should start with you instead?' she said with a lift of her brows.

The morning dragged on. Millie idly practised drawing the human heart on a corner of her notebook as they went around the class introducing themselves.

And then it came to her neighbour's turn.

'My name is Dora Doyle, and I come from Bethnal Green.' She said it with an air of defiance, her chin lifted, her unmistakable cockney accent ringing around the room.

All eyes turned to Millie then. 'Amelia Benedict,' she introduced herself. 'But you can call me Millie.'

'You most certainly cannot,' Sister Parker snapped. 'All nurses are to be addressed by their surnames at all times.'

As the girl behind her started to recite her name, Millie noticed a girl with plaited brown hair in the front row turning to look at her with interest. She stared at her for such a long time that Millie glanced down at the bib of her apron to check she hadn't spilled anything down herself.

They stopped for a tea break in the middle of the morning. As the other students chattered together, Millie noticed Dora Doyle standing by herself, looking out of the window over the courtyard, lost in thought.

She was so intriguing, the way she scowled out at the world from under that extraordinary red hair of hers, as if she was afraid of nothing and no one. And yet the way she had screamed out in the night, anyone would think the Devil himself was after her.

Millie went over to her, determined to break the ice. But before she'd had a chance to say hello, the girl with the plaits elbowed her way between them.

'It's Lady Amelia, isn't it?'

'Millie, actually.'

She smiled triumphantly. 'I thought I recognised you! You were presented at Court last year, weren't you?'

Millie frowned at her, trying to place her face with its turned-up nose and pert mouth. 'Were you there?'

'Well, no, actually – but I saw your photograph all the time in *Tatler*. My mother and I follow the Season every year. I'm Lucy Lane, by the way. My father is Sir Bernard Lane. Lane's Lightbulbs?' She waited expectantly. Millie tried to

69

look impressed.

'I was thinking of doing the Season myself last year,' Lucy went on, 'but the headmistress of my school was determined I should stay on. She wanted me to take the Common Entrance Exam, you see. She told my father I was easily bright enough for Oxford...'

Millie put on her best listening expression, the one she had cultivated from endless cocktail parties, while she searched for Dora out of the corner of her eye. She was nowhere to be seen.

'...and I have to share a room with the most dreadful Irish girl. So common, I can't tell you,' Lucy droned on. 'Terribly religious, too. I could hardly sleep last night for the sound of those rosary beads clicking. Who are you sharing with?' she asked, pausing for breath at last.

'Doyle.'

'Really? Poor you!'

'Why do you say that?' Millie asked, puzzled.

'Well, it's obvious, isn't it? She's hardly our sort, is she?' Lucy gave her a conspiratorial smile.

'Our sort?'

'You know what I mean.' Lowering her voice barely a fraction, she added, 'I wonder if we could get Doyle to swap with me? I'm sure she and O'Hara would get on. Then we could share. It would be so much fun, wouldn't it?'

Millie couldn't think of anything worse. But mercifully she was saved from replying as they were summoned back into the classroom.

Chapter Seven

By the time they returned from their break, the bookseller had set up his stall in the classroom, with boxes full of textbooks on display. The new girls swarmed all over them. Millie, who already had all her books from her first stint in PTS, sat at her desk watching them.

'Sister Tutor says we don't need to buy all of them, but I thought I might as well.' Lucy Lane sidled up to Millie, her arms full of books.

She nodded politely but her eyes were fixed on Dora as she picked up one of the books, flipped it open then quickly shoved it back into the box again.

'I know what you're thinking,' Lucy gave her a knowing smile. 'It's pitiful, isn't it?'

Millie glanced at her. 'What is?'

'Doyle, of course. Look at her, staring at those books. Like a starving dog at a butcher's shop window. It's obvious she can't afford to buy anything.'

Millie looked back at Dora. Poor girl. She herself was so used to having anything she wanted, it hadn't even occurred to her that someone might not be able to buy a few books.

'Look, Sister Tutor is talking to her now.' Lucy craned forward eagerly. 'I bet she's asking her why she hasn't bought anything. Let's listen.'

'I don't want to,' Millie said, turning her head

71

away. But it was impossible to miss what was being said.

'You know, Doyle, if you are unable to afford new textbooks, we do have a few available second-hand. They're rather worn and a little out of date, I'm afraid, but at least they are better than nothing.'

Her words made all the other girls stop dead and turn around.

'Oh, heavens, how embarrassing!' Lucy giggled. 'I'd simply die if that were me, wouldn't you?'

Millie felt mortified for Dora, whose face flooded with colour up to the roots of her fiery hair. She couldn't hear her mumbled reply, but Sister Parker said, 'Very well, but you will need textbooks if you are to continue with your preliminary training. And you will certainly need them if you are to pass your state examinations.'

'Honestly, I really don't know what some people are even doing on this course if they can't buy a couple of books.' Lucy tossed her plaits indignantly. 'If you ask me, she's taking a place that should have been given to someone who can afford to be here.'

She said it so loudly Dora whipped round to look at them. Millie found herself caught in the full force of her baleful stare.

'Oh dear, do you think she heard us?' Lucy smiled maliciously.

Soon afterwards it was time for lunch. Millie immediately made a beeline for Dora, but she was out of the classroom before she could catch her.

Unfortunately, she wasn't fast enough for Lucy Lane, who followed her into the courtyard. 'I've been thinking,' she said. 'About us sharing a room–'

'Then please don't,' Millie cut her off sharply, and hurried to the dining block, leaving Lucy standing open-mouthed behind her.

Dora didn't go to the dining room for lunch, but she returned for the practical session that afternoon. Her defiant expression was back in place, her mouth a tight line. But as Millie edged her way between the other students to stand beside her, she could see the wariness in her green eyes.

The practical sessions took place in a room, which was set up like a small ward with eight beds, a sterilising room and a sluice room. At one end of the ward was a cupboard containing bowls, instruments and linen. Screens and stainless-steel two-tier trolleys were parked at the other end. Large, colourful diagrams of various parts of the human body decorated the walls.

'Today we will be teaching you how to make a bed, with and without a patient in it,' Sister Parker announced.

Sister Sutton will be pleased, Millie thought. Maybe if I learn to make my bed properly this time she'll stop stripping it off every day.

She watched carefully as Sister Parker placed two chairs at the end of the bed. Then she and her assistant began to strip the bed, taking off the sheets and blankets one at a time, folding them in three and draping them carefully over the chairs. As they worked, she kept up a running commentary.

'You notice how we shake the sheets and blan-

73

kets as little as possible? That is to avoid creating dust in the air and spreading infection.' She placed the last blanket over the chairs and surveyed the stripped bed with satisfaction. 'Now we will show you how to make it,' she said.

Once again, she and her assistant moved in perfect time with one another, like partners in a graceful dance, drawing the sheet tight, tucking in perfect corners and turning down the counterpane so that it was completely even.

'You see how we are pulling the sheet tight, so there are no wrinkles?' She demonstrated with a sweep of her hand. 'Does anyone know why we need to do this?'

'So it looks tidy?' one of the students ventured.

'Because it prevents pressure sores,' Lucy piped up.

'Very good, Lane. Pressure sores are the result of bad nursing, nothing else. While on the wards, we expect you to be absolutely vigilant.'

After the demonstration, the Sister Tutor paired the students up to try it for themselves. Naturally, Lucy Lane put herself forward first. She looked annoyed when Sister Parker paired her with Jennifer Bradley.

'Poor girl,' Millie whispered to Dora. 'I wouldn't like to be Lane's partner.'

'Really? I thought you two were the best of friends,' Dora replied coldly.

'Shhh! Quiet, Nurses! You should be watching and taking notes, not gossiping!' Sister Parker frowned at them.

Lucy already looked every inch the professional nurse in her immaculate uniform, her cap set

74

straight on her smooth chestnut-brown hair. And she performed the whole procedure perfectly, her movements brisk and assured.

Unfortunately she was let down by her partner. Jennifer Bradley was a bag of nerves. Sweat gleamed on her brow as she struggled to keep up with Lane's fast, fluid movements. By the time they'd finished, it looked as if they'd been fighting on the bed, not making it.

'Hardly a good first effort,' Sister Parker tutted. 'You should learn to work together. It is not only easier on your back, it will also make the whole process much faster and smoother.'

'That was all your fault,' Lucy hissed as they rejoined the group and another pair took their place.

'I – I'm sorry.' Jennifer's lip trembled.

'Leave her alone,' Millie said.

'But she was useless!'

'She was doing her best. You can see she's nervous.'

'She shouldn't be here if she's not up to it.'

'If it was up to you, none of us would be here,' Dora muttered.

'Nurses, please!' Sister Parker shot them a warning look. 'If I hear another word you will all be going to explain yourselves to Matron.'

Lucy glared at Dora, but said nothing.

Sister Parker and her assistant then demonstrated how to make a bed with a patient in it, using Mrs Jones, the life-sized dummy. Millie groaned. She had done battle with Mrs Jones during her previous stint in PTS, and always came off worst.

Sister Parker knew it too. 'Benedict, you can go first. As you've already spent three months training, you should be able to show everyone how to do it.' Her eyes gleamed with malice behind her pebble spectacles. 'Doyle, you can be her partner.'

'Look, about earlier...' Millie tried to say as they took their places, but Dora cut her dead.

'We're supposed to be getting on with this, remember?' she hissed back.

They faced each other across the bed, ready to begin.

'Remember to speak to the patient,' Sister Parker reminded them. 'You must explain every procedure as you do it.'

Millie eyed Mrs Jones apprehensively. She seemed decidedly uninterested in what was about to happen to her.

She took a deep breath. 'Now, Mrs Jones, Nurse Doyle and I are going to change your bed for you,' she said brightly. 'So if you could just move your arms and legs for me ... that's wonderful.' So far so good, Mrs Jones seemed to be co-operating for once, her limbs tucking in nicely around her. Encouraged, Millie grasped her shoulders. 'Right, now I'm going to turn you on to your side towards me – oh, bugger!'

Just as it all seemed to be going so well, Mrs Jones took on a life of her own. Millie made a lunge for her as her dead weight tipped forward, slipped out of her grasp and started to roll off the bed. It was only Millie's knee catching the dummy under the chin that stopped her from hitting the ground head first.

She froze there, legs buckling under Mrs Jones'

weight, still propping her up by one knee. She looked across the bed and saw Dora standing there frozen with the draw sheet in her hands.

For a second they stared at each other in horror. Then the corners of Dora's mouth began to twitch.

'No, Benedict, that isn't the way to do it,' Sister Parker sighed. 'Try it again, only please avoid kicking the patient in the face this time. And no profanity!'

Millie heard a snort from the other side of the bed. When she looked up, Dora was busily tucking in the sheet, her head down. But her shoulders were shaking. Millie desperately tried to hold in her own laughter, but when she looked down and saw Mrs Jones staring up at her, her glassy smile still in place, she broke down.

'Are you quite all right, Benedict?' Sister Parker asked.

'Sorry, Sister ... choking fit ... be all right in a minute.'

'Really, Nurse, I hardly think it's appropriate to cough all over the patient, do you?' Sister Parker frowned. 'Go to the sluice and fetch a glass of water. Go with her, Doyle.'

'Yes, Sister.'

They didn't dare look at each other until they were safely in the sluice. Then they both burst into fits of laughter.

'Oh, my God.' Millie leant against the door, holding on to her aching stomach. 'I think I've given myself an internal haemorrhage.'

'That's nothing to what you've done to poor Mrs Jones,' Dora replied.

'It'll take more than a clean sheet to put her right, that's for sure!'

They doubled up, helpless with laughter, hands over their mouths so no one would hear their muffled shrieks. They were still giggling five minutes later when Katie O'Hara knocked on the door.

'Sister Tutor wants to know if you've choked to death?' she called out.

At least the disaster helped break the ice. As they filed off to the dining room for their tea break, Millie made sure she gave Lucy Lane the slip and joined Dora instead. A few of the pros from her previous PTS set had come down for their tea, and Millie felt a twinge of envy as she listened to them swapping excited stories about their first day on the wards.

'Don't you wish you were with that lot?' Dora asked, helping herself to a slice of bread and jam.

Millie nodded. 'I feel such a fool, having to repeat PTS. I haven't even dared tell my family yet.' She could guess what her grandmother would say about it. 'It isn't fair. I could have passed if only it hadn't been for...'

'What?' Dora asked.

'I can't tell you. It's too awful.' Millie shook her head, trying to suppress the memory. 'It was the worst moment of my life.'

'Oh, go on. You can't leave me in suspense!'

Millie hesitated. If she didn't tell Dora herself, she was bound to hear it from someone else. Like so many of her mishaps, it had already passed into hospital legend.

'During the final practical test, I had to

78

demonstrate a soap enema solution,' she said.

'And?'

'And I did it very well. I got it all right until the last minute, and then–'

'Go on.'

She closed her eyes, shuddering at the memory. 'It wasn't my fault. The wretched syringe just sort of exploded in my hands. It went off all over the place. The poor examiner was covered.'

'You didn't!' Dora put her hand over her mouth.

'I did.' Millie nodded. 'It wouldn't have been so bad if the examiner hadn't been Sister Hyde.'

'Who's she?'

'She runs the Female Chronic ward here. A real dragon, everyone is simply terrified of her. And with good reason, too. If it had been down to her, I would have been straight out of Nightingale's after that exam. But luckily Matron gave me another chance. I don't think Sister Hyde was very pleased about it.'

Dora laughed. 'You're a card, d'you know that?'

Millie smiled back. She was used to people laughing at her. And she didn't mind Dora doing it if it meant they could be friends.

As they walked back to the practical room, Dora said suddenly, 'I don't mind, you know. If you want me to swap with her?'

'Who?'

'Your friend Lane. I mean, it makes sense, doesn't it?' She didn't look at Millie as she spoke. 'You two have got such a lot in common–'

'Are you saying I'm a horrible little snob? Thanks a lot!'

'No, but–'

Millie stopped in the corridor, forcing Dora to turn and look at her. 'Promise me you won't even think about leaving me with her?' she said solemnly. 'I don't think I could cope with her droning on about how rich and clever she is.'

Dora didn't say any more until they'd reached the practical room. 'So you don't mind sharing a room with me, then?'

'That depends,' Millie said.

'On what?'

'On whether you're going to give me the silent treatment like Tremayne all the time.'

Dora smiled reluctantly. 'I'll try not to. Although it's difficult to get a word in edgeways with you!'

'I know,' Millie sighed. 'My grandmother always says I should try to maintain a dignified silence, but I can't.'

They made sure they sat together at supper. Grey mince and hard-boiled potatoes again, Millie thought. She tried not to imagine the succulent roast her father and grandmother would be sitting down to at Billinghurst.

A group of second-year students were whispering at the next table. Planning a party, Millie guessed, smiling to herself. Sister Sutton might think she had them all under control, raiding their rooms and prowling the corridors with that wretched dog of hers, sniffing out their misdeeds. Not to mention Mr Hopkins and his army of porters standing guard at the hospital gates. But they would have been astonished at how much mischief went on right under their noses.

'But it seems so mean not to ask her,' one of the

students was saying.

'If you ask her, no one else will come,' another said. 'They'll all be too scared she'll tell her mother. She wouldn't come anyway. She never joins in with anything. All she ever wants to do is stay in her room and study.'

'It sounds as if they're talking about Tremayne?' Millie said to Dora.

'That girl Hollins warned me about her last night,' Dora said, refilling her mug with cocoa. 'She said she wasn't to be trusted. But she seems all right to me. A bit quiet, but there's nothing wrong with that.'

'Oh, she's not bad. I feel sorry for her actually.' No matter how hard training might be, Millie had made some very good friends at Nightingale's. They gathered in each other's rooms to gossip and study, took trips to the cinema and treated themselves to tea in the local cafe if they were feeling flush.

But as far as she knew, Helen Tremayne had no friends. Millie had done her best to include her, inviting her on various outings. But Helen had said no so often she had given up asking.

After supper they went back to their room. Millie had arranged to go out with some of her friends to hear how they had got on during their first day on the wards.

'Why don't you come with us?' she asked Dora, pulling the pins out of her hair and enjoying the blissful freedom of it tumbling around her face.

'Thanks, but I'd rather stay here. Anyway, I'm a bit short until we get paid.'

'I'll treat you,' Millie offered.

Dora's smile tightened. 'No, thanks,' she refused politely.

Millie watched her unlacing her shoes. She had been thinking about what Lucy had said all afternoon, and knew she had to speak up.

'Look here – about your books.' She saw Dora's shoulders stiffen but carried on. 'I know you're a bit short of money, so I was thinking – what if I gave you mine? I could easily order some more, and we could share until they arrive.

She hadn't expected any thanks for her offer, but she certainly didn't expect Dora's stony expression as she turned around to face her.

'Do you think I'm a charity case?' she said coldly.

'No, not at all. I just thought–'

'You thought because you're rich and I'm poor, I'd be grateful for your cast-offs? Well, let me tell you something. My family have never accepted charity in our lives and we're not going to start now.'

Dora turned away to finish unlacing her shoes. Millie felt hot shame wash over her.

'I – I'm sorry,' she mumbled. She'd put her foot in it as usual. How could she be so stupid? Dora was right, it was very high-handed of her to go around bestowing her bounty on all and sundry. She was as bad as her grandmother, ordering their kitchen scraps to be distributed among the estate workers and then expecting them to be grateful.

Millie got changed in silence. She felt so wretched, she couldn't even summon up any anger when she realised Sister Sutton had been in her drawers again and confiscated her lipstick.

She was leaning on the chest of drawers, trying to dab some powder on her face, when she heard the creak of floorboards behind her and saw Dora's face reflected behind her shoulder.

'I'm sorry,' she mumbled.

Millie met her eyes in the mirror. 'So am I. I didn't mean to offend you, truly.'

'I know. You only wanted to help, and I shouldn't have flown off the handle like that.' Dora smiled sheepishly. 'Can we start again? Be friends?'

She held out her hand. Millie took it gratefully. 'Yes, please. And I promise I won't ever try to offer you anything again.'

'Oh.' Dora's mouth twisted. 'Well, that's a shame, because I wouldn't say no to borrowing those books? Just a loan, mind, when you're not using them?' she added hastily.

'Please, have them...' Millie began, then stopped herself. She could see from the proud tilt of Dora's chin that she would never accept anything that even hinted at charity. 'Just borrow them whenever you like,' she offered.

Chapter Eight

Every Thursday, Veronica Hanley met Sister Parker and Sister Sutton to make a quilt.

None of them could remember how long they had been doing it, or why they had even started. But that didn't matter. What Miss Hanley and the two elderly nurses looked forward to most

83

was making themselves comfortable in the over-stuffed armchairs of Sister Sutton's cosy sitting room and putting the world to rights while they snipped and stitched. The arrangement suited Veronica Hanley, who couldn't abide idleness in any form. She would never have allowed herself to sit and drink tea and gossip for the sake of it. But cutting out neat squares of fabric, hemming and pinning then stitching them together, gave her a sense of purpose.

She knew the other sisters looked forward to their weekly get togethers as much as she did. Florence Parker and Agatha Sutton had been staff nurses when Veronica Hanley first came to the Nightingale as a student. They were sisters of their own wards by the time she had qualified, and she had worked as a staff nurse on Male Medical under Sister Parker for many years.

Now the pair were in their sixties and app-roaching the end of their nursing careers, they had been given the less arduous jobs of looking after the students. It was a great kindness on the part of the old Matron, and so typical of her, thought Miss Hanley. She could never imagine Miss Fox, with her mad passion for modernising everything, sparing much thought for two elderly ladies. She would have retired them a long time ago, thrown them out like an old hospital mattress that had served its purpose and was no longer of any use.

Miss Fox was all for doing away with anything 'antiquated', as she called it. Why, only this morning – Veronica Hanley stabbed agitatedly at the square she was hemming as she remembered the discussion they'd had.

'Are you quite well, Veronica?' Florence Parker enquired in her soft Scottish accent. 'You're wielding that needle like Brutus on the Ides of March.'

'I am well, thank you, Florence.' She stared down in frustration at the big, ugly stitches she had just made. She was determined not to allow that wretched woman to ruin her enjoyment of her afternoon, sitting with her friends around the crackling fire, Sparky dozing on the rug at their feet. Outside, the November wind howled, hurling rain like pebbles against the window.

And yet she couldn't forget about it.

'I suppose this is something to do with our new Matron?' Florence Parker regarded her shrewdly over the rim of her spectacles. 'Come along, my dear, you may as well spit it out. What has she done now?'

Veronica pressed her lips tightly together in an effort not to speak. It wasn't her way to whinge and complain. Her father would never have tolerated it. Even when her mother died in India while she was away at boarding school, she wasn't allowed to shed any tears.

'We'll have no weeping and wailing in front of the servants,' her father had declared briskly, as they followed the funeral cortège under the baking Bombay sun.

But this wasn't complaining for the sake of it, she decided.

'She has done away with the bath book,' she said.

Silence fell. Veronica waited for an explosion of outrage from the other sisters.

'Is that all?' Florence said, returning to her

85

stitching. 'Really, Veronica, from the way you were talking, I thought it must be something truly serious.'

'But this *is* serious.' Veronica stared at her in disbelief. How could she not see how serious it was? For as long as she could remember, each ward had kept a detailed ledger recording when each patient was given a bath. It was an absolute cornerstone of care on the wards, enshrined in many years of tradition. The very idea of getting rid of it was sacrilege.

'Well, I can't see the harm in it,' Florence said. 'I must say, I'm surprised we still have them at all. I've always thought it was a rather silly system, and such a waste of time. Surely a sister should know if one of her patients hasn't had a bath in three days? It's a poor show on her if she doesn't.'

'But ... but...' Veronica's mouth opened and closed but no sound came out. For someone who had trained at the very nursing school that Florence Nightingale had set up at St Thomas' Hospital, and who had even met Miss Nightingale herself, Sister Parker took a rather surprising attitude towards standards, she decided.

'Well, I agree with you, Veronica. It's an absolute disgrace,' Agatha Sutton declared, her chins wobbling as she cut herself another slice of seed cake. 'It's the way we've always done things here, and Miss Fox should respect that.'

'Exactly.' Veronica nodded in agreement, trying not to notice that Agatha was dropping crumbs all over her sewing.

'There's nothing wrong with change, Agatha. If we insisted on continuing to do things the way we'd always done them, then we would still be sawing off people's legs without anaesthetic, and drilling holes in their heads to let out the bad humours,' Florence Parker put in.

'That isn't the same thing at all,' Agatha Sutton exclaimed crossly.

'Isn't it? The world is changing, whether we like it or not. We need to embrace the new ways, or get left behind. Not all change is bad, you know.'

'Well, I don't hold with any of it.'

Veronica Hanley fixed her gaze on the mantelpiece as the sisters bickered. A stuffed magpie trapped under a glass dome stared glassily back at her. Agatha had a mania for knick-knacks. Every table and inch of sideboard seemed to be crammed with china ornaments, glass paperweights, toby jugs, and a curious creature made from polished shells, with 'A Gift from Hastings' printed on it.

It was all far too sentimental for her taste. She had no time for fanciful gew-gaws. As the daughter of a British army officer, travelling from one continent to the other, she had learnt early on not to become too attached to anything.

'I think it can only lead to laziness,' Agatha declared.

'I agree,' Veronica said firmly. 'And I'm sure Mrs Tremayne will feel the same way when I tell her about it.'

Florence Parker put down her sewing and looked up sharply. 'You're going to tell Mrs Tremayne?'

'Why not? She is on the Board of Trustees. She should know about anything that affects the reputation of the hospital.'

'I agree, but surely it is Matron's place to tell her, not yours?'

Two bright spots of colour burned in Veronica's cheeks, and not just from the warmth of the fire. It was only a mild rebuke, but it hit home.

'Mrs Tremayne would want to know,' she insisted stubbornly. Constance Tremayne had confided as much herself, when she had graciously invited Miss Hanley out for tea shortly after Miss Fox had been appointed.

'I can assure you, Miss Hanley, that had the decision been left to me it would be you at the helm,' she had said, as she poured tea into delicate china cups. She was so gracious, so elegant, with her fine bones like a ballerina.

They had first met when Veronica Hanley was a young girl. Before she'd started her training at the Nightingale, she had spent two years as a cadet nurse in a small hospital in Ipswich, where Constance Tremayne was a young staff nurse.

Not that Mrs Tremayne remembered her. Veronica hadn't liked to mention their earlier acquaintance. She guessed Constance would have no interest in remembering those early days.

'I daresay Nightingale's is in for a rather bumpy voyage with Miss Fox,' Mrs Tremayne had continued. 'But I hope I can rely on you to help keep our little ship on an even keel. And if you should ever find something amiss, you know you can always bring it to my attention...'

Veronica knew exactly what she meant. She didn't hold with spying, or any other underhand behaviour. But she didn't believe there was anything underhand about Constance Tremayne's request. She knew Nightingale's meant as much to Mrs Tremayne as it did to her. She was only asking this for the good of the hospital.

'I will do my best, Mrs Tremayne,' she had promised solemnly.

Constance Tremayne had laughed lightly. 'Constance, please. We are friends, after all.'

Veronica was so flattered and flustered she had slopped tea into her saucer. She'd thought about reminding her just how far back their acquaintance went, but had a feeling Mrs Tremayne wouldn't want to know.

'Quite right, too,' Agatha said now, sucking the end of her thread. 'Really, Florence, I am most surprised at you. Veronica understands how things should be done. She has dedicated her whole life to the Nightingale. We don't want some chit of a girl coming in and ruining everything.' She squinted up at the light as she tried to thread the needle with her short, fat fingers. 'Where is she from, anyway? Does anyone know anything about her? She's Irish, isn't she?'

'I believe she's from somewhere in the north,' Veronica said. 'Lancashire, I think.'

'Well, that's just as bad,' Agatha Sutton said. 'She doesn't know how we do things here. Whereas Veronica–'

She suddenly broke off, threw down her sewing and hauled herself to her feet. Veronica and Florence exchanged wry looks as she trundled across the room, Sparky at her heels, threw open the door and bellowed, 'You! Yes, you girl. Did I hear you running just then? Don't argue with me,

89

I trust my own hearing more than I trust you. No, I don't want to hear your feeble excuses. I'm not interested in them. If I catch you running one more time, I will send you to Matron. And I dare say you won't be in such a hurry to get to *her* office.'

She slammed the door shut, bustled back to her armchair, lowered herself into it and picked up her sewing as if nothing had happened.

'Nothing gets past you, does it, Agatha?' Florence Parker said, amused.

'Indeed it doesn't. One has to be absolutely firm with these girls. Heaven knows, some of them need it. You can't imagine the lack of discipline when they arrive here. Some of them are little better than savages. It makes me wonder what their mothers have been doing all these years.' She went back to trying to thread her needle, until Veronica took it from her.

'I have to agree,' Florence said. 'It's very difficult getting them to concentrate in the classroom. It's taken this past two weeks to get the silliness out of them. And some of them still haven't lost it.'

'What are they like, the new set?' Veronica asked, handing the threaded needle back to Agatha.

'A rather mixed bag, I'm afraid. Some are very bright, but there are one or two others who leave me rather despairing.'

'Let me guess – Benedict?' Agatha Sutton shook her head. 'She is simply the most frivolous girl I have ever met. I rather thought she might have gone home after failing preliminary training first time. After all, it's not as if the girl needs a career.'

'I must say, I was surprised to see her return,'

Florence agreed. 'Perhaps she has more spirit than we give her credit for? She certainly tries hard enough. Although she does tend to lack concentration.'

'Not what we want on the wards,' Veronica said firmly.

'I thought putting her in a room with Tremayne would calm her down, but it doesn't seem to have worked,' said Agatha.

Veronica smiled approvingly. Helen Tremayne would be a good influence on anyone. Her mother must be so proud of her. 'I'm surprised Matron allowed her a second chance,' she said.

Florence sent her a sharp look. 'I dare say she had her reasons.'

'I'm sure you're right. But I must say, she has made some rather odd decisions with this new set.' Veronica paused. 'Speaking of which, how is that other girl getting on? The one with the ginger hair?'

'You mean Doyle? She's very bright.'

'Really?' It wasn't the reply Veronica had been expecting. She'd thought Florence Parker would roll her eyes and despair of Matron's poor judgement. 'We are talking about the same girl, aren't we? The common one? Rather plain?'

Florence frowned. 'Really, Veronica, you seem to have formed a very poor opinion of her. But I can assure you, Doyle is extremely hard-working, and shows a great deal of natural ability. I would go as far as to say she is a born nurse.' She sighed. 'Unfortunately, though, it may be that she won't make it beyond preliminary training.'

'Why not?'

'She has no books. She makes all kinds of excuses, but it's plain she can't afford to buy them. I have offered her secondhand books, I have even wondered about providing some kind of bursary for her, with Matron's approval, but she won't have it. Absolutely refuses anything approaching charity. She has a stubborn East End pride that I'm afraid will be the undoing of her.'

'I hardly think the people of the East End have anything to be proud about.' Veronica's lip curled. She caught the reproachful look Florence gave her. 'It's true,' she insisted. 'You know as well as I do how these people live. How many years have you spent, washing grimy bodies that have never seen hot water, shaving and sulphur-bathing children crawling with lice, scabies and ringworm? Not to mention patching up tarts riddled with disgusting venereal diseases?' She shuddered.

'If you dislike them so much, I wonder why you've stayed here so long?' Florence Parker said, her eyes back on her sewing. 'I would have thought a comfortable convalescent home with nice, clean patients and respectable diseases would have suited you much better?'

Veronica felt Agatha's tiny raisin-black eyes swivel towards her. 'I felt it was my duty to stay here,' she said stiffly. 'After all, Miss Nightingale herself worked hard to establish excellent standards amid filth and hardship.'

Florence's mouth curved. 'I hope you're not comparing Nightingale's to the field hospital at Scutari?'

Veronica flushed. She respected Florence Parker, but sometimes felt she could be rather

92

mischievous. 'Of course not,' she said. 'I'm merely saying Miss Nightingale didn't shirk from her duty, and neither do I.'

But it was more than duty that kept her at the Nightingale Hospital. It was the only home and family she had known for more than thirty years.

'Anyway, if you ask me, it's an outrage.' Agatha Sutton brought the subject back to Dora Doyle. 'The girl should never have been allowed to come in the first place if she can't afford to be here.'

'I do agree it seems rather cruel, to offer her this chance, knowing she won't be able to see it through,' Florence Parker sighed.

Veronica Hanley ducked her head and smiled down at her stitching. Another of Matron's ridiculous ideas, she thought. Just like getting rid of the bath book.

Chapter Nine

Nurse Tremayne was one of the few students of whom Head Porter Edwin Hopkins approved. He prided himself on his high standards, even if his raggle-taggle regiment of porters sometimes didn't. Old habits died hard; he had been an officer's batman in the 38th Welsh Division during the Great War, and sixteen years later he never turned out for duty looking less than parade-ground smart, with a shine on his shoes, his brown overalls pressed, moustache perfectly trimmed, and what was left of his hair slicked carefully into place with a generous dollop of Brylcreem.

He appreciated neatness, order and punctuality, and Nurse Tremayne had all those qualities. Every morning, rain or shine, he would see her heading across the courtyard towards his lodge to hand in a letter for posting. Regular as clockwork she was, while he was having his morning cup of tea and a look through the *Daily Sketch*. And every morning she would greet him with a very polite, 'Good morning, Mr Hopkins.'

'Good morning, Nurse,' he would reply. 'Another letter, is it? There's lovely.' Then he would look at the envelope, to check the stamp and the address. It was always the same. 'I bet there's a lot of mothers wish they had a daughter like you, writing every day. I'm sure she appreciates it.'

And Nurse Tremayne would always give him that same sad little smile.

'I do hope so, Mr Hopkins,' she'd say. And then she was off, head down, walking briskly across the courtyard towards the ward block to begin her day.

Nurse Tremayne had manners. Very poised and ladylike and never a hair out of place, not like some of them he saw scuttling across the courtyard when they thought they wouldn't be seen, pinning their caps into place and fastening up their collars and cuffs as they went. Unlike most of them, he had never caught Nurse Tremayne trying to sneak past his lodge after lights out or scrambling through a window someone had left open round the back of the nurses' home. As far as he knew, she had never even asked for a late pass. And quite right too, in his opinion; girls who roamed the streets at that time of night were after getting themselves into serious trouble.

He'd caught another bunch of them the previous night, tipsy as you like, giggling as they tried to give each other a leg up the drainpipe. They were all up in front of Matron this morning, of course, but it could have been a lot worse. The state they were in, they could have broken their necks.

But not Nurse Tremayne. She wasn't the type to gad about and get herself in a drunken state. He doubted if she even knew what a good time was. She always had that worried furrow between her brows, her shoulders hunched as if she had the weight of the world on them.

No wonder she didn't turn heads the way the other students did. His porters would often hang about in the lodge just to watch the nurses go by and pass comments on their favourites. Hopkins didn't hold with it, but some of these East End lads hadn't been brought up to respect ladies the way he had. The saucier nurses even played up to it as they sauntered past, glancing over their shoulders to give them the eye.

But they never commented on Nurse Tremayne. Most of them barely seemed to notice her as she slipped by, her head down, cloak pulled around her.

Mr Hopkins sighed to himself. As he often said to Mrs Hopkins, he did not hold with gadding about. But if ever there was a girl who deserved a bit of gadding, it was poor Nurse Tremayne.

Helen walked to Holmes, the Male Surgical ward, worrying about what she'd just done. She always panicked after she'd posted a letter to her mother, just in case she'd accidentally let anything slip. She tried to be careful, but it was difficult to think straight when she was tired after a long day on the wards.

Not that it really mattered what she wrote. Whether it was a few scribbled lines or several pages detailing all the medical procedures she had learnt and all the praise she'd received in the ward report for her hard work, her mother would still be bitterly disappointed in her.

Helen was fourteen years old when her mother told her she was going to be a nurse. It didn't occur to her to argue. Her mother chose her hairstyle, her clothes, friends, and everything else, so why should her future be any different? Like her mild-mannered father, Helen had understood early on in life that her mother did not appreciate anyone's opinion but her own, and that the quickest way to stop any unpleasantness was just to give in straight away.

And having decided that her daughter was going to be a nurse, Constance Tremayne wouldn't even consider the idea of her training anywhere but the Nightingale.

'It has an excellent reputation,' she'd said. 'And since I'm on the Board of Trustees, I can keep an eye on you,' she'd added sternly.

'But what if I don't get in?' Helen had asked.

Her mother had stared at her as if this were the most ridiculous question in the world. 'Of course you'll get in, you silly girl,' she'd said. 'I'll see to that.'

And she had. Helen had sat mute during the

interview as her mother made all kinds of promises on her behalf to be a good, upright, moral
character. She sang her daughter's praises so
highly Helen almost didn't recognise herself. She
certainly didn't sound like the same girl her
mother was always criticising for being lazy, untidy
or walking with hunched shoulders.

Her interview had happened before the old
Matron left, which was just as well as Helen suspected that her mother didn't have a great deal of
time for the new one. She had been most put out
when the rest of the Board of Trustees had
overruled her and appointed Miss Fox. Helen
wasn't sure her mother would ever be able to
forgive them or the new Matron for it.

But the old one had been cut from the same
cloth as Constance Tremayne. Together they had
shaken their heads and tutted over the dreadful
state of young women these days, and Constance
Tremayne had assured Matron that her daughter
wasn't like that at all, that she was an upright,
God-fearing young woman who went to church
every Sunday, worked hard at her school studies
and had no social life at all.

When the interview was over Matron had said,
'Well, Mrs Tremayne, I hope Helen becomes as
excellent a nurse as her mother obviously was.'

And Constance Tremayne had simpered and
preened and thanked her for her time. And then
she had dragged Helen to Bentalls in Kingston
and kitted her out with stout black shoes, a watch
with a second timer, and half a dozen sets of
dreadful combinations which she insisted Helen
should wear even though she loathed the very

sight of them.

She didn't think she would ever be as good a nurse as her mother had been. Constance Tremayne was a woman of such energy and high moral character, her daughter was only ever going to be a disappointment by comparison.

From far away came the faint rumble of thunder. Helen looked up at the pewter-coloured sky, still dark and heavy with clouds. It was nearly seven o'clock on what promised to be a damp, grey November Sunday morning.

She wondered whether it was raining over in Richmond, and whether anyone would venture to church for her father's service. She hated to think of him working so hard on his sermon and no one being there to appreciate it.

'Helen, wait!' She glanced over her shoulder at the young man hurrying towards her, his white coat flapping.

She suppressed a sigh of irritation as he fell into stride beside her. She was tall but he stood half a head above her, all lanky angles, his dark hair sticking up in untidy tufts, defying his attempts to comb it.

'I've been looking for you,' he said.

'What do you want, William?'

He looked hurt. 'Can't a chap show an interest in his sister without having an ulterior motive?'

'Not in your case.'

Fat drops of rain began to spatter down on the cobbles. Helen quickened her pace but William pulled her into the shelter of the trees in the centre of the courtyard.

'I can't stand here, I'll be late,' she protested.

98

'You're not due on the ward for another ten minutes.'

'We're not supposed to talk to men.'

'I'm your brother, I don't count. Anyway, I want to ask you a favour.'

A couple of other nurses had also taken shelter under the plane trees. Helen pretended not to notice as her brother gave them an appreciative once over. She tapped her foot and peered up at the sky. Another couple of minutes and she ran the risk of being late. What would Sister Holmes say then?

William, on the other hand, seemed in no hurry to go anywhere. He stood there whistling, his hands in the pockets of his white coat, unconcerned by the needs of his waiting patients. Such was the life of a senior houseman, Helen thought.

'Heard from Mother?' he asked.

'I had a letter yesterday.'

He grinned. 'Let me guess. Several pages of closely written script, warning you against everything from fraternising with medical students to not wearing your combinations?'

'It's not funny. Anyway, you're the one she should have her eye on, not me. Why don't *you* ever get letters from her?'

'I do get letters from her. All the time. But I can't help it if I'm too busy saving lives to answer them, can I?' His expression of mock innocence made Helen smile in spite of herself. William could charm the birds out of the trees. He was certainly doing a good job on the nurses, who were smiling at him through the dripping branches of the plane trees.

He did an equally good job with their mother.

He charmed and flattered her so much, Constance Tremayne was as blind to her son's true nature as she was suspicious of Helen's.

'And she believes that, does she?'

'She's very impressed with my dedication,' William said piously.

'I wish I was as good a liar as you.' Helen even felt guilty when she was telling her mother the truth. Constance Tremayne had a way of looking at her that made Helen feel as if her head was made of glass and all her thoughts were visible for her mother to probe and pick over.

She turned to face him. 'So what favour do you want? Money? Or have you accidentally killed a patient and need my help covering it up?'

'Helen! I haven't killed anyone in months and you know it.' William's thickly fringed dark brown eyes twinkled. 'But now you mention it, I am rather strapped for cash. If you're offering?'

'I wasn't.' She peered out from under the dripping branches at the rain hammering off the cobbles and wondered if she should make a run for it.

'Please, Hels. Just a few bob till payday? I wouldn't ask, but I am in great need. You know I get paid a pittance.'

'You get paid more than me.'

'Yes, well, you're so much better at managing money than I am. Come on, Hels,' he wheedled. 'I know you've got it all stashed away in a Post Office account somewhere. I mean, it's not as if you go anywhere to spend it, do you?'

'Unlike you.' William spent every penny he earnt, and more besides.

'Actually, the money's not for me. It's for Bessie.' He lowered his voice. 'I'm afraid she's very sick.'

Helen sighed. 'What is it this time? Blown gasket? Exhaust pipe dropped off? Honestly, Will, why don't you just get rid of the wretched car?'

William reeled back. 'How can you even say that? Bessie means everything to me. And I'll have you know there's plenty of life in the old girl.'

'If she's got such a long and happy life ahead of her, it won't hurt her to stay off the road for a couple of weeks until you get paid, will it?'

'Ah, well, yes. That might be possible, except–' He smoothed down a cowlick of dark hair, which sprang straight back up again. 'I sort of promised someone a trip to the coast next weekend.'

Helen rolled her eyes. 'How did I know there would be a girl involved?'

'She's not just any girl. I've been trying to get her to agree to go out with me for weeks. I think she may be the love of my life,' he confided.

'You said that about the last one. And the one before that.'

'I can't help it if I lose my heart easily, can I?'

'It's not *your* heart I'm worried about.' She glanced at the two nurses, still smiling shyly at William. They might feel flattered, but what they didn't realise was that William was as fickle and easily bored as he was charming. There were many casualties of his affections among the nurses of Nightingale's.

'I suppose she knows what she's letting herself in for?' Helen sighed.

'I'm not that bad, Hels.'

'I know exactly what you're like. You might be

able to fool Mother and half the nurses in this hospital, but you can't fool me, remember?'

William's confident smile slipped a fraction, and Helen knew he was thinking about all the times she'd got him out of a mess in the past. It was hard to be annoyed with him for long, she thought. Underneath all that charm, William had a good heart. It was a pity no girl had managed to reach it yet.

Helen sighed. 'I can spare two pounds. But I want it back.'

'You'll get it back, Sis, I promise. Every penny. With interest.' William's brown eyes sparkled. 'You're the best sister a chap ever had.'

'And you're the worst brother!'

As he walked jauntily away, hands thrust into the pockets of his white coat, she called out to him.

'William? You will be careful, won't you?'

Her grinned back. 'You know me, Hels.'

Yes, I do, she thought. That's the trouble.

Chapter Ten

Helen had been assigned to Holmes, the Male Surgical ward, for the next three months of her training. Another senior student, Amy Rollins, had been assigned with her. Helen had hoped that by working together they might become better friends. But no matter how friendly she tried to be, Amy treated her with the same mistrust as all the other girls did.

102

She was in a particularly bad mood on that morning, as she and some of the other second years had been caught by Hopkins the Head Porter coming home from celebrating Ellis' birthday, and they had all received a dressing down from Matron.

'I hope you didn't have anything to do with it?' she hissed at Helen as they served breakfast to the patients.

'Why should I want to get you into trouble?' Helen asked.

'It wouldn't be the first time, would it? We haven't forgotten what you did to Peggy Gibson.'

Helen sighed. That name had haunted her for over a year. 'Peggy Gibson was dismissed because of her own stupid mistake–'

'Which you couldn't wait to tell your mother about!' Amy snapped back. 'She'd still be here, if you hadn't betrayed her.'

'Hollins! Tremayne! Stop gossiping and take this to Mr Nicholls in bed five. You can discuss your social life in your own time,' Sister Holmes snapped at them.

What social life? Helen thought, ignoring the black look Amy sent her as she whisked past with a tray. She was never included in the other girls' plans. And even if she had been, her mother would never have allowed her to go anywhere.

'Your mate's a little ray of sunshine this morning, isn't she?' Mr Denton commented later when Helen arrived with her trolley to dress his leg. 'Practically threw my breakfast at me, she did.'

'I'm sorry, Mr Denton. I'm afraid she's – um – had some bad news.' Helen pulled the screens around the bed. It wasn't really a lie, since Amy and the others had had their leave cancelled as punishment.

'All the same, that's no reason to take it out on the rest of us. Some of the poor old crocks in here aren't exactly having a picnic themselves,' Mr Denton said. 'Take that Mr Bennett. Now he really has got something to moan about, wouldn't you say, Nurse? I'd like to see your pal Nurse Hollins have to put up with his piles for a week.'

So would I! Helen thought, keeping her head down, arranging bowls and swabs on her trolley so Mr Denton wouldn't see her smiling to herself at the thought.

But he did. 'That made you laugh, didn't it?' He grinned. 'Don't worry, Nurse, I won't tell anyone. I've seen the way she snaps your head off, too. I don't know why you don't clock her one sometimes. I reckon you must have the patience of a saint.'

'I don't know about that, Mr Denton. Now let's take a look at that leg, shall we?'

Helen carefully took off the splint and steeled herself to examine what was left of Mr Denton's leg. He had undergone an emergency amputation a week earlier after trapping it in machinery at the timber yard where he worked. He should have been on the Orthopaedic ward, but he'd been transferred to Surgical due to a lack of beds.

Even after seeing it every day, uncovering the red, angry-looking stump was still a shock to her. He seemed to read her thoughts. 'Not a pretty sight, is it?' He smiled grimly.

'It's getting a lot better. The wound is clean and

there's no sign of infection around the stitches,' Helen said briskly. 'It'll be even better after I've cleaned it up for you.'

It was just such a tragedy to happen to a young man, she thought as she cleaned it carefully with soap and water. He was only twenty-three, fit and strong. Life could be so cruel sometimes.

Not that Mr Denton saw it that way. He was grateful just to be alive.

'So it's looking all right, is it, Nurse?' he asked, as he always did.

'Fine, Mr Denton. Healing up very nicely.'

'That's all down to you, that is. You really look after me.' He watched her dabbing the wound gently. 'You're an angel, you know that?'

'It's my job, Mr Denton.'

'I wish you'd call me Charlie.'

'You know that's not allowed.' Helen finished cleaning his wound and reached for the bottle of methylated spirit. 'Now brace yourself, Mr Denton. This might sting a bit.'

'Sting, she says!' he hissed between clenched teeth, as Helen applied the spirit. 'Forget what I said about you being an angel, Nurse T. You're a demon, that's what you are!'

Helen smiled. He cursed her every time. 'Don't be such a baby, Mr Denton. It's for your own good.'

'True enough, I suppose.' He watched her as she applied powder to his leg to dry it. 'When d'you reckon I'll be up and about?'

'You'd have to ask the doctor that. But we usually aim to get you exercising as soon as possible after your wound has healed, and you'll

105

be fitted with a temporary prosthetic after about a month,' she quoted the chapter of the medical book she'd been studying the night before. She hadn't done a stint on Orthopaedics yet, but she'd been reading up on amputations since Charlie Denton had arrived on the ward.

'A month!' he groaned. 'Oh, well, I suppose it's not that long when you think about it. I'm a lot better off than that poor bloke who came in last night.'

Sister Holmes had told them about the emergency head injury that had been admitted the previous evening. A young man, Mr Oliver, had been brought in with a compound depressed fracture. He'd been in theatre for most of the night and was now recovering in a private room at the far end of the ward.

'Motorbike accident on the Mile End Road, so I heard,' Charlie Denton said. 'How is he, do you know?'

'He's as well as can be expected,' Helen replied. Not that she knew much about it – only the staff nurses were allowed to nurse the patients in the side wards.

'Well, I hope he pulls through. Poor bloke, I don't think he's any older than me. It just goes to show, doesn't it? You have to make the most of every minute, because you never know if it's going to be your last.'

He was silent while Helen replaced his splint, lost in his own thoughts. But by the time she'd finished he'd cheered up.

'Anyway, nothing can upset me today,' he said brightly. 'It's visiting day. My Sal's coming in to see me.'

Helen had heard a lot about Charlie Denton's Sal in the week he'd been on the ward. He talked about his fiancée all day, every day. She had never met a man so besotted.

'I can't wait for you to meet her, Nurse,' he said, as Helen pulled the screens back. A few beds down Amy was doing the drinks round, reciting the list to Mr Bennett.

'We've got tea, coffee, cocoa, hot milk, cold milk, Ovaltine...' she intoned in a bored voice.

'I'm telling you, I was a lucky man the day she agreed to marry me,' Charlie Denton said.

'I'm sure she's a lucky woman, too.' He seemed like quite a catch to Helen, well built and handsome, with coppery-fair hair and warm blue eyes that crinkled when he smiled.

His smile faltered now. 'I dunno if she thinks she's so lucky. Reckon she might think she's got a pretty bad deal, what with my one leg and all.' He looked down at it. 'She didn't bargain for that the day she said she'd marry me, did she?'

'What do they say, Mr Denton? "In sickness and in health"?' Helen reminded him, carefully arranging his covers and tucking them in around him.

'I hope you're right, Nurse.'

Amy arrived at the end of the bed next to his. It was occupied by Mr Nicholls, a very elderly hernia patient who was also very deaf.

'What do you want to drink?' she bawled at him.

'What have you got?' he bawled back.

'Same as we had yesterday. And the day before. And the one before that, you silly old goat,' Amy muttered. Then she pasted a smile on her face

107

and said aloud, 'We've got tea, coffee, cocoa, hot milk, cold milk, Ovaltine–'

'What?'

'Tea, coffee, cocoa, hot milk–'

'What?'

'I said hot milk–' Amy was getting red-faced with the sheer effort of shouting.

'Did you say Bovril?'

'No, I said–'

'I'd like a Bovril, dear, please.' Mr Nicholls settled happily back against his pillows. Helen and Charlie exchanged amused glances.

'You'll have a bloody tea and like it.' Amy sloshed some into a cup and shoved it at him, then moved on to Charlie Denton.

'What do you want to drink?' she asked.

'What have you got?' he asked.

Amy jerked her head towards the next bed. 'Didn't you hear me telling him?'

'Sorry, Nurse, I don't like eavesdropping on other people's conversations.'

It was all Helen could do to keep a straight face as Amy rolled her eyes and began, 'We've got tea, coffee, cocoa, hot milk, cold milk, Ovaltine–'

'I don't think I fancy anything, thanks, Nurse.'

'Then why did you make me go through the list?'

'I thought you might have something different.'

'Well, we haven't. And you'd better get a move on, Tremayne. Sister Holmes says it's nearly time for Sunday prayers.' Amy shot them both a dirty look and then moved on.

'It wouldn't hurt her to crack a smile, would it?' Charlie said.

'I told you, she's had bad news.'

'All the more reason to do it. It makes you feel better, doesn't it?' He looked at Helen consideringly. 'Like you. You're always smiling. And yet I can see you don't feel like it half the time.'

'I don't know what makes you say that.' Flustered, Helen tidied her trolley. 'Anyway, Nurse Hollins is right about one thing, I can't sit here all day. I've got to get on if we're going to have this ward ready for visitors.'

'Quite right.' Charlie grinned. 'I need a wash and brush up if I'm going to be seeing my Sal. She doesn't like a man looking scruffy. Don't want her to think I can't look after myself, do I?'

After they had said Sunday prayers and sung a hymn with the patients, the rest of the morning was spent cleaning the ward, changing beds and smartening up the patients ready for visiting hour. By two o'clock, the visitors had started to arrive. Wives, girlfriends, mothers, fathers, friends, all gathered outside the closed doors, their faces pressed eagerly against the glass, smiling and waving at their loved ones inside the ward. Sister Holmes was on the other side of the doors, checking her watch and ignoring the imploring looks of the people outside.

'Still three minutes until two o'clock.' She looked up and down the ward, satisfying herself that everything was as it should be, and that both ward and patients were ready to receive visitors.

It should be, Helen thought. The floors shone, the windows sparkled and the beds were all neatly made, with each sheet folded down exactly ten inches, thanks to Sister Holmes and her tape

109

measure. The whole ward smelt of polish and disinfectant. The patients had all been scrubbed and polished ready for inspection too. They were sitting up in bed in their fresh pyjamas, hair neatly combed, waiting for their visitors to arrive.

If they ever arrived. Sister Holmes took great pride in her ward and was fussy about who came in. She insisted on inspecting every visitor as they walked in. If they were too scruffy, they had a whiff of alcohol about them or she didn't feel they had a good enough reason to be there, she would send them away.

'Now remember, Nurses,' she warned them. 'You must be on your guard and vigilant at all times. No more than two visitors to a patient, and if you see anyone sitting on a bed, they must be ejected at once.'

The clock struck two. With obvious reluctance, Sister Holmes opened up the doors and began issuing the visitors' cards. Each patient had two cards; if more than two visitors had the audacity to turn up, one had to wait outside until another came and handed over their card, like a relay race. Helen had known fights to break out in the corridor when one loved one felt another had overstayed their time.

There were also nurses strategically placed up and down the ward to spy on the patients and make sure the rules were kept. They had to keep an especially careful eye out for any food being handed over. Fruit and sweets were allowed, unless the patient's diet forbade it – and it was amazing how many soft-hearted friends and relatives tried to bring them in anyway, thinking they were doing them a kindness – but other food had to be taken straight to the ward kitchen. If not it would end up rotting, and Helen had scraped mould out of patients' lockers too often to want that to happen.

She was told to station herself at the linen cupboard. As she headed up the ward, Charlie called her over.

'Nurse! Sorry to trouble you, but could you do me a favour?'

'What is it, Mr Denton?' Helen approached, praying he wouldn't ask for a bottle or a bedpan. Sister Holmes expressly forbade any to be given out during the two-hour visiting period, because it made the ward look untidy. Poor patients who missed her strict deadline had to cross their legs and hope for the best.

'Could you help me sort these covers out, please? I want them arranged to hide – you know, make it less obvious. Could you do that?' He looked at her pleadingly.

'Of course I can.' Helen carefully arranged the covers around him to disguise his missing leg.

'Thanks, Nurse. Don't want to scare my Sal first time, do I?' He beamed gratefully at her. 'Got to give her a chance to get used to the idea, like.'

'That's very thoughtful of you, Mr Denton.'

'She's not here yet.' His gaze strayed to the doors. 'She's meant to be coming in with my mum. I expect their bus is late again.'

'I expect so.'

As she counted and recounted the linen in the cupboard, Helen kept an eye on Charlie Denton. Once or twice she saw him sit up as a woman

111

walked through the doors at the far end of the ward, only to slump back again when she headed for someone else's bed. Helen found herself watching the doors too.

After half an hour she was about to go over and ask if he would like a cup of tea, when a large, handsome, middle-aged woman strode into the ward. From her ruddy cheeks and the sandy hair curling out from under her hat, Helen guessed this was Mr Denton's mother.

'Charlie love!' her voice boomed out. Sister Holmes looked up from her desk, eyes narrowing beadily on the woman who had dared to disturb the peace of her ward. Even during visiting time, it was as quiet as a library.

Helen watched her pull up a chair at her son's bedside and begin unloading her bulging shopping bags. Magazines, a tin of toffees, a bag of grapes, apples and bananas, were all piled on to Charlie's bedside locker. But when she pulled out a bottle of stout, Sister Holmes swooped in.

Helen was watching the ensuing altercation when Amy appeared from the other side of the linen cupboard.

'Sister wants you to do the tea round.'

'But she told me to stay here and keep an eye on everyone.'

'Well, she's changed her mind, hasn't she?' Amy said nastily. 'Anyway, I did the wretched round this morning, so you can have the pleasure now.'

Reluctantly, Helen took herself off to the kitchen to put the water on to boil and get the tea ready. She did it far more quickly than usual, almost scalding herself as she poured boiling water into the urn in her rush to get back to the ward.

Serving the visitors tea was a new idea Matron had come up with. Usually Sister Holmes would have resisted anything that involved making them feel remotely welcome. But Matron was allowing them to charge visitors a few pennies a cup, which went towards raising funds for Christmas decorations and gifts.

As she clattered the trolley from bed to bed, serving tea to the patients and their visitors and collecting the money in a tin, Helen kept trying to steal glances up the ward towards Charlie Denton. He and his mother were deep in conversation.

'You've short changed me,' a voice complained, bringing her back to the present.

'Pardon?' Helen looked around vaguely. A woman was holding out her hand. In her palm were two large copper pennies.

'You've given me tuppence,' she repeated. 'I gave you sixpence. That's threepence change.'

'Oh. Sorry.' Helen absently reached into the tin, took out a threepenny bit and handed it to her.

'What's this? Not Tremayne making a mistake, surely?' Amy sidled up to her, smiling nastily. 'What's got into you today?'

Finally Helen reached Charlie Denton's bed.

'Nurse T!' He smiled up at her, but his blue eyes had lost some of their sparkle. 'Mum, this is the nurse I was telling you about. The one who's been looking after me.'

'I'm pleased to meet you.' Mrs Denton caught Helen's hand in an iron grip. Her own hands were as big and rough as a man's. 'I can't tell you how grateful I am to you for looking after my

113

Charlie. When he had that accident, I really thought I'd lost my little boy for sure...' She let go of Helen's hand and fumbled for a handkerchief in her coat pocket.

'Come off it, Mum! You'll make me a laughing stock.' He rolled his eyes at Helen. 'Does your mum ever embarrass you like this?'

You have no idea, Helen thought. 'Would you like a cup of tea, Mrs Denton?' she offered soothingly.

The bell for the end of visiting time rang out a few minutes later, and the visitors filed out. Helen didn't have the chance to speak to Charlie until it was time to serve the patients their evening meal.

She made sure she served Charlie. She was worried about him. Since his mother left, he had flicked listlessly through his magazines and not said a word to any of the other patients.

She wondered if she should mention his fiancée. But as she put his plate of boiled fish and mashed potatoes in front of him, he blurted out, 'Sally decided not to come. Reckons she just can't face seeing me in pain like this.'

'Oh. I'm sorry.'

'I don't blame her. I'd be the same if it was her in this hospital bed.' His eyes grew misty. 'She's such a soft-hearted girl, my Sal. She cares too much, you know what I mean?'

Helen knew it was wrong to judge. 'Judge not lest ye be yourselves judged', as the Bible said. But she couldn't help thinking that if her fiancé had just survived a near-fatal accident, wild horses wouldn't have kept her away from his bedside.

Chapter Eleven

Having worked alongside hospital consultants for twenty years, Kathleen Fox was used to people who thought they were God. But she had never met anyone quite so convinced of her omnipotence as Constance Tremayne.

She reminded Kathleen of a picture she had once seen in a children's book of the first Pilgrims to cross the Atlantic in *The Mayflower*. She bristled with righteousness from her tightly wound bun to her functional shoes.

It was eleven o'clock in the morning and Kathleen should have been getting on with her ward rounds, or checking the new duty rotas, or, God forbid, actually dealing with some medical matter. But instead she had been sitting in the Trustees meeting for almost two hours, justifying to this woman in the tiniest detail how she chose to manage her hospital.

First it was a lengthy discussion over the abolition of the ward bath book. And now they were arguing over, of all things, Christmas.

Every Christmas the Nightingale held a small concert for staff and patients. Afterwards, the junior staff were invited to a small supper dance in the dining room, funded by the Trustees in gratitude for their hard work throughout the year.

Kathleen had assumed everyone agreed this was a good idea. Until she saw Mrs Tremayne's tight-lipped expression.

'As you all know, I have been of the opinion for some years now that the tradition of the Christmas Dance should cease.' A faint groan rippled around the table, but Constance Tremayne ploughed on regardless. 'I hardly feel it is appropriate that the trustees should be spending money that has been entrusted to them for the care of patients on diversions for the staff!'

'For heaven's sake, we're not talking about hiring Billy Cotton!'

Kathleen hadn't realised she'd spoken aloud until she saw the startled looks on the faces of the other Trustees.

Mrs Tremayne faced her across the table, the light of battle gleaming in her eyes. 'I beg your pardon, Matron? Did you say something?'

Kathleen glanced around the table. Philip Enright, Chairman of the Trustees, smiled sympathetically back at her. He was head of the local council and a successful businessman with a string of draper's shops to his name. But faced with Mrs Tremayne with a bee in her bonnet, even he could do no more than shrug his shoulders.

The other trustees were little help either. Reginald Collins had his head down, busily pretending to add up a list of figures. He was an accountant and far too timid ever to challenge the formidable Mrs Tremayne. Lady Fenella Brake, the wife of an elderly peer, was too deaf and too dotty to know what was going on. And Gerald Munroe, the local MP, barely paid any attention during meetings, unless there was a chance of getting his name or his face in the newspapers.

The only person paying attention was the Chief Consultant, James Cooper. He met Kathleen's eye and gave her an encouraging nod, silently urging her to go on.

'I agree with you, Mrs Tremayne, patient care should come first,' she began. 'But the patients at the Nightingale Hospital are very well cared for, unlike many of the staff. Our nurses in particular work extremely long hours, often in harsh conditions. Surely it wouldn't harm to reward them with a little entertainment at Christmas time?'

'Bit of the old festive spirit, what?' Gerald Munroe put in. Mrs Tremayne silenced him with a withering look.

'Matron, may I remind you that we are running a hospital, not the Ritz? Yes, perhaps nurses do have to endure a little hardship at times,' she conceded, 'but that is no bad thing in my opinion. They should remember that they are also receiving some of the best nursing training in the country, and be grateful for it. A good nurse should be dedicated enough without needing to be rewarded by – entertainment.' She fingered the gold cross around her neck, her only adornment against her sober fawn suit. 'When I was training–'

'My nurses are dedicated,' Kathleen cut her off before she went into another long-winded story about the good old days. Irritation prickled up her spine. 'But they are also young women. Most of them will be spending Christmas working on the wards, away from their loved ones. Your own daughter among them, I have to say.'

Mrs Tremayne's jutting cheekbones were tinged with pink. 'And I'm sure my daughter will be only

117

too glad to do her duty,' she said stiffly.

Kathleen caught the amused glint in James Cooper's eyes. 'I dare say she will, Mrs Tremayne. As will our other nurses,' she agreed patiently. 'But that is exactly my point. While you are sitting down to enjoy your Christmas dinner, they will be on their feet for fourteen hours, cheerfully changing beds, cleaning out sputum mugs and fetching bedpans, or trying to bring some comfort to a dying woman who knows she will never spend another Christmas with her children. Perhaps you would like to explain to them why you feel they do not deserve a little diversion?'

'Hear hear,' James Cooper muttered.

'Indeed,' Gerald Munroe agreed. 'And I for one quite enjoy the Christmas Dance. A chance to see all the young ladies dressed up in their finery. Very pretty girls, some of them, I must say.'

He glanced around the table. Everyone stared back at him without commenting.

'Shall we take a vote?' Philip Enright suggested, with a touch of desperation.

In the end, Mrs Tremayne was defeated. Only Lady Fenella voted with her, although Kathleen suspected she didn't quite understand what she was voting for.

'Someone will not be getting a Christmas card from Mrs Tremayne,' James Cooper observed when the meeting finally broke up and they were heading back to the wards.

'I'm sure I can contain my disappointment.' Kathleen looked rueful. 'I really wish I knew why she disliked me so much,' she sighed.

James Cooper's brows rose. 'I would have

118

thought it was obvious. You stand up to her, unlike the rest of us. You must remember, Mrs T is accustomed to having her own way in these meetings. She certainly isn't used to anyone leading a rebellion against her.'

'I'm not interested in leading any kind of rebellion,' Kathleen said. 'I thought we were all supposed to be on the same side?'

'Only if that side happens to be Mrs Tremayne's.'

Kathleen massaged the tense muscles at the back of her neck. 'At least she didn't get her way over the Christmas Dance. I'm very glad about that. Apart from anything else, I think it's an excellent way of improving relations between the staff.'

'I think it's the "relations" she's worried about.' Mr Cooper smiled as he opened a door for her. The expression 'tall, dark and handsome' could have been invented with him in mind, she decided. 'Mrs Tremayne prides herself on being the hospital's moral guardian, don't forget. She thoroughly disapproves of anything that encourages fraternisation between the male and female staff. She believes all doctors are sex-crazed beasts in white coats. And the nurses aren't much better, either.'

'If doctors and nurses are going to fraternise at all, I would far rather it happened under the watchful eye of the senior staff than locked away in the basement by the stoke hole!'

'By the stoke hole, eh?' Mr Cooper looked amused. 'I do hope that isn't the voice of experience, Matron?'

'That would be telling, Mr Cooper.'

'I'm deeply shocked.' His eyes were extraordinary, she thought. A clear, sapphire blue, fringed with very long dark lashes. She could imagine they had a devastating effect on his female patients.

They reached the other side of the courtyard and Mr Cooper turned to her. 'This is where I have to leave you. I'm due in theatre, and thanks to Mrs Tremayne, I'm already at least two hysterectomies behind on my list.'

'And I'm late for my ward round.'

'I hope you make sure all those patients have had their baths, since you've wilfully done away with all the written records?'

'Don't.' Kathleen shook her head. Mrs Tremayne couldn't have been more shocked if she'd announced she was doing away with all the beds. Kathleen wasn't sure how she'd found out but she suspected Miss Hanley might have had a hand in it. She'd already made it quite clear where her loyalties lay.

Kathleen tried to forget the unpleasantness of the meeting as she headed off to do her ward rounds. She knew the nursing staff dreaded her daily visit, but she enjoyed meeting the patients and satisfying herself that they were being cared for properly. She tried not to give the harassed nurses too hard a time. Unlike the former Matron, who she'd heard wasn't averse to tossing poorly patients out of bed so she could lift the mattress and inspect the bedsprings for dust.

As she headed down the warren of corridors, she could hear a tide of whispering and scurrying feet going before her. She knew each ward would be ringing the others to warn them of her impending arrival. Even so, she usually managed to surprise a couple, and it amused her to see them all fluttering around like startled birds when she appeared in the doorway. Once she had found Sister Wren with her feet up in her sitting room, reading *Peg's Paper.*

Matron started with Blake, the Male Orthopaedic ward. It was usually a cheerful place, filled with good-humoured patients who were more bored with being laid up than gravely ill. The sister who ran Blake, Frannie Wallace, was an old friend of hers. They had worked together in Leeds, and it was Frannie who had written encouraging her to apply for the position of Matron at the Nightingale. She was one of the few friendly faces who greeted Kathleen on the wards.

But as she entered Blake today, Frannie was nowhere to be seen. There was no expectant line of nurses either, apart from a solitary pro scurrying up the ward with a bedpan. When she saw Matron she gave a squeak of terror and abruptly fled. Kathleen watched her dive through the screens around one of the beds, then appear a moment later, followed by Frannie and her staff nurse, an Irish girl called Bridget O'Hara.

Frannie smiled when she saw Kathleen. 'Matron, what a pleasant surprise,' she said, wiping her hands on her apron. 'What can I do for you?'

'I've come to do the ward round, Sister Blake.' Kathleen remembered to address her by her proper name. Sisters always took on the name of the ward they ran. 'I'm sorry I'm late. I was in a meeting that went on for rather a long time.'

'But I thought–' O'Hara blurted, until Frannie silenced her with a look. Kathleen glanced from her to the pro, who stared down at her sensible black shoes and looked as if she might cry.

'Is something wrong?' she asked.

'No, Matron, nothing is wrong,' Frannie said smoothly. 'The patients are ready for you, if you'll come this way?'

But Kathleen had an uneasy feeling as she followed Frannie to the first bed. As she talked to an elderly patient about his painful hip, she was aware of the pro whispering to Staff Nurse O'Hara behind her.

'But I don't understand. Miss Hanley–'

'Shut up!' O'Hara hissed back. 'Just get down to bed four and pray to God that enema hasn't worked yet!'

Kathleen watched her hurry away. 'Is there something you're not telling me?' she hissed to Frannie out of the corner of her mouth as they moved together to the next bed.

'Miss Hanley came and did your rounds earlier. She said you'd asked her to do it.' Frannie paused at the foot of the next bed. 'This is Mr Fletcher, who really should be in bed,' she announced, giving a mock severe look to the man who sat in the chair beside it, reading his newspaper.

'But, Sister, I'm much more comfortable here,' he protested.

'That's as may be, but you're not doing that arthritis any good in the long run.' Frannie plumped up his pillows, the crisp starched cotton crackling in her hands. 'Nurse O'Hara, please see that Mr Fletcher gets back into bed. After he's finished his newspaper,' she added, with a little smile in his direction.

122

'Thanks, Sister,' Mr Fletcher said gratefully. 'You're a sport.'

'Now, Mr Fletcher. I don't want nasty rumours like that getting around to the other patients.' As she walked away from the bed, she said to Kathleen, 'I don't blame him. It must be very painful to lie flat in his condition.'

'Yes, indeed.' But Kathleen could barely hear what Frannie was saying for the angry buzzing inside her head.

How dare Miss Hartley take it upon herself to do her rounds for her! No wonder the nurses had been so perplexed to see her. Now she was wasting their time forcing them to accompany her around the ward again. Either that or admit she'd got it wrong and make herself look foolish.

Either option made her blood boil.

Frannie must have noticed her silently fuming. When the round was over she said quietly, 'I wonder, Matron, if you could spare me a moment in private? There's a matter I wish to discuss with you.'

'Of course.'

Kathleen followed her into her sitting room, a comfortable little area just off the ward. She waited until Frannie had closed the door, then sank down into one of the armchairs that flanked the fireplace.

'Would you like some brandy? I keep it locked away in the kitchen for emergencies.' Her dark eyes were full of merriment as usual. 'On second thoughts, perhaps tea might be a safer bet.' She summoned the ward maid and asked for a tray to be brought in. Then she sat down opposite Kathleen. 'I take it you didn't know Miss Hanley was doing your rounds?'

'Indeed I didn't!' Kathleen replied. 'That woman really is the living end.'

'Perhaps she was trying to be helpful?' Frannie suggested.

Kathleen glared at her. 'You don't believe that, do you?'

'I suppose not,' Frannie conceded. 'Miss Hanley hasn't exactly been helpful to you so far, I must admit.'

There was a tap on the door and the ward maid entered with the tray. They both waited until she'd gone before Kathleen went on.

'I could cope with her being less than helpful. But it's the deliberate attempts to trip me up I can't stand. That and the constant bleating to Mrs Tremayne.'

'Ah, yes. Mrs Tremayne.' Frannie poured them both a cup of tea. 'They do seem to be as thick as thieves at the moment.'

'I'm sure she has Miss Hanley spying on me,' Kathleen said. 'She knew all about me getting rid of the ward bath book. That could only have come from Miss Hanley.'

'Are you sure about that?' Frannie sipped her tea. 'I wouldn't put it past Mrs Tremayne to have spies all over the hospital. Any one of the sisters could have told her.'

'Well, that's just marvellous, isn't it?' Kathleen's china cup rattled in its saucer as she put it down. 'So you're saying I have enemies everywhere?'

'Not enemies, Kath.' Frannie's voice was soothing, as if she was talking to a patient. 'But you're in charge, and not everyone is going to approve of all your decisions.'

'Maybe I shouldn't try to make any changes?' Kathleen said gloomily. 'Maybe I should just allow this place to go on the way it always has. That would please everyone, including Mrs Tremayne.'

'It wouldn't please you, though, would it? And it wouldn't do this place any good, either.' Frannie sighed impatiently. 'For heaven's sake, Kath, why do you think I talked you into applying for this job?'

Kathleen smiled wanly. 'Because you have some long-held grudge against me?'

'Because I knew you could make a difference. God knows the Nightingale needs shaking up, even if no one here would ever want to admit it. And you're just the one to do it.'

'Am I?' Kathleen allowed her gaze to drift towards the window. A nurse hurried past, her hand pressed against her cap to stop it blowing off. 'I'm not so sure any more.'

'Stop being so wet. It doesn't suit you.' Anyone outside on the ward would have been utterly shocked to hear a sister address the Matron in such a sharp and disrespectful way. But Frannie was one of Kathleen's oldest friends.

Frannie refilled her cup and stirred it thoughtfully. 'Do you remember the Matron back in Leeds?' she said after a moment.

'You mean The Monster?' Kathleen shuddered. 'She was utterly terrifying, wasn't she? I hope I never end up like her.'

'But that's just it. You've got to be. What do you think she would have done if she'd found Miss

125

Hanley had done her rounds for her?'

'Crushed her to dust, probably.'

'She would make sure she didn't do it again, that's for certain. And that's what you've got to do, Kath. Show them all who's boss. Including Constance Tremayne.'

Kathleen stared down into her empty teacup. It wasn't that simple, she thought. The Monster had been so old and wise. Sometimes when Kathleen saw the nurses' expectant faces looking to her for guidance, she felt as if she knew no more than they did. 'I'm scared, Fran,' she said.

'I know you are, ducks. But you can't let anyone see that.' Frannie smiled sympathetically and re-filled her cup. 'Like it or not, you're The Monster now.'

Kathleen returned to her office ten minutes later to find Miss Hanley sitting at her desk, rifling through some papers. 'Find anything interesting, Miss Hanley?'

A mottled flush crept up her flabby cheeks. 'I was – um – looking for the laundry order. It needs to be signed off, and since you were so late back from your meeting–'

'I did it yesterday.'

'Ah. Of course. That explains why I couldn't find it.' Miss Hanley shifted awkwardly from Kathleen's seat.

'I think you'll find the laundry orders are usually filed in there.' Kathleen nodded towards the filing cabinet on the other side of the room. 'In the drawer marked "Laundry Orders".'

Miss Hanley pursed her lips. 'I will try to remember that.'

As she headed for the door, Kathleen called after her, 'Thank you for doing the ward rounds for me, by the way. It was very thoughtful of you.'

'I was only doing my job,' she replied stiffly.

'Actually, Miss Hanley, you were doing *my* job. And I would appreciate it in future if you could let me know beforehand when you intend to take over any of my duties. If you don't mind?'

Miss Hanley's broad, square face twitched. 'I'll remember that,' she snorted.

And I'll make sure you do, Kathleen thought as the door banged behind her.

Chapter Twelve

It was the Saturday before Christmas, and Millie had been looking forward to going up to Oxford Street with some of the other students after they'd finished their morning lectures. But at the last moment Lucy Lane had been beastly to Jennifer Bradley, and both Jennifer and Dora had refused to go on the outing.

Millie would have refused to go too, but it was Katie O'Hara's first Christmas in London and Millie knew how much she was looking forward to seeing the festive lights in all the big shops.

'You've got to come with me,' Katie had pleaded with her. 'Please don't leave me with Lane! I don't think I could stand her bragging if you weren't there.'

It was bitingly cold and a thick yellow fog was curling off the river as they hurried to catch their bus. Millie and the others jammed their hats down over their ears and pulled up their scarves so they didn't have to breathe in the cloying, metallic-tasting air.

'I expect we'll have a lot of bronchitis cases turning up after this,' Katie predicted, her voice muffled through thick layers of wool. 'My sister says they have chest infections queuing up outside the gates once the winter fog comes down.'

The air was clearer in Oxford Street, which bustled with Christmas shoppers. On the corner with Regent Street a brass band was playing Christmas carols, and the smell of the roasting chestnuts offered by street vendors filled the air.

Millie was glad she'd made the effort to come when she saw Katie's face light up in rapture at the sight of the brightly lit department-store windows.

'I've never seen anything like it,' she breathed, her face pressed against the glass at Marshall & Snelgrove to admire the glittering decorations. 'Back home we only have old Mr McGoogan's shop, and that tight-fisted old goat wouldn't even light an extra candle, let alone make his window as gorgeous as this. Have you ever seen a Christmas tree that big? It's like it came straight out of a forest.'

'Actually, the one we have at home is much bigger,' Lucy announced loftily. 'But I suppose when you have a house as large as ours, a small tree would just look ridiculous.'

And then she was off, bragging again. Millie and Katie exchanged long-suffering looks as Lucy described in detail the lavish Christmas her mother had planned. No expense was to be spared for the food, the decorations or the presents.

'My mother knows how to entertain,' she boasted. 'On Christmas Eve my parents throw an enormous party and all kinds of important, wealthy and famous people come. You'd simply be amazed. I expect it's the same for you at Billinghurst?' She casually dropped the name of Millie's family home into the conversation.

'Not really.' Millie glanced sideways at Katie, who was pretending to watch the model train that whizzed in and out of a toy display. She was painfully aware that the Irish girl was feeling fed up because she couldn't go home at Christmas, and the last thing Millie wanted was to make her feel even more homesick. 'My father and grandmother prefer a quiet Christmas, just the three of us.'

'Oh, come on! You must have some other plans?' Lucy nudged her conspiratorially. 'You can't tell me you sit at home playing chess all day. Aren't there lots of house parties?'

How her father would laugh at the idea of her playing chess, Millie thought. She never seemed to find the concentration to finish a game. 'My friend Sophia's family is having a house party over the New Year,' she conceded reluctantly.

Lucy's eyes gleamed with excitement. 'Is that Lady Sophia Rushton? Daughter of the Duke and Duchess of Claremont?' Millie nodded. 'Oh, how thrilling! I was only reading about her in *Tatler* the other day.' Lucy sighed. 'I'd love to meet her. Perhaps I could come down to Billinghurst sometime?'

'Perhaps.' Over my dead body! Millie thought. She could just imagine what her grandmother would make of Lucy. She was what the Dowager Countess would call 'an arriviste', which in her eyes was even worse than being a communist.

Millie took Katie's arm and steered her towards the ornate brass-trimmed doors. 'Let's go inside, shall we? It's freezing out here.'

Knowing Katie was short of money she'd expected to do nothing more than browse, but Lucy had other ideas. They trailed after her as she bought gloves and stockings, then proceeded to try on hats in the millinery department.

'What do you think of this one?' she asked, turning her head this way and that to admire a green feathered creation from every angle as the salesgirl fussed over her.

'You look as if a parrot's landed on your head,' Katie muttered. Millie spluttered with laughter.

Lucy turned around sharply. 'I'm sorry? Did you say something?'

'I said it's a shame Doyle couldn't come with us. I bet she would have loved an outing,' Katie said, meeting her eye boldly.

'If you ask me, she didn't want to come because she knew she couldn't afford it.' Lucy adjusted the hat a fraction and pouted at her reflection. 'She's so poor she probably couldn't even afford the bus fare!' She laughed unkindly.

'She didn't want to come because you were so beastly about Bradley,' Millie said.

'She deserved it.' Lucy pulled off the hat and tossed it back dismissively at the salesgirl. 'She's an idiot.'

130

'She's not an idiot. She tries very hard, she's just terribly nervous and shy. And you don't make it any better, picking on her constantly.'

'I can't help it if she's incompetent, can I?'

'Stop it, you two,' Katie broke in. 'If we're all going to fall out we might as well have stayed at home. We don't get that much time off and I want to enjoy it, not bicker all the time.'

'You're right.' Millie looked at Lucy.

'Fine by me,' Lucy shrugged, putting on her beret and smoothing down her chestnut hair. 'Let's hurry. I want to buy some more presents before the shop closes.'

It was dark by the time they got back to Bethnal Green, and the fog was a dense, cloying blanket, pierced only here and there by the sulphurous glow of the streetlamps. Millie, Lucy and Katie stood for a moment at the bus stop, trying to get their bearings.

'Holy Mother of Jesus, I've never seen anything like it,' Katie declared. 'How are we going to find our way back to the hospital?'

'We can manage,' Millie said bracingly. 'We'll edge our way along the wall like this, you see?' She groped until her fingers found the rough brick-work. 'If we hold on to each other we should be all right.'

They made their way slowly down the street, clutching each other's hands in case they became separated in the dense fog. Figures shuffled past them, emerging briefly like ghosts from the gloom then disappearing again, shoulders hunched against the cold. From the road to their right came the mufflled clip-clop of heavy horses and the rattle of carts making their way cautiously homeward.

They reached the corner of the road and stopped. Opposite them they could make out two pools of dull light from the lanterns on top of the gateposts at the Nightingale.

'See?' Millie said. 'I told you we'd find our way.'

She stepped off the kerb and almost immediately a car loomed out of the darkness. There was a squeal of brakes, a glare of headlights, and the next thing Millie knew she had landed in an undignified heap.

'Sweet Jesus, I can't look. Is she dead?' Katie whimpered, covering her face.

'Of course she isn't!' Lucy snapped back. 'Do pull yourself together, O'Hara. I thought you were supposed to be a nurse?'

The car door slammed and the driver appeared out of the fog. He was tall, dark-haired and not much older than Millie.

He looked very shaken when he saw her sitting in the gutter. 'Are you all right? Oh, God, what happened?'

'I'm not sure. One minute I was crossing the road, the next you came out of nowhere and nearly ran me over.' Millie cautiously inspected herself for damage. Her stockings were torn and her knees were skinned and muddy. But her pride was what hurt most of all.

She started to struggle to her feet but the young man grasped her shoulders with his bony hands, holding her down.

'No, don't get up. You might have hurt yourself. I'm a doctor,' he said. 'I should examine you, make sure you're not injured.'

'I'm a nurse, and I'm telling you, I'm quite all right.' Millie shook off his hands and scrambled to her feet. 'No thanks to you,' she added, brushing mud off her coat. 'What were you thinking, driving like a maniac?'

'You stepped out in front of me!'

'You might have been able to stop in time if you hadn't been speeding!'

They glared at each other. In spite of her anger, Millie wanted to laugh at the young man's comically furious expression, and the way his hair stuck up, as if he'd just tumbled out of bed.

'You ought to be more careful,' he said. 'You're not safe to be out on the street.'

'And you're not safe behind a wheel.'

'Is that so? Well, let me tell you I happen to be–'

His words were drowned out by a sickening crunch of metal, so loud Millie almost jumped into his arms. The young man swung round and gave a cry of despair. 'No!' he moaned. 'Oh, no! Bessie!'

Another car door slammed. 'What's going on?' a man's irate voice yelled. 'What idiot has parked their car in the middle of the road?'

The young man forgot about Millie and rushed off to inspect the damage to his rear bumper.

'Serves him right for being such a dangerous driver,' she said to Katie and Lucy as they watched the two men arguing in the middle of the street, all raised voices and pointing fingers.

'He must be a doctor at this hospital.' Katie glanced back at him over her shoulder. 'I wonder who he is?'

'Whoever he is, he owes me for a new pair of stockings,' Millie replied.

Dora was waiting for them in the sitting room. She was perched on the edge of the settee, arms wrapped around herself, staring into the empty fireplace. She got to her feet when she saw Millie.

'Jennifer Bradley's going home,' she blurted out.

Millie frowned at her. 'But Christmas isn't for another week?'

'No, I mean she's leaving. For good. Her parents are here. They're waiting in the car while she packs. They wanted to come in but Sister Sutton wouldn't let them. "Strictly no visitors allowed in the nurses' home",' she parroted the Home Sister's instructions in disgust.

'Poor Bradley.' Millie glanced up at the ceiling. 'Maybe we could talk to her, try to change her mind?'

'I've tried.' Dora shook her head. 'She's got the idea she's not good enough to be here.' Her eyes shifted past Millie to fix coldly on Lucy, standing in the doorway.

Half an hour later Jennifer left. They watched her from the sitting-room window as she trailed miserably to the car, her head hanging low in shame. She didn't even look back as her father loaded her trunk into the boot.

'What a pity,' Katie sighed. 'She was a grand girl, once you got to know her.'

'And she tried so hard,' Millie put in.

'I really don't know why you're all looking so long-faced,' Lucy said. 'She was never cut out to be a nurse here. Surely it's far better she goes now

134

than wastes her own time and everyone else's.'

'You're all heart, aren't you?' Dora said in a low voice.

Millie glanced warily at her. She was standing at the window, green eyes blazing in her pale, set face. Her very stillness was menacing.

Lucy didn't seem to notice. 'I'm just telling the truth, that's all,' she said, flipping her plaits haughtily. 'I can't help it if some people just aren't supposed to be here, can I?'

'I suppose that includes me?'

Lucy shot her a superior look. 'If the cap fits,' she said.

'Now, girls, what's going on in here?' Sister Sutton bustled in, Sparky wriggling in her arms. 'I don't know why you're all standing around being idle. There's always studying to be done and I'm sure none of you is so clever you couldn't benefit from a few extra hours with your books.'

'If some of us had books,' Lucy murmured under her breath. Sister Sutton didn't hear her, but Dora did. Millie saw the colour rise in her face, flooding up from her neck to her hairline.

'Go to your rooms, you're making the place look untidy,' Sister Sutton dismissed them.

They filed past her. None of them dared to mention that it was their day off, to do with as they please. For once Millie was grateful to see the bullying Home Sister. From the way Dora and Lucy had been looking at each other, she was worried a fight was about to break out.

'Take no notice of Lane, she's just a cat,' she warned Dora as they went back to their room.

'I don't care about her,' Dora said defiantly. But

135

Millie could tell from the dejected droop of her mouth that Lucy's spiteful barb had hit home.

She knew Dora wouldn't forget it, either. There was unfinished business between her and Lucy. And next time Sister Sutton might not be there to stop it.

Chapter Thirteen

It was the week before Christmas, and many of the patients on Holmes were getting ready to go home. It was the consultant's policy to send as many men as possible back to their families, to give them and the medical staff a chance to enjoy a good Christmas.

There was a definite festive atmosphere in the air. The long, cavernous ward had been brightened up with streamers, paper chains and sprigs of holly. A couple of the nurses had optimistically stuck some mistletoe over the doors, too, but Sister Holmes had ordered it to be taken down in case it gave patients the wrong idea.

That afternoon, once visiting time was over, the porters would bring in the tree and the nurses would decorate it.

'But I don't want any mess in the ward,' Sister Holmes warned them all severely. 'The first sign of a dropped needle and that tree goes out, Christmas or no Christmas.'

Helen hummed to herself as she went about her tasks. She enjoyed Christmas at the Nightingale.

Everyone was in such good spirits. Even the patients were happy, laughing and joking amongst themselves. Fortunately, they were all on the mend and there had been no dramatic admissions over the past week, apart from Mr O'Sullivan and his internal haemorrhoids. But a week after surgery, even he was feeling better.

Charlie Denton was improving, too. His wound had healed up nicely and his splints and supporting pillows had been taken away. Now all he needed was regular massage and movement to keep his leg muscles working before his temporary prosthetic was fitted. With any luck he would be back on his feet by the New Year.

Helen watched him as he helped Mr Stannard with his crossword.

'I wonder if she'll turn up today?' Amy Hollins voiced the thought that had been going through Helen's mind at that exact moment.

Charlie Denton's fiancée Sally had been in to visit him once in the five weeks he'd been in hospital. Helen had taken an instant dislike to the brassy-looking blonde who'd spent ten minutes admiring herself in her compact mirror before announcing she had to go and catch her bus.

Every week Charlie looked for her, and every week there was another excuse for her not coming. One week her mum was poorly, the next she had to go and see her sister in Clacton. He tried to hide his disappointment as best he could, but Helen could see the light fading from his eyes when the doors opened and she wasn't there.

Bitterness had got the better of him the previous week, when another visiting time was almost over and there was still no sign of his fiancée.

'I know it's tough for my Sal, having to see me like this,' he'd said to Helen. 'But all the same, you'd think she'd make the effort for my sake, wouldn't you? I mean, look at Percy over there.' He'd nodded towards Mr Oliver, who had been moved to the main ward now he was beginning to recover from his head injury. He sat propped up against the pillows, staring glassily into space, almost unaware of the pretty dark-haired girl who sat at his bedside, tenderly stroking his face. 'His girl comes in to see him every visiting time, even though he doesn't know she's there half the time. And I reckon she'd come every day if she could. They say head injuries change people, don't they? Make them moody, like? That poor girl doesn't even know if he's going to be the same bloke when he gets out of here. And yet she still comes, still loves him with all her heart. You only have to look at her to see that.'

He turned to Helen, blue eyes full of despair. 'I'm not like that, am I? I haven't changed. I'm still the same bloke Sal fell in love with. It's only my leg that's gone, not up here.' He touched his finger to his temple.

Helen wished she could say something to comfort him and bring the smile back to his face. But she couldn't. She could tend his wounds, keep him clean and comfortable, but she couldn't mend his broken heart. Only Sally could do that.

As another visiting time loomed, Helen hoped his fiancée wouldn't let him down. She was almost as thrilled as he was when Sally appeared shortly after the visiting bell rang. Helen saw Mr Denton's face light up when he saw her strutting down the ward towards him in her smart red coat, her hat arranged at a rakish angle on her blonde head. She carried a wicker basket full of fruit – an offering from his mum, Helen guessed. Mr Denton's father was a costermonger in Columbia Street market, and every week his mum would turn up for visiting time with a basket overflowing with apples, pears, bananas and oranges, which Mr Denton'd kindly distribute among the rest of the ward.

She watched Sally place the basket down beside the bed, lean over and kiss her fiancé on the cheek. It didn't look like the warmest kiss Helen had ever seen, but since she had never been kissed herself she was no judge.

'Tremayne?' Sister Holmes jolted her back to reality. 'While we're quiet, I want you to go down to the basement and fetch the box of tree decorations. The porters will be bringing the tree up after visiting time.'

'Shall I go with her, Sister?' Amy Hollins offered. 'It will be quicker with two of us.'

'Good idea, Hollins.'

Helen was surprised at Amy volunteering for extra work. But she found out why as soon as they got down to the basement and Amy disappeared off to the stoke hole for a sneaky cigarette, leaving Helen to search for the box by herself.

The air in the basement was musty, and so cold Helen could see her breath curling in front of her. The feeble electric light barely pierced the gloom, casting long shadows over the bare brickwork.

Helen inched her way between shelves that were crammed with boxes and long-forgotten medical equipment. Old desks, chairs and trolleys covered in dustsheets made sinister shapes that rose out of the shadows at her, making her jump at every turn.

'I see your Mr Denton's fiancée has turned up,' Amy remarked, her voice carrying from the far end of the basement where she perched cosily beside the stoke hole.

'He's not my Mr Denton.'

'Really? You seem to take quite an interest in him. I thought you two were the best of friends.'

Helen bent double to squint at the rows of boxes on the lower shelves, trying to make out their labels in the darkness.

'She's probably ditching him,' Amy said.

Helen stood up so quickly she backed into a drip stand, sending it clattering. 'That's an awful thing to say!'

'Why? It's what I'd do. What good is a crippled husband to her? Better to end it now than go on with it out of pity, I say.'

'If she loves him, she'll stay with him whatever happens.'

'Then she's daft. He'll drag her down and ruin her life.' Amy appeared at the far end of the basement, cigarette in hand. 'Think about it. He'll never be able to work or provide for his family. And as for wanting to go to bed with someone like that–' She shuddered. 'No, she's better off finding a real man who can look after her.'

'Charlie *is* a real man!'

Helen felt herself blushing as she blurted out the words. Amy's brows rose questioningly.

'It's Charlie now, is it? You really are interested

140

in him, aren't you? Fancy that – the oh-so-perfect Tremayne falling for a patient. Bet your mother wouldn't like *that.*' She smiled wickedly. 'Maybe someone should tell her? Give you a taste of your own medicine.'

'Don't be ridiculous,' Helen protested.

'Oh, don't look so panic-stricken. We're not all tell-tales like you.' Amy took a long pull on her cigarette. 'Anyway, you'll get your chance with him soon enough. Trust me, I know about these things. I bet you sixpence she'll finish with him today.' She looked up at Helen through a curling plume of smoke. 'Have you found those decorations yet? Better get a move on before Sister She-devil sends someone down to look for us.'

I'd find it a lot quicker if you were helping me, Helen thought.

She finally located the battered, dust-covered cardboard box on a top shelf at the far end of the basement.

'About time, too.' Amy stubbed out her cigarette and tossed it into the stoke hole as Helen appeared, staggering under its weight. 'And you've got dust all over your apron,' she added casually. 'Sister isn't going to be too pleased about that.'

Visiting time wasn't yet over by the time they returned to the ward, but Charlie Denton's fiancée had already gone.

Staff Nurse Lund intercepted Helen as she was changing her apron. 'Can you keep an eye on Mr Denton, Tremayne? We think he might have had some bad news.'

Helen's heart sank. Ignoring the knowing look Amy sent her, she went to Charlie Denton's bed.

141

A newspaper lay open at the crossword page, but he wasn't looking at it. One look at his hollow-eyed face, and Helen knew Amy Hollins was right.

She offered the only comfort she could. 'Would you like a cup of tea, Mr Denton?'

He turned to look at her, his smile wobbling. 'No, thanks, Nurse. But I wouldn't mind something a bit stronger, if you've got it?'

'Why? Has something happened?'

'You could say that.' He took a deep breath. 'Sal's called off the engagement.'

'What happened?'

'Oh, she was nice enough about it. Shed a few tears, said how sorry she was and all that. But the bottom line is, she reckons she can't cope with the idea of me being disabled. Doesn't want a cripple for a husband.' He pleated the sheet between his fingers. 'Can't say I blame her. I'm not looking forward to it much myself.'

'Oh, Mr Denton, I'm so sorry.' Helen fought the urge to reach for his hand. 'Perhaps when she's had time to think about it, she'll realise she's made a mistake?'

'I doubt it, Nurse T. From the sound of it, she's already found someone else.'

'Do you know who it is?'

He nodded. 'One of my best friends, as it happens.' He tried to smile, but his voice was thick with emotion. 'I don't really blame her. Sal's young, full of life. She wants someone who can take her out dancing, someone who can provide for a family. And let's face it, I'm never going to trip the light fantastic around the People's Palace any more, am I? No, it's better that she finds someone who can look after her. And I know my mate Sam will do that. I'd like to think my Sally will be well looked after.' He opened his hand. A ring with a tiny diamond chip glinted in his palm. 'Although I don't suppose she is my Sally any more, is she?'

Helen felt a lump rising in her throat. But before she could say any more, Sister Holmes summoned her to help decorate the tree.

Charlie Denton smiled wanly. 'You'd best get on, Nurse. I've taken up too much of your time. That tree won't decorate itself, will it?'

Helen had been looking forward to decorating the Christmas tree. But now, as she perched on a chair to hang glittering stars from its branches, she had never felt less festive in her whole life. She kept stealing glances over at Charlie. Mr O'Sullivan in the next bed was trying to regale him with the details of his recent operation. But even though Charlie was smiling and nodding, she could tell he wasn't listening to a word.

'I do wish you'd pay attention, Tremayne,' Sister Holmes scolded, as another bauble shattered on the ground. 'If you drop anything else it will come out of your pay.'

'Yes, Sister,' Helen said miserably.

Amy sidled up to her smugly, a glass angel in her hand.

'Told you, didn't I?' she said. 'That's a tanner you owe me.'

Helen ignored her. Turn the other cheek, the Bible said. But sometimes the urge to shove Amy's face in a bedpan was almost overwhelming.

Chapter Fourteen

'Dunno about being a White Christmas, but I reckon it's going to be a wet one!'

Nanna Winnie peered through the net curtains at the rainwashed backyard. It had been pouring down for days, and even though it was only mid-afternoon the sky was a sullen grey that promised no relief.

But it was Christmas Eve, and not even the constant rain could dampen Dora's spirits as she sat at the kitchen table with her mother, slicing carrots for their tea.

It was the first time in seven weeks that she had been home. Most nurses didn't get the luxury of Christmas Day off once they were on the wards, so she was making the most of this chance while she was still training.

It felt good to be able to relax back into the comforting familiarity of home. The kitchen was cosy and festive, festooned with bright paper chains and sprigs of holly. A welcoming fire crackled in the grate, filling the room with light and warmth. Dora and her mum had been busy cleaning all day to get the house ready for Christmas, and now as they sat down to prepare the tea, the air was filled with the smell of Mansion Polish, mingling with the delicious aroma of mince pies baking in the oven.

'When will they be ready?' Bea asked for the

third time. She was playing schools with Little Alfie in front of the fire. He was her only pupil and she was bossily making him do his letters on an old piece of slate.

'Give us a chance, they've only just gone in!' her mum laughed.

'But I'm hungry!'

'You're always hungry. I dunno where you put it all. You must have hollow legs,' Nanna grumbled.

Little Alfie looked up suddenly, his round face anxious. 'Father Christmas?' he said hopefully. At two years old, he was just getting used to the idea of Christmas and stockings and presents.

'Not yet, Alfie.' Josie ruffled his hair. 'He won't come till you're fast asleep. You have to leave a pillow case at the end of the bed, and then while you're asleep he'll come down the chimney and bring your presents.'

'I'm not sure he's real,' Bea announced in a loud voice. 'Terry Jacobs at school says he's just made up.'

'If he hears you saying you don't believe in him then he definitely won't come,' Dora warned her.

She and Josie smiled at each other. She was relieved that her worries about Alf getting his hands on her sister had been for nothing. Josie was the same happy, carefree girl she'd always been.

'I reckon we've all heard enough about what Terry Jacobs thinks,' her grandmother put in.

Rose smiled across the table at Dora. 'I bet this must seem like a mad house, after that nice, quiet nurses' home of yours?' she said.

'It's different,' Dora agreed. 'But I've missed being here.'

145

'Do you have to work really hard?' Josie asked.

'Well...'

'Hard work, my backside! Sitting at a desk all day isn't what I'd call real work,' Nanna Winnie said.

'It's not just sitting behind a desk, Nanna. We have to practise all sorts of stuff, too. Taking temperatures, and samples, and changing dressings.'

'The glue factory. Now that's what I call real work,' Nanna grumbled on, not listening. 'You spend ten hours a day boiling down animal bones, then you'll know you've done a hard day's graft.'

'Go and put the kettle on, Mum, for Gawd's sake. I'm spitting feathers.' Rose rolled her eyes at Dora as Nanna shuffled off. 'Take no notice of her, girl. She's as proud as punch about you being a nurse. You should hear her telling all the neighbours. I don't think there's a single person in Bethnal Green who doesn't know you're the next Florence Nightingale!'

Dora was silent, thinking of her textbooks. She was barely scraping by in the weekly tests through lack of studying, and Sister Parker had more or less told her that if she didn't get her books within the next two weeks she would fail preliminary training completely. She'd been pushing the thought from her mind, but she knew she had to do something about the problem soon.

'Penny for your thoughts?' Her mother was watching her anxiously.

Dora forced herself to smile. 'It's nothing, Mum.' She refused to allow her worries to ruin anyone's Christmas. There was nothing she could do about them anyway.

Nanna Winnie brought the tea in, and as they drank it Dora told them all about the other girls in her set.

'They all sound a bit posh to me.' Nanna Winnie sucked on a digestive biscuit. Her false teeth had been giving her gyp again.

'They are a bit,' Dora admitted. 'One of the girls I share a room with is an earl's daughter.'

'Never?' Nanna Winnie stopped eating, her biscuit halfway to her mouth.

'It's true. Her name's Lady Amelia and she lives in a castle down in Kent. Her father owns a lot of the hop farms down there, too.'

'Imagine that! I bet we've been hopping down on one of his farms, don't you, Mum?' Rose said.

Nanna looked doubtful. 'What does an earl's daughter want to be wiping people's backsides for, then?'

'Search me, Nan.' Dora was mystified too. She'd tried asking her about it, but Millie had gone into a long explanation she didn't follow about wanting to be independent and make her own way in the world before she married some rich lord.

As if there was anything good about working your fingers to the bone, Dora thought. She knew a few women who would gladly give it up for a life of idle luxury and no bills to worry about.

'Hello, what's he doing out there?' Nanna said, twitching back the net curtain to peer outside.

'Who? Who's out there?' Bea was first at the window, pressing her nose against the steamy glass to see. 'Oh,' she said, disappointed. 'It's only Danny Riley.'

'What's he doing?' Rose asked.

147

'Just sitting on the coal shed. He does it sometimes.' Bea went back to bossing Little Alfie.

'In the rain?' Dora said.

Bea shrugged. 'I don't think he notices. It's 'cos he's funny in the head.'

'Beatrice Doyle! You'd better not let his brother hear you saying that!' Rose said.

'Why not? It's true. Anyway, Nanna says it.'

'I do not!' Nanna Winnie looked indignant.

'You do! You said–'

'That's enough. I don't care who said it, I don't want it repeated,' Rose said firmly. 'The poor boy's got enough to cope with, without the likes of us going round calling him names.'

Dora pulled back the net curtain and peered through the rain streaming down the window pane. Danny Riley sat on top of next door's coal shed, his knees tucked under his chin, staring with vacant, glassy eyes, oblivious to the rain that plastered his hair to his face.

Dora caught his eye and waved. He gave her a shy, lopsided smile and ducked his head away.

'Poor little bleeder,' Nanna said. 'When I think about what a bright little boy he used to be, running around playing games in the street with our Josie.'

He was fifteen years old, but he had the mind of a child. No one really knew what had happened to make Danny Riley the way he was. His mum June always said it was an accident, a bad fall when he was eleven years old. Whatever it was, it caused bleeding in his brain that had almost killed him.

As usual in Griffin Street, there were rumours. Everyone knew June's husband Reg had been handy with his fists. But whatever had happened to poor little Danny, it must have terrified his father because the day his son was rushed to hospital Reg had disappeared, never to be seen again.

'He can't sit out there in the rain, he'll catch his death,' Rose declared. 'Call him in, Dora.'

She went to the back door and called out to him through the rain, 'Where's your mum, Danny?'

'Out shopping.'

'Shopping, my eye! Down the pub, more like!' Nanna Winnie muttered from inside the house.

Dora ignored her. 'Do you want to come in and get warm by our fire?' she said.

He eyed her warily from beneath his dripping fringe. 'Nick says I'm not to go nowhere with no one.'

'Nick won't mind you being with us. Come inside and dry off,' Dora coaxed him. 'We'll listen out for Nick coming home and let him know where you are.'

Reluctantly, Danny slithered down from his perch and edged through the gap in the broken fence. He stood dripping on the kitchen rug, a forlorn sight with his bony wrists poking out of the shrunken sleeves of his jersey.

'Come on, Danny, let's get that jumper off you,' Rose said. 'Josie, run and fetch one of Alf's old shirts from the mending.'

Five minutes later Danny was huddled by the fire, steam rising gently from his sodden trousers. Alf's shirt swamped his scrawny frame.

'Ugh, he smells!' Bea whispered loudly, her nose wrinkling.

'So would you, if your mother didn't look after

149

you properly,' Rose hissed back. 'Now be quiet, or Father Christmas might decide to give this house the go-by!' She beamed at Danny. 'Time for those mince pies to come out of the oven, I reckon. Are you hungry, Danny?'

He nodded, his eyes round in his pale, narrow face. A thin trail of saliva dribbled from the corner of his mouth.

'Look at him,' Nanna said pityingly as he tucked into a hot mince pie. 'I wonder when the poor little sod last had a decent meal? He's all skin and bone.'

Danny ate half the pie, then pulled a grubby handkerchief out of his pocket.

'What's he doing?' Bea watched, fascinated, as he wrapped the other half of the pie in the handkerchief and tried to stuff it in his trouser pocket.

He noticed them all watching him, and a deep flush spread up his face. 'It's for Nick,' he explained in a quiet, fearful voice.

'It's all right, ducks, you can finish that one. We'll give one to Nick when he gets in,' Dora reassured him.

Danny ate the rest of his pie happily while he watched Bea and Little Alfie play schools.

'Do you want to play?' Bea asked.

Danny eyed the piece of slate she offered him and shook his head. 'I'm not g-good at reading or writing,' he stammered.

'I'll teach you,' she said.

'Why don't we play something else?' Dora suggested quickly, seeing his look of fear. The last thing a timid boy like Danny needed was her bold as brass sister bullying him. 'How about

Snakes and Ladders?'

Dora sat with Danny and helped him. He liked rolling the dice and watched her with round, curious eyes as she carefully counted out the squares for him. Every time anyone reached a snake or a ladder he would let out a bellowing laugh and clap his hands.

As he began to relax, he started to chatter.

'My brother is going to fight Max Baer,' he whispered to Dora.

'Oh, yes? Who's he when he's at home?' Dora rattled the dice in her hands. Probably some local lad who'd caused offence, if she knew Nick Riley.

'He's a boxer. The best in the world, Nick s-says. Except f-for him.' He beamed proudly.

'Your Nick's good with his fists, I'll give him that.' There weren't many men who'd willingly take him on in a fight. She threw the dice. 'Another six,' she said. 'You must be lucky, Danny.'

'And we're going to live in a big house in America, and we'll have a car, and Nick's going to pay a doctor to get me straight. But it's a secret so you're not allowed to tell Mum,' Danny confided in a loud whisper.

'Right. Best not say any more then, eh, ducks?' Dora whispered back, as Bea leant in closer to listen.

The game was almost over when they heard the Rileys' front door bang, followed by Nick's heavy footsteps thundering down the passage next door.

'These walls are like paper,' Nanna Winnie grumbled. 'You can hear everyone's business.'

'As if that that ever worried you!' Rose laughed.

'Sounds like your brother's home.' Dora got to

151

her feet. 'Better go and let him know where you are.'

She went out into the yard just as Nick came flying out of his back door, his face white. 'Have you see Danny?'

'He's with us. He was sitting out in the rain, so we brought him in–'

But Nick had already vaulted the broken-down fence between them and shouldered past her into their kitchen. Danny saw his brother and his face split into a big grin.

'I'm playing a game. I'm winning, look!'

'Never mind that. What have I told you about wandering off on your own?' Nick snapped.

'He was safe with us,' Dora said.

Nick ignored her, his gaze focused on his brother.

'Come on, we've got to go,' he ordered.

Danny's grin turned into a stubborn pout. 'I'm playing,' he insisted.

'And I'm saying come home now!'

'It's all right, love,' Dora said quickly, seeing Nick's frown. 'We've got to pack it away, anyway. Let's say you won, shall we?'

There was a flurry of activity as they packed up the game and helped Danny back into his almost dry jersey. Nick watched, unsmiling, from the doorway. Dora couldn't imagine two brothers more different. While Danny was so happy, child-like and trusting, Nick seemed permanently guarded and watchful. Physically they were very different too: Danny pale and slight, Nick dark-haired and muscled like a fighting dog.

They were already in the yard before Dora

remembered the pies her mother had wrapped up for them.

'Wait!' She caught up with them. 'These are for you.' She tried to hand Nick the package, but he eyed it suspiciously. 'What is it?'

'Don't worry, it's not a gun, it won't go off in your hand!' She laughed at his wary expression. 'It's just a couple of mince pies Mum promised Danny.'

'We don't need hand-outs,' Nick said gruffly.

'It's not a hand-out. Call it a Christmas present. Anyway, they're not for you, they're for your brother.' Dora turned, smiling, to Danny. 'You'll take them, won't you love?'

Nick scowled as his brother grabbed the parcel eagerly.

'Th-thank you,' he stammered.

'You're welcome. Happy Christmas, ducks.'

Dora watched Nick lift Danny over the broken fence and propel him back into their house, his hand fixed on the back of his brother's neck.

'And Happy Christmas to you too, Nick,' she called.

He didn't reply.

Chapter Fifteen

Christmas Day was as bleak as any other for the Riley boys.

Danny had wet the bed again. Nick woke up to find him whimpering in the corner, tears running

153

down his face.

'S-sorry, Nick,' he sniffed, wiping his nose on the frayed cuff of his pyjamas. 'It was a accident.'

'I know, mate. Don't take on about it, there's no harm done. We'll get this lot washed in no time.' He forced a smile for his brother's sake.

As he dragged the sodden sheets off his brother's mattress, Danny whispered, 'Y-you won't t-tell Mum, will you?'

'Don't worry, I won't disturb her beauty sleep.'

Nick hauled the washing into the sink and ran the cold tap, barely able to contain his anger. It was Christmas Day, but you'd never know it. There were no decorations, no tree, no presents. The old Ovaltine tin where his mother kept the housekeeping money was empty, but there wasn't a scrap of food in the house apart from half a stale loaf and a sweating lump of cheese in the cupboard.

He thought about the Doyles' warm, cheery kitchen, so full of laughter and happiness. They would be next door unwrapping their presents now, all excited about the day ahead. Rose Doyle would probably already have a chicken in the oven, its delicious aroma drifting through the house.

And where was his mum? Still in bed, sleeping off last night's bender.

He rolled up his sleeves and plunged the sheets into the freezing water. This was all his mother's doing. She hadn't come home until the early hours, even though she knew it upset Danny.

'Sh-she will come home, won't she, Nick?' he'd asked, over and over again, as they lay side by

154

side on their mattresses in front of the dying fire.

''Course she will, mate,' he'd replied cheerfully, while inside he seethed with anger. His mother had gone out yesterday and left Danny on his own again. She'd promised faithfully she wouldn't, not after the last time he'd gone wandering and that policeman had picked him up near the canal.

Nick shuddered to think about what might have happened if his brother hadn't been found then. Now he worried every time he went to work, spending all his shift with his stomach churning. Every time he turned the corner into Griffin Street he expected to find a policeman waiting for him.

It won't always be like this, he told himself as he wrung out the sheets and draped them on a clothes horse in front of the dying embers of the fire. As soon as I've saved up the money, we're getting out of this dump.

As if he could read his thoughts, Danny said, 'D-do they have Christmas in America, Nick?'

''Course they do, mate. Better than we have over here, I reckon.'

Danny emerged timidly from his corner to watch as Nick stoked up the fire with the last of the coal. 'Can we have a Christmas tree when we live there?'

'The biggest one you've ever seen. With presents piled high under it.'

Danny's eyes shone. 'What kind of presents?'

'What do you fancy?'

His brother thought about it for a moment. 'A motor car,' he said.

Nick poked at the fire, stirring it back into life.

'Not sure we'd be able to fit one of those under the tree. But maybe Father Christmas could leave it outside with a ribbon round it, eh?'

Danny sighed with pleasure. 'I reckon Mum would like a motor car.'

Nick straightened up, massaging the aching muscles in his back. 'What did I tell you, Danny? This is meant to be a secret, all right? We're not going to tell Mum about it, are we?'

Danny nodded. 'It's going to be a surprise for her.'

'It will that, mate.' You don't know the half of it, he thought. With any luck, by the time she found out about it they'd be long gone.

He'd heard a lot about what life was like in America, and he'd also heard they had doctors over there who might be able to help Danny. If there was even the slightest chance his brother might be right again one day, he had to take it.

Every week Nick saved some money out of his wages to get them to America. And the cash prizes he won from his fights went into his savings, too. His trainer Jimmy reckoned he was good enough to make the big time as a boxer, and Nick was determined to be as rich and famous as Max Baer one day.

It was the only thought that kept him going when life in Griffin Street was really grim.

Their mother finally surfaced just before midday. She drifted into the living room, her woollen dressing gown pulled tight around her thin body. Nick could smell the stale booze on her from the other side of the room.

'H-happy Christmas, Mum.' Nick watched Danny rush to greet her, winding his skinny arms around her neck and planting a sloppy kiss on her cheek. He wished he could be so forgiving.

'Happy Christmas, son.' She and Nick shot each other resentful looks across the room. 'Any chance of a cup of tea?' she asked.

'That's about all there is.' Nick filled the kettle under the tap. 'There's no food, that's for sure.'

His mother pulled a packet of Woodbines out of the pocket of her dressing gown. 'Here we go,' she sighed, lighting one with an unsteady hand. 'Your brother never misses a chance to have a go at his poor old mum, does he?' she said to Danny. 'Even on Christmas Day, he can't let it lie.'

'So you've noticed it's Christmas Day, then?' Nick lit the gas. 'I wasn't sure, since we've got nothing to show for it in the house. Unless you've got a chicken and a load of sprouts hidden away somewhere?'

June Riley narrowed her eyes at him through the curling plume of cigarette smoke. She had been pretty once, but drink and resentment had etched deep lines in her face. 'Maybe there would be, if you gave me a bit more money?'

'What, so you can go and spend it all down the Rose and Crown? You'd have enough money if you didn't drink it all away.' He turned to face her. 'I s'pose there's no point in asking where you were last night?'

'I'm entitled to a life, aren't I? They'd banned slavery last time I looked.'

'It wouldn't hurt you to do a bit of slaving once in a while. Have you seen the state of this place?'

June rolled her eyes at Danny. 'Your brother's giving me earache again, Danny boy. When's he going to change the record, eh?'

'I'll change it when you start listening to me.' Nick sat across the kitchen table from her, forcing her to look at him. 'Look, I don't care where you go, or what you do. You can go to hell for all I care. It's Danny I worry about. You know I don't like him being left on his own. Anything could have happened to him.'

'It didn't though, did it?'

'No thanks to you. You know what he's like.' Nick lowered his voice. 'Doesn't it bother you that he could have wandered off and ended up in the river, or under a tram?'

June turned her head slowly to look at him, her red-rimmed eyes mournful. A thin stream of cigarette smoke escaped from one corner of her mouth. 'Might be a blessed relief if he did,' she muttered.

Her words hit Nick like a punch in the stomach. 'You wicked cow!'

'Wicked, am I? Look at the poor little sod.' She glanced at Danny, who sat at her feet, looking up at her with adoring eyes like a spaniel. 'He doesn't understand half of what we're saying. What kind of life is that for him? Who's going to look after him for the rest of his days?'

Not you, that's for sure, Nick thought.

'You don't know how hard it is for me.' There was a catch in his mother's voice as she turned her face away. 'Four years I've had to struggle on my own.'

'You, struggle? Don't make me laugh! You

haven't been on your own, have you? You've had us. Except you've never given Danny and me a thought in all that time.'

Nick watched her fish in the pocket of her dressing gown for a handkerchief, unmoved by her self-pity. It was the same every time she'd had a drink

Danny rushed to comfort his mother, clumsily trying to dry her tears with his sleeve. 'L-leave her alone, Nick,' he begged.

'You wouldn't say these things to me if your father was here,' she wept.

'Well, he's not here is he?' Nick said.

'Because you drove him away. You sent away the only man I ever loved!'

'And do you know what? I'd do it again tomorrow.'

'That's your father you're talking about. You should show some respect.'

'Did he show us any respect when he blacked your eyes and cracked my ribs or–' Nick broke off. He couldn't bring himself to talk about Danny. His brother didn't understand what had happened to him, and Nick would never say it.

But he remembered only too clearly that day four years ago when he'd come home from work and found Danny lying like a broken doll on the floor, his face a mashed-up pulp, blood seeping from his ears and nose. And Reg Riley, the evil swine Nick couldn't even bring himself to call his father, standing over him, his fists balled, acting the big man because he'd smashed into a skinny, helpless little boy.

Nick never knew what his brother had done

wrong. Danny was only eleven, such a quiet lad who never got into trouble or said a cheeky word to his father. Not like Nick. But Nick was sixteen, and so big and strong that even Reg Riley wasn't stupid enough to pick a fight with him. Nick had tortured himself ever since, wondering if his father had decided to punish Danny instead.

Nick had carried his brother's broken little body across the park to the Nightingale himself. It was the worst moment of his life. He had no use for religion, but he had prayed that night, traded his soul, his future and everything he had, if the Almighty would just let his little brother live.

And he had. But no one had promised what kind of life he would have.

Once he knew Danny was going to pull through, Nick had left his mother crying crocodile tears over her son, and gone out looking for Reg Riley. He'd found him hiding in the pub, dragged him outside and given him a taste of what he'd given his youngest boy. Such was Nick's white-hot anger he would have killed him stone dead if some other men hadn't dragged him off.

But Reg Riley had got the message. That night, while Nick and his mother were at the hospital, he had come home, packed his bags and left.

Nick had thought his mother might be grateful that her bullying husband was out of her life. But once the shock of what had happened to Danny had passed, June Riley quickly forgot who had been to blame for it.

'You don't know what it's like,' she wept now. 'I need someone to look after me.'

'Don't cry, Mum. We'll look after you.' Danny

hugged her tighter, burying his face in her neck. June pushed him away impatiently.

'Get off me, for Gawd's sake. You're smothering me.'

Nick saw his brother's trembling lip and his heart hardened. 'I don't know why you even bothered to come back,' he said. 'Why didn't you stay out drinking with your pals at the pub?'

'Oh, believe me, I would if I could. Anything not to stay here in this dump and look at your depressing bloody face all day.' June took a vicious drag on her cigarette. 'I know it's Christmas but they don't give drinks away.'

'You mean you couldn't find some desperate bloke to buy them for you? You must be slipping.' Nick's lip curled. He reached into his back pocket and took out his wallet. He could feel his mother's eyes watching him keenly as he took out a ten shilling note and dropped it on the table in front of her.

'I don't want your money!' she hissed.

'Fine, I'll take it back–' He reached for the note, but June snatched it away before he could reach it.

'I'll take it for housekeeping,' she sniffed through her tears. 'You keep me short anyway. Someone has to put a roof over our heads.'

We wouldn't have much of a roof if it was left to you, Nick thought. He'd been the man of the house since long before his useless father slung his hook, dodging school to do all kinds of odd jobs and errands. He'd sold scrap metal, worked as a bookie's runner, even collected and sold horse manure. Anything to make a few pennies.

But not for much longer. One day soon he and

161

Danny would be on their way to a better life in America. And his mother would have to find someone else to pay for her gin.

'For the last time, Mum, will you come and have your dinner?' Rose Doyle said in exasperation.

Nanna Winnie reluctantly put down the glass she had been holding up to the wall. 'I'm only interested,' she grumbled.

'So am I,' Bea piped up. 'What's going on, Nan?'

'It's none of our business,' Rose said shortly. 'Now, everyone, sit down at the table.'

Her mother had done them all proud again, Dora thought, as she watched Alf pick up the carving knife. All day the house had been filled with tempting aromas, and now the table groaned with a feast of chicken, stuffing, roast potatoes, parsnips, carrots and Brussels sprouts. It was a far cry from the poor food she was used to at the nurses' home, all greasy grey stews, bullet hard potatoes and burnt porridge.

It was a far cry from the kind of Christmases they'd had after her father died, too. Dora could still remember how bleak it had been, with barely any money for coal on the fire or food on the table, let alone presents. Her mum had done her best for her kids, working all the hours she could and going without herself to provide for them. She kept a cheerful smile painted on for her family, but at night, after they had gone to bed, Dora had often heard her crying through the paper-thin wall that separated them.

It was a different story now. Dora looked around at her brothers and sisters all crowded around the small table, their faces lit up with anticipation, and at her mother, smiling as she served the dinner to her family. She was in her element, radiantly happy to have all her kids around her. Even Dora's elder brother Peter, just twenty and newly married, was there with his young wife Lily. She looked around shyly, not used to such a big, noisy gathering. She had been brought up in an orphanage, and had no family of her own.

'This is for you.' Alf's eyes met Dora's as he passed her plate down the table to her, shattering her moment of happiness. Just being in the same room as him made her skin crawl. She wished she could scream out, tell everyone what a monster he was. But as Alf knew only too well, she could never admit her shame to anyone, or destroy her family's happiness.

The sound of the Rileys' front door crashing shut made the windows rattle. Everyone jumped. 'Sounds like June's going out for another session,' Nanna Winnie said, helping herself to sprouts.

Rose shook her head pityingly. 'What those poor boys have to put up with. It's terrible, it really is.'

Dora saw the thoughtful look on her mother's face, and knew what was coming next. Everyone else knew it, too.

'No, Rose,' Alf said. 'We're not taking in any waifs and strays.'

'They're not strays. They're our neighbours.' Rose looked at her husband pleadingly.

'As if we've got room for visitors,' Nanna grumbled. 'The house is like the Black Hole of Calcutta as it is.'

'I'm not sitting here stuffing my face while

163

those boys are next door starving, Mum,' Rose said, putting down her knife and fork. 'Sorry, but it wouldn't feel right. I know what it feels like to go hungry, and I wouldn't want to see anyone else's kids go through it. We'll find room for them somewhere. Dora, go and fetch them in.'

She climbed the broken fence and knocked on the Rileys' back door, almost certain it was a fool's errand. If Nick was reluctant to accept a couple of mince pies, he certainly wasn't going to come and have Christmas dinner with them!

He opened the door a crack and scowled out at her. 'What do you want?'

Nothing, if you're going to talk to me like that, she thought. But she suppressed her irritation. 'Mum says to invite you in for your dinner.'

'We don't need no charity.'

Dora looked at his stubborn face. She couldn't really blame him for his pride, she was guilty enough of it herself.

'It's not charity,' she said. 'It's just families helping each other out like we always have. But you please yourself,' she shrugged. 'If you want to go hungry because of your pride, then that's your business. But I don't think it's fair to make your brother go without, just because you can't accept a bit of kindness from a neighbour.'

As she turned to go, Nick suddenly said, 'Wait.'

She looked back at him. His dark features were gathered in a frown, as if he was wrestling with his inner feelings. 'We'll come,' he said finally. 'For Danny's sake.'

Don't do us any favours, will you? Dora felt like saying. But she bit her tongue, knowing the door was likely to be slammed in her face if she did.

The Riley boys came into the kitchen warily, looking around them as if they'd arrived in a foreign country.

'Don't just stand there, boys. Come and have something to eat.' Rose beamed at them. 'Have you got those plates, Josie? Set a couple of places over there, next to you. Nick, you sit next to Dora.'

Rose piled their plates full of food. Danny fell on his immediately but Nick was more cautious.

'Look at that poor little bugger,' Nanna Winnie said in a loud whisper. 'Anyone would think he hadn't eaten for a week.'

Dora shot her grandmother a silencing look, but she and Bea were too busy staring at Danny in fascination, as if they were watching a wild animal in the zoo.

Dora and Nick didn't speak or make eye contact all the way through dinner but she was aware of him crammed in beside her, so close she could feel his broad shoulder brushing against hers. She was also conscious of Nanna watching them both with interest.

After the meal was over, Nick helped clear the table. He and Dora carried the plates through to the scullery while Danny sat on the rug in front of the fire with Little Alfie, helping him construct a tower with his new bricks.

'I'll help wash up,' Josie offered, but Nanna stopped her.

'Leave them be,' she said, in another loud whisper. 'You never know, they might want to be alone together.'

Dora felt a cold trickle of horror run down the

back of her neck. Please, Nanna, don't, she prayed.

'Why?' Bea asked.

'Because it's about time our Dora started courting. And I reckon Nick Riley's as good a bet as any of 'em around here.'

Dora didn't dare turn around. She was aware that Nick had suddenly gone very still beside her.

'But you said Nick Riley was a dirty little sod who wasn't safe to be left alone with any girl!' Bea reminded her loudly.

'That's as may be, but I reckon our Dora should be all right. She's a sensible girl. And anyway, she can't afford to be too fussy!'

Dora flushed crimson as they stood at the sink in silence, her washing the dishes, Nick drying. She was so mortified she couldn't even bring herself to look at him. She was so flummoxed that she didn't think about what she was doing. As she went to put a plate on the draining board, it slipped out of her hands and smashed to pieces on the stone-tiled floor.

'Bugger!'

She crouched to pick them up but Nick was there before her. 'Let me,' he said. 'You might cut yourself. You fetch some newspaper.'

Dora found some old newspaper in the kindling basket, and spread it out on the tiled floor. Nick carefully picked up the pieces.

'Sorry,' she said.

He shrugged. 'One less to dry up.'

They both knew she wasn't talking about the smashed plate.

She glanced sideways at him. The curve at the

corner of his mouth might not have counted in most people, but it was the closest she had ever seen Nick Riley come to a smile.

Chapter Sixteen

Christmas Day on Holmes had started with the laying out of a corpse.

When Sister Holmes arrived on the ward that morning, her main concern was what kind of mess the night staff had left in the ward kitchen. They were careless enough at the best of times, but on Christmas Eve night there was bound to be some extra merriment. Some of the nurses had been particularly giddy as they'd done their traditional Christmas Eve carol singing around the wards, their cloaks turned inside out to show the red lining, each carrying a candle glowing inside a jam jar. She only hoped none of them had found their way into the locked cupboard where she kept the emergency brandy supply.

But there was no giddiness, just sombre faces all round as the Night Sister told her Mr Oliver had died just after dawn.

It was the last thing Sister Holmes was expecting. After recovering so well for weeks he had taken a sudden turn for the worse during the night. Everyone said after his accident he was lucky to escape death; now it seemed death had come to claim him after all.

Sister Holmes looked around the nurses who'd

come on duty an hour earlier. Young Tremayne and Hollins were white-faced and shaken. Even Staff Nurse Mary Lund, who had been her right-hand woman for five years, was downcast. Although as an experienced nurse, she did a better job than the students of not showing it.

'I know this is a sad time for all of us but remember we have a duty to our other patients,' Sister Holmes reminded them all when she handed out the work lists for that day. 'It's Christmas Day, and these men are away from their loved ones, lonely and in pain. We must be professional and put aside our own feelings. Try to make the day as pleasant for them and for ourselves as possible.'

'Yes, Sister,' they chorused.

'Hollins, I want you to perform last offices.'

Hollins looked up sharply. 'But Sister–'

'I don't believe I asked for a debate, Hollins.' She shot the student a sharp, silencing look.

'Are you sure I shouldn't do it, Sister?' Mary Lund asked as the girls headed for the sluice. 'He's only a young man, not much older than they are...'

'They are nurses, Lund. They must learn to do their duty whatever the circumstances.'

'Yes, but–'

'It's a hard lesson, Lund, but this is a hard profession. The sooner they realise that, the better.' Especially Hollins, she thought. If she put as much care and thought into her work as she did into flirting with the young doctors, she might even manage to pass her state exams.

Mary Lund lowered her eyes. 'Yes, Sister.'

Sister Holmes went to her office and closed the door. Sitting down at her desk, she loosened the strings of her starched bonnet from under her chin and massaged her pounding temples. Less than half an hour into her duty and she was already exhausted. She had no idea how she was ever going to get through the next twelve hours, let alone stay cheerful for the patients.

All her strength had been spent on her mother. She had been awake most of the night, in and out of bed, pacing the floor of her bedroom, wandering on the landing, searching for her dead husband. She had fought as her daughter tried to comfort her.

'Who are you? I don't know you. Get out!' she'd screamed.

'Shhh, Mother. It's me, Miranda.'

'You're not Miranda.' The old woman shrank away from her, her face contorted with horror. 'Miranda is at school. You're not my daughter!'

And then she had had to calm and coax and whisper to her, until the moment came when her mother finally remembered again. It saddened her so much to see the confusion and panic in her face as she realised that more than twenty years had somehow slipped by, and she was no longer Elise Pallister, the beautiful and celebrated stage actress, but an old, sick woman whose husband was dead and whose daughter was a grown woman she barely recognised.

Miranda had put her mother back to bed and rocked her like a child until finally she fell asleep just before dawn. Then she had left her in the care of their housekeeper Mrs Jarvis and come on duty.

It was almost a relief to step inside the gates of

the Nightingale, where she could cease to be Miranda Pallister with all her worries and heartache and become Sister Holmes instead. Here, on the ward, she could impose order. She had patients to care for, and nurses who needed her calm authority. For a few hours at least, she had the perfect excuse to switch off and forget all about what was happening at home.

Except she never did. The sadness and anxiety were always there, tugging at the corners of her mind.

A soft tap on the door disturbed her thoughts.

'Sister?' Staff Nurse Lund called. 'Mr Hopkins is here to take Mr Oliver away. Shall I deal with it?'

'I'm just coming.' Sister Holmes quickly re-arranged her cap, fastening the strings with shaking fingers. She gave herself a careful once over in the looking glass to make sure she looked as immaculate as ever. Her nurses and patients expected nothing less than perfection from her.

As she practised a smile at her reflection, she remembered how she used to watch with fascination as her mother put on her make-up, sitting at her dressing table surrounded by powder and paint.

'You have to put on a face for your public, darling,' she'd always said.

Sister Holmes adjusted her cap and went out to meet her public.

Helen couldn't stop thinking about Mr Oliver as she did TPRs. She couldn't begin to imagine how his family would feel, waking up on Christmas morning to the news that their son was dead. And what about his girlfriend, that poor girl who

170

had sat so devotedly at his bedside, stroking his hand and telling him she loved him?

And the fact that it happened on Christmas Day, a day that was supposed to be so full of hope and expectation, just made it seem even more cruel somehow.

His passing cast a shadow over the rest of the ward. As the news rippled through the rest of the patients, the men became subdued. There was none of the usual banter and merriment that usually accompanied the early morning routine. Everyone had taken Percy Oliver to their hearts, willing him to get better. Not just because he seemed like a nice lad, but because his miraculous recovery from surgery gave them all hope that they would pull through, too.

The only one who didn't seem troubled about it was Amy Hollins. She was too preoccupied with what she was going to wear to the Christmas Dance.

'I don't know whether to go with the pink or the green,' she mused. It was unusual for Amy to give her the time of day, so Helen guessed her need to gossip outweighed her aversion. 'My pink dress is new, but the green one is prettier. Actually, it's not really green, more a sort of eau de nil ... what are you wearing?'

'I'm not going.' Helen held up a thermometer to check the reading.

'What a surprise.' Amy rolled her eyes. 'I suppose you don't like dancing, as well as everything else?'

'I just don't see the point.' The truth was, she'd never danced in her life. And she wasn't about to try it, since her mother had forbidden her to go.

171

'I will not have you associated with it,' she'd declared. 'It's a waste of hospital funds, and it encourages over-familiarity among the medical staff.'

Looking at Amy's expression now, it was clear she was expecting a great deal of overfamiliarity. Indeed, she would probably be bitterly disappointed if it didn't happen.

'You're so wet, Tremayne,' Amy accused her. 'But then, I don't suppose you're too worried about meeting anyone at the dance, are you? You've got your eye on someone else.'

'I don't know what you mean.'

'Oh, come on! We all know you fancy Charlie Denton!'

'I do not!' Helen could feel the colour rising in her face.

'Then why are you always hanging around him? "Would you like a tray, Mr Denton? Can I plump up your pillows for you, Mr Denton?"' she mimicked Helen's voice.

'I'm just trying to be a good nurse.'

'Really? I don't see you plumping up Mr Boyd's pillows every five minutes. Oh, no, I forgot. He's just a smelly old bloke with a prostectomy, not a handsome young man whose fiancée has just left him.' Amy laughed unkindly. 'Fancy yourself as her replacement, do you? Reckon you stand a chance with him, just because he's lost his leg and no one else will have him?'

'That's a horrible thing to say.' Helen hurried to the next bed, keen to put as much distance between herself and Amy Hollins' smirking face as she could.

172

It was traditional for the nurses to have their own celebration in Sister's sitting room on Christmas morning. Sister Holmes served them all coffee and handed out the small gifts she had bought for them all. In spite of their downcast mood, they all oohed and aahed dutifully over their bottles of scent and tins of talc, and Sister Holmes looked just as pleased with the ashtray they'd all clubbed together to buy her. By the time she'd added a dash of weak brandy to their coffee from the bottle she kept in her emergency cupboard, and they'd cracked open the boxes of chocolates and dates given to them by grateful patients, their good humour was almost restored.

When the porters arrived with their Christmas dinner, the men were in good spirits too. For once, anyone who could get out of bed gathered around the table in the centre of the ward to watch Head Porter Edwin Hopkins carve the turkey. He enjoyed the importance of the moment, and insisted on saying a lengthy Grace before starting to carve. Helen was used to prayers before meals at home, but the men started shifting restlessly and clearing their throats, and Sister Holmes sent him a sideways look over her clasped hands

'Blimey, tell me he's not a surgeon!' Mr O'Sullivan joked as Mr Hopkins inexpertly hacked off a wing and served it up on to one of the waiting plates.

As Helen helped pass the plates down the table, she noticed one seat was empty. Charlie Denton was still slumped in bed, staring into space.

She went over to him, smiling brightly. 'Not joining us, Mr Denton? I thought you'd be keen to try out your new leg?' He'd been fitted with a temporary prosthetic the day before, but it had lain unused ever since.

He gazed past her listlessly. 'I'm not hungry.'

'But you must eat. I can bring your dinner over for you, if you like?'

'I told you, I'm not hungry,' he snapped. Helen flinched. She had never known him raise his voice, he was always ready with a smile for everyone.

She went back to the table. 'Everything all right, Tremayne?' Sister Holmes said.

'Mr Denton doesn't feel like eating.'

Sister Holmes looked over at him, slumped against his pillows. 'Well, he'll just have to miss out, then,' she said briskly. 'This is a hospital, not a hotel. We can't serve patients their food whenever they feel like it.'

As they handed the plates around, Amy Hollins sidled up to Helen. 'You must be losing your touch,' she said. 'Your Mr Denton doesn't feel like flirting with you any more.'

'I don't know what you're talking about.'

As she walked away, she heard Amy say, 'Looks like even cripples have standards.'

Helen tried to ignore the nasty remarks, and kept her eye on Charlie Denton all afternoon. The other men played dominoes and cards at the table, but despite their urging he refused to join them.

At three o'clock they all gathered around the wireless to listen to King George giving his broadcast to the nation.

'I'll never get used to hearing his voice,' Mr O'Sullivan said. 'Imagine him, sitting there in Sandringham at this very moment, talking to us here. It makes you proud, doesn't it?'

'I'd sooner be where he is than where I am,' one of the other men joked.

'I don't know as I would. Poor devil hasn't had an easy time of it, has he? What with the war and then all the trouble in Ireland, and the General Strike, and then the economy collapsing round our ears.'

'I haven't noticed him standing at the dock gates looking for work.'

'That's not the point,' Mr O'Sullivan insisted stoutly. 'And he's not been well himself either. He hasn't been right this past ten years–'

'Will you shut up about the bloody King?' Charlie Denton shouted, shocking them into silence. 'It's bad enough we have to lie here and listen to him droning on about this and that, without you lot joining in as well!' He lay back against the pillows, exhausted by his outburst.

Sister Holmes tutted. 'Really, someone is not feeling in a festive mood at all, are they? Go and see to him, Tremayne. And try to offer some words of comfort if you can, before he upsets the whole ward.'

Aware that Amy was watching her, Helen made a cup of tea and carried it down the length of the ward to where Charlie lay, staring up at the ceiling. All the life and hope that had kept him going through the bad days after his accident seemed to have drained away, leaving him a husk of misery.

'Here you are, Mr Denton.' She forced brightness into her voice. 'I've made you a nice cup of tea.'

'Tea?' He stared at her, his blue eyes cold. 'That'll make everything all right, will it?'

'It can't make things any worse.'

'No, you're right there.' He shifted his gaze towards the window. Rain streamed down the panes of glass. 'They couldn't get much worse, could they?'

'Oh, I don't know,' she said. 'At least you can get up and about now you've got your new leg.'

'That thing?' Mr Denton looked in disgust at the plaster contraption, with its complex straps and splints. 'Not exactly a leg, is it?'

'I admit it's not the prettiest thing in the world, but it gets the job done. And you'll have a permanent one once you've mastered getting around on this one.' Helen put the cup down on his bedside locker. 'How about we give it a try now? I could help you get it on?'

He turned his gaze back towards the window. 'What's the point?' he said listlessly.

'Well, you need to keep your muscles properly exercised if they're going to support you enough to walk again–'

'Yes, but I'm not going to walk again, am I? You keep talking about my new leg, and being up and about again, as if this useless bloody stump is suddenly going to grow back again and I'm going to be as good as new. But that's not going to happen, is it?'

Helen glanced around her, uncomfortably aware of all the glances in their direction. 'Keep your voice down, Mr Denton. You're disturbing the other patients.'

'I don't care. Don't you understand that, Nurse?

176

I don't bloody care!' His eyes blazed with anger. 'I didn't just lose my leg in that accident, I lost everything. And I'm sick of putting a brave face on it, pretending it's all a big lark, and that everything is going to be hunky-dory again. Because it isn't, is it? When I get out of there, what have I got? I'll tell you, shall I? Nothing. No job, no future, no girl to marry. Everything I dreamed of, everything I hoped for, just gone. When that machine took my leg, it took everything else with it. I wish it had finished the job. If I'd known what was going to happen to me, I would have chucked myself in.' A muscle flickered in his tense jaw. 'So no, Nurse, I don't want your false leg or your false smiles or your false bloody promises. And I don't want your bloody tea, either!'

He knocked the cup off his locker with an angry sweep of his arm. Helen tried to dodge but the hot liquid caught her square in the chest.

For a moment no one moved. She looked down at the spreading brown stain on the bib of her apron.

Mr Denton's anger quickly turned to horror. 'Nurse Tremayne, I'm sorry. I didn't mean–' he started to say, but something inside Helen snapped.

'Sorry? You *should* be sorry!' The voice that came out of her was louder and harsher than she had ever heard herself use before. 'How dare you sit there and say you wish you were dead? A young man lost his life this morning. Somewhere out there, there's a family mourning their son. And there's your family, sitting down to their dinner and giving thanks that theirs is still alive.'

She was aware that Sister Holmes, halfway down the ward towards them, had stopped in her tracks. 'Do you think Mr Oliver wanted to die? With his serious head injuries God knows what kind of life he would have had if he'd survived, and yet he was fighting for it right up until the end. Because he knew that any life is better than no life at all.' She felt hot tears of anger spring to her eyes. 'So don't you ever, ever sit there full of self-pity and moan about your life. Because someone out there decided that it was worth sparing. And there are some people who aren't nearly as fortunate as you.'

In the deafening silence that followed, the only thing Helen could hear was her own breathing, hard and ragged.

She felt a hand on her shoulder. 'Go and compose yourself, Tremayne,' Sister Holmes said quietly. 'Hollins can clear up this mess.'

Helen left the ward in a daze, aware of every single pair of eyes on her. Outside in the courtyard the cold rain hit her like a slap in the face, bringing her sharply to her senses.

What had she done? She had allowed her feelings to get the better of her, and now her anger was ebbing away she felt thoroughly ashamed.

'Hels?' She glanced around. William was hurrying through the rain towards her. 'I was just playing cards in the porters' lodge when I saw you rush past. What are you doing out here? What have you done to yourself?'

Helen looked down at the stain on her apron. She'd forgotten all about it. 'There was an accident,' she said, shivering in the rain. 'I need to go and change–'

'Not until you tell me everything.' William grasped her wrist. 'You're shaking like a leaf. Calm down and tell me what's happened.'

They took shelter in a doorway, and Helen explained about losing her temper with Charlie Denton. William listened intently.

'And he threw a cup of tea over you?' His jaw was set with anger. 'I'm going to have a word with him–'

'No, don't,' Helen pleaded. 'He was just upset.'

'He'll have something to be upset about when I've finished with him. How dare he do that to my sister?'

'I think I've already said enough to him,' Helen said. 'There's no point in both of us getting into trouble.'

'Good for you. It sounds as if he had it coming.'

'But I behaved in an unprofessional manner,' she said miserably. 'I'll probably be sent to Matron.'

'It won't come to that,' William soothed.

'It will. And then Mother will find out about it, and then...' she trailed off. And then she would never, ever hear the end of it, she thought.

Once she'd calmed William down and reassured him that she didn't need him to go into battle with Charlie Denton, Helen went back to the nurses' home to change into a fresh apron. Then she returned to the ward.

She crept back full of trepidation, ready to apologise to anybody and everybody. She had barely got through the doors before Sister Holmes stepped into her path.

'Feeling a little calmer, Tremayne?' Her brows rose questioningly.

'Yes, Sister. Thank you, Sister.' Helen hung her head, ready to say the speech she had been practising in her head all the way back from the nurses' home. 'I am so sorry, Sister. It was very wrong of me to speak out of turn like that. I will apologise to Mr Denton, of course.'

'Before you do, Tremayne, perhaps you had better take a look?'

Sister Holmes stepped aside. Helen lifted her head warily. There, at the far end of the ward, Mr Denton sat in the chair beside his bed, doing a crossword, his temporary prosthetic propped up on a stool in front of him.

'It seems your little lecture did him the world of good,' Sister Holmes said. 'But please don't make a habit of it, will you, Tremayne?'

'No, Sister.'

She didn't approach him straight away. Sister Holmes might have forgiven her, but she wasn't sure Charlie Denton ever would.

Finally, she could avoid it no longer. She and Amy were doing TPRs again, and it was just her luck he was last on her list.

'Nurse T,' he greeted her quietly.

'Mr Denton.'

They were both silent as she checked his pulse. It wasn't until she'd recorded the number on the chart at the bottom of his bed that he finally said, 'Thanks.'

'What for?'

'Giving me a kick up the backside.' His eyes met hers. 'I reckon I needed it.'

Helen's head spun with all kinds of emotions. There was so much she wanted to say, but this time she managed to stay professional.

'Would you like that cup of tea now, Mr Denton?' she asked.

'Thank you, Nurse. That would be very nice indeed.'

She went to great lengths to lay out a tea tray nicely with a pretty coloured cloth and a Christmas cracker. As she tucked a spring of holly into his saucer, she told herself that Amy Hollins was wrong. She would do the same for any patient, even Mr Boyd.

Chapter Seventeen

Lucy Lane sat at her dressing table, admiring her Christmas gift in the mirror. The pearls glowed prettily against her skin, three strings fastened together with a diamond-encrusted clasp. Her father assured her they were from the South Seas, so they were the best money could buy. They would go perfectly with the new dress her mother had had made for her, shimmering silver-grey satin and chiffon, cut on the bias so it skimmed over her slim curves before falling in delicate bead-trimmed points almost to the ground. With matching silver slippers, white satin evening gloves and her mother's silver fox stole, she would steal the show at the Christmas Dance that night, she decided.

What a pity it was just a silly hospital do and not a really grand occasion where she might be photographed. But even if she didn't make it into the pages of *Tatler*, at least she'd have the satisfaction of seeing the other girls sick with envy. Most of them couldn't even afford a new pair of stockings for the occasion, let alone a dress designed by Hartnell.

Downstairs, her parents were arguing. It had been brewing like a storm since the last guest left their party on Christmas Eve. Throughout Christmas Day the dark clouds had been building, tension gathering, with long, oppressive silences punctuated by the odd sniping comment. It was almost a relief when finally the storm broke and the heavens opened in a spite-filled rage of shouting, screaming and breaking glass that had lasted all afternoon. It had been going on for so long Lucy barely noticed it any more as she sat at her mirror, turning her head this way and that to catch the pearls' iridescent sheen, lost in her own world of dresses and dancing.

Soon, she knew, it would all be over. The storm would blow itself out, the screaming and smashing ornaments would stop, and peace would be restored. In a couple of days her father would appease her mother with a gift, some diamonds from Asprey's perhaps, or a new fur, and then it would be all smiles again. Until the storm clouds gathered once more.

The front door crashed, making her jump. A moment later she heard her father's car roar away. She steeled herself, still fingering the pearls. A flicker of dread uncurled itself in the pit of her stomach.

Sure enough, a few minutes later music from the crackling gramophone drifted upstairs. *It had to be you*. Lucy knew what song it would be long before she could make out the tune. Her mother always played it when she was drunk or unhappy, or both.

Lucy stared at her reflection in the mirror, wondering how long she could stay out of her way. She hated it when her father ran off, leaving her to deal with her mother. Although she didn't blame him at all. She'd wanted to run away herself often enough.

Finally, she could avoid it no longer. With a heavy sigh, she took off her pearls and headed downstairs.

She found her mother in the drawing room, glass of wine in one hand, bottle in the other, swaying gently to the music. Still dancing, she swung around slowly and saw Lucy. 'Darling! Come and dance with me.'

She held out her arms, long and slender as a ballerina's. It was five o'clock in the afternoon, and she was still wearing last night's ivory satin evening gown, her feet bare. Her make-up was smudged like bruises under her eyes.

'Where's Daddy?' Lucy asked.

'How should I know? I'm only his wife.' Her mother turned languorously in time to the music. The gown plunged deeply at the back. She was so fashionably thin Lucy could make out every bone down the length of her spine. 'I don't give a damn about him anyway. I just want to dance and be happy and forget everything.' She twirled, flinging her arms wide, carelessly slopping wine.

'Give me that.' Lucy stepped forward and took the bottle from her, uncurling it from her long, bony fingers. 'You're ruining the rug.'

Clarissa Lane gave a brittle laugh. 'You sound just like your father. Don't do this, don't do that, remember who I am... As if I could ever forget!' She faced Lucy, her eyes glittering dangerously. 'Look at you. So disapproving. Such a daddy's girl. You take after him far too much,' she accused, pulling a face.

I'm glad I don't take after you, Lucy thought as she watched her mother sway, humming the dying bars of the music.

She couldn't remember when it had all gone wrong. One minute she was a little girl with two loving parents who treated her like a princess. The next she was caught between a father who preferred to be anywhere but at home, and an angry, bitter mother who drank to stop herself caring.

The music died away. Her mother carried on dancing. 'Put it on again,' she said dreamily, her eyes closed.

'No. It gives me a headache.'

'Well, I like it.'

Lucy watched her cross the room unsteadily. She dragged the gramophone needle across the record with an ugly screech. Then she was off dancing again, waltzing with an unseen partner, eyes closed, lips moving to the words.

'This was our favourite song,' she said. 'I remember him singing it to me one night in Paris ... oh, God, I need more wine.'

'No, Mummy. Please.' Lucy rushed to stop her before she could ring for the butler. 'It will only make it worse,' she pleaded.

She held on to her mother's arms, feeling the

fragile slenderness of skin and bone. For a moment their eyes locked and Lucy held her breath in fear, waiting for her to react. Either she would fight and claw, or...

Clarissa suddenly went limp in her arms, like a puppet whose strings had been cut. Her mouth drooped dejectedly.

'Oh, God,' she wailed. 'Why did he stop loving me?'

Lucy caught her as she fell into her arms, comforting her like a child. 'He does love you, Mummy.'

'Then why does he have to treat me like this? I can't bear it, Lucy, I can't.'

Lucy helped her over to the chaise longue and sat with her, holding her as she wept.

She didn't know who was to blame. All she knew was that she desperately wanted it to stop. She loved both her parents and hated seeing them both so unhappy.

'Don't cry, Mummy,' she pleaded. 'It will all be all right, I promise.'

Her mother clung to her. 'You won't leave me, will you, Lucy? I don't think I could bear it if you left too.'

Lucy thought of her pearls, so glowing and beautiful. How she'd looked forward to showing them off to the other girls at the dance. Proof yet again of how much she was loved.

But tonight wasn't the night.

'No, Mummy,' she sighed. 'I'm not going to leave you.'

Chapter Eighteen

'Cecily Ridgemont's finally managed to get herself engaged to Viscount Tarlington, I see.' The Dowager Countess of Rettingham scanned the Announcements column of *The Times* with an expression Millie had come to dread. 'I dare say her mother will be utterly insufferable now.' She peered at Millie over the top of the newspaper. 'You do realise that could have been you, Amelia, if only you'd tried harder?'

Millie sighed. 'Granny, I only ever met Freddie Tarlington once, and he was completely mad.'

'Don't exaggerate, child.'

'I'm not. Don't you remember, he threw his shoes out of the window at the Grosvenor House Ball, then spent the evening sobbing behind a curtain?'

'That was nothing more than high spirits,' her grandmother dismissed.

'He was taken away in a private ambulance, and not seen for the rest of the Season.'

Lady Rettingham's mouth tightened. 'I admit he is a rather – unfortunate young man,' she conceded. 'But when he stands to inherit an estate half the size of Somerset, one can surely overlook a little eccentricity. Cecily Ridgemont certainly can, it seems.'

Millie caught her father's eye across the breakfast table and smiled.

'I'm glad you two can find humour in the situation,' her grandmother snapped. 'I sometimes feel as if I'm the only one who takes Amelia's prospects seriously.' She laid aside her newspaper and frowned at her granddaughter as she rose from her seat and headed for the sideboard. 'Another helping? Really, Amelia, do you have to eat so much? It's most unbecoming.'

'Sorry, Granny.' Millie served herself more scrambled eggs and devilled kidneys from the silver chafing dishes. 'But I really am starving.'

'Doesn't that wretched institution feed you at all?' Her grandmother made a face of disgust as Millie returned to the table with a laden plate.

'Barely.'

'Well, it's too bad.'

'There's nothing wrong with having a healthy appetite.' Millie's father winked at her.

'It's not just her appetite. Look at her, Henry. Look at her hair, look at her hands. They belong to a housemaid, not a lady.'

Millie looked down at her work-roughened hands. It was difficult to keep them white and soft when they were in water and disinfectant all day.

'That's what comes of putting them to better use than flower arranging, I expect,' her father said.

The Dowager Countess sighed. 'Really, Henry, I would have thought I could count on you for your support. It's bad enough that you've allowed her to stay here over the New Year, rather than insisting she goes to the house party at Lyford.'

Millie rolled her eyes. Her grandmother hadn't stopped talking about the fact that Millie had turned down an invitation to a country house

187

party given by the Duke and Duchess of Claremont. 'Granny, I didn't want to go. I'd rather stay at home than spend three days shooting.'

'That's as may be, but one doesn't turn down an invitation from the Claremonts. Especially not when there will be so many eligible young men in attendance.'

'Perhaps you should have gone in my place, then?' Millie suggested crossly. 'You could have picked one out for me.'

'I have already selected several. Much good it has done me, since you continue to show a wilful lack of interest in your future.'

'I've already decided what my future is going to be, Granny,' Millie reminded her. 'I'm going to be a nurse.'

'Pshh!' Her grandmother curled her lip.

'Please, can we stop arguing?' Henry Rettingham intervened. 'Amelia has agreed to go to the Claremonts' New Year's Eve Ball with us, Mother. I'm sure there will be plenty of opportunity for her to find her Prince Charming there.'

Or another chance to be paraded around in front of potential suitors like a prize cow at a meat market, Millie thought, spearing a mushroom in disgust.

At least her friend Sophia, the Claremonts' daughter, would be there. They had been at boarding school together, and jointly endured the London Season – although with more success for Sophia, who had managed to fall in love with the Duke of Cleveland's son and heir.

Millie was also looking forward to seeing Sophia's brother Sebastian. He had initially escorted his sister to many of the Season's endless events. But since Sophia had proved so immediately popular, he had gallantly offered to squire Millie instead.

They had had so much fun, laughing at the ridiculousness of it all as they stumbled and blundered their way around the dance floors of Mayfair and Belgravia. As a mere second son, Seb had been spared much unwelcome attention from ambitious debutantes and their mothers. And he had done a good job of protecting Millie from the few unwelcome suitors who came her way, too.

But the idea of a ball was simply too exhausting. It was the first time she had been home to Billinghurst in months, and she had been looking forward to exploring the estate and getting to know her old home again.

'We shall have to prepare,' her grandmother said briskly: 'We must decide on a suitable dress this morning, and then we shall have to try to do something with your hair...'

'Actually, Mother, I was planning to take Amelia out with me,' her father said. 'I have to see a few of the tenants, and I know she will benefit from some fresh air after being in London for so long. That is, if you can bear to spend a couple of hours with your dull old father?' He smiled questioningly at her.

'Oh, yes, please!' Relief flooded through her at the chance to escape.

'As long as it is only a couple of hours.' Lady Rettingham looked askance at her granddaughter's hair. 'I can see already we have a great deal to do.'

'In other words, she wants to dress me up like a doll in a shop window,' Millie said as she and her father rode out of the stableyard together, she on her favourite roan Mischief, and her father on Samson, his hunter.

'You are her hobby, Amelia. Everyone must have an interest,' he pointed out mildly.

Out of the stableyard, she dug her heels into Mischief's plump flanks and took off down the lane, her blonde curls flying. Samson thundered behind her, easily keeping pace.

Further down the lane she turned off and galloped up the ridge of hill that looked over Billinghurst.

Millie took a deep breath of clean, fresh country air. How she'd missed it in the sooty grime of London.

She loved the hustle and bustle of the city, and the freedom from her grandmother's watchful eye. But sometimes the narrow streets and dirty buildings seemed to close in on her. Then she longed to be back here, where the sky was so vast above them, like a great cloudless blue canopy, with fields and trees stretching as far as she could see.

From the top of the ridge, she had a wonderful view down over Billinghurst. It sat square and solid, straight out of an Arthurian fantasy with its crenellations and mullioned windows, its thick stone walls burnished golden by the wintry sunshine.

Her father sent her a sidelong glance as they sat side by side, looking down on the magnificent house. 'Do you miss it?' he asked.

'Very much,' Millie admitted with a sigh.

'You don't have to go back, you know.'

Just for a moment, she was desperately tempted. It would be so easy to sink back into her old life. No more rising at dawn to queue up in freezing bathrooms, no more being shouted at or coming home to find Sister Sutton had upended her bed again.

But no hope of having any life of her own either.

'Do you want me to come home?' she asked.

'Only if that's what you really want.'

'I don't have much choice, do I? Grandmother is right, I have to marry for the sake of Billing-hurst.'

'You always have a choice, Amelia.' Her father was silent for a moment, gazing out over the estate. 'I admit, I would like to think of you here one day with a husband and a happy family of your own. But at the end of the day it's just a house. Bricks and mortar are not what's important in life. What's truly important is having someone to love and grow old with.'

She looked across at his strong, handsome profile and knew he was thinking about her mother. Even after nearly twenty years, his sadness still lay heavy on him.

Her mother, Charlotte, Countess of Retting-ham, had died of fever two days after Millie was born. It had broken her father's heart and even now he found it difficult to talk about her. Millie had found out nearly all she knew of her mother from talking to her grandmother and the servants. According to them, Charlotte Rettingham was beautiful and graceful, a gifted artist and musi-cian. So far as she could tell, Millie's only resemblance to her mother was her curly blonde hair and blue eyes.

Despite being alone for so many years, her father had never considered remarrying. But that didn't stop him being the target for many ambitious women. Millie wasn't surprised. As well as being one of the wealthiest landowners in the county, Henry Rettingham was still a very handsome man.

'I don't think Grandmother sees it that way!' she said.

'You have to make allowances for her. Things were very different in her day. Making a good marriage was the ultimate goal for girls of your age. Which is why she's so determined to help you.'

No one could doubt the Dowager Countess had done her best, Millie thought. She had been well educated, sent to finishing school in Switzerland, where she had been taught to dance and arrange flowers. Before the Season, she had taken endless lessons in how to curtsey at Madam Vacani's school in Kensington.

And yet, despite all her new-found talents, she still hadn't managed to find a husband.

'I don't understand it,' her grandmother had said. 'It's not as if you're a pauper. You would think someone would want to marry you for your money, if nothing else.'

'I must be a great disappointment to her,' Millie said ruefully now.

'You're certainly not a disappointment to me.' Her father reached across and took her gloved hand in his. 'You're a fine young woman, Amelia. I'm very proud of you, and I know your mother

192

would have been proud too.'

Millie's smile trembled as she squeezed his hand. She wished more than anything she could have known her mother. It would have meant everything to her to see her face for herself, instead of having to make do with just a few old photographs and a portrait hanging over the fireplace in the great hall.

'Anyway,' her father said, brightening. 'I'm not planning to drop dead just yet. You've got plenty of years to carry on nursing before you have to think about providing a son and heir for Billinghurst!' He pulled at Samson's head to turn him around. 'Now let's go and take a look around the estate, shall we? If we're not back for luncheon I feel sure your grandmother will not be very happy with me.'

Millie was enjoying herself so much, she was very reluctant to head back to the house, knowing what lay in store for her. Sure enough, as soon as luncheon was over, her grandmother ushered her up to her room to start getting ready for the Claremonts' New Year's Eve Ball.

Millie wasn't looking forward to the preparations but she was looking forward to spending time with her maid Polly and catching up on all the gossip below stairs. So she was disappointed when she found her grandmother's maid Louise waiting for her instead.

Louise was in her fifties, French and very proper. She had been with the Dowager Countess since she was a girl, and now fancied herself almost as grand as the old lady herself.

'Where's Polly?' Millie asked.

'Drawing a bath for you, my lady. Her ladyship thought that you might both benefit from my experience in the matter of preparing for this evening.'

Millie found Polly in the bathroom, looking resentful as she filled the tub with steaming water.

'Her ladyship doesn't trust me,' she grumbled.

'No, Polly, I'm afraid it's me she doesn't trust.' Her grandmother clearly wasn't taking any chances on Millie making it through the evening without disaster.

Louise was as tyrannical as her mistress. She bullied them both mercilessly, sending Polly scurrying here and there while she tutted and fussed over Millie at the dressing table with powder and lipstick and hairpins.

'What have you done to your hair?' she demanded, dragging an ivory-handled brush through what was left of Millie's curls.

'I didn't have time to go to the salon, so I cut it myself.' Millie enjoyed seeing the shock on both their faces, reflected in her dressing-table mirror. 'It was terribly easy, I just chopped a bit off here and there so I could get it all under my cap. It's an awful nuisance otherwise.'

Millie hoped she might at least have some say in what she wore for the evening, but Louise had already consulted Grandmother on the matter. She couldn't fault their choice. Her dress was heavy crêpe, cut fashionably on the bias. The blush-pink colour flattered her pearly skin and blonde hair perfectly.

Millie twirled in front of the cheval glass. It was a long time since she'd worn anything vaguely

194

becoming, let alone pretty. Her kid shoes were so light after the stout, sensible black shoes she usually wore, she felt as if she could dance all night.

Meanwhile Louise continued to tut and fuss over her appearance. Her hair was still all wrong, she didn't hold herself like a lady, and how was her diamond necklace supposed to look right with those awful red marks around her neck?

'It's where my collar rubs all day,' Millie explained. 'I've tried putting Vaseline on my skin, but it didn't really help.'

She saw the shocked looks Louise and Polly exchanged, and knew exactly what they were thinking. She was treated worse than her father's staff.

Her grandmother came in just as Louise was rearranging her hair for the third time.

'Well? Will I do, Granny?' Millie waited anxiously for her approval.

The Dowager Countess's gaze swept over her. 'Louise has done a good job, I suppose,' she conceded stiffly. 'Now hurry along, or the year will have ended before we get there.'

Chapter Nineteen

The Claremonts' family home, Lyford, was some thirty miles away. It was a beautiful Georgian house, far grander than Billinghurst, with its elegant symmetry and imposing frontage of Corinthian columns sitting in the centre of beautifully manicured parkland, surrounded by intricate flowerbeds and topiary.

As Felix the chauffeur drove the Daimler through the gates and up the sweeping drive illuminated by flaming torches, Millie could almost feel her grandmother's bristling resentment. She and the Dowager Duchess of Claremont were distant cousins, and there were rumours that Grandmother and the old Duke had once been romantically involved before Cecilia swept in and snapped him up.

Millie understood why her grandmother might covet such a grand house, but she much preferred the homeliness of Billinghurst.

As she stepped from the car, her grandmother said, 'Now remember, Amelia, Richard will be here this evening. I hope you will make a point of speaking to him?'

'Try to catch his eye, you mean?'

'Don't be vulgar, child. But if you must put it that way – why not? He is Claremont's eldest son, and one day all this will be his. And he always had rather a soft spot for you, as I recall. Don't look at me like that,' she added, as Millie frowned at her. 'I dare say there will be a great many young women here tonight hoping to catch his eye, as you so crudely put it.'

Then they're welcome to him, Millie thought. Sophia's older brother Richard was an officer in the Guards, and one of the most pompous men Millie had ever met.

She had visited Lyford many times as a guest of her friend, but the impressive entrance hall, with its grand sweeping staircase, still took her breath away. It looked even more beautiful this evening, lit by the glow of hundreds of candles. The sound of a string quartet mingled with laughter and chatter and the clink of glasses from the ballroom beyond.

The Duke and Duchess greeted their arrival. Caroline Claremont was in her late forties, elegant and even more regal than Millie's grandmother, if that were possible. Millie could never meet her without fighting the urge to bob a quick curtsey.

'Rettingham, how wonderful to see you.' The Duke was a very genial man, and a close friend of her father's. They had served as officers together during the Great War. But unlike her handsome father, years of good living had left Claremont with a rounded figure and a red, hearty face. 'And Lady Rettingham, you're looking very well.'

'Thomas,' her grandmother greeted him. 'How is your dear mother?'

'Alas, she is indisposed and will not be joining us this evening.'

'Oh, how very sad.' Only Millie spotted the slight lifting of the corners of her grandmother's mouth. 'Do give her my very best wishes, won't you?'

'Amelia, how wonderful that you could join us.' Millie felt unnerved as their host looked her up and down with a speculative gleam in his eyes. She was well aware of the Duke's reputation as an old roué.

'We were rather afraid you would be too busy nursing the sick to join us this evening.' Caroline Claremont looked amused.

'I'm still training, they haven't let me loose on any sick people yet,' Millie replied.

'How fascinating. We can't wait to hear all about

197

it.' Then, just in case Millie thought she meant it, the Duchess immediately changed the subject. 'Sophia is longing to see you. I believe she has some rather exciting news for you.' She gave Millie a meaningful look.

Millie could already guess what it might be. But she didn't have to wait long to find out as Sophia rushed up to greet her as soon as she entered the glittering ballroom.

'I'm engaged!' she blurted out, waggling her left hand under Millie's nose. The impressive diamond sparkled in the light of the chandeliers.

'That's wonderful!' Millie embraced her friend. 'When did it happen?'

'On Christmas Eve. Oh, Millie, it was so romantic. We were walking on the terrace, and suddenly he just took my hand, and...' She sighed with happiness. 'I can't believe it.'

'Why not? Anyone can see he's besotted by you.' And rightly too, she thought. Sophia was every inch the duchess in waiting, so beautiful and graceful and as elegant as her mother. Everything Millie wasn't, in fact. She also understood her duty and was happy to submit to it in a way that Millie never would.

But it wasn't just duty with Sophia. She was genuinely in love with David, and probably would have been even if he hadn't been the son and heir of the Duke of Cleveland.

'I want you to be a bridesmaid,' Sophia said, her dark eyes shining with excitement. Millie stared at her.

'Are you sure? I'm terribly clumsy, you know. I'll probably trip over your train and ruin everything.'

198

'You won't.'

'How can you be so certain? Remember the awful hash I made of my presentation?'

'How could I forget?' Sophia giggled.

Millie blushed at the memory. It had sounded so simple. Make one curtsey to the King, then rise, step to the side and make another to the Queen. Except somehow she had become entangled in her own train and almost pitched headlong at Her Majesty's feet.

She didn't know which infuriated her grandmother more, her dreadful faux-pas or the fact that she'd laughed about it so much afterwards.

They were still laughing when Sophia's brother Seb joined them.

'What are you two giggling about, as if I couldn't guess?' He was a year older than Sophia, and in his last year at Oxford. He was as good-looking as his sister, but as fair as Sophia was dark. He reminded Millie of a poet, with his fine-boned, sensitive face, long thin nose and clear grey eyes.

'Your sister has just made the mistake of asking me to be her bridesmaid,' Millie said. 'Although now I come to think of it, I think it's only fair I should ruin your day, since you're ruining my life,' she added. 'You do realise that once news of your engagement gets out, my life won't be worth living?' she explained, as Sophia looked puzzled. 'My grandmother will be completely relentless in her pursuit of a husband for me.'

'Perhaps we should help her?' Seb looked around the room. 'Is there anyone you like the look of?'

'I don't know about that, but I have been told

to keep my eye on your brother,' she said.

'Oh, God, not you too?' Sophia laughed. 'Richard is awfully popular, isn't he?'

'Undeservedly so,' Seb said. 'He's a frightful bore. But it seems wit and intelligence count for very little compared to a title,' he sighed. 'Which is probably why I'm destined to spend the rest of my life on the shelf.'

'At least you'll have me for company,' Millie grinned, taking his arm.

'Unless Miss Farsley has other ideas,' Sophia said mischievously. 'Don't look now, Seb darling, but she's just walked in.'

'Oh God,' Seb groaned.

Millie followed their gaze to where a tall, raven-haired beauty stood in the doorway surveying the crowd. 'Who is that?'

'Georgina Farsley,' Sophia said. 'She arrived in England this summer with her family. American, and disgustingly wealthy.'

'Obscenely,' said Seb.

'Her father buys his darling Georgina everything she wants. Except the one thing she really craves, that is.'

'Which is?'

Sophia looked at her brother. 'Have a guess.'

'You mean Seb?'

'Don't sound so surprised.' Seb looked hurt.

'She's been pursuing him around Lyford like a hound after a hare for the past two days,' Sophia said. 'It's simply too funny to watch.'

'The poor girl,' Millie said.

'Poor girl? What about poor me?' Seb said, outraged. They went in to dinner shortly afterwards, and as she'd hoped, Millie found herself seated beside Sebastian.

'Are you terribly disappointed?' he asked. 'I could arrange for you to sit next to Richard, if you'd prefer?'

'That's quite all right. I can make my play for him after dinner. I shall dazzle him with my dancing.'

'That should be entertaining. Richard is an even worse dancer than you are.'

It was fun, sitting next to Seb. He wasn't like the usual men one met during the Season, great bellowing bores who talked about nothing but hunting, shooting and fishing, and expected girls to hang on their every word. Seb was intelligent, witty and well read. He rode and loved the outdoors as much as Millie, but not to the point of being tedious. He was also interested in her nursing, something everyone else seemed to regard as rather an embarrassment. Millie entertained him with tales of her training, and he filled her in with lots of amusing gossip about his undergraduate friends.

After dinner, it was time for dancing.

'Please tell me your dance card isn't already full?' Seb said as he escorted her in to the ballroom.

Millie pulled a face. 'It's completely empty, I'm afraid.'

'Then allow me.' Seb took out his pen and scribbled his initials gallantly beside every dance.

'You really don't have to, you know. I'll only stamp all over your toes,' Millie warned him as they took to the floor.

'Sooner me than some other poor blighter.'

'Miss Farsley looks as if she is far lighter on her feet than I am,' Millie commented, as the mysterious Georgina skimmed around them, whirled around the floor by another admirer. 'Are you sure you wouldn't rather dance with her?'

'Even having my feet crushed by you is preferable to fighting off her attentions, I assure you.'

'Why don't you want to marry an American heiress? It might be rather fun.' Millie glanced at Georgina as they whisked by each other. 'And she is very beautiful.'

'So is a Ming vase, but I wouldn't like to be married to one. Although come to think of it, I would probably get more entertaining conversation out of a piece of ancient pottery than I ever would out of Miss Farsley.'

Finally, after an exhausting couple of hours' dancing, the clock struck midnight and they all poured out on to the terrace to watch the firework display the Claremonts had arranged.

'Happy New Year,' Millie said to Seb.

'It will be for some people.' He nodded over to where Sophia was entwined in the arms of her fiancé David, their happy faces illuminated by bursts of colour overhead.

'Perhaps it will be for you, too?' Millie smiled. 'I think nineteen thirty-five will be the year someone finally notices your excellent qualities.'

He smiled back at her in the moonlight. 'We can but hope,' he murmured.

Chapter Twenty

'Today I will be explaining the human repro-
ductive system.'

A ripple of nervous giggles ran through the
classroom, quickly silenced by Sister Parker's
stern look.

'Really, Nurses, I fail to see what is so amusing.
Reproduction is simply a function of the human
body like any other. I don't recall anyone being
this giddy when I explained the digestive system,'
she reminded them. 'Now, turn to page seventy
three in your textbook. We'll begin with the male
sexual organs...'

There was a rustle of pages, and Millie pushed
her book across the desk towards Dora. But she
couldn't bring herself to look down at the
diagram in front of her.

'As you can see, the male genitalia is comprised
of the following...'

Someone in the back row gave an embarrassed
cough. In front of her, Dora could see the tips of
Katie O'Hara's ears glowing red. Lucy Lane was
making feverish notes, her pencil flying over the
page as if her life depended on capturing every
word.

Dora kept her gaze fixed on the colourful diagram of the respiratory system that was pinned to
the wall opposite. She tried to fill her head with
the song one of the older girls had been thumping

203

out on the piano the previous night. Anything to tune out the words Sister Parker was saying.

Millie nudged her sharply. 'You're supposed to be writing all this down,' she hissed out of the corner of her mouth.

Dora stared down at the blank page of her notebook. As she did, she caught sight of the diagram in the textbook.

A sudden, horrible image of Alf Doyle came into her mind, grunting like an animal as he pushed himself insistently against her. She clamped her lips together to stop the tidal wave of nausea that swept up into her throat.

The room was chilly but she could feel perspiration standing out on her brow. She gulped for breath, but the air was suddenly filled with the smell of Alf's stale sweat and cigarettes.

'Is something the matter, Doyle?'

Sister Parker was staring at her across the classroom, her brows meeting in a frown over the top of her pebble spectacles.

'I – I don't feel very well, Sister,' Dora whispered.

'For heaven's sake!' The Sister Tutor tutted. 'I might've known someone would have the vapours, but I didn't think it would be *you*. Go outside and get some fresh air, girl. But be quick about it.'

Dora stumbled to her feet and hurried out of the classroom. As soon as she felt the slap of the icy January air on her cheeks she felt foolish. Fancy feeling sick at the sight of a drawing in a medical book! If she was like this now, how would she be when she reached the wards?

Of course Lucy Lane had a field day afterwards, regaling everyone who'd listen about Doyle turning queasy at the facts of life lecture.

'I told them all it must have been something you ate,' Millie told her loyally in their room later. Dora had escaped there as soon as the morning lectures had ended, unable to face lunch in the dining room with the others. Millie had taken the big risk of smuggling her a slice of bread and marge, even though it meant sneaking it past Sister Sutton's room and Sparky's keen nose.

'Thanks.' Dora nibbled on the crust. It might have been true, she reflected. She was usually ravenous by lunchtime, but it was all she could do to swallow past the solid lump of misery in her throat.

Millie watched her, her wide blue eyes sympathetic. 'It is all rather beastly, isn't it?' she said. 'All that business Sister Parker told us about, I mean. Glenda Pritchard actually fainted when she told us during my last stint in PTS. So I think you did rather well, under the circumstances.' She shook her head. 'It seems so terribly complicated, doesn't it?' she whispered, her voice hushed with awe.

Dora put down her piece of bread, her appetite deserting her. 'I don't know and I don't want to know,' she said firmly. Then she added, 'I think I should just pack it in and go home.'

Millie stared at her. 'Why? Not just because you went a bit wobbly in a lecture, surely? I told you, Glenda Pritchard was far worse than you–'

'Not just because of that,' Dora said. The truth was, she didn't feel as if she really belonged at the Nightingale. She'd really tried to fit in, but she was always painfully aware of the differences between her and the other pros. They were all well-to-do, well educated girls who knew so much more than she did. Not just the subjects they learned in class, but all the other things books didn't teach. The unwritten rules, like which knife and fork to use, how to pour a cup of tea, how to speak properly. They talked in a language she didn't understand, about ballet lessons and boarding schools.

And none of them understood her, either. None of them had lived the life she had, working in a sweat shop and dodging the rent man.

Not that she could explain that to Millie. She was the poshest of the lot of them, but she was also the nicest. She was so used to being pretty and popular, she simply wouldn't be able to imagine what it must be like to feel like an outsider.

'I'm going to fail PTS,' Dora said. 'The exams are only a couple of weeks away, and I still don't have my books. I'll never catch up at this rate.'

'I'm sure they'd let you take PTS again, like they did me,' Millie said cheerfully.

Dora smiled, but didn't reply. They might give an Earl's daughter a second chance, but she doubted if they'd do the same to an East End girl who'd barely scraped in the first time round.

'Anyway, I've already said you can have my books,' Millie went on.

'And I've already said thanks but no thanks.'

'There must be some way you can get the money to buy them?'

'I don't have rich relatives like you, more's the pity.'

'My relatives aren't that rich, most of them are in

hock up to their eyeballs just to keep – that's it!'
Millie's eyes lit up. 'You could pawn something!'

Her pretty, innocent face was so earnest, Dora
couldn't help laughing. 'And what does an Earl's
daughter know about pawning things?'

'You'd be surprised,' Millie said. 'My third
cousin Lord Lumley had a terrible gambling
habit. He was forever heading up to London with
a suitcase full of the family silver.'

'It's a pity I don't have any silver to pawn, then!'
Dora said wryly.

'What about that charm your friend gave you?'

'My hamsa? I can't get rid of that.'

'You wouldn't be getting rid of it. You could get
it back when you get paid next month.'

Dora considered it. Esther had told her to use
it whenever she needed a bit of luck. Perhaps it
would turn out to be lucky for her after all...

'Can you pawn this for me?'

Nick examined the tiny silver hand Dora had
given him. He'd never seen anything like it
before. 'What is it?'

'My lucky charm.'

'Why do you want to get rid of it, if it's that
lucky?'

'Because I need the money to buy books. If I
don't get them, I'll need more than a charm to
get me through preliminary training.'

They stood on the patch of waste ground
behind the nurses' home. Nick had been intrigued when Dora had asked to meet him there.
He'd tried to imagine what she might want, but
this hadn't even occurred to him.

'Why come to me?' he said. 'Why not take it down to Solomon's yourself?'

'I don't get another day off until next month and I need the money before then.'

'Why don't you ask your dad?'

'Why don't you mind your own business?' The vehemence of Dora's reply shocked him. 'I don't want to ask him for money, all right? I've got my reasons.' Her eyes met his. 'Now, will you help me or not?'

Anyone else and he might have said no, especially after the way she'd just spoken to him. But Dora had always been good to him and Danny, and Nick didn't forget a kindness.

'I s'pose I could nip down there on my way home,' he conceded grudgingly. He looked at the charm nestling in his palm. 'How much do you need?'

'The books cost just over a fiver new, but I might be able to get some secondhand for cheaper.' She looked up at him anxiously. 'Do you think I might get that much?'

'From old Solomon? You'll be lucky!' he laughed, then saw the disappointment in her face and added, 'I'll see what I can do, all right? But no promises.'

'I understand.'

She smiled that strange, lopsided smile of hers. No one in their right mind could ever call Dora pretty, but there was something about her.

He remembered her nanna's words on Christmas Day: 'Dora can't afford to be fussy.' And the way she'd turned red, and he'd pretended not to hear so she wouldn't be embarrassed.

208

He liked Dora. She had a dream, just like him. He could imagine telling her about his plan to go to America, knowing she wouldn't laugh at him.

As she walked away, he called after her, 'How do you know I won't just nick it and keep the money?'

She looked back over her shoulder at him. 'I trust you,' she said simply.

Her words haunted him all the way home. People didn't trust Nick Riley. They either respected him because he was a hard grafter, or they feared him because he was good with his fists.

But no one had ever trusted him before. It was a strange, heady feeling.

He reached Solomon's just as the old man was shutting up shop for the night.

Mr Solomon emerged from the curtained-off back room at the tinkle of the bell over the front door. He was a wiry little man, with a face as wrinkled as a walnut and shrewd brown eyes.

'Nicky boy! To what do we owe this pleasure?' He rubbed his hands together. 'How's your mother? Well, I hope? I haven't seen her in here for a while.'

That's because we've got nothing left to pawn, Nick thought.

The musty smell of the cramped little shop made him feel sick As a small boy it had seemed like a place of wonder, its shelves lined with all kinds of strange and magical things – old paintings, antiques, curios, children's toys, even a stuffed cat once. And then there was the glass cabinet, crammed with watches, rings, necklaces, brooches, like a pirates' treasure chest. He remembered spending hours just staring at them while his mother argued with old Solomon.

'A tanner? Is that the best you can do you tight old sod? How am I going to feed my kids?'

'That's your husband's job, Mrs Riley, not mine,' Mr Solomon would always reply.

But somehow the deed was always done in the end and his mother would drag Nick back to Griffin Street by the hand, complaining bitterly all the way about how she'd been robbed.

Ten years later she was still pawning everything she could get her hands on.

'Got something for me, have you, Nick?' Mr Solomon's eyes gleamed with anticipation.

Nick reached into his pocket and pulled out Dora's chain. 'What can you give me for this?'

'Well, well. What have we here?' Mr Solomon dangled the chain from his fingers, admiring the charm as it swung gently before his eyes. 'Now what's a *goy* like you doing with a thing like this, Nicky boy?' He looked up at him sharply. 'You didn't pinch it, did you?'

'No, I didn't.' Nick glowered back at him. 'It belongs to someone I know. Are you interested, or what?'

'That depends, doesn't it? I need to examine the merchandise closely first.'

Nick tried to control his impatience as Mr Solomon fetched his magnifying glass from under the counter and began scrutinising the charm against a square of green baize. He took ages doing it, turning it this way and that.

'Well?' he said.

210

'In a hurry, aren't you? Are you sure you didn't nick it?' The old man set down his magnifying glass and looked up at Nick. 'It's not a bad piece, I suppose. I'll give you a pound for it.'

'A quid? You must be joking! Anyone can see it's worth more than that.'

'They're not standing here, though, are they? I am. And that's my offer. So what do you say?' Mr Solomon's bright eyes fixed on him expectantly, waiting for his next move.

'I say you're a robbing...'

'Now, now, Nicky boy, that's no way to talk, is it?' The old man looked more amused than insulted. He had been called a lot worse in his shop over the forty years he'd been trading in Bethnal Green. 'Look, since your mother is such an old and valued customer of mine, I'll be generous with you. How about I make it a nice round guinea?'

'I need a fiver.'

'Then you need your head looked at!' Mr Solomon cackled. 'Look, the chain's a piece of cheap tat, worth next to nothing. The hamsa – well, it's a nice piece, but nothing special. I'd be cutting my own throat if I offered you any more. I'm practically robbing myself as it is!'

I doubt that, Nick thought. If old Solomon was offering a guinea then it must be worth three times that at least.

Nick looked down at the charm lying on the green baize mat. Maybe a guinea would be enough for Dora to get her books secondhand?

But then he thought of the way she'd looked at him. 'I trust you,' she'd said. He couldn't let her down.

211

'Well?' Mr Solomon's bright brown eyes were fixed on him keenly. 'Do we have a deal, Nicky boy?'

Nick looked from the charm to the old man and back again. 'No chance.' He picked it up off the counter. 'I'd sooner chuck it in the Thames than let you have it.'

'Suit yourself.' The old man shrugged his narrow shoulders. 'But you'll be back, I'm sure. Turn the sign round on your way out, will you? And give my regards to your mother,' he called after Nick as he slammed the door behind him.

Nick walked back through the market. The traders were packing up their wares on to barrows, leaving only the wooden skeletons of their stalls behind. A little boy, eyes bright in his grimy face, oversized trousers rolled up to reveal worn out boots, dodged and weaved his way between them, swooping in under the stallholders' feet and the rumbling barrow wheels to gather up the squashed, bruised fruit and veg that had fallen on the cobbles.

'Watch it!' one of the stallholders shouted, as he narrowly missed being run over to rescue an apple. 'Do you want to get yourself killed, son?'

He picked an orange off the stall and tossed it to him. The boy caught it with one hand.

'Thanks, Mister.' He grinned cheekily and darted off, his bounty gathered up in the tails of his grubby shirt.

That was me once, Nick thought as he watched him go. Ducking and diving around the stalls, looking for something to bring home. Or roaming the streets, collecting bottles to get the deposit, or even shovelling up horse manure to sell. Anything to earn a few pennies to keep his mum happy and his dad from using his fists.

Dora's charm was still clenched in his hand. He'd let her down. She'd trusted him to get the money for her and he'd failed. He couldn't bear to think of the disappointment in her eyes when he told her he hadn't got the money for her books.

'All right, Nick?' He looked round. Ruby Pike was picking her way across the cobbles towards him, spectacular curves swaying. She was dressed up to the nines as usual, her blonde hair carefully waved. She looked as if she was coming back from a night out, not a day at work.

He carried on walking and she caught up with him. 'Lovely day, innit? Not that I've seen much of it, stuck behind that machine all day. Honestly, it could be blowing a gale or anything outside, and we wouldn't know about it...' She chattered on, oblivious to the fact that Nick had stopped listening.

He was lost in his own thoughts, still thinking about Dora.

He would give her the money himself. It was as simple as that. He had always made a strict rule not to take anything out of his American fund, but he knew Dora would pay him back. And besides, his dream was still a long way off. Dora needed the money now or her dream would be over.

'Are you listening to me, Nick Riley?' Ruby blocked his path, hands planted on her rounded hips.

'What?'

'I knew it. You haven't listened to a single word

I've said, have you?' Ruby pouted her full lips. 'Here I am, giving you the chance that a lot of men round here would give their right arm for, and you're not even paying me a bit of attention. I've a good mind to tell you to forget it.'

'Forget what?' He frowned at her.

'Taking me out, of course.' She raked her scarlet-tipped hand through her blonde curls. 'I'm free tonight, as it happens. Do you fancy taking me out dancing?'

'I don't like dancing.'

'Maybe you just haven't found the right partner?' She flashed her eyes at him. Nick moved past her and went on walking.

Ruby fell into step beside him again. 'Oh, all right,' she said. 'If you don't fancy dancing, how about the pictures? They're showing the new Errol Flynn down at The Rialto. I love Errol Flynn, don't you?' she sighed.

'He's not my type,' Nick muttered.

Ruby laughed and batted him playfully on the arm. 'Oh, you're a funny one, you are, Nick Riley! Come on, let's go to the pictures. I'll even sit on the back row with you, if you like?'

He looked her up and down. She was everything a man could ever want, with her pin-up girl curves and saucy smile. She was right, there were a lot of men in Bethnal Green who would love to get an offer like that from Ruby Pike.

But not him.

'Some other time,' he said.

As he walked on, Ruby called after him, 'How do you know there'll be another time? I might change my mind, you know.'

But I won't change mine, Nick thought as he headed home, Dora's charm still clenched in his fist.

Chapter Twenty-One

Dora squeezed her eyes shut, trying to memorise the bones of the foot.

'Calcaneus, talus, navicular, cuboid, cuneiforms, metatarsals, phalanges...'

She paused, trying to make the words sink in, but they just seemed to fall away into nothingness.

'Each toe has three phalanges – proximal, middle, and distal – except the hallux, or big toe, which has only two – proximal, and distal. The hallux ... proximal and distal...'

Across the room in the darkness she could hear Millie and Helen's soft breathing as they slept. She longed for sleep too, but the PTS exams were two days away, and there was still so much to learn.

At least she had her books now. She'd been surprised when Nick gave her the money. Old Mr Solomon had been more generous than she'd hoped, giving her enough money to afford brand new books.

But that was where her luck had run out. The past week had been spent reading far into the night, trying desperately to catch up and cram her brain with all the information the other girls had been able to study for the past three months.

All the time, the picture of her family haunted

215

her, smiling through their disappointment as they welcomed her back home. Just like Jennifer Bradley's parents had as they bundled her into the car that day.

And then there was Alf. It didn't even bear thinking about, being back under the same roof as him.

Dora lay back on the bed and rubbed her eyes. They felt gritty and sore from studying. How blissful it would be to just let them close and allow herself to drift away...

The squeak of the doorknob shocked her awake. She sat up quickly as the door opened and Alf Doyle stood there. His looming dark bulk filled the doorway.

Dora's mouth went dry with fear. 'Go away,' she whispered. 'You don't belong here.'

Alf leered at her. 'Not until I get what I've come for,' he said softly. 'You know what I've come for, don't you, Dora love?'

He came towards her, undoing his belt. Dora shrank back against the hard wooden bedhead. 'Leave me alone,' she whimpered. 'You don't belong here. I need to study...'

'I know what you need.' His hands gripped her shoulders, pushing her down on the bed. She struggled against him, but his weight pressed down on her so she couldn't breathe...

'Doyle? Doyle, wake up.'

When she opened her eyes, it wasn't Alf's leering grin she saw, but the concerned faces of Millie and Helen looking down at her.

'You had a nightmare,' Millie told her kindly. 'You were thrashing about and shouting.'

216

'Sorry. Did I wake you?'

'Us and half the mortuary too, I shouldn't wonder.' Helen padded back across the room to her own bed, yawning.

Dora gulped in a deep, calming breath and felt her racing heartbeat slowing down.

'What were you dreaming about?' Millie asked.

'I don't remember,' she lied.

'You kept telling someone to leave you alone?'

She saw Millie's frown of concern and panicked. Had she given herself away? 'It was probably something to do with the PTS test,' she said. 'I've been worrying about it a lot.'

'Haven't we all?' Millie said.

'Can we go back to sleep now?' Helen mumbled sleepily from the other side of the room.

They went back to bed, and moments later Dora once again heard the soft breathing that told her her room-mates were fast asleep.

She lay awake, staring up at the ceiling. Tired though she was, she was too terrified to close her eyes in case she cried out again and gave herself away. Alf Doyle, she thought bitterly. Even now, he still made her too afraid to sleep.

The four sisters who filed into the student block could not have looked more unfriendly if they'd tried. The students watched them arrive from the window of the nurses' home.

'Is Sister Hyde with them?' Millie whispered anxiously. 'Oh, please God, don't send her again. If I even see her in that examination room, I'll just fall to pieces, I know it.'

'I'm going to fail anyway,' Katie groaned. 'I'll be

217

the only O'Hara girl not to qualify. I'll be sent back to Ireland and my mammy will die of shame.'

'I don't know what you're all getting so worried about.' Lucy, as ever, was perfectly calm and poised. 'It's only a couple of tests. You should pass it easily, as long as you've prepared.'

Dora was glad she wasn't the only one who gave her a black look. Lucy's perfection had started to grate on all of them over the past few days.

Sister Parker didn't help their nerves, either, fussing over them like an anxious mother hen.

'Make sure you arrive promptly for each of your tests, and don't address the examiners unless addressed by them,' she'd warned them over and over again. 'Remember to bring a clean apron in case of accidents. And, Doyle, can you please do something about your hair?'

Dora tucked her curls under her cap. She could understand Sister Parker's anxiety. It reflected badly on her if her students didn't do well in PTS.

There were two days of tests for the students, a practical and oral test followed by a written examination. For days they had been practising their bandages, taking each other's temperatures, checking pulses and respiration and swotting up on the bones and organs of the human body and their various functions. But as she made her way unsteadily to the student block with the seven other students from her set, Dora could feel all the knowledge she had worked so hard to cram into her head slowly ebbing out like a retreating tide.

They waited in the classroom to be called. Finally the first four were summoned, two into the kitchen and two into the practical area.

Millie followed her partner, Gladys Brennan, into the practical area as if she were going to the gallows. 'I'm going to get a capelline bandage, I just know it,' she hissed to Dora.

Dora smiled, but the smile was wiped off her face when she was summoned to the kitchen with Lucy Lane.

Why did it have to be her? she thought wretchedly as she followed her down the corridor. No matter how good she tried to be, Lucy would make her look hopeless by comparison. They were given the task of preparing a meal for a patient on a Sippy diet. Lucy immediately knew what to do, moving with practised efficiency around the kitchen, pulling out pans, peeling vegetables and chopping up beef, while Dora stood motionless at the stove and tried to get her dull brain to think straight.

Slowly it started to come back to her. Sippy diet, that meant very bland, lots of milk and cream, suitable for a patient recovering from a gastric ulcer.

She mentally went through a list of suitable dishes. Boiled fish would be bland enough, with mashed potatoes and a spoonful of pureed vegetables, and junket to follow.

Lucy was already busy stirring something on the stove. Beef consommé, by the delicious smell filling the kitchen. Dora hoped her humble offering wouldn't pale in comparison.

For the next few minutes they were both busy, working in purposeful silence while the sisters looked on from the other side of the room. They didn't seem to be paying too much attention to

219

their cooking, thank goodness; Dora knew she would be all thumbs if they'd stood over them all the time.

She had boiled her vegetables and potatoes, put her junket aside to set and was lighting the gas ready to cook her fish when she heard Lucy cry out. Dora turned around. Lucy was standing at the next stove, staring into the pan with a look of utter despair.

Dora's eyes darted to the sisters, still conferring quietly at the far end of the room. 'What's wrong?' she hissed out of the corner of her mouth.

Lucy tipped the pan towards her. The soup had boiled down to almost nothing, a couple of spoonfuls of rich brown syrup. 'I must've lit the gas under the soup again, instead of under the vegetables. It's ruined.' Her usual composure had disappeared, and her voice was thick with tears.

Serves you right, Dora thought. She had a sudden mental image of the sisters looking into the pan, then putting a big cross next to Lucy Lane's name. That would stop her bragging, she thought.

At the other end of the room the sisters were beginning to stir. Any moment they would look up and realise something had gone wrong.

'Put some boiling water in it,' Dora whispered. 'Hurry up, before they come.'

'But it'll taste awful.'

'It can't be any worse than it is now, can it? Just boil up a kettle and hope their taste buds are too numb to notice.'

Lucy shook her head mournfully. 'I didn't light the gas for my vegetables either. They're not even cooked.'

'Then you can share mine. Now quickly, get that kettle on while they're still having a chin wag over there.'

Her face still blank with shock, Lucy did as she was told while Dora strained and pureed her vegetables and mashed her potatoes. Before the sisters came to inspect their trays of food, she quickly dolloped a spoonful of veg on to Lucy's plate.

They both held their breath as the sisters sampled their dishes. When Dora glanced across, she saw Lucy had her eyes tightly shut, her lips moving in a silent prayer.

After a long time, one of the sisters put a tick on her clipboard.

'Thank you, Nurses,' she said. 'Please send in the next pair.'

It took Millie several minutes to take in what Sister Parker had said to her. Even then she'd had to show her the printed result sheet before she would allow herself to believe it.

'I'm sorry, Sister, I'm just so surprised I've passed,' she said.

Sister Parker regarded her severely over her spectacles. 'Believe me, Benedict, no one could be more surprised than I am,' she said with feeling.

The others had all passed too, and there was much excitement in the nurses' block as they swapped horror stories.

For once Lucy seemed oddly quiet, Millie noticed. She hadn't bragged about how well she'd done, or how easy the test had been. She hadn't made a single nasty remark. During supper, she had even offered Dora the cocoa jug first for

221

once, instead of grabbing it for herself.

'What's the matter with her, I wonder?' Millie mused.

Dora shrugged. 'Maybe the test has brought her down to earth?'

'I doubt it. You wait, she'll be full of herself again by tomorrow.'

'You never know,' Dora said. 'She might be different once we start training on the wards.'

'The wards!' Excitement bubbled inside Millie. 'Just think, we're going to be real nurses.'

'Steady on, we've got another three years of training before then.'

'But at least from now on we'll be on the wards, dealing with real patients.'

'Yes, and have you seen the state of some of them?' Dora laughed. 'I bet after six months we'll be longing for Mrs Jones again!'

'Well, she did it. I don't know how, but somehow she managed it.'

'Oh? What's that?' Veronica Hanley looked up from her quilt-stitching and pretended not to know what Sister Parker was talking about.

'Young Doyle. She passed her preliminary training. More than passed, in fact. Her marks were excellent. They might have been even better if she'd had access to books earlier.'

Veronica gave her a tight smile. 'She is a tribute to your excellent teaching, Florence.'

'She's a very bright girl,' Florence Parker corrected her, a touch of irritation in her voice. 'Even if some people would have dismissed her out of hand,' she added pointedly.

'You're talking as if she's already a qualified nurse,' Sister Sutton said, leaning over her sewing to pass a biscuit to Sparky. 'She still has three years and several more examinations to go before we can say that.'

'Indeed,' Miss Hanley agreed. 'Girls can change a great deal in three years.'

They lapsed into tense silence. Veronica had the feeling Florence was bursting to say something more, but manners prevented her. She was surprised at her friend. She had always thought Sister Parker had standards. Now she was beginning to sound like some kind of socialist.

'What about Benedict? Did she pass?' Sister Sutton asked.

Florence Parker thought about it for a moment. 'She scraped through, yes.'

'Well, I hope *she* changes in the next three years,' Agatha Sutton said with feeling. 'Otherwise God help our poor patients!'

Chapter Twenty-Two

Having tea with her mother was always an ordeal for Helen. Constance Tremayne criticised everything, from where they were seated – 'Not a corner table, please. And not over by the window, either' – to the quality of the sandwiches. 'I hope they are freshly made?' she frowned at the waitress, who stood with her notepad poised.

'Yes, Madam. Freshly made to order.'

'Then we shall have an assortment and a pot of tea for two.' She snapped her menu shut.

'Any cakes, Madam?'

Constance looked down her nose at the girl. 'Did I order cakes?'

'No, but–'

'Then obviously we do not require any. And make sure the pot has been warmed and the water is boiling,' she called after the waitress.

Helen put down her own menu. There wasn't much point in looking at it, since her mother always ordered for her anyway.

It was a cold, wet January afternoon, and Helen was on her break. She was due back on the ward at five o'clock, and felt guilty that she was already counting the hours. She found herself thinking about Charlie Denton. He was due to go home that day, and Helen had hoped she might be there to see him off. But Sister Holmes had put her down on the rota to take her break from three till five, and then her mother had summoned her for afternoon tea, and Helen couldn't possibly say no to either of them.

The waitress returned with their tea and sandwiches. Helen cringed as her mother inspected everything. It took her some time, but finally Constance found something that wasn't to her satisfaction.

'Waitress! Over here, if you please.'

The girl came over, her expression resigned. 'What can I do for you, Madam?'

'You can take this teacup away and bring me a clean one. Look at it, it's revolting.' She shuddered with distaste.

The waitress peered into the cup. Helen prayed she wouldn't argue; she could already see the light of battle gleaming in her mother's eyes.

'Very well, Madam.'

Helen caught the waitress' scowl as she took the offending cup away. The poor girl might feel put upon, but at least she only had to put up with Mrs Tremayne for half an hour or so. Helen had been under her thumb for the last twenty years.

'That's better,' Constance said, when the waitress had returned with a spotless cup. She turned her attention back to Helen. 'Now, where were we?'

Helen folded her hands in her lap and waited patiently for her own inspection. She was certain that, unlike the second teacup, she would not pass muster.

She could feel her mother's gaze, raking her up and down. Finally, Constance said, 'Have you cut your hair?'

'Just a couple of inches.' Helen fingered the ends of her hair uncertainly. 'But I was thinking of having it cut a bit shorter,' she ventured. 'A lot of the other girls are having theirs done, and–'

'No, I don't think so,' her mother cut her off.

'But it's all the fashion. And it would be a lot more practical.'

'Short hair looks fast.'

Helen watched her mother pour the tea. It was a waste of time to argue. Constance Tremayne had spoken and that was the end of the matter.

She allowed her thoughts to drift back to Mr Denton, or Charlie as she called him in her head. He had been in an odd mood as she'd helped him to pack that morning, as if he had something weighing on his mind.

Helen did her best to cheer him up. 'I bet you're looking forward to getting out of here?' she'd said, as she carefully folded his spare pair of pyjamas.

'I don't know about that. I'm not sure I'm ready for the big wide world yet, Nurse T.'

'You'll be fine,' she reassured him. 'You've learned to cope really well with your new leg.'

'Oh, I can manage all right in here. But what's it going to be like when I get out there?' He turned his gaze towards the window.

'You're bound to feel a bit nervous at first,' she said briskly. 'But I bet in a couple of weeks you'll be happily drinking pints in the Rose and Crown and won't even remember this place!'

'I won't forget you in a hurry.'

Helen was on her hands and knees, clearing out his locker. She was glad he couldn't see her blushing face.

'Helen? Have you listened to a word I've said?'

She looked at her mother across the table. 'I'm sorry?'

'I thought not.' Constance's mouth pursed with irritation. 'I hope you're more attentive than this when you're working on the ward?'

'Yes, Mother.'

'I'm sure I don't need to remind you that you're representing me at the Nightingale. I do not expect you to let me down.'

'No, Mother.'

'And if you make a mistake, be sure I will find out about it.'

'I know, Mother.'

As they nibbled their sandwiches, her mother quizzed her. How were her studies? What had she learned? Was she doing better than the other students?

Helen did her best to answer tactfully. But she made a mistake when she tried to tell her mother a funny story about one of the pros on her ward who had got confused by Sister's instructions to give a patient an air ring to sit on after his haemorrhoid operation.

'She thought Sister meant give him an airing. The Staff Nurse caught her trying to drag him outside, howling in pain!'

She hoped her mother would laugh, but Constance Tremayne's face grew serious.

'Really, Helen, I see nothing to laugh about,' she said sternly. 'A patient's life could have been put at risk.'

'He only had haemorrhoids!' Helen protested.

'Perhaps, but tomorrow it could be someone with a heart condition or a head injury. You may smile, Helen, but I'm serious. Quite honestly, I don't know what you young nurses are thinking about these days. When I was training—'

Helen mentally tuned out, playing with the crumbs on her plate. It was going to be a long afternoon, she could tell.

She hurried back to the ward just before five, but Charlie had already gone. Two pros were making up his bed with fresh sheets, ready for the next patient.

'He left half an hour ago,' Amy Hollins told her. 'If you ask me, he couldn't wait to see the back of this place.'

'I don't blame him,' Helen sighed. But she couldn't help feeling a pang of disappointment that she'd missed saying goodbye.

The following morning Helen was surprised to see him coming through the doors as she was taking TPRs at the other end of the ward. Charlie was leaning heavily on his stick while balancing an enormous bunch of chrysanthemums in his free hand. She felt a sudden wave of panic and lost her count while taking Mr Stannard's pulse.

'Looks like someone's got a secret admirer.' Mr Stannard grinned at Helen, showing off his few remaining teeth. 'Who's the lucky girl, I wonder?'

'I really wouldn't know.' Helen quickly copied the previous figure on his chart and moved away. Her own pulse had started racing so hard she couldn't keep count of that, either. She tried to ignore the conversation that was going on at the other end of the ward between Charlie Denton and Staff Nurse Lund. They talked for a minute or two, then he left. Shortly after, Lund summoned Helen over.

'Mr Denton brought these flowers in to thank us for looking after him. Isn't that kind?' she said.

'Very kind, Staff. Shall I put them in water?'

'Good idea, Tremayne. But be sure you're back before Sister returns from her break, won't you?'

Helen didn't understand the look Lund gave her until she found Charlie Denton waiting for her by the sluice-room door.

'The nurse said I could have five minutes with you.' He looked so different all dressed up in a

228

suit and shirt, his red-gold hair brushed back off his smiling face. So handsome, too. Helen nervously checked the thought, as if he could somehow read her mind.

He was looking at her expectantly, but Helen didn't know what to say. Finally she asked, 'How's your leg?'

'All right, thanks. Takes a bit of getting used to, but it's not as bad as I thought.'

'That's good.' She moved awkwardly past him into the sluice room. Mr Denton followed her.

'Cold in here, isn't it?'

'That's because there's no glass in the windows.' Helen pointed at the high screen-covered gap above their heads. 'It's better for ventilation. But it does get freezing in the winter.'

'Is that right?'

It seemed so ridiculous, having a chat about the sluice-room window. But Helen had no idea what else to say. She could feel him watching her from the doorway as she found a vase in the cupboard and filled it under the tap.

'I've missed you,' he said at last.

'You've only been gone a day!'

'I know, but it feels strange, not seeing your smiling face when I wake up.'

The silence stretched between them. Helen glanced down at the watch pinned to her bib. Another minute and she'd have to go back to the ward.

'I'm making a right mess of this, aren't I?' Charlie Denton ran his hand through his sandy hair. 'I had it all planned on the way here, but now it's all gone out of my head.'

'What did you want to say?' Helen could hear her heart beating in her ears.

He smiled at her, his blue eyes warm. 'I don't suppose you'd think about coming out with me one night?'

Her surprise must have shown on her face because he went on quickly, 'No, sorry, forget I asked. I don't know what I was thinking. You've probably got dozens of lads after you. Why would you want to have anything to do with me?'

'I haven't, honestly,' Helen blurted out.

His face brightened. 'So does that mean you'll come out with me?'

'I'm sorry, I can't. I'm going on nights from tomorrow.'

'How long for?'

'Three months.'

'Three months! That's a long time to wait for a night out at the pictures!' Charlie Denton thought about it for a moment. 'But I reckon you're worth waiting for,' he said cheekily. 'So what d'you reckon? Will you go out with me then?'

Helen hesitated. She longed to go, but... 'My mother wouldn't like it.'

'I'm not asking your mother. I'm asking you.' He grinned. 'And I'm warning you, if you say no, I'll come back in three months and ask you again!'

'You're very persistent.'

'I am when I want something, Nurse T.' He frowned. 'I can't keep calling you that, can I? Can I at least know your name?'

'Helen.'

'Helen.' He paused for a moment, savouring it. 'I knew you'd have a beautiful name. A beautiful name for a beautiful girl.' He smiled. 'And I reckon now I'm not a patient any more, you can call me Charlie.' He took her hand and shook it. 'I'll see you in three months, Helen.'

'If you say so ... Charlie.'

But as she watched him walk away, Helen knew she would never see him again. In three months' time he would have gone back to his old life and forgotten all about her.

Which was probably just as well since her mother would never allow her to have a boyfriend.

She smiled to herself as she carried the vase back to the ward. But it was still a nice idea while it lasted.

Chapter Twenty-Three

'See anything you like, young lady?'

Mr Solomon crept from behind the curtained-off area at the back of the shop, his tread so soft Dora hadn't heard him approach. 'Or perhaps you have something you wish to offer me?' he suggested

'I'm looking for something...' She peered into the glass-fronted case, crammed full of watches, rings, brooches and trinkets, each with its own sad story to tell. How desperate did a woman have to be to part with her wedding ring, or a man to hand over his precious war medals, knowing they might never see them again?

'So you have something special in mind?' He

231

took a jingling ring of keys out of his pocket and selected one. 'A ring, perhaps? Or a bracelet? I have one here that might suit you...'

'A necklace,' Dora said. 'A – friend – brought it in last month. You gave him money for it.'

'And now you want it back?' He opened up the case. 'A necklace, you say? What does it look like?'

'It's silver, shaped like a little hand. But I don't see it here...'

'Ah, you mean the hamsa?' Mr Solomon smiled. 'I remember it now. That Riley boy brought it in a few weeks ago.'

Dora nodded eagerly. 'That's it. Do you have it?'

'I'm afraid not, young lady. I made young Nick an offer for it, but he turned me down. Seemed to think it was worth more than I was offering. Cheeky little *ganef* thought he could swindle me in my own shop.' He cleared his throat in disgust and spat into a grubby handkerchief.

Dora began to panic. 'So where is it now?'

'How should I know? Knowing that boy, he probably flogged it down the Rose and Crown.' Mr Solomon shrugged. 'You'll have a job getting it back, I reckon. He should have sold it to me,' he called after her, as she rushed out of the shop. 'At least I would have kept it safe for you.'

Dora was seething as she stomped back through the market. It was a Saturday afternoon, and the street was busy. On one side, people picked and argued over secondhand clothes spread out on canvas sheets across the pavement. On the other side were stalls selling fruit and veg and seafood. The sharp, salty smell mingled with the tang of fried onions and the tempting aroma of freshly baked bread. Usually Dora loved the sights, sounds and smells of the market, but today she was too furious to notice them.

Mr Solomon was right, she stood no chance of getting her hamsa back. It could be anywhere. The thought of it hanging round the neck of one of Nick Riley's tarty girlfriends made her feel sick. I should never have trusted him, she thought. Now she'd lost her precious hamsa and let Esther Gold down, and it was all *his* fault.

Back at the Nightingale, she headed straight for the porters' lodge.

Mr Hopkins was very put out when she marched in. 'What's the meaning of this?' he spluttered. 'You can't come barging in here...'

'I'm looking for Nick Riley. Where is he?'

'Having his tea break. But you can't go in there!' he shouted after her as she marched past him. 'I'll tell Matron. This area is restricted to porters only, not nurses. You have to go through the proper channels...'

Nick was in the back room, playing cards around an upturned tea chest with a few of the other porters.

'I want a word with you,' Dora said.

'All right, Nick? What you been up to then?' one of the other porters cackled.

'Hope you haven't been a naughty boy?' another laughed.

'Wouldn't be the first time if he was, would it?'

Nick threw down his cards, rose to his feet and followed Dora out, to a chorus of cat calls from the other porters.

Outside it was cold, damp and already growing dark even though it wasn't yet four o'clock. Nick lit a cigarette and took a deep drag. 'What's this all about?' he asked gruffly.

'Where's my necklace? And don't bother lying to me, I've been down to Solomon's and he says he hasn't got it. So where is it?'

He stared at the glowing tip of his cigarette. 'It's safe.'

'Why didn't you pawn it like I asked you to?'

'Because he offered me next to nothing for it.'

'So you thought you'd sell it to one of your mates instead?'

He didn't meet her eye. 'What do you care? You got the money for your books, didn't you? More than old Solomon would have given you.'

'That's not the point. You knew what it meant to me, and you knew I'd want it back. How am I supposed to get it if you sold it?'

'Who said I sold it?'

'Don't be clever with me, Nick Riley. I don't want to hear any of your lies.' Dora stared at his rigid profile. He couldn't even look her in the eye. 'You really don't care, do you? You knew how much that necklace meant to me, and you just handed it over to any old Tom, Dick or Harry,' she raged.

'I got you the money, didn't I?' he growled.

'So you say. I wouldn't be surprised if you'd sold it and kept some for yourself!'

He turned slowly to look at her. 'Are you calling me a thief?'

Anyone else might have been put off by his icy anger, but Dora was too furious to care.

'I wouldn't put anything past you, Nick Riley. I was wrong about you, wasn't I? Everyone said you weren't to be trusted, but I didn't believe them. I thought you wouldn't let me down–'

There was a jingling sound at her feet. Dora looked down. The hamsa lay glinting in a dirty puddle of water.

'I do know what it meant to you,' Nick said gruffly. 'Why else do you think I kept hold of it?'

'I don't understand.'

'No, you don't, do you? Looks like I was wrong about you, too.' As his eyes met hers, Dora caught the flash of hurt.

'Nick...' she began to say, but he was already walking back towards the porters' lodge, hands thrust in his pockets, head down.

The first ward allocations went up that night. Dora and the rest of her set gathered eagerly around the noticeboard outside the dining room to find out where they would be spending their first three months as probationers.

'Not that it really matters,' Katie O'Hara said, as they all crowded around the list of names. 'Wherever we are, all we'll be doing is cleaning. Junior pros get all the dirty jobs no one else wants to do.'

'I don't care so long as I don't get Female Chronics,' Millie whispered, her hands clasped together in fervent prayer. Female Chronics was presided over by Sister Hyde, the sister Millie had soaked with enema solution.

'I don't care where I am, so long as I'm not teamed up with Lane,' Dora said.

'It's all right, she's on Gynae with you, Benedict.'

'Oh, dear,' Millie sighed. 'I wonder if I wouldn't have been better off with Sister Hyde?'

'Where am I?' Dora craned her neck to look.

'Let's have a look ... stop shoving, you lot!' Katie ran her finger down the list. 'Ah, here we are. Doyle, Dora ... Blake. That's Male Orthopaedics. That's Bridget's ward!' She laughed. 'Good luck, Doyle. You'll need it, being ordered about by my big sister for the next three months.'

'I won't be the only one,' Dora said. 'Look who's down for Blake with me.'

She could hardly stop herself from smiling as she watched Katie peer at the list, her expression changing from puzzlement to complete horror.

'No!' She shook her head. 'There must be a mistake. I can't be going to Blake... I can't be. Lord, Bridget's going to love that,' she sighed.

Chapter Twenty-Four

Blake, the Male Orthopaedic ward, was as cavernous as a cathedral, with high, echoing ceilings and tall windows on either side. A strong smell of disinfectant hung in the air.

Beds lined the walls, about thirty in total, stretching the length of the ward. Nurses darted to and fro, some in the striped uniforms of students, one or two in the royal blue of staff nurses. Dora wondered if she would ever be that efficient or confident. She certainly didn't feel like it at that moment.

Down the centre of the ward were various cupboards, trolleys and pieces of equipment, with Sister's desk at the far end.

'What do we do?' she whispered to Katie.

'Go and say hello, I suppose. Oh, God, there's Bridget. Don't catch her eye, whatever you do.'

Dora's legs felt like jelly as she walked down the length of the ward, her stout shoes squeaking on the highly polished linoleum. Katie followed behind, nose stuck in the air, staring straight ahead of her.

Dora could feel the men's eyes following them speculatively.

'Aye-aye, a couple of new ones. This should be fun,' she heard one of them say to another. 'What do you think?'

'The dark one's pretty. I like 'em with a bit of meat on their bones.'

'Not sure about the ginger one, though. She looks as if she'd put up too much of a fight!'

Sister Blake sat behind her desk in the centre of the ward, surveying her domain. She was the first ward sister Dora had ever met apart from the sisters who had marked her PTS practical. She had heard so many stories about how fierce they could be and how they regularly made nurses' lives a misery, but Sister Blake looked nice enough.

'Don't look so terrified, Nurses. I'm not going to beat you with a stick. Unless you don't come up to my standards, that is, in which case I might.' Sister Blake was small and slim with lively brown eyes that sparkled with fun. Dark hair curled out from under her cap, which was fastened with a bow under her pointed chin. 'That was a joke, by

237

the way,' she said to Katie, who looked pale enough to faint.

'Yes, Sister.' Katie bobbed a small curtsey, which seemed to amuse Sister Blake.

'Since this is your first day on the wards, you'll need to know who you'll be working with. My name is Frances Wallace, but you must always refer to me as Sister or Sister Blake. Then there are two staff nurses on this ward, O'Hara and Martin. Although I don't suppose I need to tell you that, do I?' Her brown eyes twinkled as she looked at Katie who kept her gaze on the floor, too terrified to meet her eye.

'The staff nurses are the sister's second-in-command. They are in charge when I am not here, so you must take orders from them.' Dora heard Katie's faint groan. 'Below the staff nurses are the students. These range from seniors, who are in their last year of training, down to pros like yourselves. We have another student starting today. Her name is Pritchard and she is in the set above yours, as I'm sure she will make clear to you.' Sister smiled. 'We all have our own duties to do, but our main concern is the welfare of our patients. So please don't wait to be asked. If you see a patient who needs help or a job that needs to be done, tell me or one of the staff nurses immediately. Now, are there any questions?'

She looked from one to the other of them. Dora and Katie exchanged sidelong looks and both shook their heads.

'Goodness, I've never seen students so quiet,' Sister Blake commented. 'I suppose your first time on the ward can be rather daunting.'

You're telling me, Dora thought. She hardly dared look round at all the beds. For the first time it struck her these were real people, and she was supposed to care for them.

'Remember, no one is expecting you to know everything,' Sister Blake went on. 'If you have a problem, or you need to know something, please ask. We are here to help you become the best nurses you can be, and you can't do that unless you learn.'

'She seems nice,' Dora said, as she and Katie headed back down the ward to the sluice with their work lists for the day. As Katie had predicted, their chores mainly consisted of washing bedpans and cleaning lavatories.

'Don't let appearances fool you,' Katie replied wisely. 'Bridget reckons she can be as snappy as the rest of them if things aren't done her way. Ah, here we are.' She pushed open the door to the sluice. 'Welcome to our new home for the next three months. Fat lot we'll learn in here, washing bedpans!'

The sluice room was freezing. February had brought grey skies and frost, and the wind whistled through the open grating that covered the high window. Pritchard, the other pro, was already at the sink, rinsing out a bedpan under the tap. She was gangly, with buck teeth and spectacles.

'Thank God you're here.' She thrust the bedpan at Dora. 'You can take over with these while I go and finish the round.'

'What are we supposed to do with them?'

'Empty them down that sink, of course, and then wash them out. And be sure you do it properly,' she added bossily. 'I'll be back to take the clean ones out again in a minute.'

'Listen to her! I bet she was doing all the dirty jobs herself until we came along,' Katie said, as they unfastened their cuffs and rolled up their sleeves. 'Now she thinks we're her slaves.'

'I reckon we're everyone's slaves.' Dora finished washing the bedpan and turned to face the others piled up beside the door. 'I suppose we'd better get on with this lot,' she said dubiously.

Sister Parker had told them all about cleaning and sterilising, but she hadn't prepared them for how awful the job would be.

'Jesus, the smell!' Katie pinched her nose. 'I think I'm going to be sick!'

'Just hold your breath.' Bracing herself, Dora grabbed the first bedpan and swung it at arm's length towards the big hole in the middle of the sink.

'I'm going to close my eyes too.' Katie picked up a bedpan and aimed it towards the sink.

'Watch it!' Dora jumped out of the way just in time. 'Do you think you could keep your eyes open? That nearly went over my shoes.'

'You two! Stop chattering.' Staff Nurse O'Hara stood in the doorway, her arms folded. She looked like Katie, with her dark hair, round blue eyes and plump figure. But her frown was all her own. 'You're not in PTS now, you know. This is not the place for gossiping.'

'Oh, go and boil your head!' Katie muttered as her sister bustled off.

But no one had told Glenda Pritchard it wasn't the place for gossiping. Speaking in a rushed, excitable whisper, just low enough to escape the staff nurses' sharp ears, she kept up a constant stream of chatter to Dora and Katie as she rushed in and out with the bedpans.

'I can't tell you how relieved I was when I found out I was coming here. Everyone says Male Ortho-paedics is the best ward. I've heard it's full of handsome young men with sports injuries, all laid up with nothing to do but flirt with the nurses.' She blushed. 'It's a bit different from Gynae, I can tell you. Oh, poor you, having to wash all those bedpans! I'm so glad I don't have to do it any more. What do you think of Sister? She's lovely, isn't she? So much nicer than Sister Wren on Gynae. She was utterly spiteful. You're meant to warm those bedpans under the hot tap, by the way...'

Dora allowed Glenda's voice to wash over her as she got on with washing the bedpans. Her arms were pimpled with cold, and she had to grit her teeth together to stop them from chattering.

After the bedpan round, she and Katie were sent to scrub out the bathrooms and clean the patients' lockers. Then they had to pull the beds into the middle of the ward to clean behind them.

'I thought they had a ward maid to do the cleaning?' she whispered to Katie.

'They do, but the nurses still have to do a proper clean at least once a week,' Katie replied, clattering her mop into the galvanised bucket, which earned her a sharp look from her sister Bridget.

'Do you have to make so much noise? You're disturbing the patients,' she warned.

'Look at her. Thinks she's the Rose of Tralee.'

Katie pulled a face. 'I wish she'd skid on this wet floor. That would give me a laugh! Is it lunchtime yet? I'm starving, and I think my back's going to break.'

Dora was used to hard work, so the cleaning didn't bother her. And the patients were so friendly, it made her job a lot easier. Most of them were recumbent on iron frames, or encased in plaster. Many had nothing more serious than a sports injury, while others had congenital deformities. Denied even the chance of sitting up and looking around them, they were dependent on the nurses for entertainment. They chatted to Dora as she went about her work.

Sister Blake seemed pleased with her. 'You're doing a good job, Doyle,' she complimented her. 'As you've probably gathered, most of the patients on this ward get rather bored and starved of excitement. They welcome a friendly face and a bit of chat. It's a very important part of nursing, keeping their spirits up. But just be careful, some of the younger ones can get cheeky sometimes,' she warned.

Dora didn't understand what she meant until later that afternoon. She was carrying a pile of fresh linen from the cupboard when Mr Hubbard, a young man with a dislocated shoulder, called her over.

'Can you spare a minute, Nurse?' he asked.

Dora glanced around. There were no other nurses in sight.

'Shall I fetch someone?' she asked.

'No, you'll do. Could you take a look at something for me? Only I'm a bit worried.'

Dora looked around again. Sister Blake and Staff Nurse O'Hara were behind the screens with another patient. Staff Nurse Martin was in the kitchen. Even Glenda Pritchard and Katie were nowhere to be seen.

She remembered what Sister Blake had said about them all working together to help the patients. Taking a deep breath, she walked over to his bed, feeling very important in her uniform.

'What is it you wanted me to look at?' she asked, in her best bedside manner voice.

'This!' Mr Hubbard threw back the covers. He'd unfastened his pyjama bottoms to expose himself. 'I think you should give it a close examination, Nurse.'

Dora took one look at the naked white appendage hanging there limply and jumped back in panic, sending his water jug flying. Laughter exploded all around her, ringing around the ward. Everyone was in on the joke.

'What's going on?' Sister Blake appeared from behind the screens. 'Nurse, explain yourself!'

'Sorry, Sister, it was my fault,' Mr Hubbard grinned, whipping the sheet back to cover himself. 'The other lads put me up to it. We were just having a bit of a laugh with the new nurse, that's all.'

'Really, Mr Hubbard, that is hardly a gentlemanly thing to do to a young student on her first day!' Sister Blake eyed him sternly. 'Doyle is very shaken, as you can see.'

'Sorry, Nurse.' Mr Hubbard didn't look at all sorry. It was all he could do to stop himself smiling. 'It was just a joke. No harm done.'

Sister Blake turned to Dora. 'Are you all right,

243

Nurse?' Dora nodded, still shaken. 'Go and get a cloth and get this mess cleaned up. Really, Mr Hubbard, anyone would think we had nothing better to do!'

Dora rushed off to the sluice, a chorus of laughter still ringing in her ears.

She stood at the sink, trying to calm herself down. It was a joke, she told herself over and over again. Just a joke.

'Have you got that cloth yet?' Staff Nurse O'Hara appeared in the doorway. 'For heaven's sake, Doyle, don't look so terrified. They were only having a laugh. And they'll probably do it again, too, if they get a reaction like that out of you. You've got to toughen up, or you won't last five minutes on this ward.'

Only having a laugh? Dora thought as she wrung out a cloth. Maybe it was just a bit of fun for anyone else. But for her, it brought back too many horrible memories ever to be funny.

Chapter Twenty-Five

'I have a very important job for you to do and I want you to listen carefully while I explain it.'

Millie was surprised. Her first three days on Wren hadn't been a spectacular success. As far as Sister Wren was concerned, she seemed to make a mess of everything.

'Why are you taking so long?' she'd demanded that morning, as Millie returned from collecting

244

up the breakfast dishes. 'You're here to work, not gossip with the patients.'

But Millie couldn't help it. The women were so much fun, and terribly keen to stop her for a chat. It seemed rude to hurry by, and Millie did feel for them, being stuck in bed away from their families. It must be so terribly boring, she thought, seeing the same faces day after day.

Sister Wren didn't see it like that, unfortunately. Millie had only been working with her for a few days, but she had already realised that Sister had little time or sympathy for most of her patients.

Given their dismal relationship so far, it was very surprising she should be entrusting Millie with an important task now.

'Yes, Sister.' She stood to attention.

'The consultant, Mr Cooper, is doing his round later this morning,' Sister Wren explained. It might not have been her real name, but she lived up to it perfectly. She looked exactly like a bird, with her tiny frame, beaky nose and dark, darting eyes. The thin hair under her cap was a dusty brown colour, like a sparrow's wing. 'It's very important that when he arrives everything is in order. Mr Cooper is very particular, and I do not want any complaints from him.' She eyed Millie severely. 'When he arrives on the ward he likes to wash his hands straight away. So I will need you to have a basin of water ready for him.'

'Yes, Sister.'

'It must be waiting by the door, with a towel over it. The water must be neither too hot nor too cold. Is that understood?'

'Yes, Sister. Not too hot and not too cold.'

'Good. See that it's done correctly, please.'

She started to walk away. 'Sister?' Millie called after her, puzzled.

Sister Wren turned slowly back to face her. Too late Millie remembered that humble pros were not supposed to speak unless spoken to.

'Yes?' she said icily.

'What is the important job?'

Sister Wren stared at her. 'I've just explained it to you. Don't tell me you need telling again?'

'No, I just–' Millie had had visions of being called on to give her opinion on some medical matter, or at least being allowed to pass the consultant some notes. 'I just didn't think fetching a basin of water was that important, that's all.'

Sister narrowed her eyes. 'You get it wrong and you'll see how important it is,' she said.

After the bedpan round it was time to clean the ward. As Millie and Lucy Lane swept, polished and buffed every inch of floor space, Millie kept her eyes fixed on the doors.

'Why do you keep staring like that?' Lucy asked.

'I don't want to miss the consultant when he arrives.'

'Don't worry, you won't. I heard the staff nurses talking. Apparently someone always rings from another ward to warn us when he's on his way.'

Reassured that she wouldn't be caught unawares, Millie was able to relax and get on with her cleaning. She was determined to make a perfect job of it, to show Sister Wren she could be a good nurse.

'Watch it, love, you keep on polishing it like that you'll wear a hole straight through the floorboards!' one of the women cackled cheerfully as Millie skimmed around her bed with the mop.

'Really?' Millie said anxiously. 'This is how they taught us to do it in training. Have I got it wrong, do you think?'

'Bless you, love, you carry on.' The woman beamed at her. 'You can go round and do mine afterwards. God only knows what state it's got in since I've been in here. I don't suppose that old man of mine has lifted a finger.'

Millie finished the polishing, which passed even Sister Wren's eagle eye.

'You took your time about it, I must say,' was her only comment. 'Now get the patients washed and ready. And see you're a bit quicker about it this time.'

Millie loaded up a trolley with combs, flannels, towels and a bowl of water, and she and Lane made their way around, taking one side of the ward each. Every patient had to be washed, their hair combed, put into a clean nightdress and generally made presentable for Mr Cooper's arrival.

This is very nice, I must say,' said Miss Desmond, as Millie carefully combed through her bleached-blonde curls. Blanche, as she liked to be called, was a voluptuous woman, her fleshy curves barely contained within the richly patterned red silk nightdress she wore. She was due for a hysterectomy to get rid of her fibroids. 'So what's all this in aid of? Are we going for a night out?'

'No such luck, I'm afraid, Miss Desmond. The consultant is doing his rounds.'

'Ah. That explains why Sister is all of a twitch this morning.' Blanche nodded knowingly. 'She's got a soft spot for Mr Cooper,' she explained, when Millie looked blank.

'Surely not!'

'Where do you think she's gone now? Off titivating herself in that sitting room of hers, I expect,' Blanche said. 'You watch her when he turns up. She'll go all fluttery and girlish. And then she'll try and lure him back to her sitting room for tea and biscuits. Although I reckon it'll take more than a cup of Earl Grey to get him interested in her!'

She roared with laughter. Millie caught the staff nurse's warning frown and quickly gathered up the washing things, guilty at being caught idling yet again. Lucy was making much faster progress up her side of the ward, she noticed.

'Mind you, I can't say I blame her. He is a handsome devil,' Blanche went on. 'And he's got a lovely speaking voice, too. I wouldn't mind having a crack at him myself.' She turned to Millie. 'Reach into my locker and get my make-up bag, will you love? Can't have him seeing me looking a state, can I?'

Millie watched in fascination as Blanche applied deep red lipstick to her generous mouth. 'Not that I know why I'm bothering,' she said. 'There's only one part of my body that man ever looks at, and it ain't my face!' She laughed so hard her hand shook, wobbling her lipstick. 'Sounds like every man I've ever met!' She winked at Millie.

'I don't know how you can bring yourself to talk to that woman.' Lucy fell into step beside Millie as she wheeled her trolley back down the ward. She had already finished and tidied her own trolley away, as usual.

248

'You mean Blanche? She's lovely. And she makes me laugh. Besides, she likes the company. None of the other women seem to want to talk to her for some reason.'

'I'm not surprised. Who'd want anything to do with someone like her?' Lucy frowned at Millie. 'You do know what she does for a living, don't you?'

'She runs her own business from a flat off the Mile End Road, she told me.' Millie noticed Lucy's expression. 'What's so funny?'

'You are. God, you're such an innocent, Benedict!' Lucy lowered her voice. 'She's a tart. A prostitute. She sells her body for money.'

'That's not true!'

'Ask her, if you don't believe me. Ask anyone,' Lucy shrugged. 'Everyone knows what she is. Everyone but you, that is,' she said with a smirk.

Millie glanced back over her shoulder at Blanche Desmond. Among all the drab, worn-out women she shone like a bright flame with her blonde hair and scarlet satin gown.

'Well, I don't care,' she declared. 'I still think she's delightful.'

'My mother would die if she knew I was having anything to do with women like her.'

'And my father says we should treat everyone with respect unless they give us a reason not to,' Millie said firmly.

They were interrupted by Staff Nurse Cuthbert, stepping in front of them.

'When you've quite finished gossiping, Sister wanted to know if you've finished with the patients?' They both nodded. 'You've washed them, combed their hair, changed their night-gowns? What about their teeth?'

Lucy nodded. Millie looked blank. 'What about them?'

Cuthbert stared at her. 'Don't tell me you haven't done their teeth? You have to take them out and clean them,' she explained with exaggerated patience.

Millie glanced at Lucy. Her expression was smug, as usual.

'What, all of them?' Millie looked up and down the ward in horror. 'That will take forever.'

'Well, you'd better get on with it, hadn't you?'

'You could have told me I had to clean their teeth,' she whispered to Lucy as she clattered back down the ward with her trolley.

'I thought you knew,' the other girl said carelessly.

'Won't you help me?' Millie pleaded.

'Not a chance. I've done my bit. And hurry up about it! They'd better be cleaned and put back in before Mr Cooper shows his face or there'll be real trouble.'

Millie felt close to tears as she hurried back to the sluice. With so much to do and no one willing to give her a hand, she had horrible visions of not getting the job done in time and ending up in Matron's office yet again.

She was filling the basin with water when she had a brainwave. She didn't have to go round to every bed, cleaning each set of teeth individually. Surely all she had to do was collect up all the teeth and clean them at the same time?

Pleased with herself, she hurried back down the

ward with the trolley, collecting up everyone's teeth and throwing them into the basin of water as she went. Most of the women in the ward had false teeth – during training Sister Parker had explained how East End women often had their teeth removed at an early age to save on expensive dental treatment when they got older. When she had a basin full Millie carried them carefully back to the sluice, briskly trotting as fast as she could get away with, without breaking into a run.

She was just rinsing the last of the teeth under the tap and feeling rather pleased with her own ingenuity when Lucy appeared in the doorway to the sluice.

'What are you doing now?' she demanded. Millie suppressed her annoyance. Lucy had become insufferably bossy since they'd started work on the ward.

'Cleaning the teeth. Look.' Millie showed her the basin. But instead of being incredibly impressed by her timesaving brainwave, Lucy just stared at the bowl then at Millie and back at the bowl again.

'How are you going to tell which teeth are which?' she asked.

'That's easy, I'll just...' Millie's smile faltered slightly '...I mean, I'll...'

Then full realisation hit her and she stared in horror at the assortment of teeth in the bowl. They all seemed to be grinning up at her.

'Oh, Benedict, what have you done now?' Lucy put her hand over her mouth, her eyes as big as saucers above it. They stared at each other for a moment.

Then the phone rang.

'Mr Cooper's on his way.' Lucy thrust the basin at her. 'Get this lot handed out stat.'

'But how will we know who to give them to?' Millie asked.

'I don't know, do I? You'll just have to guess for now and sort it out later.'

Fortunately Staff Nurse Cuthbert was busy and Sister Wren had retired to her sitting room, so they didn't witness Millie hurtling up and down the ward, skimming false teeth into the laps of surprised patients.

By the time she had reached the other end of the ward, Sister Wren had emerged from her sitting room, her ashy brown hair looking suspiciously teased under her starched cap. The staff nurses and Lucy had already gathered at the doors to the ward, ready to greet their illustrious visitor when he arrived.

'Benedict!' Sister Wren snapped at Millie. 'Is that the basin for Mr Cooper? Put it down at once.'

'But Sister–'

'I said, put it down!' Sister Wren hissed furiously. 'Roll your sleeves down, put your cuffs on and come over here.'

With a quick, guilty glance at Lucy, Millie hastily put the bowl on the stand at the far end of the ward, covered it with a towel and hurried back to join Sister Wren and the other nurses, who were busy patting their hair and smoothing down their aprons. All she could hope now was that Mr Cooper didn't mind too much that the water in the bowl was stone cold.

She was still fastening the studs on her cuffs when the doors swung open and the Great One himself entered, followed by his firm, a procession of two registrars, a pair of senior housemen and several medical students. Millie could immediately see why Blanche had put on lipstick and Sister had teased her hair. Mr Cooper looked like Errol Flynn in a white coat.

'Sister Wren,' he greeted her with a nod.

'Mr Cooper,' she simpered. Her voice was high and fluttery, and nothing like the sharp tone she took with her nurses. 'Your water is ready, if you would care to step this way?'

'Thank you.' Millie and Lucy exchanged panicked looks as he strode over to the basin, his retinue following behind. Millie crossed her fingers behind her back. The whole ward seemed utterly, deathly silent, although she guessed that was because they had been struck dumb by their ill-fitting teeth.

Mr Cooper hitched up the sleeves of his white coat, flicked the towel aside and plunged his hands into the water. Millie closed her eyes and prayed.

Please don't let it be too cold, please...

For a moment nothing happened. Then Mr Cooper said in his deep voice, 'Sister, would you mind explaining why there is a set of false teeth in the bottom of this bowl?'

Sister Wren opened her mouth to speak, but before she could utter a word, a voice rang out from the far end of the ward.

'Oh, they'll be mine, Doctor. The nurse forgot to give me back my set.' They all turned to see Blanche grinning toothlessly at them all. Her

253

bright red lips only emphasised the gaping cavern of her mouth.

The silence seemed to go on forever. Millie could feel everyone staring at her, but she couldn't look up from the shiny floor. She'd done a good job of polishing it, she thought. But it would take more than a spot of cleaning to save her now.

'Nurse ... my office ... immediately.' Sister Wren turned on her heel and stalked out of the ward. Millie trailed after her.

She braced herself as best she might, but couldn't have prepared herself for the full force of Sister Wren's wrath. 'Never ... in my whole career ... utterly humiliated.' Cords of suppressed rage stood out on her thin neck. 'Dumbfounded ... disgrace to nursing...' Millie let the words wash over her, until finally the storm blew itself out.

'Well? What have you to say for yourself?' Sister demanded when she finally paused for breath.

'It was an accident, Sister.'

Sister Wren closed her eyes, mentally composing herself. 'You,' she said, enunciating slowly and carefully, 'are one big accident waiting to happen. I would send you to Matron but I'm sure she's already seen more than enough of you. Now please get out of my sight. And be sure I will be mentioning this in my ward report. How we are going to survive the next three months with you on my ward, I have no idea.'

Lucy was waiting for her in the sluice when she returned. 'What happened?'

'I don't want to talk about it.' Millie's hands shook as she washed them under the tap. 'Has Mr Cooper gone?'

Lucy nodded. 'He said he'd come back and continue his round when Sister had finished dealing with you. He didn't look too pleased.'

'Oh dear.' He would probably go straight to Matron too. Millie had a sudden, horrible vision of being packed off unceremoniously back to Billinghurst. Her grandmother would be delighted. 'What do you think I should do?' she pleaded.

'I'd stay out of everyone's way, if I were you.' Lucy could barely hide her glee.

But first Millie had to sort out the puzzle of the teeth. She was so miserable she could barely speak as she trailed up and down the ward with her bowl. But the women did their best to cheer her up.

'Don't worry about it, love, worse things happen at sea,' Blanche said. 'Besides, it gave us all a right good laugh. And they say that's the best medicine, don't they?'

It was kind of them to try and make her feel better, Millie thought as she washed the bowl in the sluice room sink. But she still felt utterly foolish.

'Really, Millie, you must try to think in future,' she warned herself.

'Did you know that talking to yourself is the first sign of madness?' a voice said behind her.

Millie swung round. A young man stood in the sluice-room doorway. She recognised him as one of the housemen she'd seen with Mr Cooper that morning.

'Of course, presenting a bowl of false teeth to the hospital's Chief Consultant in full view of his entire firm may also be considered an act of insanity,' he drawled.

His grin irritated Millie. 'Have you come to gloat?' she snapped.

'I've come to tell you not to take it to heart.' He wasn't much older than she was, tall and lanky in his white coat, his dark hair flopping into his eyes. There was something familiar about him, but she wasn't sure what. 'If it's any help, I actually think Cooper was secretly quite amused.'

'Sister certainly wasn't.'

'Sister Wren has no sense of humour.'

Millie frowned at him. 'Do I know you?'

'I don't think we've been introduced. I'm William. Will, to my friends. And you are?'

'Benedict.'

'No first name?'

'You can call me Nurse Benedict, if you like?'

He smiled. He had a nice smile, Millie thought...

'Thanks for trying to make me feel better,' she said.

'I'm a doctor. It's my job.'

I'm a doctor. Something about the way he said it made her think. She looked up at him, more closely this time. The last time she'd seen that tall, lanky figure it had been looming out of the fog towards her...

'It's you!' she cried. 'You ran me over!'

'I'm sorry?' He frowned. And then, slowly, it dawned on him. 'You!'

'You owe me a new pair of stockings.'

'And you owe me a new rear bumper. But we could call it quits if you promise to come out with me one night?' he added cheekily.

Millie had opened her mouth to reply when she

heard voices in the corridor.

'Sounds like Mr Cooper's coming back,' said William.

He ducked out of sight, then stuck his head round the door again. 'It's been nice meeting you, Nurse Benedict. Perhaps I'll run into you again sometime.'

'Not literally, I hope!' Millie was still smiling to herself as his running footsteps echoed away down the corridor.

Chapter Twenty-Six

At nine o'clock, just before the day staff went off duty, Sister Hyde gave her final report to the night nurses who were taking over the Female Chronics ward.

'Mrs Tyler in bed two has been in a great deal of pain from her arthritis today. Dr Grange has prescribed Cincophen, but she may need extra pain relief during the night.' Like the other sisters, Sister Hyde didn't need to consult any notes. She knew by heart the state of every patient on her ward. 'Miss Fletcher in bed four suffered a convulsion at ten-past four this afternoon. She has been quiet since, but you must keep an eye on her. And we have had one admission today. Mrs Mortimer, bed six.' She swept them with a warning glance. 'You may need to watch her. She has been rather trying.'

Helen glanced across at Amy Hollins, who was

257

barely listening. She had hoped that after their three months on Male Surgical they might get a break from each other. But here they were, stuck on night duty together, with only a solitary pro to keep them company. And even she was acting as a runner between several wards.

Sister Hyde finally went off duty, after leaving a long list of jobs to keep the nurses busy.

'She'll be lucky,' Amy whispered as the doors closed behind her. 'Come on, let's get this lot settled quickly and then we can relax.' She stretched and yawned.

Helen suspected Amy hadn't been to bed. After their shift finished at seven in the morning and they'd had breakfast, they were sent straight to bed in the night nurses' block, where a sister prowled the corridor to make sure they didn't get up before noon. Helen usually couldn't wait to crawl into bed, but she knew some nurses were more interested in their social lives than sleep, and managed to evade Sister's beady eye to go off for the day with their boyfriends.

She would have asked Amy, but the other girl would probably think she was prying. Better just to stay out of her way, Helen decided.

'I'll make a start on the drinks round, shall I?' she offered.

'I suppose so. Where's that runner got to?'

'Gone over to report to Male Chronics, I think.'

'Well, I hope she comes back soon. We need her far more than they do. If she isn't back in five minutes you're to go and find her,' she instructed Helen. 'It's not fair she should leave you to do the drinks round on your own.'

Helen smiled as she headed for the kitchen. It wasn't like Amy to be so considerate. Although her consideration didn't stretch to helping with the drinks herself, she noticed as she put the kettles on.

Amy had disappeared by the time she returned with the trolley, so Helen did the drinks round by herself. It took a long time, as most of the elderly women needed help with feeding cups. Almost half an hour had passed by the time she reached the new patient in bed six. Mrs Mortimer sat up ramrod straight, her long white hair beautifully brushed over the shoulders of her spotless nightgown.

'Would you like a drink, Mrs Mortimer?' Helen spoke to her slowly and encouragingly, as she did to all the women on the ward. 'A nice cup of tea? Some Horlicks?'

Mrs Mortimer gave her a withering look. 'Good gracious, girl, why are you speaking to me like that?' she said sharply. 'It's my body that's afflicted, not my mind.' She peered at the trolley, unimpressed. 'I don't suppose you have anything as civilised as a brandy, do you? No? I thought it was rather too much to hope for.' She sighed heavily. 'In that case, you may go.'

She dismissed her with an imperious wave of her hand. Helen stood there, nonplussed.

'Well? Was there something else?' Mrs Mortimer said, as if she were addressing a rather dim servant. Helen shook her head. 'Then I suggest you get on with your work, girl, and stop staring at me like a stunned trout.'

Helen slunk off, pushing her trolley. No wonder

Sister Hyde had called her 'trying'. She could imagine the pair of them clashing terribly if Mrs Mortimer used that tone with her.

Amy returned as she was pushing the drinks trolley back to the kitchen. She was herding the pro back in front of her like a lost lamb.

'Look who I found,' she said. 'Gossiping on Male Chronics, she was. Not a thought for us, slaving away here on our own.'

Helen's brows rose but she said nothing.

For the next hour she and Amy handed out medication with the Night Sister, changed dressings, straightened sheets and shook pillows, generally making the patients comfortable for the night. Then they turned off the lights and Helen and the pro went around pinning little green cloths over the lamps above patients who needed special care, and the one on the sister's desk.

After that, the pro headed off to catch up with her duty list on Male Chronics, leaving Helen and Amy alone.

'Right, that's it. I'm off for a rest,' Amy announced.

Helen sat down at the desk in the middle of the ward. 'I'll keep an eye on this lot and let you know if Night Sister turns up.'

'She doesn't do her rounds until well after midnight. Why don't you come and have a cup of tea in the kitchen?' Amy offered.

If Helen hadn't already been sitting down, she'd have fallen over in a faint. Ever since they'd started on night duty, Amy had entertained a string of junior doctors in the kitchen. But Helen had never been invited to one of her midnight soirees.

'Why?' she asked blankly.

'No reason. I just thought you could do with a break,' Amy shrugged. 'It's so tedious sitting here night after night with this lot.' She nodded around the ward. 'You could come and have a laugh with us for a change.'

Then, just as Helen was beginning to wonder if she'd fallen asleep and was dreaming it all, Amy added, 'Your brother said he might drop in later.'

Ah, so that's it. Helen saw the studied nonchalance on Amy's face and realised the real reason why she was suddenly being so nice to her. She was interested in William, and she'd decided she should start sucking up to his sister.

As if that would make any difference, thought Helen. She tried to keep as far away from William and his love life as she possibly could.

'That's very kind of you,' she said, 'but I'd better stay here, just in case any of the patients needs anything.'

'The only thing this lot need is a good undertaker,' Amy said. 'Don't look at me like that, they're all at death's door anyway. Although I hope none of them decides to die before tomorrow morning. If I'm late going off duty because I have to lay someone out, I won't be very happy about it.'

'I'm sure none of them will be that inconsiderate,' Helen murmured.

Once Amy had gone, she started on the list of jobs Sister Hyde had left for them to do. She had just started mending the linen when she saw three housemen creep past. Her brother William was one of them. He smiled and gave her a sheepish

261

wave as he followed the others into the kitchen.

Helen settled down to her stitching by the dull light of the shaded desk lamp. All around her was the creak and rattle of bedsprings, mingled with the noises made by the patients. Many of the elderly women on Hyde were disturbed, their minds gone with age and illness. At night they became even more restless and agitated. While other wards slept on peacefully, Female Chronics rang with the sound of whooping, sobbing, wailing and groaning, at least until the effects of their bedtime sedatives took over and an uneasy peace descended for a few hours. Helen was used to the noise. She didn't find it nearly so disturbing as the muffled shrieks and whoops that came from the kitchen.

'Nurse?' Mrs Mortimer's voice startled her, coming out of the darkness. Helen hurried over.

'What can I do for you, Mrs Mortimer?'

'You can tell that rabble to keep their voices down. It's difficult enough to sleep in this madhouse, without being disturbed by that racket,' she grumbled.

'I'm sorry, Mrs Mortimer. I'll tell them immediately.'

She walked into the kitchen to find them all drinking cocoa and listening to William telling a lurid ghost story about a former patient who haunted Hyde ward.

'And they say that on dark, still nights you can still see her in her blood-stained nightgown, wandering up the ward,' he intoned in a grave voice.

'Do you mind?' Helen interrupted him sternly. 'You're disturbing the patients. And you can put that down, too.' She snatched a slice of bread out of her brother's hand. 'That's supposed to be for the patients' breakfast.'

'Don't be such a spoilsport, Tremayne,' Amy said sulkily.

'She's right,' William said. 'We'll keep the noise down,' he promised.

As she left, Helen heard Amy saying, 'Honestly, Will, I can't believe she's your sister. She's nowhere near as much fun as you.'

Back on the ward, Helen found one of the women had wet her bed and was busy dragging off the sopping sheets, draping them like washing over the sides of her cot. As Helen went to stop her, the woman grabbed her cap, ripping it off her head and sending pins scattering everywhere. Helen was still desperately groping around in the dark, trying to gather them up, when the runner scuttled into the ward to tell her Night Sister was on her way to do her round.

'Oh, Lord, she's early.' Helen retrieved the last pin from under the patient's bed and got to her feet. 'You'd better warn Hollins.'

The next minute was a desperate scramble as Amy smuggled the doctors out and tidied the kitchen while Helen tried to refasten her cap as best she could.

She had just fixed the last pin in place when Night Sister appeared. By the time her soft tread was heard outside the ward doors, Amy and Helen had managed to get themselves into some kind of order. Helen could feel her cap slipping down over one ear, but fortunately Night Sister was summoned to an emergency in Female

Surgical and didn't stay long enough to notice.

Amy was even nicer to Helen for the rest of the shift. For once she helped pack the drums with dressings and swabs, ready for the porter to take off for sterilising when he came back on duty.

'Are there any doctors you fancy?' she asked, as they worked.

'No.'

'Surely there must be one you like?'

'Can't say I've noticed them.'

Amy sent her a shrewd look. 'You're not still pining over Charlie Denton?'

Helen ducked her head, blushing furiously. Three weeks after starting night duty, she had heard nothing from him. She hadn't expected him to remember her, but she still felt a pang of disappointment.

'Don't be ridiculous,' she snapped.

'Pardon me for breathing, I'm sure.'

Helen wished she hadn't been so sharp. She longed to say the right thing, to make Amy like her more. But she didn't know how to gossip like the other girls.

There was a long pause. Helen could tell what was going through Amy's mind long before she said, ever so casually, 'Does your brother have a girlfriend?'

'You'd have to ask him that.'

Another pause. 'Do you think he likes me?'

Amy didn't look up as she said it, but Helen could feel her anxiety. She suddenly felt sorry for the girl. She wanted to warn her that she was wasting her time, that William would get bored once the chase was over. 'I'm sure he thinks very highly of you,' she said tactfully.

Amy went off for her midnight meal shortly afterwards, leaving Helen alone on the ward again. She did a quick round with her torch to check on the patients, trying not to think about the story William had told about the ghostly woman who haunted Hyde. After she'd satisfied herself that the patients were sleeping peacefully – or as peacefully as they could in a ward full of whistles, groans and snoring – she went into the kitchen to slice and butter more bread for the patients' breakfasts. If she knew William and the other junior doctors, they would have finished off the last lot.

Cockroaches scuttled for cover as she switched on the light. They'd frightened her the first time she saw them, but now she barely noticed them. She heard someone come into the kitchen behind her.

'That was quick,' she said, thinking it was Amy.

'I didn't know you were expecting me?' She swung round. William lounged in the doorway.

'Hollins has gone for her break,' she told him. 'You'll have to come back if you want to see her.'

'I didn't come back to see her. I wanted to talk to you.'

'Oh, yes?' Helen eyed him warily.

'Why do you always look so suspicious when I say that?'

'Because it usually means trouble.' She slapped his hand away as he reached for a slice of bread.

'This time I need your advice.' He perched himself against the stove. 'Do you know a pro who's just started on Wren? Blonde, very pretty–'

'You mean Benedict?'

His dark eyes lit up. 'You do know her, then?'

'I share a room with her. Why?' Helen didn't need to ask the question. One glance at his face told her all she needed to know. 'Oh, Will,' she sighed.

'What? You don't even know what I'm going to say yet,' he protested.

'I know that look on your face.'

He picked up a teacup and traced the pattern on it with his finger. 'She seems like a nice girl,' he said.

'So are lots of other nurses in this hospital. So is Hollins. Why can't you go out with her instead?'

'I'm not interested in Hollins.'

'Will, you promised.' Helen put down the knife and looked at him appealingly. 'After all that business with Peggy Gibson, you promised me you'd never get involved with one of my friends again.'

She saw him wince at the mention of Peggy's name. 'This is different,' he said quietly. 'Anyway, all that business with Peggy was a long time ago. Can't you ever let me forget it?'

No one lets me forget it, she thought. She knew he felt guilty about what had happened with Peggy. But he didn't have to face the other girls' scorn every day. He didn't have to endure everyone thinking she was to blame.

She picked up the knife again. 'Sorry, William, I don't want to get involved,' she said.

Just at that moment Amy appeared in the kitchen doorway. 'What are you doing in here? Why aren't you–' She saw William and smiled. 'Hello, are you looking for me?' She batted her eyelashes flirtatiously.

266

'Who else?' William gave her a winning smile in return. Helen wrung out a teatowel, put it over the plate of bread and butter and left them to their flirting.

Whatever happened, she didn't want to be part of it.

Chapter Twenty-Seven

'Let me be clear on this.' Kathleen Fox struggled to control her rising temper as she looked at the rows of figures in front of her. 'You are telling me there is no money available for new linen on the wards because you have decided to spend it all on a party?'

She fixed her gaze on Reginald Collins, Treasurer of the Hospital Trustees and the man responsible for drawing up the figures. He squirmed in his seat and examined the papers in front of him.

'It's not my doing,' he huffed. 'I simply present the facts. The other Trustees...'

He shot a quick, guilty look at Constance Tremayne, seated to the right of the Chairman, Philip Enright. Philip might as well not have been there, Kathleen decided. They all knew who was really in charge of the Nightingale.

'Matron, you do make it sound so frivolous,' Constance Tremayne observed. She was dressed for battle in a stiff tweed suit, her hair scraped back in its usual tight bun which drew her skin taut across her cheekbones, making it difficult for her to smile. Not that she ever did.

'Isn't it?' Kathleen said coldly.

'Of course it isn't. The annual Founder's Day celebration is a big event for the Nightingale Hospital. And as this year is our fiftieth anniversary, we wanted to make it even more special. All we've done is make a temporary allocation in the budget to cover expenses. I think we all agree that is reasonable?'

She looked around the table. No one spoke.

'Mrs Tremayne is right,' Gerald Munroe said finally. 'The Nightingale Hospital is a very important aspect of the lives of the people in this area. It's our duty to allow everyone to celebrate it.'

Kathleen stared at him. She might have known he'd vote for anything that involved him getting his face in the newspapers yet again.

'And exactly how many people from this area will we be inviting to celebrate?' she asked pleasantly. 'I take it we'll be throwing the gates open to everyone?'

There was some coughing and shuffling of feet around the table. 'Of course we will have to restrict the guest list to local dignitaries, senior staff and their families,' Mrs Tremayne said.

Of course, Kathleen thought. Constance Tremayne wouldn't want any East End riff-raff at her grand garden party.

'It will be a very prestigious event,' she added.

'I see. And while you're enjoying this prestigious event of yours, our patients will be sleeping on thin sheets which the nurses are having to patch and mend constantly.'

'You didn't seem to mind spending money on the Christmas dance?' Mrs Tremayne reminded her.

'The Christmas dance cost next to nothing compared to this extravaganza you're planning.'

All eyes turned to Constance Tremayne.

'Then the nursing staff will just have to practise economy.'

Blood sang in Kathleen's ears. 'My staff are hardly spendthrift, Mrs Tremayne,' she bit out. 'They waste nothing. Dressings are boiled and re-used until they fall apart, everything that can be used again is kept and cleaned and mended. Go and ask any of the sisters here. They will tell you. And while you're at it, perhaps you'd like to explain to them why you feel it necessary to spend this hospital's money on champagne and canapés while they have no clean sheets to put on the patients' beds? See if they understand this fur coat and no knickers approach of yours, because I certainly don't!'

Mr Cooper gave a muffled snort of laughter from across the table. Mrs Tremayne turned white-faced with shock.

'Did she say knickers?' Lady Fenella asked, baffled.

'Perhaps we should move to a vote?' Philip Enright suggested quickly.

'I think even Mrs Tremayne was lost for words in there!' James Cooper fell into step beside Kathleen as she made her way back to her office ten minutes later. 'You have a very lively turn of phrase, Matron. Very ... vivid, shall we say?'

269

'I didn't intend to be vivid,' Kathleen snapped back. Usually she enjoyed the few moments of banter she had with Mr Cooper as they left the Trustees meeting, but this morning she wasn't in the mood. 'I merely wanted everyone to see how perfectly ridiculous they were being. How on earth can they call this a prestigious hospital when our linen cupboards are empty? Can't they see the irony?'

'I don't think irony is Mrs Tremayne's strong point.' James Cooper pulled a wry face. 'Look, you did your best,' he said. 'You can't expect to win every fight.'

'But I should have won this one!' She swung round to face him. 'This was important. My nurses were relying on me to argue their case for them.'

'And you did. Admirably.'

'I still failed though, didn't I?'

'There is one consolation.'

'Which is?'

'I'm sure you'll get an invitation to the party.'

Kathleen's mouth tightened. 'I can't wait.'

There was a student waiting outside her office with a broken thermometer. Under normal circumstances, Kathleen would have put it down to an accident and given her a small fine to cover the cost. But this time she harangued her about carelessness and waste until she was hoarse and the poor girl was close to tears.

She was mindlessly shuffling papers on her desk, still trying to calm herself down, when Miss Hanley came in. Kathleen groaned inwardly. The last thing she needed in her present mood was

270

the Assistant Matron's oppressive presence.

'Did you have a good meeting?' she asked politely.

Kathleen looked up at Miss Hanley, towering over her, as solid and unyielding as a block of granite. Usually she would have made some anodyne reply, but for once she was too angry to lie.

'No, since you ask,' she snapped.

'Oh?' Miss Hanley did her best to mould her features into an expression of concern.

'I'm afraid we will not be getting the new requisition of linen we ordered. You will have to go and tell the sisters they're to go on making do and mending.'

'Oh.' This time Miss Manley's concern seemed genuine. 'But our linen stock is very low, Matron. Last time I checked–'

'Then perhaps you'd better tell Mrs Tremayne that?' Kathleen cut her off abruptly. 'She's the one who's put her foot down. She thinks the money would be better spent showing off to the local dignitaries at a Founder's Day garden party.'

She could see Miss Hanley's features twisting in confusion as she struggled to justify her friend's actions.

'Well, I suppose Founder's Day is an important occasion...' she began doubtfully.

'More important than looking after our patients?'

'Of course not.' For once Miss Hanley wasn't wearing her usual look of self-assurance. 'I'd better go and talk to the sisters,' she said.

'You do that, Miss Hanley.' And good luck, Kathleen added silently.

Veronica Hanley caught up with Constance Tremayne just as she was leaving.

'May I have a word, Mrs Tremayne?' she asked.

'Of course, Miss Hanley.' Mrs Tremayne gave her a charming smile. 'I would have come and said hello but I had no wish to see Miss Fox again. One meeting with her was more than enough for today.' She shuddered delicately. 'I can't tell you how rude and insulting she was to me this morning. Even the other Trustees were shocked. Between you and me, I think they're beginning to see our new Matron's true colours.' She laid a delicate hand on Veronica's arm. 'How I wish you were Matron, Miss Hanley. I'm sure we could conduct business in a far more civilised way if we were working together.'

Miss Hanley blushed. For a moment she was too sidetracked by Constance's flattery to continue. But then she remembered why she'd sought her out.

'I have to admit, for once Miss Fox has a point,' she said, trying not to meet Mrs Tremayne's eye. She couldn't bear to see that warmth replaced by a look of frosty disapproval. 'We really do desperately need more linen...'

'And you'll get it, of course,' Mrs Tremayne assured her. 'But I'm afraid you'll have to wait a little longer, that's all.' She looked disappointed. 'You know how much I care about this hospital, Miss Hanley. It means as much to me as it does to you. Do you think I would do anything to damage the Nightingale's excellent reputation?'

'Well, no. But...'

'I want everyone to look at this hospital and see it for what it is: a shining beacon of excellence. That's why I so want this Founder's Day celebration to be a success. So we can make the Nightingale a hospital to be proud of. You want that too, don't you, Miss Hanley?' Her fingers tightened on Veronica's arm, her eyes glittering with fervour.

'Of course,' Veronica agreed cautiously. 'But I must insist...'

'You must insist that patients' welfare comes first,' Mrs Tremayne finished for her. 'I do agree with you, Miss Hanley, I really do. And I have to say, this problem with the linen is not entirely of the Trustees' making. In fact, you could have had your order before Christmas, if only...' She let her voice trail away.

'If only what, Mrs Tremayne?'

She glanced one way and then the other before leaning forward and whispering, 'I'm not sure I should tell you. It is a matter for the Trustees, after all. And everyone else agreed with it at the time. Apart from myself, of course,' she added.

'Agreed with what, Mrs Tremayne?' Miss Hanley's eyes narrowed. 'Is there something we are not being told? If it concerns the running of this hospital and the welfare of the patients, then we have a right to know.'

Mrs Tremayne paused for a moment. 'There was money for the linen requisition before Christmas,' she said. 'I was all for putting it through – the patients' comfort is paramount, after all. But Matron insisted the funds must go instead on providing some kind of – entertainment – for the nursing staff.'

'What kind of entertainment?'

'The Christmas dance. I made my feelings very clear at the time, warned her that funds were low and questioned the wisdom of frittering money away on such a frivolous activity. But Matron would have her way. Which is why we find ourselves in such a perilous financial situation now.' She looked up at Miss Hanley, her face full of regret. 'We mustn't blame Miss Fox,' she said with every appearance of sincerity. 'She is new and inexperienced. She has no idea of our values, the way we do things at the Nightingale. If she chooses to spend hospital funds on allowing the nurses to get tipsy and cavort with the junior doctors, while vital stocks run low, well ... what can we do?'

What indeed? Miss Hanley thought.

Chapter Twenty-Eight

'Don't look now, duchess, but your young man's got his eye on you again.'

Millie looked over her shoulder to where William stood hovering by the end of a patient's bed at the far end of the ward, pretending to check their notes. He had taken to turning up at different times of the day, ostensibly checking on patients, taking an unusual interest in their welfare.

'He's persistent, I'll say that for him,' Blanche commented. 'That's the third time today he's been to see Mrs Ruddock. The poor woman will start thinking she's for the high jump if he keeps frowning at her notes like that.'

'I do wish he'd go away,' Millie sighed.

'Go on, you must have a soft spot for him? He's a handsome lad. I wouldn't kick him out of bed, that's for sure. Mind you,' added Blanche, 'I wouldn't kick anyone out of bed, would I? I'd be skint otherwise!'

She cackled with laughter, and Millie joined in. In the six weeks she'd been on Wren she had learnt a lot from the women on the ward. And not just medical knowledge, either. Her grandmother would be shocked by some of the ideas she'd picked up.

William turned at the sound of their laughter, and smiled. Millie hurriedly went back to her polishing, in case the ward maid reported her again. The ward maids were the eyes and ears of the sisters, and Sister Wren's maid Lettie Pike was especially vigilant.

'Poor Dr Tremayne,' Blanche said. 'I s'pose you'll be after marrying a lord or summat, won't you, love?'

Blanche had been fascinated to find out about Millie's family background. She'd laughed out loud at the idea of having methylated spirit rubbed into her backside by an Earl's daughter.

Millie kept her entertained with stories about the balls and parties she had been to, and the grand families she mixed with. She was worried it might seem like bragging, but Blanche reckoned that listening to her was better than the films.

'I'm not sure I want to marry anyone just yet,' Millie said, rubbing hard at a tarnished spot on the brass plate beside Blanche's bed. If only the local dignitaries who donated to the hospital knew how long the poor pros spent polishing their blessed name plaques, she thought, they might think twice about handing over the money.

'Quite right, too,' Blanche said, checking her lipstick in her mirror compact. 'You should play hard to get. Don't make the same mistakes I did, love. Not that there's much chance of that, you being a real lady and everything.' She smiled wryly.

'You're a real lady too, Blanche,' Millie said.

'Bless you, lovey.' Blanche blushed pink with pleasure. 'Ain't nobody called me that in a long time. But that's all going to change, see? Once Mr Cooper's fixed me up and I'm out of this place, things are going to be different. I'm going to make a new start.'

'On your sister's farm?' Millie had heard the story several times, but she knew Blanche never tired of talking about it. Her sister's husband had just died, leaving her with five children and a rundown farm in Essex to look after. She'd asked Blanche if she would move down there and help her.

Millie could hardly imagine Blanche tottering around a farmyard in her high heels and red lipstick, but the idea seemed to cheer her up so much she didn't want to dampen her spirits.

'I can't wait to get out of this place,' Blanche said firmly. 'This will be a new lease of life for me, with Elsie and the kids.'

'It sounds wonderful,' Millie agreed.

'You never know, I might meet a nice farmhand and settle down.' Blanche opened her bedside drawer and took out a brown paper cone. 'Humbug, love?' She proffered the bag to Millie.

She eyed the bag longingly. 'I can't.'

'Go on. One won't hurt.'

'We're not supposed to eat on the ward.'

'I won't tell.'

Millie quickly took the humbug before Sister Wren noticed. It tasted divine. It was so strange – not so long ago she would have taken such pleasures for granted. But now a sweet or a piece of toffee or just the chance to sit down for a minute in her long day was a real pleasure to be savoured.

'Benedict!'

No sooner had she put the sweet in her mouth than Sister Wren's voice rang out from the other end of the ward, summoning her. Millie made her way as slowly as she could down the length of the ward, desperately trying to finish the humbug before she got to Sister Wren. But somehow it seemed to have swelled to giant proportions, and her throat was so dry she couldn't swallow it.

'Hurry up, Nurse. I don't have all day!'

As she approached, she could see Sister Wren's eyes narrowing on her. Matron's office, here I come, she thought miserably.

Just at that moment William stepped out in front of her, so quickly she almost collided with him.

'Sister,' he said. 'May I ask you something?'

Sister Wren tutted. 'What is it now, Dr Tremayne?'

'I wonder if I might take a look at Miss Fletcher's wound?'

'Must you? We've only just put on a new dressing.'

'I am rather worried about it.'

'Mr Cooper seemed perfectly satisfied when he did his rounds yesterday.'

'All the same, I would like to take another look.'

'Very well, then.' As Sister Wren turned away, Millie quickly spat the humbug into her hand and looked around desperately for somewhere to deposit it.

The only place she would find was Sister Wren's prize aspidistra. She had just dropped her sweet into the pot when Sister Wren swung round again.

'Benedict, perhaps you could assist Dr Tremayne? I'm far too busy.'

'Yes, Sister.'

As they walked away together, Millie whispered, 'Thank you.'

'I'm sure I don't know what you mean,' William replied innocently. 'Although if it puts you forever in my debt, then I'm happy to accept your thanks.'

'How will I ever repay you?' Millie smiled.

'You could have dinner with me tonight?'

'I can't,' she said. 'I already have plans.'

'Then cancel them.'

'I can't.'

'But you would if you could?' His dark eyes teased her.

'I certainly wouldn't.' They reached Miss Fletcher's bed, and Millie pulled the screens around it.

'Then we'll just have to make it another night,' he said in a low voice.

'What makes you think I'll say yes another night?'

'Because you find my charm irresistible. And if you don't, I'll tell Sister Wren who buried a humbug in her aspidistra.'

Helen hurried across the courtyard towards the porters' lodge with her head down, her cloak pulled around her against the cold March wind. It was five o'clock and darkness was gathering. The shivering plane trees stood stark against the purple-grey sky. Lights from the ward windows above her cast long shadows across the wet cobbles.

'Good evening, Nurse Tremayne. Nasty cold one, isn't it?' Mr Hopkins greeted her in his sing-song Welsh accent. The porters' lodge seemed warm and welcoming after the cold darkness. A hearty fire burned in the grate and the kettle sang on the gas ring. In the room beyond, Helen could see a few of the porters reading their newspapers and playing cards. 'I still can't get used to seeing you in the evenings and not the mornings. Throws my routine right out, so it does.'

'I'm sorry about that, Mr Hopkins.' Helen pulled her letter out from under her cloak and handed it over.

'It's nice, though, that you still find time to write to your mother, even when you're on night duty.'

I don't have much choice, Helen thought. If she didn't, her mother would be up at the hospital gates in no time, demanding to know why.

She was just about to turn away when Mr Hopkins said, 'Hold on, Nurse. I've got one for you, too.'

Helen frowned. Her mother was usually far too busy to write letters in return. And she couldn't imagine why her father would want to write to her.

But it wasn't from either of her parents. Her

heart leapt as she studied the spidery, unfamiliar scrawl. She didn't dare hope who it might be from.

'Everything all right, Nurse?' Mr Hopkins was watching her carefully.

'Yes, yes Mr Hopkins. Everything's fine. Thank you.'

Edwin Hopkins saw the little skip in Nurse Tremayne's step as she crossed the courtyard. It was lovely to see the way her eyes lit up as she saw the letter. That young man who'd come in to deliver it must mean a lot to her, he decided.

'Is that kettle boiled yet, Mr Hopkins?' One of the porters called out from the back room.

'I'm doing it now.' He smiled to himself as he turned off the gas and warmed the teapot. Maybe Nurse Tremayne would get to do a bit of gadding after all, he thought.

Helen could feel her letter burning a hole in her pocket all the way through the first two hours of her duty. She didn't dare get it out and read it, although she was absolutely desperate.

Her first emotion when Mr Hopkins had given her the letter was of happiness that Charlie Denton had remembered her. But by the time she'd reached the ward, she'd already convinced herself that it must be bad news. He had changed his mind about taking her out, and was trying to extricate himself as best he could from an awkward situation. For all Helen knew, Sally might even have decided to give him a second chance.

Helen didn't blame him. She knew all about patients who formed romantic attachments to the nurses who cared for them, only to realise their

280

mistake once they returned to their real lives. She should just be grateful that he had thought enough of her to set her straight, she decided firmly.

That night she couldn't wait for Amy to go off for her midnight rendezvous in the kitchen with the junior doctors, so she could have some time to read her letter in peace. She sat at the ward desk and read by the dim green-shaded light. All around her, the women filled the air with their low moans, but Helen was too lost in her letter to notice.

Dear Helen,

I hope you don't mind me writing to you. I bet you thought you'd seen the last of me, but here I am, turning up like a bad penny. I just thought I'd let you know how I'm getting on.

I've settled back into my old life, enjoying seeing my mates and going to the pub, just like you said. No work yet, but that's to be expected, I suppose. I'm sure something will come along. Anyway, I'm getting around a lot on the new leg, and surprising everyone with what I can do. My dad reckons it won't be long before I'm playing for Orient. Mind you, the way they've been playing lately, I reckon even a bloke with one leg would be an improvement! I still get a bit down sometimes, but whenever I start to feel sorry for myself, I hear your voice in my head, telling me to count my blessings. I reckon I needed that kick up the backside you gave me, although I can't say I was happy about it at the time!

Listen to me, rabbiting on about myself. How are you getting on? How is night duty? It's only another six weeks till you finish, isn't it? You see, I'm counting the days. I still want to take you out when you get off.

281

I want to show you how well I'm doing – you never know, I might even take you dancing by then!

Seriously, Helen, I know you've probably forgotten all about me – heaven knows, you must have patients asking you out all the time. But it really would mean a lot to me if you gave me a chance. Promise me you'll think about it, anyway.

I'll be in touch again next month. In the meantime, I'll have my fingers crossed you'll say yes.

Yours,

Charlie Denton

P.S. Sorry for writing to you at the hospital. I hope it doesn't get you into any trouble with your Matron.

Helen laid the letter in her lap and paused for a moment, savouring it. The paper was smudged with ink and covered with crossings out, but to her it was as beautiful as one of Shakespeare's sonnets.

Charlie Denton hadn't forgotten her. He still thought about her, and he was counting the days until he could take her out.

She could never accept, she knew that. Her mother would never allow it. But it was still nice to know that somewhere out there, someone cared.

'Nurse? Nurse, come here at once!' Mrs Mortimer's voice rang out imperiously from the darkness, breaking into her pleasant thoughts. Helen put her letter down and tiptoed down the ward.

'What is it, Mrs Mortimer?'

'I can't sleep.'

'I'm sorry, Mrs Mortimer. Here, let me try to make you more comfortable.'

'More comfortable? These wretched pillows feel as if they've been stuffed with coal. And I don't know what you're grinning at.' She glared at Helen through the darkness. 'Are you an idiot, girl?'

'No, Mrs Mortimer.' Helen tried hard not to smile as she plumped up the pillows. Charlie Denton hadn't forgotten her, and not even Maud Mortimer could wipe the smile off her face tonight.

Chapter Twenty-Nine

'What exactly do you think you're playing at, Nurse Doyle?'

Dora squirmed under Sister Blake's withering gaze. 'I'm sorry, Sister,' she mumbled. 'I thought it was a joke.'

'A joke?' Sister's voice rose in disbelief. 'Do I look as if I'm laughing, Doyle? Does poor Mr Wenham look as if he's laughing?'

'No, Sister.' Dora kept her gaze fixed on the white-tiled wall of the sluice. The last half-hour had been a slowly unravelling nightmare.

It'd all started when Mr Wenham had asked her for help with his urinal. 'It's a bit awkward with my poorly back.' He winced. 'If you could just reach down there and arrange it all, so to speak...'

But Dora had already caught the twinkling eye of the man in the next bed as she took the bottle behind the screens, and knew this was yet another of their pathetic jokes. Two months after she'd started on the ward, the men still hadn't stopped tormenting her. Blushing, she'd panicked and thrust the urinal under the covers then shot off through the screens as fast as she could. It wasn't until she had been summoned to account to Sister Blake for why she had refused to help an immobile patient, that she'd realised it wasn't a joke.

Cleaning up wasn't a joke, either. Dora was too mortified to meet Mr Wenham's eye as she stripped off the soiled bedding. The poor man didn't know where to put himself. 'Sorry, Nurse,' he kept mumbling.

'This is not the first time this has happened, is it, Doyle? I seem to recall several similar incidents when you've left a patient struggling.'

Heat spread up her chest, flooding her neck and face. 'I'm sorry, Sister.'

'Is there something I should know, Doyle?'

Dora looked up sharply. 'I – I don't know what you mean, Sister.'

'I mean, do you have some kind of problem dealing with men?'

Sister Blake's keen eyes were fixed on her, as if she could see right into her head. Dora dropped her gaze quickly.

'N-no, Sister.'

'I'm glad to hear it.' When Sister Blake spoke again, her voice was gentler, more understanding. 'Look, I was a student myself once. I realise that dealing with male patients can be embarrassing and alarming for a young girl, but it is a very necessary part of nursing.'

'Yes, Sister.'

'I also realise that you seem to have had more than your fair share of teasing from some of the young men on the ward. They seem to regard you as particularly good sport, so I've heard?'

Dora allowed herself to look up at Sister Blake. Her brown eyes were full of sympathy.

'You do realise they only pick on you because they know they can get a reaction? If you can manage to conceal your feelings and laugh it off, the teasing may stop.' Sister Blake laid a hand on her arm. 'Try to play them at their own game, Doyle. For your own sake,' she advised. 'I would hate to have to put this incident in the ward report.'

Dora thought about her words all the way through dinner. As the other pros excitedly swapped stories of their experiences on the wards, she sat mute with misery. If she didn't buck up her ideas, she would never be a nurse. But how could she ever overcome her terror of touching a man's body? If she wasn't careful, Alf Doyle's poison was going to seep in and infect her future, just as he'd infected her past.

The sound of laughter from the far end of the table made her look up. She saw Lucy Lane's face and realised the joke was directed at her.

'O'Hara's been telling us about your latest mess in Male Orthopaedics,' she announced down the length of the table. 'Really, Doyle, how do you expect to make a nurse if you can't even give someone a bottle?'

Dora stared at her coldly. She knew they would never be friends, but had hoped after saving Lucy's bacon during the PTS exam that the other girl might stop taunting her. But no such luck. It was as if she had pushed the whole incident to the back of her mind, pretending it had never happened.

'We can't all be top of the class like you, can we?' replied Dora. 'You'll have to give me some tips. I've heard you're a dab hand in the kitchen?'

Lucy's cheeks coloured, and Dora knew her barb had hit home. Lucy left her alone for the rest of the meal, although Dora had to listen to her bragging to the other girls about how Sister Wren had praised her bed-making skills.

'Sorry.' Katie O'Hara caught up with Dora as they left the dining room. 'I didn't mean to make fun of you, honest to God. I was only telling the girls what had happened.'

'It's all right.' Dora shrugged. 'I know what Lane's like. She never misses a chance to have a go at me.'

'She's got a mouth on her, right enough,' Katie said. 'Listen, are you coming to sit with us tonight? We all finish at six so we're going to do a bit of studying in Brennan's room. Lane won't be there,' she reassured Dora hastily. 'She reckons she doesn't need to revise as much as us slowcoaches.'

'She wants to revise some manners,' Dora said. For all her airs and graces, Lucy Lane knew nothing about being a lady.

'True enough. So are you coming or not?'

'Later,' Dora said. 'I want to go to the porters' lodge first.'

'Oh, yes?' Katie wiggled her eyebrows. 'You've been paying a few visits there lately. Got your eye on someone, have you?'

'Hardly. I owe someone a favour, and it's about time I paid him back.'

'Aye aye, Mr H. Here comes your mate!'

286

Edwin Hopkins looked up from tuning his radio, irritated at the interruption. He'd been looking forward to hearing Marjorie Westbury and the BBC Orchestra.

He was even more irritated to see that wretched ginger-haired nurse stomping across the court-yard towards the lodge again. Now he'd miss Marjorie completely.

'What does she want this time?' he sighed.

'Same as she wanted all the other times, I expect.' Percy Carson grinned. 'Our Nick.'

'No prizes for guessing why, I suppose,' Edwin Hopkins muttered to himself. Nick Riley was a hard enough worker, but he had trouble written all over him.

'How many times has she been round here? Must be at least once a week. You'd think she'd take the hint by now, wouldn't you?' Davey Johnson said.

'Maybe she's in trouble?' Percy suggested.

'Wouldn't be the first time a nurse has found herself in bother,' Davey agreed.

'No wonder Nick runs a mile, then!'

'Now, I won't have that kind of talk in here,' Edwin Hopkins warned them. He didn't hold with bad-mouthing young ladies. Even if some of them were no better than they ought to be.

He glanced at the ginger girl. He almost felt sorry for young Nick if she got hold of him. She struck him as a bit of a firecracker.

He met her at the door to the lodge. 'Before you ask, he's gone. And you needn't think about barging your way in to look for him the way you did before, because he's not here, see?' Hopkins

287

sidestepped to block Dora's way as she craned her neck to look over his shoulder.

'I don't believe you,' she said bluntly.

'I'll have you know, I've never told a lie in my life, young lady.' Edwin Hopkins' moustache bristled with indignation. 'If I say he isn't here, then he isn't.'

The girl frowned. She didn't look like Nick's type, thought Hopkins. He usually went for the pretty ones, the ones who fluffed and primped and giggled. Not ones with sturdy legs, frizzy hair and an expression that looked as if they were wondering who to hit next.

'Did he get my letters?' she asked.

Edwin Hopkins nodded. 'Of course he did. I handed them over right away.' He didn't like to tell her Nick had stuffed them straight in his pocket without even looking at them. He didn't reckon Nick Riley was much of a reader.

The wind whipped the girl's red curls across her face and she pushed them back, tucking them behind one ear. She stood there, looking around her, at a loss for what to do next.

Edwin felt a lurch of pity for her. For all her front, she was only young. He hoped she wasn't in trouble, poor girl. If she was, she wouldn't get much help from Nick Riley.

'Look, Miss, if you've got any sense, you'll stop coming around here looking for him,' he said kindly. 'It's plain he doesn't want to see you. And it's unladylike to go around chasing after a man, especially when he's not interested.'

The girl stared at him blankly. 'You think I'm interested in Nick Riley?'

288

'Why else would you be coming round here all the time?'

Her mouth firmed. 'That's none of your business. Do you know where he might be?'

'No, I don't,' Edwin Hopkins replied huffily, all his fatherly concern gone. 'What he does in his own time is his concern, not mine – or yours either, come to that.'

'Have you tried the boxing club on Ratner Row?' Percy Carson came up behind them. 'Nick usually goes down there to train on a Tuesday after work.'

Edwin Hopkins shot him a frowning look. Carson always had a bit too much to say for himself.

'Ratner Row, you say? Thanks very much.'

'You didn't want to be telling her that,' Hopkins scolded as she walked away.

'Come on, Mr Hopkins, have a heart. Can't you see the poor girl's desperate?'

'That's as may be, but I don't hold with young ladies chasing after men.'

'Looking like her, I don't s'pose she's got much option but to chase them!' Davey put in unkindly.

'There's no need for that either.' Edwin Hopkins shot a quick glance at the girl, hoping she hadn't heard. It wasn't right for a young lady to hear that sort of remark.

The boxing club was in a basement under the King's Arms pub, a rough old dive near the canal. A narrow door led down from the street.

Dora paused for a moment before going inside. This was the last place she wanted to go, but she had no choice. Nick had been avoiding her for weeks, ever since their argument over the hamsa.

She'd tried everything to talk to him, even risked catching his eye while they were on the wards. But he'd just walked by with his face turned away.

Now, two months on, she was determined to track him down and pay him back the money she owed him, no matter what it took.

She stepped carefully down the steep staircase and found herself in a dingy, low-ceilinged room reeking of stale sweat. In the centre of the floor two men were slugging it out in a boxing ring, while all around the room other men were exercising with weights or working on punchbags hung from the ceiling.

She was still peering around, trying to find Nick, when a man came up to her. He was middle-aged, with the broad shoulders and flattened features of a boxer.

'Excuse me, Miss, but you can't come in here.' His voice was gruff. 'This club is for men only.'

'But I'm looking for someone—'

'I don't care if you're looking for the Prince of Wales, you can't come in here. Now, if you don't mind...'

As he started to hustle her out, Dora suddenly spotted Nick over in the corner, head down, driving his fists into one of the heavy punchbags.

'Nick!' She dodged past the man and darted towards him.

Nick looked up sharply. 'Dora?' His dark hair hung damply in his eyes and he pushed it back with a gloved hand. 'What are you doing here?'

'Looking for you. Same as I have been these past two months.'

The other man appeared behind her. 'I've told

her she can't come in here, Nick, but she won't listen. Do you want to throw her out or shall I?'

Nick looked from him to Dora and back again. 'Five minutes, Jimmy? Please?'

The man sighed. 'Five minutes. But then I'm coming back and I'm putting you over my shoulder.' He pointed a warning finger at Dora.

The shadow of a smile crossed Nick's face. 'He means it, too.' He turned back to his punchbag. 'You shouldn't have come here.'

'I needed to find you. Didn't you get any of my notes?'

'I got 'em all right.' He drove his fists into the punchbag. Sweat gleamed on his powerful muscles, clearly outlined under his thin vest.

'It would have been nice of you to answer instead of ignoring them.'

'Wasn't that answer enough for you?'

'Maybe you don't want this, then?' Dora reached into her pocket and drew out the money she'd been keeping carefully in an envelope. 'Maybe you're so loaded you can afford to give your money away?'

She held it out to him. Nick glanced down at it, then took it. 'You could have left it at the porters' lodge.'

'I didn't want some toerag to nick it, did I?' She hesitated. 'Besides, I wanted to apologise. I shouldn't have flown off the handle at you like that. I was wrong, and I wanted to say sorry.'

Nick stared at her for a moment. It was hard to work out what was going on behind those hooded eyes of his. She thought he might reply, but he just turned around and thudded his fist squarely into the middle of the punchbag. 'Was that it?' he said gruffly. Dora nodded. 'You'd best get off, then, hadn't you, before Jimmy comes back.'

He turned his back on her and carried on aiming punch after punch into the heavy sandbag, his fists thrusting like pistons. Dora watched him for a moment.

'Blimey, Max Baer doesn't stand a chance, does he?' she said.

Nick stopped dead. 'What do you know about Max Baer?'

'Danny said you wanted to go to America and fight him one day.' She saw his quick frown. 'It's all right, he said it was a secret. I'm not going to tell anyone.'

Nick's eyes met hers, then he turned back to the punchbag. 'It's just a stupid dream,' he muttered.

'I don't think it's stupid.' Dora watched the muscles of his back working under his sweat-slicked vest. 'I reckon you could do it.'

'Oh yeah? Expert on boxing now, are you?'

'No, but I know determination when I see it. And I don't reckon it's stupid to have a dream. Sometimes dreams are all that keep you going. You can't give up on them, can you?'

His leather-gloved hands closed around the bag, stopping it dead. 'I'm not ready to give up on anything,' he said.

'All right, you two.' Jimmy came up to them, his meaty arms folded across his chest. 'Time's up. If you want to whisper sweet nothings to each other go down the Palais like everyone else.'

Dora glanced at Nick. 'No, you're all right,' she said. 'I reckon he's got two left feet anyway.'

Nick gave her the ghost of a smile. 'You'll never know, will you?'

I'm not ready to give up either, Dora thought the following morning, as she walked on to the ward. She could already feel several pairs of eyes swivel towards her, anticipating the fun and games they would have.

But this time Dora was ready for them. She'd been thinking about it all night. Nursing was her dream, and she wasn't going to let anyone stand in her way. Especially not the likes of Alf Doyle, or a bunch of bored men who wanted to act like schoolboys.

Their first job was the bedpan and bottle round. As Dora approached Mr Hubbard's bed, he was already grinning.

'Sorry, Nurse,' he said. 'I'm having a bit of trouble with the bottle. I wonder if I could ask you to help me put it in? You know, my...'

Dora smiled sweetly. 'Of course, Mr Hubbard,' she said.

His eyebrows shot up. 'Really?' he said. Dora understood his surprise. Usually she would flee in confusion when he had made the same request, almost knocking over the screens in her haste to get away.

But this time she'd come prepared. Still smiling, she reached into her pocket and pulled out a large pair of rat-tooth forceps.

'Now,' she said brightly, snapping the spiked jaws in front of his face. 'Let's see if we can help you, shall we?'

'Ooh, no, no, it's all right, Nurse. Do you know

293

what? I think I can manage after all,' he reassured her hastily, his eyes round as he stared in fear at the forceps.

Dora smiled. 'I thought you might.'

As she walked away, Sister Blake approached her. 'Doyle, did I just see you threaten a patient with a pair of forceps?' she asked.

Dora gulped, her moment of triumph vanishing like mist. 'Y-yes, Sister.'

A slow smile spread across Sister Blake's face. 'Excellent work. Perhaps we might make a nurse of you yet,' she said.

Chapter Thirty

Blanche Desmond went down to surgery on a trolley, like Cleopatra going down the Nile on her barge.

'Well, this is it.' She winked at Millie. 'I'm glad you're coming with me, love.'

'So am I.' Usually it was a senior's job to accompany patients down to Theatre, but Blanche had insisted she wanted Millie with her.

'A lot of those other nurses walk by with their noses in the air and won't give me the time of day. But our Millie's different,' she'd told Sister Wren.

Sister was outraged – she was the one who gave orders on her ward – but as it happened one of the seniors had been taken to the sick room with a fever and they were short-staffed, so it suited her to give Millie the job.

'But I'll be having words with you later about allowing patients to call you by your Christian name,' she'd warned ominously.

They made their way through the grey-painted corridors, a porter pushing the trolley, Millie walking beside Blanche. She felt terribly important in her uniform. It helped her walk with her head held high, in a way that Madame Vacani's deportment lessons had never managed to teach her.

'Hold my hand, would you, love?'

Blanche reached out to her. Millie took her hand and curled her fingers around it.

'Silly, isn't it? But I can't help feeling a bit nervous now it's all happening,' she whispered.

Millie squeezed her hand. 'You'll be fine, Blanche,' she reassured her.

'I hope so, love. Funny thing is, I had a dream last night that I wasn't going to make it. A what do you call it? Premonition.'

'Everyone feels nervous before an operation,' Millie said.

'Let's hope the surgeon doesn't!' Blanche managed a wobbly smile. She looked so vulnerable without her usual mask of powder and scarlet lipstick.

'You've got nothing to worry about,' Millie reassured her. 'This is a routine operation, and Mr Cooper knows what he's doing. You'll be as right as rain when he's finished with you.'

'I hope so, love. It's not been much of a life, but I'd be sorry if this was my lot.'

'It won't be,' Millie said. 'Just think, in a few weeks' time you'll be chasing chickens around your sister's farmyard and wondering what you were ever worrying about!'

Blanche smiled, and this time her smile reached her eyes. It crinkled the skin at the corners, showing her age.

'I'll have a good send off before then, I hope,' she said. 'A party in the King's Arms, and you can all drink to my good health. You'll come, won't you, love?'

'I'd love to,' Millie said. 'I've never been to a pub before.'

Blanche's mouth fell open. 'You what? How old are you?'

'Nineteen. Nearly twenty, actually.'

'Blimey, love, by the time I was your age, I was – well, never mind what I was,' said Blanche hastily. 'Let's just say I'd seen the inside of a fair few pubs by then. Next you'll be telling me you've never had a port and lemon?'

Millie shook her head. 'I haven't. But I'll try anything once.'

'Don't be saying that, girl. You don't know what trouble you'll end up in!'

They both laughed. Then Millie remembered the porter was listening, and started to blush.

Blanche gazed at her fondly. 'You're a lovely girl, do you know that? You've been very good to me while I've been here. And you're a bloody good nurse, too.'

'I don't think Sister Wren would agree with you!'

'Sister Wren doesn't know her arse from her elbow, if you'll pardon my French.'

'Let's hope the surgeon does, or you'll be in trouble,' the porter said cheekily.

Blanche stared at him for a moment, then burst

out laughing. She suddenly seemed more like her old self again, her hearty, wheezing laughter ringing out down the corridor.

William was waiting for them on the other side of the double doors to the theatre.

'There you are, Miss Desmond,' he greeted her with a smile. 'We were wondering what had happened to you. We thought you might have changed your mind and stood us up?'

'Stand up Mr Cooper? Not a chance. Although I feel a bit strange, seeing him without my lipstick on. I don't suppose there's any chance you could...'

'Sorry, Blanche, it's against the rules,' Millie said. 'But I'll make sure you're wearing it when you come round.'

'Promise? I feel naked without my lipstick.'

'I promise,' Millie said.

'You look beautiful without it anyway,' William put in gallantly.

'Ooh, listen to you!' Blanche chuckled. 'You'd better watch out, Millie love. Looks like your young man's got his eye on me now!'

Millie couldn't bring herself to look at William as colour scalded her face. 'This is where I have to leave you,' she said.

'Don't.' Blanche was suddenly serious, her fingers tightening around Millie's. 'Stay with me,' she pleaded.

'I'm sorry, I can't. I'm not allowed.' Millie felt suddenly flustered. 'But I'll be waiting with a nice cup of tea when you wake up.'

'And I'll take good care of you in the meantime,' William put in.

As the porter wheeled her away, Blanche called back, 'You will make sure I've got my lipstick on when I come round, won't you? I don't feel right without it.'

They were the last words Millie ever heard her say.

Millie was due to take her break from three until five. She had arranged to meet Sophia at the dressmaker's for a fitting that afternoon, but was determined to be back on the ward in time to keep her promise to Blanche.

She changed out of her uniform and ran to catch the bus up to Piccadilly. By the time she arrived, puffing for breath at the top of the stairs to the dressmaker's atelier, Sophia's cousin Margaret was already standing in the middle of the room wearing a calico toile of her bridesmaid's dress while two of the dressmaker's assistants knelt at her feet, busily pinning and adjusting.

Millie was surprised to see Georgina Farsley was also there.

'She invited herself,' Sophia whispered as she kissed Millie in greeting. 'Thank God you turned up – I think she was about to offer to take your place.'

The dressmaker's studio was a large, sunny, white-painted room looking out over Green Park. Millie gazed out over the well-dressed people strolling in the park and sighed happily. It felt almost decadent to be somewhere that didn't smell of disinfectant, where there wasn't always someone calling for her, or watching for her every mistake.

It felt just like old times, laughing and gossiping with Sophia as the dressmakers fitted her dress. Her friend, as she'd expected, was full of chatter about the plans for her forthcoming wedding.

'We're having it at St Margaret's, of course. Mother's already tying herself in knots, trying to make sure it's the biggest and grandest wedding they've ever seen. I think she'd even try to outdo Princess Marina if she could!'

'Oh, but she looked beautiful on her wedding day, didn't she?' Georgina sighed. 'Edward Molyneux really did her proud with that design. So simple, but so stunning. Are you having a tiara like her, or flowers?' she asked Sophia.

'Flowers, I think. Although I dare say Mother has it all planned.' Sophia smiled wistfully. 'I don't really care what I wear or where I get married, as long as I'm marrying David.'

'And becoming the next Duchess of Cleveland,' Georgina said eagerly.

The other girls looked at each other uneasily. 'I'm not marrying him because of his title,' Sophia said.

'Of course you're not,' Georgina said quickly. 'But it doesn't hurt to have people referring to you as "Your Grace", does it?' She saw their expressions. 'Oh, come on! What girl doesn't want to marry a man with a title?'

'Poor Seb,' Millie whispered to Sophia as the dressmaker's maid arrived with more tea. 'He really doesn't stand a chance, does he?'

'She's certainly determined,' Sophia agreed.

'I'm surprised she hasn't set her sights on marrying Richard, if she's so keen to marry into

299

a title?'

'She did, at first. But he made it clear he wasn't interested, so she had to turn her attention to poor Seb instead. I think she's secretly hoping a terrible accident will befall Richard once she and Seb are safely married.'

Millie was scandalised, until she remembered her grandmother would probably think in exactly the same way.

The conversation turned to Millie. Sophia and Margaret were horrified and fascinated when she told them all about her work on the Gynae ward.

Georgina looked repelled. 'And you actually have to touch these women? With all those nasty diseases and things?' She wrinkled her nose in disgust.

'How else are we supposed to nurse them?' Millie asked. 'They're just people, like the rest of us.'

'Maybe, but I wouldn't want to clean up after them. Can you imagine?' Georgina shuddered.

Millie saw the looks of revulsion on her friends' faces and realised they probably couldn't imagine anything like it. Much as they enjoyed squirming and giggling over all the gruesome details, she knew they would never feel anything but horror at the idea of cleaning toilets or mopping up someone's vomit.

Once she would have felt the same, but now, after a couple of months on the ward, she barely thought about it. It was only seeing her friends' expressions that made her realise how distant she had grown from them. She had seen and experienced things they could never imagine in their worst nightmares.

And it worked the other way, too. As they gossiped about the latest scandal in their circle, and excitedly planned what they were going to wear to the next country house weekend, Millie couldn't help feeling how trivial and tedious their lives were. She missed her old life back at Billinghurst, but she knew she'd miss being a nurse even more.

After the fitting, the other girls were going for tea at Fortnum and Mason's.

'Why don't you come with us?' Sophia asked.

'Sorry, I have to catch my bus back to the hospital. I'm back on duty at five.'

'Those backsides won't wipe themselves, will they?' Georgina smirked.

Millie scowled back at her. She sincerely hoped she didn't manage to ensnare Seb. Her friend deserved far better.

It was twenty to five when she hared through the hospital gates. She headed straight for the nurses' home, praying Sister Sutton wasn't around to delay her. But as she put her foot on the stairs, she heard Sparky yapping and a moment later the door to Sister Sutton's room swung open.

'Where do you think you're going, Benedict?'

Millie's shoulders slumped. 'I'm going to get changed, Sister.'

Sister Sutton gasped as if this were the greatest impertinence she had ever heard. 'And where have you been? I hope you haven't been out gallivanting?' she said suspiciously.

Millie was about to point out that it was her afternoon off and she could gallivant if she wanted to, but thought better of it. She already had less than ten minutes to change and get back to the ward.

There was nothing she could do but to stand and submit to Sister Sutton's scrutiny as she looked her up and down.

'Your bed was a disgrace again this morning,' was all she could finally find to say. 'Make it properly before you go on duty.'

'Yes, Sister.' To hell with the bed, thought Millie as she raced up the stairs, already tearing off her coat. She was more afraid of Sister Wren than she was of Sister Sutton.

But it wasn't just fear that made her hurry, clumsily pulling on her black stockings and ramming her feet into her shoes. She was anxious to keep her promise to Blanche, to be there with her lipstick, ready for when she woke up.

Mr Hopkins gave a disapproving shake of his head as she hurried past the porters' lodge a few minutes later, still buttoning up her cuffs as she went. No one noticed her when she arrived breathless on to the ward. She slid past Sister Wren's gaze and hurried to Blanche's bed at the far end of the ward.

As she drew closer, her smile froze on her face. There was no sign of Blanche, and her bed had been stripped down to the mattress.

'There you are.' Sister Wren stood at her shoulder. 'You do realise you are two minutes late?'

'Where's Blanche?' Millie blurted out without thinking.

Sister Wren blinked. 'I beg your pardon? Were you addressing me?'

'I'm sorry, Sister.' Millie lowered her gaze

302

humbly. 'I just wondered what had happened to Blanche – I mean, Miss Desmond?'

Sister Wren pulled herself up to her full height, which was still barely taller than a child's.

'Miss Desmond died earlier today,' she said.

'Died?' Millie could hardly manage the word.

'Yes, Nurse Benedict. Don't look so surprised. This is a hospital. Regrettable as it may be, people do die here from time to time.' Her face registered no more emotion than if she'd been talking about the leaf wilt on her aspidistra. 'Now, when you're ready, the bathrooms need cleaning.'

She turned on her heel and stalked off, hands clasped behind her back, leaving Millie numb with shock.

'Hard-hearted cow,' the woman in the bed next to Blanche's muttered. 'I know you've got to be in your job, but she really takes the biscuit. Poor woman.' She turned her gaze to Blanche's stripped bed. 'It's a real shame, I reckon. She didn't deserve to go like that.'

How would you know? Millie felt like snapping back at her. You never had a kind word to say to her when she was here. Poor Blanche. She'd often lain in bed, watching the other women and longing to join in their chat, but no one ever gave her a smile or the time of day. She never had any visitors, either. Millie was the only company she'd had.

Lucy Lane was in the bathroom, scrubbing out the bath with Vim. She sat back on her heels, brush in hand, when she saw Millie.

'There you are,' she said. 'I've been waiting for you. I was supposed to go off duty ages ago. But

303

Sister Wren said I wasn't allowed to leave until you came back.'

'Blanche is dead,' Millie cut her off.

'Who? Oh, you mean the prostitute? Yes, I heard she died during the op. Turned out she had some kind of heart defect, I think. Couldn't cope with the anaesthetic.' She dropped her scrubbing brush into the tin bucket and stood up, brushing down her knees.

'Who did last offices?' Millie asked urgently. 'Did they remember her lipstick?'

'As far as I know, she was taken straight down to the mortuary. What are you talking about, anyway? What lipstick?'

'I promised her… I promised I'd put her lipstick on for her.'

'I don't suppose she's in any position to hold you to your promise.' Lucy shrugged. She picked up her bucket and handed it to Millie. 'Anyway, you need to take over. I'm off. And do try to cheer up,' she called over her shoulder. 'Sister Wren will have a fit if you go around with a face like a wet weekend.'

Chapter Thirty-One

'I don't understand it,' Lucy Lane said. 'Why do you want to go to some old tart's funeral?'

'Blanche wasn't an old tart. She was kind, generous, warm-hearted…' Everything you're not, Millie almost added.

304

'I don't think your family would approve of you going to the funeral of an East End prostitute,' Lucy said. 'And I doubt Matron would like it either.'

'It's my day off, and I can do as I please,' Millie retorted. 'If I want to pay my respects at someone's funeral, I can.'

But it was about more than paying her respects. She still felt guiltily that she'd somehow let Blanche down.

'I'll come with you,' Dora offered. 'I'm on a split shift today. I don't have to be back on the ward until five.' She glared at Lucy, defying her to argue.

'Thanks,' Millie said gratefully. 'I was a bit nervous about going, actually. I've never been to a funeral before.'

'You've never seen anything like an East End funeral,' Dora promised her. 'It's a big occasion round here. Bigger than weddings, sometimes. People who don't have two halfpennies to rub together get into debt so they can give their nearest and dearest a good send off. Carriages drawn by horses decked out in black feathers, strings of mourners in top hats, the lot. And then there's the big party afterwards!' she said.

But there was no horse-drawn carriage at Blanche's funeral, nor any black feathers, nor mourners in top hats. Only a handful of people were gathered around her graveside in the damp, grey afternoon. There was Blanche's sister Elsie and her five children, and a couple of tired-looking women Millie guessed must be Blanche's old friends from the docks. A young man stood with them, looking smart in his dark suit, head bowed

305

at the graveside. Millie felt a jolt of recognition.

'That's Tremayne's brother, isn't it?' Dora whispered as they approached the grave. 'What's he doing here? I wonder.'

'Same as us, I suppose.' Millie avoided William's eye as she and Dora took their places beside the grave.

The service was short and to the point. Even the vicar seemed impatient to get it over with, rushing through the formalities as the drizzle dampened his cassock.

Millie kept her gaze fixed on the coffin as it was lowered into the ground. She wondered what Blanche looked like. She hoped someone had dressed her up nicely in her favourite bright colours. Blanche wouldn't have liked to go into the hereafter looking less than her best.

She thought about the lipstick, and a lump rose in her throat. She took a deep breath, sniffing back tears. Immediately she felt a handkerchief pressed into her hand.

'Here,' William whispered.

'Thanks.' She took it, feeling foolish. No one else seemed to be crying, not even Blanche's sister. Why did she have to be so sentimental?

Afterwards, her sister approached them. 'Excuse me, I'm Mrs Wilkins. Were you friends of my sister?' she asked. She was nowhere near as showy as Blanche in her plain black coat, her mousy hair tucked into a limp felt hat. Her eyes, green like Blanche's, were full of suspicion.

'Yes. I mean no ... not friends exactly...'

'We're from the Nightingale Hospital,' Dora explained, as Millie scrabbled for the right words.

306

'My friend nursed Miss Desmond.'

Mrs Wilkins' eyes lit up, and suddenly she looked more like Blanche. 'Are you Millie? Blanche wrote to me about you. She told me there was a nice young nurse on her ward she'd made friends with. She thought a lot of you.'

'Did she?'

'Oh, yes. Reckoned you were the best of the lot. Treated her right, she said.' Mrs Wilkins lowered her voice. 'There weren't many who did that to my sister, her being what she was.'

Millie lowered her gaze, embarrassed by the hot tears that sprang to her eyes.

'Bless you.' Mrs Wilkins smiled fondly at her. 'My Blanche told me you had a soft heart.'

Please stop it, Millie begged silently. She didn't want to hear any more about what Blanche thought of her. Not when she'd let her down so badly.

William joined them. Elsie Wilkins was most impressed when he introduced himself.

'A doctor, eh? Blimey, Blanche had some friends in high places, didn't she? Do you lot always turn out for patients' funerals?'

William shot Millie a sidelong look. 'Blanche was very special,' he said.

'Well, she'll be pleased you came.' Mrs Wilkins started looking around for her children, who had wandered off to explore the churchyard. 'Now if you'll excuse me, I'd best be going. We've got a train to catch.'

'You're not having a send-off then?' Dora frowned.

Mrs Wilkins shot her a guilty look 'I didn't

think I'd bother with all that,' she said. 'My sister didn't have many friends – not the kind I'd want to associate with anyway. Besides, funerals cost money, and it's not as if Blanche left us anything for the expenses.' Her chin lifted defensively. 'It's been very hard on me, you know. I only lost my husband a few months back. I've had to get someone to look after the farm while I came all the way up here, and that costs money too...'

'Of course.' William switched on the easy charm that worked so well on his patients. 'We understand, Mrs Wilkins. You need to get your children home. It's been a long day for all of you.'

'That it has.' The woman looked mollified. 'I would have done something for Blanche,' she said to Millie and Dora. 'But I have to put my family first.'

'Blanche was family too,' Millie muttered, as they watched Mrs Wilkins head off towards the gates of the churchyard, leading her string of children.

'I've known families pawn everything they had to give someone a decent funeral,' Dora agreed.

'And there's no reason why we can't do the same.' William looked at them both. 'We don't need Blanche's sister to give her a good send-off. I don't know about you, but I'm going to the King's Arms to drink to her. Would you care to join me?'

Millie glanced at Dora.

'Don't look at me,' she said. 'I have to be back on duty at five. Sister Blake might be a nice woman, but I doubt she'd understand if I went back stinking of drink!'

'I'll come with you,' Millie told William.

'Are you sure?' Dora frowned. 'East End pubs can be a bit rough at the best of times, and the King's Arms has a bad reputation...'

'I'm sure William will protect me.'

Dora shot him a look, as if to say that idea was no comfort at all. 'Just see that you do,' she warned him.

They didn't mean to stay quite so long. The afternoon turned into evening and the pub became crowded with dockers, filling the hot, stuffy bar with laughter, raised voices and cigarette smoke. Over in the corner, someone was banging out a tune on an old piano.

'If you were the only girl in the world, and I were the only boy...'

William smiled. 'I can just imagine Blanche sitting at the bar, giving all the men the eye, can't you?'

'She'd be laughing and singing louder than anyone,' Millie agreed. 'No wonder she loved this place so much.' She raised her glass again. 'To Blanche.'

'To Blanche.' William's hand shook as he raised his glass to his lips. He'd lost count of how many times they'd toasted her.

Somewhere in the back of his mind, he was dimly aware that it was getting late and he should think about getting Millie back to the nurses' home. But he was enjoying himself too much to want the evening to end.

Millie sipped her drink. 'Do you know, I rather like port and lemon,' she said thoughtfully.

'You should, you've had enough of them!'

She squinted at him. 'Do you think I'm squiffy?'

'I don't know. I'm too drunk myself to tell.'

She giggled. 'Oh, dear, we're behaving rather badly, aren't we? I'm sure Blanche would approve.'

William studied her. She was unbelievably pretty, with her soft lips, small, slightly upturned nose and the bluest eyes he had ever seen.

But it wasn't just the way she looked. Millie was also the sweetest, gentlest girl he had ever met. She didn't flirt and giggle about nothing the way other girls did. She seemed genuinely interested, asking about his work and his family. For once William didn't feel as if he needed to impress her. He wanted her to know everything about him, good and bad. He even found himself telling her all about growing up in the vicarage with his gentle, henpecked father and fearsome mother.

'She watches us all like hawks,' he told her. 'No one dares put a foot wrong.'

'Even you?' Millie smiled teasingly at him.

'It's true, I get away with a lot,' William admitted, shame-faced. 'But only because I've learnt to tell her what she wants to hear. And Helen covers for me too. Poor Helen,' he sighed. 'She gets far worse treatment than me. My mother seems to set particularly high standards for her daughter. Helen works so hard to please her yet she's barely allowed to breathe without Mother's say-so. I'm sure she thinks Helen's going to run wild.'

'Perhaps your mother worries Helen will meet someone like you?' Millie suggested.

William smiled. 'I see my reputation precedes me. I'm surprised you allowed yourself to be

310

alone with me?'

'I never listen to gossip,' Millie said firmly. 'I prefer to make up my own mind about people.'

'And have you made up your mind about me?'

She gazed at him for a long time, her blue eyes searching his face. Then she pushed her glass towards him.

'Buy me another drink and I'll tell you.'

Two drinks later, they were still talking. It came as a shock when the bell for last orders rang.

'I didn't realise it was that late. You do have a late pass, don't you?' William asked. Millie shook her head.

'I never do. But I'll find a way back in, don't worry.'

They left the pub. William knew he was slightly drunk, but Millie was worse. She wobbled like a baby gazelle, stumbling against him. He put his arm around her, and kept it there as they walked back along the river. The Thames snaked like an oily black ribbon ahead of them, its cranes, docks and factories shadowy shapes looming through the darkness around them.

'I think Blanche would have enjoyed this evening,' Millie declared.

'So do I. I bet she's looking down at the two of us now and laughing.'

'Why?'

'Because she always thought we should get together.'

He waited for Millie to pull away from him, but she didn't. 'I know,' she sighed. 'She kept telling me I should give you a chance.'

'And what do you think?'

311

'I'm still considering it.' William felt the yielding warmth of her body against his, and longing hit him like a punch in the stomach.

Any other girl and he would have taken her in his arms, but not Millie. He felt protective of her in a way he couldn't have imagined possible. And he'd made that promise to Helen, too. Although out here, walking together under the stars with his arm around her, he wasn't sure he would be able to keep it.

'You're quite right to be cautious,' he said. 'In fact, you should probably stay well away from me.'

'Because of your reputation? I told you, I don't listen to gossip.'

'But it's true in my case. I'm nothing but trouble. Just ask my sister.'

Millie laughed. William wished he could have laughed with her. But for once he wasn't joking.

He usually enjoyed this part of the game, the teasing to and fro before he moved in to claim his prize. But not this time. Millie deserved more than a few days of flirtation.

And that was all he could offer. William wasn't the type to lose his heart to anyone. Most girls understood it was just a game and were happy to play along. But then there were girls like Peggy Gibson, who didn't understand the rules. They were the ones who got badly hurt.

The memory of what had happened to Peggy still weighed heavy on him. He didn't want to put anyone through that again. Especially not someone as sweet and adorable as Millie.

'I mean it,' he said. 'You're far too good for me.'

'I'll make my own mind up, thank you very

312

much.' Millie stopped and turned to face him. She was so close he could smell her flowery perfume. 'Kiss me,' she said.

William looked down at her upturned face, her innocent eyes, and felt a jolt of desire so powerful he could barely control it.

'I can't,' he said.

Her face fell. 'Don't you want to kiss me?'

'Of course I do. More than anything. But we're both extremely drunk, we're on a lonely stretch of river on a dark night, and it's all a bit too compromising.'

'I don't care.'

'No, but I do.' Any other girl and he might have taken advantage. No, he knew he would. He'd done it before. But Millie Benedict was too special. 'Besides, I made a promise to Helen.'

Millie squinted at him in confusion. 'What has your sister got to do with this?'

'She asked me to stay away from you.' William glanced down at the cobbles. 'I – I had a bit of an entanglement with a girl she used to share a room with, and poor Helen caught the flak. I don't think she wants to go through that again.'

'This is nothing to do with Helen!'

'You don't know what it was like for her. You mustn't blame her...'

He reached for Millie, but she pulled away, stiff with indignation. 'Don't touch me,' she said. 'Your sister might not like it.'

She turned and tottered off up the street. William caught up with her and tried to put his arm around her to steady her again, but she shrugged him off. They crept in through the hospital gates.

313

Millie slipped past the porters' lodge and headed purposefully around the side of the nurses' block.

'How are you going to get in?' William whispered in the darkness.

'How do you think?'

She tried the drainpipe, but William stopped her. 'You can't climb up there!' he said, appalled.

'Why not? I've done it before lots of times.' She was already taking off her shoes.

'Not after half a dozen port and lemons, you haven't. You'll break your neck...'

Regardless, she put her hands around the drainpipe and tried to wedge her foot into a piece of loose brickwork. It slipped, sending a brick rolling noisily across the path. They both tensed, waiting for a light to go on. It didn't.

He put his hand on her arm. 'Come on, we'll find another way in.'

They headed around the back of the block, trying windows. 'Everything's locked up,' Millie said mournfully. She gazed at the windows on the first floor. 'I wonder if I should throw a stone up and try to wake someone?'

'You might not get the right window.'

'Then it'll have to be the drainpipe.'

'I'm not letting you break your neck.'

'I didn't think you cared,' Millie said huffily.

'Of course I care.' Their eyes met in the darkness, and once again William felt the powerful jolt of desire.

This time it was too strong to fight. As he lowered his face to kiss her, Millie suddenly said, 'I have an idea. Come on.'

She led the way to the other side of the block.

'There's a corridor that joins the nurses' block to the rest of the hospital,' she explained. 'We're not allowed to use it, it's only for sisters. But if I could somehow get into one of the wards on the ground floor, I might be able to sneak in that way.'

William laughed. 'Break into a ward? That's even riskier than climbing up a drainpipe!' But Millie was already heading towards the courtyard, inching her way around in the shadows. He followed her.

'Millie, this is ridiculous...'

'Shhh!' she hissed at him. 'Do you want me to get caught?'

She edged round a corner and stopped beside a window. 'This will do,' she said.

'Which ward is it?'

'I can't tell.' Millie craned over and tried to peer through the window.

William counted the windows. 'I think it might be Hyde.' He judged it with narrowed eyes. 'Yes, definitely Hyde.'

Millie tested the window. 'It's unlocked. I can climb in and sneak through.'

'What if you're caught?'

'Honestly, William, where's your sense of adventure?' She smiled at him, a smile that melted his heart and made his head spin.

'This is where we say goodbye,' she said.

'Yes.' He didn't want to. His legs wouldn't move. 'Thank you for a very enjoyable evening.'

Before he had a chance to reply, Millie bobbed up and in one swift movement threw open the window and slithered through. It wasn't until she had disappeared that he realised he was still holding her shoes in his hand.

Millie landed with a soft thud in the narrow space between two beds. She crouched for a moment in the darkness, waiting for her eyes to get used to the gloom. All around her, bedsprings creaked and the air was filled with the sound of low moans and sobbing. They sounded like souls in purgatory. Millie shuddered. What an awful place to have to be.

She finally got her bearings and started to inch forward on her hands and knees to peer around the end of the bed. The doors seemed to be a hundred miles away, at the far end of the ward. She was still working out how she could crawl down the length of it when she heard the muffled squeak of rubber-soled shoes approaching. She turned around, just in time to see a tall, slender figure emerge from behind a screen, a bedpan in her hands.

Before Millie could duck back into the shadows the nurse saw her. She jumped, let out a startled cry and dropped the bedpan with a clatter. It crashed like noisy cymbals around the ward, setting all the women off in an unearthly chorus of screaming and wailing.

Millie recognised the nurse in the middle of all the chaos. 'Tremayne? It's me.'

Helen peered at her in the darkness. 'Benedict? What are you doing here?' she hissed.

Before Millie had a chance to answer, more footsteps approached.

'What's the meaning of all this noise?' Millie heard the Night Sister's voice and dived for cover under the nearest bed. She lay there, hardly daring to breathe. She could see the Night Sister's sensible shoes, just inches from her face.

'Well?'

'I ... I...' she heard Helen floundering desperately. Shock seemed to have paralysed her vocal chords.

'Speak up, girl.'

'Sister, there is a young woman under my bed,' a voice announced, clear and high, from just above Millie's head. She froze.

She heard the Night Sister's heavy sigh. 'Mrs Mortimer, there is not a young woman under your bed, just as there are no fairies prancing every night on top of Miss Fletcher's bedside locker, or men playing the bagpipes down the middle of the ward. It's all just the effect of your medication.'

'But–'

'Please, Mrs Mortimer, I don't have time for this,' the Night Sister said impatiently. She turned to Helen. 'Get this mess cleaned up immediately,' she said. 'And please quieten the patients. This ward gets more like a menagerie every night. I'm sure Sister Hyde would not approve.'

She walked away, her tread as light and soft as a dancer's.

Millie waited until she was sure the coast was clear, then stuck her head out.

'It's all right, you can come out now.' Helen squatted down to pick up the bedpan, her face stony.

She looked so furious, Millie couldn't help giggling. 'It's not funny,' Helen snapped. 'You could have got both of us sent to Matron. Honestly, it's bad enough that you come in through the window at all hours without...' She sniffed, suddenly alert. 'Have you been drinking?'

'No. Yes. A little,' Millie admitted.

'Oh, for God's sake! This is too much. First you stay out late, then you break into a ward drunk as a lord. I'll be amazed if they don't throw you out on your ear.'

'They'll have to catch me first.' Millie wriggled out from under the bed and stood up, dusting off her dress. 'I'm terribly sorry,' she said to the woman in the bed, who was watching her through narrowed eyes.

'I should think so too,' snapped Mrs Mortimer. 'Thanks to you, that wretched woman now thinks I'm as demented as the rest of them. This nurse is quite right, you should be thrown out. I will write to the Board of Trustees in the morning.'

Millie looked at Helen and another giggle escaped her.

'Just go to bed,' Helen said wearily. 'And try not to get caught.'

Lucy Lane shuffled along the darkened corridor to the toilet, still half asleep. She jumped when she heard the stairs creak and saw a dark shape appear on the landing.

'What the—' she started to say. But the shape stumbled past her and continued up the stairs to the attic. It tripped on the top step and Lucy heard a high-pitched giggle.

Millie. Lucy listened to her clattering about on the top landing, taut with resentment. No matter how hard she'd tried, Lady Amelia Benedict

318

showed no interest in being her friend. She seemed to prefer to hang around with that awful common Dora Doyle. It sickened Lucy to see them together all the time, laughing and joking.

They should both stick to their own kind, she decided. She had far more in common with Millie, but most of the time the other girl ignored her.

And she had led such a charmed life, too. Everyone adored Millie, and everything came so easily to her. Lucy couldn't imagine her losing sleep over whether her parents were fighting, or whether she was rich or popular or clever enough. Millie had never known a moment's real anxiety in her life.

Lucy smiled to herself in the darkness. Well, it was about time she learnt what it felt like.

Chapter Thirty-Two

Millie woke up the following morning with a pounding headache, dry mouth and a churning stomach, absolutely certain she was going to die. The maid's voice outside their door summoning them awake sounded like an unearthly clamour.

'I truly don't feel at all well,' she told Dora, pulling the thin covers around her, her teeth chattering. 'Do you think I should go to the sick bay? I think I might have a virus, and I don't want to pass it on to the patients.'

'I don't think what you've got is contagious.' Dora smiled knowingly as she adjusted her woollen stocking to hide a hole. 'If you ask me, I reckon you had too much to drink last night.'

'Surely not!' Millie sat up sharply and wished she hadn't, as the world lurched sickeningly around her. 'I only had – oh, heavens.' She'd lost count after the third port and lemon, but she had the awful feeling there had been many more.

Dora laughed. 'You came crashing in here, fell over the rug and passed out face down on your bed. I had to get you undressed.'

Millie clutched her head and stared at the heap of discarded clothes that lay crumpled on the floor as the previous night's events came back to her in sickening waves. Had she really climbed in through a window in Female Chronics? Worse still, had she really asked – no, practically begged – William Tremayne to kiss her?

Hot shame washed over her. She wasn't sure which was worse, her asking or him refusing.

Dora noticed her look of dismay. 'What happened last night?' she asked.

Millie couldn't meet her eye. 'What do you mean?'

'Dr Tremayne didn't try anything with you, did he? Only I've heard about his reputation with the nurses. I wasn't sure if I did the right thing, leaving you alone with him...'

'Dr Tremayne was a perfect gentleman.' Millie blushed, thinking of the bold way she'd turned her face towards his, ready for a kiss.

'How odd. From what I've heard, he never usually misses a chance to get fresh.' Dora shrugged. 'Anyway, you'd better hurry up and get dressed before Sister Sutton comes in. This room smells like a brewery.' She sat down on the bed to pull on her shoes.

'I can't.' Millie fell back groaning against the unyielding pillows. 'You don't understand. I can't ever face the world again.'

'It's not that bad.'

'But I did something terrible. Tremayne is going to hate me.'

'Why? What on earth did you do?'

Millie told her about breaking into the ward. For some reason Dora seemed to find the idea of her getting stuck under a patient's bed hilarious.

'You're a caution, d'you know that?' she laughed, wiping away a tear.

'It's not funny!' Millie insisted. 'I'm so mortified, I just want to crawl away and die.' She pulled the sheets over her head. 'Tremayne is probably writing to her mother about me as we speak.'

'Don't be daft.' Dora tugged at the covers. 'Now get up, get dressed, wash your face and come and have some breakfast.'

'Ugh! I couldn't face breakfast.'

'You must. It'll do you good.'

She was right. Even though Millie's stomach churned as she forced herself to eat tiny forkfuls of cold kipper, by the time she'd washed the last of it down with a cup of hot, sweet tea she felt less fragile.

She was still feeling a little shaky as she cleaned out the sluice and did the bedpan round. And when she had to hold a bowl for one of the women to be sick, her own stomach heaved in sympathy.

But she thought she was managing quite well until Sister Wren sought her out and told her to

321

report to Matron's office.

'Why, Sister? What have I done?'

Sister Wren looked affronted. 'Good heavens, there is so much wrong with you I would hardly know where to start,' she said. 'But for once the complaint has not come from me. Now hurry along. I want those lockers cleaned and scrubbed when you get back.'

At nine o'clock, Millie joined the line of sorry-looking nurses waiting outside Matron's office.

Matron sat behind her desk, Miss Hanley the Assistant Matron at her shoulder. Outside the harsh wind spattered rain against the window-panes like gravel against the glass. It was more of a downpour than an April shower.

Matron eyed her wearily. 'Do you recall, Benedict, the last time we met in this office I told you that if I heard one more report of your mis-behaviour, I would have no choice but to dismiss you?' she said.

'Yes, Matron.' A tiny seed of unease began to unfurl inside her.

'And if I recall correctly, you gave me your word that you would be a reformed character and apply yourself assiduously to your studies?'

'Yes, Matron. I have, Matron.'

'Indeed?' Matron's brows rose. 'In that case, why did I this morning receive an anonymous note claiming that you returned to the nurses' home late last night in a severe state of intoxication?'

Millie stared down at the parquet floor. She was too afraid to breathe, let alone speak.

'Should the allegations in this note turn out to be true, you understand I would have no choice but to dismiss you immediately from this hospital. I cannot have students behaving in such an outrageous fashion.'

'No, Matron.' This was it, Millie thought. She could already see herself travelling home on the train, Felix picking her up at the station, her father's disappointment, her grandmother's elation.

'However, as yet I have been unable to prove these accusations,' Matron continued. 'I have received no official complaint either from Home Sister, or the night porter. I cannot make decisions about a nurse's future based on gossip and rumour. And since the author of this note clearly lacks the courage to approach me personally with any proof, I am regrettably forced to give you another chance.'

Millie looked up, scarcely able to believe what she was hearing. Neither could Miss Hanley, judging by the thunderous look of outrage on her face.

'You – you mean you're not dismissing me?' said Millie.

'Not unless you wish to confess to this misdemeanour?'

Millie opened her mouth and closed it again. She knew honesty was one of her many failings, but even she wasn't silly enough to speak up now.

'I have nothing to say, Matron,' she said stiffly.

'No, I didn't think you would.' There was a glint in Matron's grey eyes. 'Very well, then, Benedict, you may go. But rest assured, I will be keeping my eye on you.'

'Yes, Matron. Thank you, Matron.'

'Oh, and Benedict?'

323

'Yes, Matron?'

'You might find a couple of Aspirin beneficial, I think.'

Millie felt as if she'd received a last-minute reprieve on her way to the gallows. Her hangover forgotten, she almost danced her way through the rest of her duties on the ward, and by lunchtime she was feeling a great deal better, even though she still couldn't face food.

She was pushing a stringy piece of meat around her plate when one of the seniors, Amy Hollins, plonked herself down in the seat next to her. Millie was shocked; seniors rarely associated with lowly pros.

'What were you doing in Hyde last night?'

Millie looked at her sharply. 'You saw me?'

'I was coming back from my break just as you were sneaking out. You weren't exactly being subtle about it. What were you up to?'

She laughed when Millie told her. Millie couldn't understand why everyone seemed to find it so amusing. 'You're lucky no one caught you.'

'They did,' Millie said miserably. 'I had to see Matron this morning.'

'I bet she was furious.'

'Actually, she was very nice about it. She said since Sister Sutton hadn't caught me red-handed, there wasn't much she could do.' Millie put down her fork, her appetite gone. 'I wish I knew who'd written that note. What a beastly thing to do.'

'I bet I can guess,' Amy said through a mouthful of food. 'It's got to be Tremayne, hasn't it?'

Millie shook her head. 'She wouldn't do a thing

like that.'

'What makes you so sure?'

'Because she's not like that. She's always covered for me in the past when I've come in late.'

'Perhaps you upset her?'

Millie thought briefly about what William had said. Helen didn't want her brother to have anything to do with Millie. She couldn't remember if she'd told Helen who she'd been with that night, but it wouldn't take a genius to work it out...

No. Millie dismissed the thought. 'Helen wouldn't do it,' she said. 'She wouldn't deliberately set out to get me dismissed.'

'Why not? It's exactly the kind of thing she'd do. She's done it before.'

Millie frowned. 'What do you mean?'

'Have you ever heard of a girl called Peggy Gibson?' Millie shook her head. 'She shared a room with Tremayne last year. She thought she could trust Tremayne too. Until she got thrown out.'

Amy reached across for Millie's plate and scraped her leftovers on to her own plate.

'What happened?'

'Tremayne told tales. She went to her mother and told her Gibson had a bottle of gin hidden under her bed.'

'And did she?'

'Well, yes. We were planning a party and she'd bought a bottle of booze to share. But Tremayne found out about it and reported her. I suppose she was just annoyed she hadn't been invited.' Amy shovelled a forkful of food into her mouth. 'And she was supposed to be Gibson's friend. The rest of us never wanted anything to do with

Tremayne because she was such a swot, but Gibson was always nice to her.'

Millie considered for a moment. 'I can't believe she'd do something like that.'

'Can't you? I can.' Amy pointed her fork at Millie. 'Ask anyone here. They'll tell you Helen Tremayne is not to be trusted.'

Chapter Thirty-Three

Helen sat bleary-eyed behind her cramped desk, fighting sleep as Sister Parker described the anatomy of the colon. Night duty or not, all students were expected to attend lectures one day a week. But it was difficult to stay awake in the stuffy, airless classroom, with Sister Tutor's voice droning on, punctuated only by the squeak of her chalk across the blackboard. Helen had to keep pinching the back of her hand to make sure she didn't nod off.

Finally the lecture finished, and she escaped into the fresh air. After days of slate-grey skies the rain had finally cleared and spring sunshine had emerged, glinting in the puddles and making the rooftops shine. The patch of grass in front of the students' block was fresh and green, studded with purple and white crocuses and yellow daffodils.

As she crossed the courtyard on her way back from her lecture, she noticed Millie sitting on the bench under the trees. Helen saw her pale, sombre face and smiled to herself, wondering if she was suffering from the after-effects of her night's drinking. Even though she hadn't been amused at the time, the thought of Millie wedged under Mrs Mortimer's bed, only inches from the Night Sister's shoes, had made Helen laugh all day. She wished she could be like her, so confident and fearless and always ready to take risks.

Millie caught her eye and waved her over.

'I've been waiting for you,' she said.

'Me?' Helen was surprised. 'Why? Is everything all right?'

She could see immediately that it wasn't. For once Millie wasn't smiling. Her pretty face was tense, brows knotted under her starched cap.

'Was it you who reported me to Matron?' she asked. 'No, don't tell me, I know it must have been you.' Millie looked up at her, her blue eyes full of reproach. 'Why did you do it? I thought we were friends?'

Helen stared at her in confusion. 'Why would I report you? You're always coming in late and I've never said anything before, have I?'

'I've never been out with your brother before.'

Helen felt her stomach lurch. 'You were with William?'

'Don't pretend you don't know!' Millie stood up to face her. 'I know you told him not to have anything to do with me. Is that why you reported me? Because you wanted to keep us apart?' Her blue eyes were cold. 'I don't know why you didn't want us to be together, but this was a nasty way of going about it. You could have got me thrown out of the hospital. Is that what you really wanted?'

'I don't know what you're talking about. I told

you I didn't report you. I wouldn't do something like that to you.'

'You did it to Peggy Gibson.'

Helen felt the blood drain out of her face. 'Who told you about her?'

'Does it matter? It's true, isn't it? I didn't want to believe it, but I can see it in your face. You got her thrown out.'

'It wasn't like that,' Helen said quietly.

'Then what was it like?'

Helen looked into Benedict's face. She wished she could tell her, make her understand. It would have been so nice just for once to stop everyone hating her so much. But she had sworn to Peggy that she would never tell.

Millie shook her head. 'And to think I actually liked you. No wonder no one else does, if that's the way you treat people.' She looked more disappointed than angry. 'Well, you've just lost another friend. Although I don't suppose you really care, do you?'

Helen watched her walk away across the courtyard. You're wrong, she thought. I do care.

Millie was counting the dirty sheets and towels before they went off to the laundry the following day when she was summoned back to the ward for Mr Cooper's round.

She had been hoping to avoid William. But as she joined the other nurses at the doors of the ward to greet the consultant, she saw him trailing along with the other registrars, housemen and students behind the great man as usual.

Millie tried not to catch his eye as she tagged

on to the end of the train that went from bed to bed. She was too mortified to face him. What on earth must he think of her, after the last time they'd met? Not a lot, apparently; everyone knew no girl was safe from William Tremayne, yet he'd turned her down flat.

At every bed Mr Cooper paused to study the notes as Sister Wren rushed around pulling the screens around the patient. He would then ask the patient how they were feeling, and question the registrars and housemen about their treatment. Occasionally he would pounce on an unsuspecting medical student and ask them how they would proceed with the treatment. If the patient's condition were very serious, they would move discreetly away from the end of the bed to discuss it out of their earshot. Millie always wondered how this was any more reassuring than telling them the facts, since they immediately knew that they were doomed.

William sidled up to her while Mr Cooper was quizzing a medical student about the appropriate surgical treatment for fibroids.

'Hello again,' he whispered. 'How are you feeling today? I don't know about you, but I woke up yesterday with a hellish hangover.'

Millie ignored him, her eyes fixed on Mr Cooper.

'And if the haemoglobin level is below forty per cent, would you still advise proceeding with surgery?' he was asking the furiously blushing student.

'Are you not speaking to me?' William looked hurt.

'I don't want to get into any more trouble,' she hissed out of the corner of her mouth.

'I certainly wouldn't want to get you into any,' he agreed solemnly. 'But, you see, I still have your shoes and I would like to return them to you.'

Millie shot him a panicked look as Mr Cooper turned to address the group. 'Quite right,' he said, his powerful voice carrying across the ward. 'In such cases surgery would carry an increased risk of post-operative complications such as embolism or femoral thrombosis. But fortunately your haemoglobin levels are perfect, are they not, Mrs Chattis?' He bestowed one of his dazzling movie star smiles on the patient, who simpered as if he'd just paid her a wonderful compliment.

'Leave them at the porters' lodge,' Millie whispered.

'And start the whole hospital gossiping about why I have them?' William looked amused.

Millie thought about it for a moment. Perhaps that wasn't such a good idea. 'Meet me in the courtyard at six o'clock.'

He was there waiting for her, sitting on a bench under the plane trees when she arrived a few minutes after her duty finished.

'I thought you weren't coming,' he said.

'Do you have my shoes?'

He handed them over, and she started to walk away.

'Wait,' he called after her. 'Is that it?' He sounded disappointed.

Millie looked back over her shoulder at him. 'Was there something else you wanted?'

'I don't know...' He looked awkward. 'I thought

you might ... you know ... want to talk about the other night?'

'Definitely not.' Millie stared at the shoes in her hand. 'In fact, I would prefer it if that night hadn't happened.'

'Oh. Right. I see.' William looked deflated. 'You do know your sister reported me, don't you?'

He frowned. 'Helen wouldn't do that.'

'She told you to stay away from me, didn't she?'

'Only because she wanted to protect you from me.' William smiled sheepishly.

'And I suppose she was trying to protect Peggy Gibson, too?'

He went very still. He had the same blank look on his face that Helen had done when Millie mentioned the name. 'What do you know about her?' he asked quietly.

'I know your sister got her dismissed from this hospital. Over a bottle of gin, wasn't it?' She curled her lip. 'I bet Helen was very proud of herself for that.'

'It wasn't Helen's fault. Peggy broke the rules–'

'Everyone breaks the rules sometimes. But we don't tell on each other. We're supposed to help each other, not stab one another in the back.'

'Helen tried to help Peggy.'

'Gosh, she's terribly helpful, isn't she? She tried to help Peggy and she gets thrown out, then she tries to protect me and *I* almost get dismissed too. She's all heart, I'd say.'

William stood up, towering over her. His dark hair still sprouted upwards, defying his attempts to flatten it. 'Look, it wasn't like that. Helen really

331

did care for Peggy. And it wasn't just a bottle of gin that got her thrown out, it was…'

'Go on,' Millie said quietly.

William paused for a long time. Millie could almost see his mind working, searching for the right words.

'I can't,' he said. 'I've already said too much. Helen would kill me if I told you.' He sounded wretched. 'All I can tell you is, you mustn't blame Helen for what happened to Peggy. They were good friends. It was because she was a good friend that Helen – did what she did.'

Millie stared at him. There was a longing in his dark eyes, just as she'd seen in his sister's. As if there was something he wanted to tell her, a secret he was desperate to share.

'You have to trust me.' He held on to her hands, gripping them tighter as she tried to pull away. 'If Helen says she didn't report you, then I'd bet my life on it that she didn't. My sister is no sneak, Millie. And she doesn't set out to hurt people either.'

'But Peggy–'

'For God's sake, stop talking about her!' William cut her off impatiently, startling her. 'Helen didn't get her into trouble. She saved her life!'

'What do you mean?' Millie asked softly.

William paused for a moment. Millie could see all kinds of conflicting emotions battling in his face. Then, finally, he took a deep breath and said, 'Peggy was a very – emotional girl. She got herself very upset about something and tried to take her own life. Helen found her just in time.

She begged Peggy to get help, but she refused. Helen was desperately worried she would try to kill herself again and next time she wouldn't be there to save her. So she did the only thing she could, and told our mother.'

'But I heard—'

'You heard she was found smuggling in a bottle of booze?' William finished for her. 'That was the story everyone came up with. Her parents were very upset, you see. They didn't want anyone to know the truth about their daughter's – distress – so everyone decided it would be best to come up with the gin story. And Helen went along with it.'

'Even though she knew everyone would think she was a sneak?' Millie could hardly believe it. Poor Helen, the other girls were so cruel to her. If it was her, she was sure she would be tempted to clear her name and tell them the truth.

William seemed to guess her thoughts. 'Now do you believe my sister can be trusted?' he said. 'Believe me, Helen knows how to keep secrets.'

There was something about the way he said it that made Millie look at him. 'What was it that upset her so much that she tried to kill herself?' she asked.

He was silent for a long time, his lips pressed together as if he was trying to hold the words in.

'She fell for the wrong man and he let her down badly,' he said.

One look at his eyes, so dark and intense, and Millie knew his sister wasn't the only one who guarded their secrets.

Chapter Thirty-Four

'Who's there? Is that you, Gwen?'

The old lady's opaque, sightless eyes searched for Helen in the darkness as she sat beside the bed, holding her hand. It felt like a child's, fragile bones under papery skin.

'It's me, Mrs Rodgers. Nurse Tremayne.'

Not that it mattered now. Mrs Rodgers was nearly eighty and beyond knowing anyone, even herself. The end was very near.

Mrs Rodgers turned her head away restlessly. In the dim light her scalp gleamed through sparse tufts of white hair. Helen was relieved she was quiet at last. All night she had been thrashing around, crying out in a panic, calling out for Gwen. Whether it was a sister or a daughter, Helen didn't know. She had done her best to calm her fears, sitting with her and holding her hand, even though Amy Hollins complained bitterly at the extra work she'd had to do.

'I don't know why you're making so much fuss,' she'd said. 'It's not as if the old girl even knows you're there.'

But Helen did it anyway, holding on to her hand and trying to reassure her. No one deserved to die alone.

Although she didn't seem to be alone. All through the night, Mrs Rodgers had talked to the invisible souls who gathered around her bedside.

'I'm not ready to go,' she insisted over and over again, her voice blurred and mumbling. 'Not until I've seen Gwen.'

Finally, as the pink light of dawn was beginning to creep around the drawn blinds, she lifted her head off the pillow and looked at Helen with such intensity that for a moment it was as if she could really see her.

Her gaping, toothless mouth broke into a smile. 'Gwen,' she said. 'You've come at last.'

She gave a sigh of contentment, turned her face away, and was gone.

Helen put her fingers to Mrs Rodgers' throat to satisfy herself there was no pulse. Then she calmly got up and pulled the screens around the bed.

Amy was very put out when she emerged from the kitchen, where she had been buttering bread for breakfast.

'Typical!' she snorted. 'Why couldn't she have hung on an hour longer? Now we're going to have to deal with it ourselves before the day staff come on.'

'I'll do it,' Helen said.

'Really?' Amy looked relieved. 'If you're sure?' she said, although it was obvious she wasn't going to volunteer to help.

Helen sent the runner to fetch the Night Sister, who in turn informed the Duty Registrar. He arrived, rubbing the sleep out of his eyes, and declared what everyone already knew, that cancer had eaten its way into Mrs Rodgers' bones, brain and every organ in her body. The porters arrived and transferred her body to the side room while Helen gathered everything she needed on the trolley, washed her hands and donned gloves and a clean apron.

She took her time, washing the old lady with care and respect. Mrs Rodgers was no bigger than a child, her wrinkled skin hanging loosely from thin bones. Helen was astonished she had managed to keep death at bay for as long as she had, when there was no strength left in her frail, emaciated body.

Sister Hyde came in as Helen was fastening the shroud. She was the most fearsome of all the sisters at the Nightingale, bristling efficiency in her immaculate grey uniform, her cap fastened in a crisp bow under her square chin. Helen fought the urge to jump to attention.

'Good gracious, Nurse, what are you doing here? Hollins went off duty fifteen minutes ago.'

'I wanted to finish preparing Mrs Rodgers before I left, Sister. Hollins offered to stay and help me,' she lied quickly.

'Did she indeed? That hardly sounds like Hollins.' Sister Hyde looked down at Mrs Rodgers' face, encircled by the white shroud. 'So she's gone at last. I hope it was peaceful?'

'Yes, Sister. Quite peaceful.'

'I'm glad. She suffered quite dreadfully towards the end.' Sister Hyde sighed, and for a moment her face lost its severe expression. Then she recollected herself and said, 'Tonight is your last night on this ward, isn't it?'

'Yes, Sister.'

'Do you know where you will be sent next?'

'Wren, Sister.'

'Gynae? That will make a change for you.

336

Rather a lively ward, so I'm told.' Sister Hyde looked thoughtful. 'It's very commendable that you should want to stay and do this. I wish all students were as conscientious as you. I shall certainly mention you in the ward report.'

'Thank you, Sister.'

It was almost half-past eight when the porter came to escort Mrs Rodgers down to the mortuary. Helen had missed breakfast, so she headed straight to bed in the night corridor. But it wasn't easy to sleep with the maid clattering noisily outside the door with her broom, and Miss Hanley stomping to and fro down the corridor to the staff linen room.

She slept fitfully, haunted by dreams of Mrs Rodgers clawing at her hands and calling out to her. She woke up at midday, stiff and aching, foggy-headed with lack of sleep. Wearily she got up and dragged on her dressing gown.

Opening her door, she didn't see the figure sitting on the floor outside her room until she fell over them.

'Oops, sorry, I didn't– Benedict?' Helen rubbed her gritty eyes. 'What are you doing down there?'

'Waiting for you.' Millie clambered to her feet, brushing herself down. 'I'm supposed to be at dinner but I wanted to see you before I went back on duty.'

Helen's heart sank. 'I'm not in the mood for another argument,' she sighed, shouldering past her.

'I don't want to argue. I just wanted to say I was sorry,' Millie said.

Helen stopped in her tracks and turned slowly to face her.

'I know you didn't sneak to Matron about me really. And even if you did, I probably deserved it.' Millie was gabbling on, the words tumbling out so fast Helen could hardly keep up with them. 'After all, I did break just about every rule in the book, stumbling around the ward like a drunken maniac...'

'I didn't report you,' Helen said.

'I know you didn't. That's what I'm trying to say although I know I'm making a frightful hash of it. I spoke to William, you see, and he told me about what happened with Peggy Gibson. He said there was no chance you would ever–'

'What did he tell you about Peggy Gibson?' Helen cut in, panic beating in her chest.

'He told me the real reason she had to leave.'

'He had no right to do that. It was supposed to be a secret.'

'It's all right, I won't tell anyone else,' Millie said solemnly. 'Don't be angry with him, he only did it for your sake.'

'Even so, he had no right to say anything,' Helen fumed. 'I made a promise to Peggy...'

'Your secret is safe with me, I swear. It's the least I can do, after the horrible way I spoke to you.' Millie looked up at Helen sheepishly from under her fair curls. 'Can you ever forgive me? I'd like us to be friends.'

It was a long time since anyone had wanted anything to do with her. Helen smiled warily. 'I'd like that too.'

'I'm so pleased!' Millie's pretty face lit up. 'And I'd really like to make it up to you, if I can. Doyle and I are planning a trip up west to have tea at the

Lyons' Corner house in The Strand as soon as we have time off on the same day. Doyle's never been, can you imagine? I'd like you to come with us.'

Helen shook her head, immediately ready to refuse. 'Oh, no, I couldn't.'

'Nonsense, it will be fun.'

Helen's mind raced. Surely even her mother couldn't object to her going out for tea with a couple of other students? 'If you're sure I won't be in the way?' she said.

'Absolutely not. It wouldn't be the same without you.'

Helen was still smiling to herself as she washed and dressed later. It was strange to think she might actually have a friend. She had become so used to being on her own, she hadn't realised how lonely she was.

It had been that way ever since Peggy Gibson left. Poor Peggy, she had been the closest to a friend Helen had had at the Nightingale. They didn't exactly have a lot in common – Peggy was as bubbly, vivacious and popular as Helen was serious, thoughtful and solitary. But like Millie Benedict, she was kind-hearted and persevered in trying to make friends with Helen.

'I don't care what you say, I'm not letting you study a minute longer,' she would say, tugging away Helen's books. 'Come on, even you can spare a few minutes to listen to music in the sitting room?'

With her being young and pretty, it was only a matter of time before William made a play for Peggy. Helen was happy for them at first, and even hoped that Peggy might be the one to make her brother settle down. But it soon became clear that Peggy was taking their romance a lot more seriously than William was. After a matter of weeks it was all over, and William was flirting with a staff nurse on Female Surgical while poor Peggy cried herself to sleep every night.

And then one evening she came home from her shift and found Peggy slumped on her bed sobbing, a bottle of Lysol in her hand.

'I – I can't do it,' she'd wept. 'I want to kill myself, but I'm not brave enough. Help me, Helen,' she'd begged. 'Please help me take the pain away.'

Helen had sat up with her all night, holding her while she cried, one minute raging, the next inconsolable with grief. All she could do was cling to her and pray she would calm down.

By the morning Peggy was subdued, but still chillingly determined to end her life. Helen tried to plead with her, to convince her that no man was worth so much misery, especially not her brother. But Peggy just shook her head and told her she wouldn't understand.

'There's nothing left for me,' she'd said. 'It's not just William. I'm so unhappy, I can't bear it any more. And if you don't help me, I'll find some other way to do it. You might have managed to stop me last night but you can't watch me for ever.'

It was that fear that kept Helen awake, watching over her as she slept night after night. But just as Peggy had said, Helen soon realised she couldn't keep an eye on her for ever. She needed to do something to make sure her friend stayed safe.

And so she did the only thing she could. She told

her mother. Peggy was diagnosed with a nervous breakdown and taken away for treatment.

She had been careful to keep William's name out of it to protect him. No one else at the Nightingale ever guessed he was part of the reason Peggy had gone.

And now he had chosen to tell Millie about her. Helen had never known him confide in anyone else before. It made her wonder if perhaps Millie meant more to him than either of them realised.

Chapter Thirty-Five

On a Saturday afternoon a week later, the three of them caught the bus into The Strand. While Dora and Millie chatted on the seat in front, Helen sat behind looking around her apprehensively. She half expected her mother to appear at any moment and send her back to the hospital.

As they passed St Paul's Cathedral, they saw workmen busy building stands along Ludgate Hill ready for the King's Jubilee. Two days later His Majesty would travel by carriage from Buckingham Palace for a thanksgiving service in St Paul's, and the whole city was in a state of high excitement. Especially Millie, who was going to watch the parade with some of her friends.

'I do hope the sun shines,' she said, looking up at the gloomy grey sky. 'It will be so much nicer if the weather's fine.'

'I know what you mean,' Dora said. 'We're

planning a street party and we don't want it to be a wash out.'

'A street party?' Millie looked intrigued. 'What is that, exactly? I don't think I've ever been to one.'

'Never been to a street party? Then you haven't lived!' Dora laughed. 'We're always having them down our way. Any excuse to get the flags out!'

'It sounds wonderful,' Millie sighed. 'I think I'd much rather come to your street party than watch the procession.'

'What, and miss the chance to see the King?' Dora looked astonished.

'But I've seen the King, remember?' Millie reminded her. 'When I was presented at court.'

'So you were. I'd forgotten you were practically royalty!' Dora laughed.

Millie twisted round in her seat to face Helen. 'What are you doing for the Jubilee?' she asked.

'Working, as usual.'

'You mean you didn't manage to get the day off? How awful for you.' Helen listened to Millie sympathise. She didn't like to tell her she didn't have any plans anyway. Everyone else in the country seemed to be having a party, or going into town with friends to celebrate, except Helen.

She felt like such dull company as she listened to them chatting away. She hoped they didn't regret bringing her along.

They got off the bus in The Strand and walked down to Lyons' Corner House. As it was a busy Saturday afternoon there was quite a queue waiting outside but Dora and Millie didn't seem to mind as they joined the end. Helen looked nervously at her watch.

'Are you sure we're going to have time?' she said. 'We've got to be back in our uniforms and on the wards by five, and it's nearly half-past three now.'

'Stop fretting, we have ages,' Millie reassured her breezily. 'Honestly, this queue will move in no time, and the service is so quick in here. They don't call the waitresses Nippies for nothing, you know!'

Helen tried to smile and to join in with their chatter and laughter, but she was beginning to feel anxious about the idea of going out. She didn't usually venture far from the hospital on her break, just in case she couldn't get back on time. Mostly she stayed in her room, studying or else writing to her mother. She had no idea when she was going to finish today's letter. Her mother would be most upset if a day went by without hearing from her.

'Here we are,' Millie said, as they approached the plate-glass doors. 'You see? I told you we wouldn't have to wait long.'

The seater showed them into the cheerful, brightly lit restaurant and guided them to a vacant table.

Helen had visited the local Corner House with her mother, but Dora had never been inside such a place before. Helen could see her trying to keep her excitement under control as she gawped around at the glowing lights overhead, and the walls which were richly decorated with pictures. Heavy draped curtains hung at the windows. A band played softly over in the corner.

'It's like a palace,' she breathed.

'Wait until you try the food.' Millie picked up a

343

menu. 'Now what's everyone having? I don't know about you, but I'm starving.'

'This all looks a lot better than the food we get at Nightingale's,' Dora said, perusing the menu.

'Ugh, don't remind me.' Millie pulled a face. 'How do you think they get their mince that awful grey colour?'

'Dunno. I reckon they must cook it in the autoclave!'

'If they cooked it in there at least it would come out hot. The stuff in the dining room is so cold it sticks hard to your plate.'

The nippy approached, looking smartly turned out in her black dress and white cap. 'What can I get you?' She smiled brightly at them.

Millie ordered sandwiches and a plate of assorted fancies.

'I told you I was starving,' she said, as Helen laughed at her.

Dora took much longer to order, frowning in deep concentration over the menu before closing it up and saying, 'Just a pot of tea, thank you.'

'You must have more than that!' Millie protested.

'I'm not very hungry.'

'But we've come all this way–'

'I told you, I'm not hungry.'

Helen caught the obstinate set of Dora's chin, and realised at once that a pot of tea was all their friend could afford. She also understood that there was no point in offering to pay her share, because Dora was far too proud ever to accept charity, no matter how well meant it was.

They had fun for the rest of the afternoon,

laughing and chatting. Helen relaxed so much she was shocked to find a whole twenty minutes went by without her checking her watch. It was such a relief to be able to enjoy eating in a cafe without worrying that her mother was going to pick on a waitress or make a scene.

Millie made them laugh with her stories about what she'd got up to as a debutante.

'Weren't you supposed to be chaperoned?' Helen asked, after she'd finished an outrageous tale about taking a dip in the Serpentine one warm summer's evening.

'Oh, yes, but we usually managed to give them the slip.'

'Sounds like good practice for Nightingale's!' Dora said, helping herself to one of the dainty cakes Millie offered her. Helen noticed Millie had pretended to be too full to finish the plate, and told her they would only go to waste otherwise.

'Yes, it is. Except unlike Nightingale's we were practically thrown at eligible young men, instead of being kept away from them.' Millie sighed. 'But I still managed to avoid getting myself engaged. Now my grandmother thinks I'm on the shelf.'

'You never know, maybe someone will take pity on you and marry you one day?' Dora joked, licking icing off her fingers.

'I hope not! Not for a while anyway. I intend to forget about men and devote myself to nursing for the next three years at least. I mean it,' she insisted, catching the smile Dora and Helen exchanged. 'Nearly getting kicked out that last time has made, me realise that nursing is really what I want to do.'

'You said that last time,' Helen reminded her. 'Although I must admit, you do seem like a reformed character. You haven't sneaked in through a window for at least a week.'

'And I definitely saw you with your nose in a book yesterday,' Dora put in.

'You may laugh, but you'll see. I'm going to be as clever as Lucy Lane.'

'Oh, no, please!' Dora laughed. 'One know-all is enough!'

'We'll be the most virtuous room in the whole nurses' home,' Millie said. 'We've got no choice really, since none of us has a boyfriend.' She gazed around the table. 'Unless anyone's got one hidden away they're not telling, me about?'

'No chance,' said Dora. Helen kept silent.

She stared down at her teacup, but she could feel Millie's gaze fixed on her. 'You've gone very quiet, Tremayne. You haven't got an admirer, have you?'

'Of course she hasn't,' Dora answered for her. 'Leave her alone. You know she's shy.'

'Actually,' Helen found her voice, 'there is someone...'

It was worth breaking her silence just to see the looks of astonishment on their faces.

'No?' Millie's jaw dropped. 'You *are* a dark horse, Tremayne. Who is he, this boyfriend of yours? Come on, spill the beans. We're utterly agog.'

'He's not really a boyfriend,' Helen admitted shyly. 'He's just someone I met when I was on Holmes ward.' Shyness crept over her. 'He sent flowers and asked me out when he was dis-

346

charged. He's written to me a couple of times since then, asking to meet up with me when I've finished on nights.'

'Oh, how thrilling! And so romantic, too.' Millie sighed.

'Love among the bedpans. That's dead romantic, that is,' Dora put in dryly.

'Oh, do be quiet, Doyle. Just because you have no poetry in your soul.' Millie turned to Helen, her blue eyes shining. 'So when are you seeing him?'

'I'm not. It was just silliness, really. I expect he's forgotten me now.' She blushed, feeling their eyes on her. 'He was probably just being polite,' she added lamely.

Millie laughed. 'Young men don't bother sending flowers and writing love letters if they're just being polite! No, if you ask me, I reckon he's smitten.'

'Do you think so?' Helen paused for a moment, enjoying the warm glow it gave her inside. Then she shook her head. 'It doesn't matter anyway. I can't possibly go out with him. My mother would never allow it.'

'Why does your mother have to know?' Dora asked.

Helen stared at her, dumbfounded. Her mother knew everything. Even if Helen didn't tell her, she would find out somehow.

And if she discovered her daughter had done anything so daring as going out with a boy, her wrath would simply know no bounds.

No, it was too big a risk to take. And Helen would never be that brave.

Would she?

Chapter Thirty-Six

Griffin Street did His Majesty proud for his Silver Jubilee. Church bells were ringing all over the city as Dora left the hospital early on that sunny May morning. She turned the corner into Griffin Street to find neighbours hanging out of the windows high above her, shouting to each other as they strung colourful bunting across the gap between them. On the street, women were busy arranging long tables, laughing as they tried to stop the tablecloths fluttering away. Children darted in and out around their feet, into everything, already over-excited.

'Dora!' Bea rushed up to her, dragging Little Alfie behind her. His chubby legs could hardly keep up with her long strides. 'Have you seen it? Isn't it grand? Mum's made a jelly and fairy cakes and sausage rolls, and later on we're going to have races and games, and look what they gave me...' She opened her palm to reveal a small silver medal on a burgundy ribbon. 'Everyone at school got one but mine's the best.'

'That's smashing, love. Be careful you don't lose it.' Dora scooped her baby brother into her arms. 'You look very pretty, too. Is that a new dress?'

Bea nodded. 'Mum made it for me. She says everyone's got to look their best for the King's Jubilee.' She tweaked her pigtails, tied up in fancy new ribbon. 'Nanna says she's going to

348

wear her fur coat, but Mum says it'd look daft. And our Josie's shut herself in her room and won't come out,' she added as an afterthought.

'Has she now? It doesn't sound like our Josie to miss a day of fun and games.' Dora hitched Little Alfie on to her hip. Except he wasn't so little any more, and weighed heavy in her arms. When did he grow so big? she wondered. 'Come on, let's go and find out what it's all about, shall we?'

The kitchen table was crammed with plates of sausage rolls and dainty little iced cakes as fancy as anything from Lyons'. In the centre a large bowl of scarlet jelly glistened like a jewel. Nanna Winnie sat at a corner of the kitchen table, making fish-paste sandwiches. She had fetched her best green coat with the fox fur collar out of the wardrobe, and the smell of mothballs filled the tiny kitchen.

'All right, Mum?' Dora greeted her mother with a kiss on the cheek. 'You've been busy, haven't you? It all looks lovely.'

'She's done enough to feed an army!' Nanna Winnie grumbled. She pointed the end of the butter knife at her daughter. 'You just be sure to bring back more than you take, that's all.'

'That's hardly the party spirit, is it, Nanna?' Dora grinned.

'Party spirit indeed! I don't hold with parties,' Nanna grunted. 'Never have, never will.'

'Come on, Nanna, you love parties! Bet you'll be the first up and dancing when the music starts.'

'Not with my back, I won't. I'm a slave to my lumbago.'

Dora set Little Alfie down on the floor and turned to her mother. 'Anything I can do to help?'

she asked.

'No, thanks, love, it's just about done now. Besides, you don't want to ruin your nice dress, do you?'

'I thought I'd make a bit of an effort.' Dora looked down at her cotton dress. Her mum had made it for her years ago and the blue flowery pattern was faded with washing, but it was still her best frock. She'd made an effort with her hair, too, smoothing down her frizzy curls and fastening them back with matching blue ribbon.

'You look lovely. Doesn't she, Mum?'

Nanna Winnie peered at her. 'She's scrubbed up all right. But you can't make a silk purse out of a sow's ear, can you?' she said, and went back to her sandwich-making.

Dora laughed. There was no point in getting offended – as her mum always said, if you took offence at everything Nanna came out with, you'd be in a huff all day.

'What's happened to our Josie?' Dora asked. 'I thought she'd be down here helping you?'

Rose and her mother exchanged looks. 'She's taken herself to bed. Says she's not feeling right.' Rose shook her head. 'I don't know, they're dropping like flies around here. Alf's been complaining about a pain in his gut all night.'

'If you ask me, there's nothing wrong with our Josie,' Nanna mumbled. 'She's been a right little madam lately. Barely speaking one minute, snapping at everyone the next. And she gave our Bea a good hiding the other day. I mean, I know she can be an annoying little bleeder sometimes, but she didn't deserve that.'

'Josie hit Bea?' She was usually the peacemaker of the family, always trying to stop fights between her brothers and sisters.

Her mother read Dora's thoughts. 'I know, it's not like her, is it? And Lettie Pike reckons she saw her in Victoria Park the other day when she was supposed to be at school.'

'That Lettie Pike's a troublemaker. I wouldn't believe anything that came out of her mouth,' Nanna said. 'Whatever else our Josie does, she'd never miss her school. She's too clever for that.'

'I wouldn't be too sure.' Rose looked worried. 'The way she's acting at the moment, I don't think I'd put anything past her.'

Fear began to uncurl in the pit of Dora's stomach. 'Shall I have a word with her?'

'Would you, love? She might listen to you.'

She took a deep breath before she stepped into her old room, steeling herself against the rush of painful memories that overwhelmed her.

Josie lay in the middle of the bed, huddled under the eiderdown, her dark head on the pillow. She turned sharply as Dora came in.

'Oh, it's you.' Her hunched shoulders relaxed.

'I brought you a cake. I thought you might want one before Bea scoffs the lot.'

'Thanks.' Josie didn't move, so Dora put the cake carefully down on the bedside cupboard.

'How are you feeling, love?' she asked.

'I've got a headache.'

'Will you be all right for the party?'

'I don't think so.'

'Blimey, you must be sickening for something if you want to miss out!' The old feather mattress sank beneath Dora's weight as she perched on the edge of the bed. 'It won't be the same without you, Jose. Mum's made all your favourites, and Nanna's all dressed up in her best fur coat like Nancy Glitters. You should see her!'

Josie didn't move. Dora stared worriedly at the back of her sister's silky dark head. 'What is it, love?' she whispered. 'What's wrong?'

'I told you, I've got a headache.'

Dora looked down at her hunched figure under the bed clothes. 'How long have you had it? You're not running a temperature, are you? Let me see...' She reached over and tried to put a hand to her sister's forehead, but Josie batted her away.

'Don't touch me! I don't need you nursing me, all right? Just leave me alone.'

The fierce look in her blazing brown eyes startled Dora.

'All right, Jose. No need to bite my head off.' She stood up. 'Come down if you feel better, won't you? We'll all miss you at the party.'

'Well?' Her mother looked up from her sandwich-making as Dora came back into the kitchen. 'How is she?'

'She says she's not well.'

'Not well, my eye!' Nanna snorted. 'If you ask me, that girl's hiding something.'

Dora chewed her lip and said nothing. She hoped she was wrong, but she had the horrible feeling that her grandmother might have hit the nail on the head.

She tried to shake her lingering worry from her mind as she got stuck in, helping her mother and their neighbours to shift food and chairs outside.

The children ran around them, tunnelling under the tables, caught up in the excitement of the day. At the other end of the street, a few of the men were bringing a piano out of one of the houses. Nick Riley was with them, his shirtsleeves rolled up, dark hair falling into his eyes. He seemed to be doing most of the heavy lifting, Dora noticed.

She caught his eye and they both looked away at the same time.

'Your Nick's a strong lad, isn't he?' Nanna remarked to June Riley, as she placed a plate of sandwiches in the middle of one of the tables.

'Nice to see he's useful for something,' June replied, taking a long drag on her cigarette.

'She can talk,' Nanna muttered to Dora. 'She hasn't lifted a finger all morning. Too busy sunning herself and making eyes at the men.' She brushed off the cigarette ash that June had allowed to fall on to the table. 'Where's your Danny anyway?' she asked.

'He's around somewhere.' June waved her cigarette vaguely, allowing another shower of ash to fall.

'Last time I saw him he was with the Pike boys,' Rose said, flicking a wasp off the jelly. 'You want to watch them, June. You know how they love to tease him.'

Sure enough, at that moment Dennis Pike came hurtling around the corner, laughing and shouting. His brother Frank came after him, followed by Danny who was doing his best to keep up, his face red with exertion.

'Come on, Danny. Catch!' Dora spotted the boy's cap flying through the air. Danny tried to grab for it but Frank got there first, snatching it out of mid-air before Danny had a chance.

'Oi, you two. Give it back!' she shouted. Dennis and Frank just laughed at her.

'We're only playin'!' Frank shouted back. 'He loves it, don't you, Danny? He knows it's just a game.' He dangled Danny's cap in front of his face, then snatched it away at the last minute. 'Gotta be quicker than that, Danny boy!'

He tossed the hat up high. It spun around in the cloudless sky, then started to come down. Dennis went to jump for it, but before he could grab it, a hand shot out and snatched it out of mid-air.

'Gotta be quicker than that,' Nick Riley said.

Dennis and Frank took one look at him, towering over them, and ran. Nick went over to where Danny was doubled up, gasping for breath, and put the cap back on his head.

'What have I told you about going near those boys?' Dora heard him say softly. 'You stay away from them, you hear me?'

'But ... they're my f-friends,' Danny said shakily, still fighting for breath.

Just at that moment the rest of the Pikes – Lettie, her husband Len and Ruby – came out of their house to join the party. Lettie carried a plate of sandwiches proudly aloft.

'Is that all she's brought?' Nanna muttered in disgust. 'Typical. That woman's as tight as a duck's–'

'Aren't you going to help me with the sausage rolls, Mum?' Rose interrupted her quickly, as Nanna and Lettie Pike exchanged evil stares across the table.

Dora was staring too, but in admiration of Ruby who looked stunning. Her fitted dress, white and covered in big splashy red roses, showed off every curve, while the daring scoop of the neckline barely contained the generous swell of her breasts.

'Oh, Ruby, you look like a film star!' she breathed.

'Thanks.' Ruby tugged at her short white gloves. Her mouth was painted the same red as her dress. 'You've got to make the effort, haven't you?'

'I feel like a right plain Jane next to you,' Dora said wryly.

'You look lovely,' Ruby complimented her absently, barely looking at her dress. 'Anyway, I'm only wearing this for one person's benefit. And that's him.'

She nodded to where Nick Riley was lifting another table into place.

'You fancy Nick Riley?' Dora said in disbelief.

'Doesn't everyone? Look at him, Dor. Look at those muscles. He's so strong. And so handsome.'

'Handsome is as handsome does, as far as I'm concerned. And Nick Riley's a right surly bugger!'

'I know. That's why I like him so much.' Ruby sighed. 'I've always liked the strong, silent type. And he's a mystery. He doesn't chase after me like all the other boys. He's hard to get. I like a challenge.'

Dora laughed. 'You mean you only want what you can't have?'

'Maybe,' Ruby conceded with a shrug. 'Except I mean to have Nick Riley. You see if I don't.'

'What are you going to do? Kidnap him and make him succumb to your womanly wiles?'

'If only! No, I'm going to work my magic on him. But I need you to help me.'

'Me? How?'

'I want to make sure I sit next to him at the party. But I know he'll want to sit next to Danny so I need you to get Danny to sit next to you instead.'

'Can't you just sit next to Danny as well?'

'Ugh! No, thanks. He gives me the creeps.' Ruby shuddered. 'Anyway, he'll only spill something or dribble down my dress. I can't have that, can I? No, it's best if you keep Danny busy. Keep him at the other end of the table, well away from us.'

'I don't think Nick likes Danny out of his sight.'

'He'll be all right about it if he knows he's with you. Nick trusts you. Anyway, I'll keep him so busy looking at me he won't even remember he's got a brother. Please, Dora? Will you do it?' Ruby batted her eyelashes appealingly.

'I suppose so,' Dora agreed. 'But I still don't know why you're bothering.'

The party was a great success. They crammed in along the length of the table, shoulder to shoulder, tucking into sandwiches, cakes, fruit jellies and blancmanges. There was lemonade for the kids, while beer flowed for the adults. They toasted the health of the King many times.

It was a pity Josie wasn't there to enjoy it, Dora thought. She still couldn't get her sister's face out of her mind. The hollow, despairing look in her eyes was one she'd seen in the mirror too many times.

She tried to push the thought from her mind

and enjoy the party. There was time to talk to Josie later, she decided.

Thanks to Ruby's deft shuffling, Nick ended up with her at the far end of the table, with Danny beside Dora at the other end. She didn't mind keeping an eye on him or helping him with his food, although she was conscious of Nick's eyes on them from the other end of the table as she cut up Danny's sandwiches and spooned out a portion of jelly for him.

Ruby, meanwhile, was doing her best to impress Nick, laughing and flirting and batting her eyelashes for all she was worth.

After they'd eaten, there were games and races for the children. Dora was dragged into joining in the three-legged race, fastened to her sister Bea, while Nick was attached to Danny. They screamed with laughter as they hobbled forward, trying to trip each other up. Dora pitched head first over the finish line, but Nick and Danny still beat them.

'Well done!' Ruby made sure she was the first to congratulate Nick, throwing her arms around him as if he'd just won the Grand National.

'All right?' Nick put out a hand to help Dora up as she struggled to her feet. 'Better luck next time, eh?'

'We'll see.' They gave each other a quick smile.

'Oi,' Ruby hissed in her ear. 'No flirting. He's mine, remember?'

Dora laughed. 'As if he'd look at me when you're wearing that dress!'

She was still laughing as she left them racing and headed back into the house to check on Josie. But her smile disappeared when she met

Alf stomping down the stairs.

Her blood turned to ice. 'Where's Josie?' she said.

'Still in bed, I s'pose. How should I know?' He shouldered past her into the kitchen. Dora followed him.

'What were you doing upstairs?' she demanded.

'If it's any business of yours, I went to get some of your Nan's indigestion pills. Got a right pain in my gut, I have.' He rubbed his hand across his belly under the stretched fabric of his shirt. 'You're meant to be a nurse. What d'you reckon it is?'

'I don't know and I don't care. What have you done to Josie?' Dora stood squarely in front of him, her eyes cold.

He stared back at her for a moment. Then a slow, nasty smile spread across his broad face. 'Why? You jealous?'

It took all her strength not to lash out at him. 'If I find out you've laid your filthy hands on her, I swear I'll–'

'All right, you two?' Rose came in through the back door, her hands full of empty plates. 'What you doing hiding in here? Why aren't you out enjoying the party with the others?'

'I came to check our Josie was all right,' Dora said, her eyes still fixed on Alf.

'Poor lamb. I'll go up to her.' Rose put the plates on the table and headed for the hall. 'You go out and check on Bea. She's howling her head off, I think she's fallen over.'

Luckily Bea was more annoyed at being pushed off a wall by the Pike boys than hurt. Dora listened to her cursing them as she examined her grazed knee.

'Don't you let Mum hear you saying words like that,' she warned as sternly as she could without smiling.

'Why not? Nanna says them all the time.'

Dora was still trying to think up a suitable reply when the back door crashed open and Rose came flying out of the house, ashen-faced.

'Come quick!' she screamed. 'Our Josie's gone!'

Chapter Thirty-Seven

The next few minutes were panic stations, as everyone ran around in different directions, all talking at once.

'She must have slipped out the back way.'

'Did anyone see her go?'

'How do you know she's run away?'

'I bet she's just gone down the shops.'

In the middle of it all sat her mother, her face drained of colour.

'I went up to check on her and she'd gone. She's taken all her clothes with her.' Her hand shook as she rubbed her eyes. Dora could tell she was trying hard not to cry in front of the neighbours.

'We'll find her, Mum. Don't worry,' she said.

Bea came running out of the house. 'I've found a note. It was under her pillow...'

Before she could give it to her mother, Alf had snatched it out of her hand. 'Let me have a look.' He ripped it open and read it. They all watched in tense silence as his eyes scanned the piece of paper, then handed it over to Rose.

'She says she thinks we'll all be better off without her.' Rose looked up at Dora. 'Oh, Dor, what can she mean? I know she's been a bit troublesome lately, but I didn't know it was this bad...'

Her voice trembled and she put her hand over her mouth. Alf came and stood behind her, resting his big paws on her shoulders. 'We'll find her,' he promised. 'I'll bring her home to you.'

I bet you were the one who drove her away. Dora stared at him, but he didn't meet her eye.

'We should split up into groups and search for her,' Len Pike suggested. 'We can cover more ground that way.'

'Good idea,' Dora's brother Peter said. 'I'll take the park.'

'I'll look in the market,' said his wife Lily.

'I'll go down by the canal,' Dora said.

'I'll come with you.' She hadn't realised Nick had come over to her side until she heard his voice behind her.

'I'll come too,' Ruby offered straight away.

'There's no need for three of us to go,' Nick turned to say to her. 'You're better off staying here in case Josie comes back.'

Dora saw the narrow-eyed look Ruby gave her, but was too worried about finding her sister to care who went with her.

The traffic seemed more noisy and threatening than usual as they ran down the main road. They vaulted over the low fence and sprinted down the canal path.

'I should have known,' Dora said as they ran. 'I

should have known something wasn't right.'

'How could you know?'

'I'm her big sister, I should have been able to see it. She wasn't herself. But I was so worried about getting to the stupid party, I didn't think...'

'Leave it,' Nick said. 'You're not doing anyone any good getting yourself in a state. Let's find her first.'

'What if we don't?'

'Someone will find her. She's got to be somewhere.'

But what if we're already too late? Panic made her run through the overgrown grass and weeds on the steep canal bank. She screamed out Josie's name over and over again, her voice echoing around the factory buildings that edged the narrow ribbon of green, fetid water.

Suddenly Nick grabbed her arm, pulling her back. Dora took one glance at his grim expression and her stomach plummeted.

Turning slowly, she saw what he was looking at. A red shape, arms outstretched, floating face down in the canal.

She recognised Josie's favourite red coat, the one she would never be parted from.

'Josie!' The scream was torn from Dora's throat. She heard Nick call her name, but was already hurtling down the bank, slipping and slithering on the damp grass. She reached the tow path and, without thinking, pulled off her shoes and dived in.

The water was dark and murky, choked with thick weeds and foul-smelling mud. Dora ploughed through it and grabbed for the coat.

Her hand closed around an empty sleeve.

'Josie!' She gulped in a mouthful of foul water. The sour, metallic taste made her gag. She could hear Nick calling to her from the bank and tried to make her way towards him. But her feet and clothes snagged on fallen branches, rusting hulks of metal and other old junk lurking forgotten beneath the murky surface, holding her back. She could feel her strength ebbing away as the churning water closed over her head.

Suddenly she felt strong hands gripping her, hauling her out of the water.

Dora sprawled, gasping, on the canal path. She could feel Nick's arms still wrapped around her. 'It's all right,' he said, over and over again, his voice thick. 'I've got you. You're safe.'

'I think I'm going to–' Dora sat bolt upright as her stomach lurched. She had barely managed to crawl into the long grass before she was violently sick.

Finally, when she was empty and wrung out, she crawled back to where he was waiting for her.

'S-sorry,' she said. Her teeth chattered so much she could hardly manage to speak. Cold seeped deep into her bones, making her whole body ache.

'Here.' Nick took off his jacket and draped it around her shaking shoulders.

'Th-thanks.' Dora tried to stand up, catching her breath as pain lanced through her.

Nick caught her as she stumbled. 'Your leg's bleeding,' he said.

She looked down at the blood trickling from a jagged cut on her calf. 'I must have caught it on a bit of metal in the water.' She touched the wound and bit her lip. 'It's not too deep, thank heavens.'

'It's bad enough,' Nick said. 'You need to go to hospital.'

'Later. I've g-got to find Josie first.' She tried again to stand, but it was too painful. As she stumbled once more, Nick's arms came around her.

'You're in no fit state. Your leg's in a right old mess. Look at you, you can't even stand on it.'

'I told you, I'll see to it later – Nick!' she yelped as he picked her up in his arms. 'What are you doing? Put me down!'

'I'm taking you to hospital.'

'No, you're bloody well not! Put me down!' Dora hammered on the hard wall of his chest, but he carried on walking, grimly ignoring her blows. 'I mean it, Nick. I've got to look for Josie.'

'There's plenty of people out looking for her already. And what good are you going to be, hopping about on one leg?'

'She's my sister. I can't just sit about doing nothing while she's out there somewhere.' Dora's voice caught on the lump in her throat.

'I'll find her,' Nick said softly. 'I promise you.' Their eyes met, and she knew he meant every word. With her arms wound around his neck, Dora could feel the warmth of his body, his muscles reassuringly solid. She felt the apprehension ebb out of her.

'Now,' Nick said gruffly, 'for once in your life, will you do as you're told?'

An hour later Dora was in Casualty, her leg stretched out in front of her as a nurse bathed the wound. She was horribly self-conscious about her wet, filthy dress, and her hair, free from its restraining ribbon, tumbled in a mass of muddy red curls.

'Ow!' Dora flinched as the salt water touched her raw flesh.

'Oh, for heaven's sake!' The boot-faced staff nurse didn't look up. 'Stop making such a fuss,' she said briskly.

Dora stared at the top of her starched cap and decided she would never, ever tell a patient not to make a fuss again.

The door opened and a bespectacled young doctor came in, stethoscope slung carelessly round his neck.

He looked Dora up and down, taking in her damp, bedraggled appearance. 'I'm Dr McKay. Would you be the young lady who's been swimming in the canal, by any chance?' he enquired in a soft Scottish accent.

'How did you guess?' Dora smiled back at him.

'Years of medical training.' He examined her leg. 'Hmm. The wound doesn't look too bad. Nurse Percival has, as usual, done a grand job of cleaning you up. But I reckon we should still give you a tetanus jab, just to be on the safe side.'

He nodded to the nurse, who went off to prepare the needle. The young man then sat down on a chair beside Dora. 'So why did you decide to take a dip? High spirits after the Jubilee, I suppose?' His eyes behind his spectacles were the warmest brown she had ever seen.

'My sister went missing.' She couldn't stop herself from blurting out the words.

'Oh.' Dr McKay looked dismayed. 'I'm sorry to

364

hear that. Has she been found?' Dora shook her head, not trusting herself to speak. 'How old is she?'

'Nearly fifteen.'

Nurse Percival returned with a tray containing the needle. Dr McKay picked it up, his eyes fixed on the narrow point as he gently thumbed the plunger. 'Now, this may sting a bit...'

Dora gritted her teeth and kept her eyes fixed on the wall as the needle went in.

'There, all done.' Dr McKay put the needle back on the tray. 'You were very brave, Miss Doyle.'

'Thank you, Doctor.'

As Dora reached the door, he suddenly said, 'She will turn up, you know.'

She turned back to look at him. 'Your sister,' he said. 'She'll come home as soon as she gets hungry. I dare say it's just a silly prank.'

He smiled encouragingly, and Dora smiled back. 'Yes, I expect you're right. Thank you, Doctor.'

But even as she said it, she knew she didn't mean it. There had been nothing high-spirited about the look on Josie's face earlier that day.

Chapter Thirty-Eight

Millie sat down on the pavement, took off her shoes and massaged her stockinged toes. Standing for hours for a glimpse of the royal procession had been almost as hard on her feet as a twelve-hour shift on the ward.

365

But she wouldn't have missed it for the world. It felt as if the whole of London had gathered to celebrate the King's Jubilee. Crowds lined the streets between Buckingham Palace and St Paul's Cathedral, old and young, families with their children perched on their shoulders to see the glittering ranks of guards on horseback and the carriages containing the Royal Family. The King was decked out in all his military finery, while Queen Mary looked as regal as ever in a plumed hat, her shoulders shrouded in pale fur. Their sons followed behind in another open carriage together with their wives, all waving as they drove past.

Millie and her friends had managed to find themselves a good spot on the stands close to Admiralty Arch, where they could watch the whole event.

'Isn't the Prince of Wales handsome?' Georgina Farsley sighed, as the carriage rattled past. 'But he looks so lonely, doesn't he? His brothers have their wives, and he has no one.'

'Don't you believe it,' grinned Sophia's fiancé David. 'He's certainly not short of female company from what I hear.'

'Mrs Simpson sees to that,' Seb added.

Millie had heard her father discussing Wallis Simpson with her grandmother. The future king's romance with 'that wretched American', as the Dowager Countess called her, was the talk of high society. Everyone had hoped that she might prove to be nothing more than a distraction, like Thelma Furness and Mrs Dudley Ward, and that the Prince would eventually grow weary of her. But a year on, her hold only seemed to grow stronger.

'I can't see the attraction myself,' Seb said. 'She always looks rather cruel to me.'

'And we all know you prefer blondes!' Sophia joked. Seb blushed. Georgina tossed her raven locks and looked furious.

'Daddy says if he doesn't come to his senses soon it might affect the succession,' Millie observed.

'I don't see why,' Georgina huffed. 'He should be allowed to marry whoever he likes.'

'It's not that simple,' Sophia explained patiently. 'Our King can't marry a divorcee.'

'Then the rules should be changed,' Georgina said firmly.

'If she really loved him, she'd give him up and allow him to do his duty to his country,' Millie said.

Georgina glared at her. 'Wallis Simpson is an acquaintance of my mother's,' she said. 'And believe me, she isn't ready to give up anyone.'

Millie caught Sophia's eye as Georgina turned her adoring gaze towards Seb. Poor Seb. Georgina Farsley was just as determined to get her man as Mrs Simpson.

Millie looked around, enjoying the spectacle of the crowds below them, and caught a glimpse of a familiar face across the road. Lucy Lane sat perched high in the stands opposite, beside a very stylish-looking woman in a fitted blue coat – her mother, Millie guessed. Their miserable faces were a stark contrast to all the cheering and waving going on around them.

Millie was waving her handkerchief and trying

to catch her eye when Sophia grabbed her arm. 'Everyone's following the procession to the palace,' he said. 'Let's go up The Mall and watch the King come out on to the balcony.'

Afterwards they joined hundreds of other revellers in St James's Park. It seemed as if no one wanted the party to end. All over the park, people were having picnics, playing games or just lazing on the grass together.

'Look at you,' David laughed, as Sophia carefully unpacked the wicker picnic basket. 'How domesticated you look. You'll make someone a wonderful wife one day.' He winked at her.

'Don't get too excited, it was our cook who prepared it all,' Sophia replied, peeling the muslin off a veal pie.

'Just think, you'll have a house and staff of your own soon,' Georgina sighed dreamily.

'Don't!' Sophia shuddered. 'I'm sure I'll be a perfectly useless housekeeper. The servants will all bully me mercilessly.'

'They won't, because they'll all adore you far too much.' David leant over and kissed the end of her nose.

'Ugh, do you have to?' Seb grimaced. 'People in love are rather sickening to watch.'

'You're just jealous.' Sophia screwed up the muslin pie wrapping and threw it at him. 'You should find a girl of your own, Seb. Then perhaps you wouldn't be so bitter.'

'And I don't think you'd have far to look either,' David added meaningfully. 'In fact, I suspect there's a girl not a million miles away who has claimed your heart already.'

'I'm sure I don't know what you mean,' Seb replied through tight lips, as Georgina simpered.

'He shouldn't tease Seb like that,' Millie whispered to Sophia as they handed round the plates. 'You know he's not keen on Georgina.'

Her friend smiled. 'I don't think David was talking about Georgina.'

Before Millie had a chance to reply, a cricket ball whistled past her ear and landed with a smack in the middle of the plate of sandwiches Sophia had just unwrapped, scattering them everywhere.

'I'm terribly sorry,' a voice called out. 'May we have our ball back, please?'

Millie looked up, squinting into the sun, as the young man jogged across the grass towards them. He was dressed casually in flannels, not a white coat in sight, but she would have known that tall, lanky frame anywhere.

'William?'

He turned around. 'Hello,' he said, breaking into a smile. 'Fancy seeing you. Although I suppose it's hardly surprising since half of London seems to be here.'

He grinned around at her friends, who were eyeing him curiously.

'Aren't you going to introduce us?' Sophia asked.

'This is William Tremayne,' Millie said. 'He's – er–' She searched for the right word. A friend? An acquaintance? Someone I tried to kiss one dark night when I'd had too much to drink?

'We work together at the Nightingale,' William finally finished for her.

'You're a doctor? How thrilling,' Georgina said.

369

'Would you like to join us?' Sophia invited graciously.

'No, thank you. My friends are waiting for me.' Far beyond them, under the trees, Millie recognised a few of the other junior doctors from the hospital, and a couple of nurses too.

Seb picked up the ball and held it out to William. 'You'll be wanting this, then?'

'What? Oh, yes. Thanks. I hope I didn't ruin your picnic?'

'I'm sure we can live without a few cucumber sandwiches,' Sophia smiled.

'William?' Amy Hollins sauntered over to them, looking pretty in a summer dress. She nodded a greeting at Millie and then turned to William. 'Hurry up. We're waiting to finish the game.'

'Just coming.' He looked down at the ball in his hand, then back at them. 'Would you like to come and play? We could use a decent bowler?'

'No, thanks,' Seb answered for them shortly.

'Oh. Well, if you're sure?' He glanced at Millie. 'I expect I'll see you back on the ward.'

'I'm sure you will. If I'm not stuck in the sluice as usual.'

'Is he an admirer of yours?' Georgina asked Millie, as they watched him walk away.

'Not at all. He's just a friend.' She kept her gaze fixed on William and Amy. She had her arm threaded possessively through his as they sauntered towards their group of friends.

'Don't be silly, Georgie,' Sophia said. 'You can see he's with that blonde girl.'

Millie turned to her sharply. 'Is he?'

'If he isn't now, he soon will be!' David laughed.

'She's certainly got her sights set on him. Poor fellow doesn't stand a chance. None of us ever do. We're just helpless victims to predatory females, aren't we, Seb?'

'If you say so,' Seb replied distractedly. His gaze was still fixed on William too.

'Are you saying I'm predatory?' Sophia pinched David's arm, making him yelp.

'What? Of course not, my darling. I'm just saying I'm helpless,' he protested.

'There's nothing helpless about William Tremayne,' Millie said quietly.

Georgina looked at her. 'Really? That sounds rather intriguing. I must say, he did seem to be devouring you with his eyes, Millie. Perhaps we should join them?' she said, glancing over to where William was going in to bat. 'After all, we mustn't stand in the way of true love, must we?'

'Do shut up, Georgina,' Millie and Seb said together.

Millie returned to the nurses' home just before nine in the evening. She hadn't been planning to go back so early, but it'd been a long day and the champagne had given her a headache. While the others went off for dinner and dancing, Millie got a bus back to Bethnal Green. She refused Seb's offer to escort her, to Georgina's obvious relief.

She was looking forward to seeing Helen's face when she walked in before lights out, and to hearing all about Dora's street party. But instead Millie walked in to a full-scale argument between her room mates.

'You can't go,' Helen was saying.

'Well, I can't stay here, can I?' Dora was shrugging on her coat. Her leg was bandaged and she was limping badly.

'And what are we supposed to say to Sister Sutton if she comes looking for you?'

'Say what you like. I'm still going.'

Millie looked from one to the other. 'What's going on?' she asked.

Helen rolled her eyes. 'Thank heavens you're back. She might listen to you. Tell her she can't just walk off into the night whenever she feels like it.'

'My little sister's missing. What am I supposed to do, sit here on my backside while everyone else goes out looking for her?'

Millie stared at her. 'Your sister's missing?'

She nodded. 'Josie disappeared during the street party. They've been out searching for her all day.' She swallowed hard. Millie could tell she was trying her best to stop herself from crying.

'I know it's awful,' Helen said. 'But you won't do any good if you–'

'Of course you must go and look for her,' Millie interrupted. 'Do you want me to come too?'

'What?' Helen's voice rose. 'Now just a minute...'

'No, thanks,' Dora said, ignoring her. 'But maybe you could leave the window open for when I get back?'

'Of course.' Millie nodded. 'Oh, and you'd better take this.' She pulled her torch out of her bag. 'It's a life-saver when you're scrabbling around in the dark, trying to find the drainpipe.'

'Thanks.' Dora tried to smile, but Millie could

see the worry in her green eyes.

'You're both mad,' Helen declared flatly. 'If you get caught...'

Dora turned to her. 'I'll deal with that if it happens,' she said grimly. 'First I've got to find my sister.'

No one was asleep in Griffin Street. Light spilled from every window and open door on to the street, illuminating the tables and chairs from the abandoned street party. People were milling in and out of the open back door of number twenty-eight. The neighbours who weren't searching the streets were gathered in the kitchen and the yard, trying to offer whatever comfort they could.

In the kitchen, Dora's mother sat like a pale, frozen statue, staring fixedly into the empty grate, her arms clenched around Bea and Little Alfie as if she were terrified to let them out of her sight. Alf and June Riley were with her, while Nanna Winnie and Dora's sister-in-law Lily bustled in and out of the scullery, keeping themselves busy brewing up tea for everyone.

Rose looked up sharply as her eldest girl came into the kitchen.

'Dora?' She looked dazed. 'What are you doing here?'

'I couldn't sit at the hospital doing nothing. I wanted to see if there was any news?' She glanced around. June Riley shook her head sadly.

'Everyone's still out searching,' she said. 'Your Peter, the Pike boys, all the neighbours, my Nick. No one's giving up 'til she's found.'

Dora turned to Alf. 'Why aren't you out look-

373

ing, too?'

He shifted his bulk guiltily in his armchair. 'Someone's got to stay with your mum, haven't they? Besides, I'm not feeling too good. My gut's still playing me up something awful.'

Dora glanced at Nanna Winnie, who rolled her eyes but said nothing.

'Well, I'm going out to look,' Dora said.

'Do you have to?' Her mother looked up, her eyes glazed with fear. 'I don't like to think of you out there on those streets at this time of night. It's bad enough our Josie's missing, but if anything happened to you, too—'

'I'll be right as rain, Mum,' Dora reassured her. 'Anyway, I can't sit around and do nothing until our Josie's home safe and sound.' Unlike some people, she added silently with a filthy look in Alf's direction.

She needed Millie's torch as she tramped the streets from the canal to Victoria Park. Now and then she met one of the neighbours or a gaggle of men from the pub or the market, all out looking too. Word had soon spread around the local area and everyone had taken to the streets to find Josie Doyle.

And they *would* find her. Dora wouldn't allow herself to think anything different. Although the image of Josie's red coat floating in the dark water of the canal still haunted her.

How many times had she stood on that canal bank and thought about ending it all herself, when she didn't think she could stand another day of Alf's abuse? She only prayed Josie hadn't got that desperate yet.

But it became harder and harder to stay optimistic as the hours went by and the dark streets began to empty. By midnight, even the most intrepid searchers were heading home to snatch a few hours' sleep before going out again at dawn.

Except one. Down on the waste ground behind the railway line, Dora spotted a solitary figure emerging from one of the disused railway sheds, silhouetted in the moonlight.

'Nick?' She called out to him and he came to her, picking his way over the rubbish-strewn ground.

'What are you doing here? Why aren't you back at the hospital–' The silvery moonlight caught the look of panic in his face. 'Josie's not...?'

Dora shook her head. 'She's not been found yet. But I couldn't just sit around and do nothing. Not while our Josie's out there on her own–' she broke off, her voice catching.

'I thought she might be hiding out down here.' She was grateful that Nick pretended not to notice her trembling lip. 'It's where I always used to come when I wanted to get away from my old man.'

Dora looked up at his haggard face, etched with exhaustion. 'You must be dead on your feet,' she said. 'Why didn't you pack up and go home with the others?'

'I promised you I'd find her, didn't I?'

His eyes met hers in the moonlight. For a moment neither of them spoke. Somewhere in the distance, a train rumbled past, making the ground tremble beneath their feet.

'We'll look together.' She pulled away from him, breaking the spell.

Even Millie's torch was no match for the darkness as the moon became shrouded in cloud. Dora tripped and stumbled over the uneven ground, and Nick put out a hand to steady her. After a while it was easier for her to go on holding on to his arm. His presence beside her made her feel safe.

But knowing that her sister had no one to hold on to made her feel even worse.

'She'll be so frightened.' She spoke her thoughts aloud. 'She never liked the dark. I used to tease her all the time about ghosts and bogey men who wandered around the streets after dark, lying in wait for kids...' She put her hand over her mouth to stifle her sob of despair.

'Shh.' Nick's arm came around her shoulders, pulling her into the reassuring, solid warmth of his body. As she leaned against him she could feel the steady beat of his heart against her cheek. 'You're tired, you should go home.'

'I'm not going anywhere until we find Josie.'

She felt the rise and fall of his chest as he let out a sigh. 'At least let me walk you back to Griffin Street,' he said. 'You never know, there might be some news.'

There was. As they turned the corner, Dora recognised the black bicycle leaning up against the wall outside their house.

'The police are here!' She pulled away from Nick and started to run, tripping and stumbling over the cobbles in the darkness.

They all turned to face her as she crashed into the kitchen. Including the policeman who stood in the centre of the room, towering over everyone

376

in his helmet, his short dark cape thrown around his shoulders.

But there was no sign of her sister.

All the terror and anxiety she'd been holding back crashed over her like a great tidal wave. She felt her legs buckle and would have sunk to the ground if Nick hadn't been there to hold her up.

Her mother came forward, tears shining in her eyes. 'It's all right,' she whispered, hugging Dora. 'They've found her. She's safe.'

'But I don't understand. Where is she...?'

'She's ended up at your Auntie Brenda's,' her mum explained. 'Can you believe she walked all the way to Loughton?'

'And now the cheeky little so-and-so is putting her foot down and says she won't come home.' Nanna Winnie folded her arms across her chest. 'If that don't beat everything, after what she's put us all through. I'll have a few words to say to her when she gets back here, I can tell you. Spoiling our Jubilee Day, and making us all in with worry–' But beneath her angry bluster Dora could see the relief on her grandmother's face.

'Stop it, Mum. It's enough that she's safe.' Rose Doyle released Dora and turned to the policeman. 'Thank you, Constable, for letting us know,' she said stiffly, remembering her manners. 'We're very grateful, we really are.'

'I'm just glad I could bring you a bit of good news.' He glanced around at them, touched his helmet and then let himself out of the back door.

'I wonder why she went all the way to Loughton?' Rose said, when he'd gone. 'It's a mystery to me, it really is.'

'It's a mystery to me why she don't want to come back,' Nanna put in.

Dora glanced at Alf. It was no mystery to her why her sister had run away. And it wasn't to him, either. She could see it written all over his face. It was all she could do not to grab the poker and smash him with it.

'We'll see about that,' he said. 'First thing tomorrow I'm going down to Loughton to fetch her. I'll bring her home, don't you worry, love,' he reassured his wife. 'Even if I have to drag her all the way–'

'No!' Dora hadn't realised she'd shouted it out until she saw the looks of surprise on everyone's faces as they stared at her.

'Why don't you let her stay with Auntie Brenda for a while?' she reasoned, forcing herself to calm down. 'Give her time to sort herself out a bit? Maybe you could take the kids over to Loughton and visit for a few days,' she said to her mother. 'You could have a proper chat with her, find out what's wrong.'

'I know what's wrong,' Nanna Winnie grumbled. 'She needs a good hiding, that's what's wrong.'

'It might be an idea to go down there I s'pose.' Rose turned to her husband. 'What d'you reckon, Alf?'

'Well–'

'I'm sure Alf wouldn't say no to the idea of you having a holiday?' Dora put in quickly. 'I reckon she deserves it, don't you?'

She looked across the room at Alf. He was gnawing at his thumbnail, a sure sign that he was aggravated.

'Well, I think it's a grand idea,' Nanna Winnie put in. 'Our Dora's right, you could do with a break, Rose. And you might be able to talk some sense into Josie, too. We'll manage all right here for a few days, won't we, Alf?' She gave her son-in-law a toothless grin.

'I s'pose.' The thwarted, angry glance he shot at Dora was enough to stop anyone in their tracks, but she didn't care. At least this way she could keep Josie safely out of his filthy hands for a while.

Behind her, Nick cleared his throat. In all the excitement she'd almost forgotten he was there. 'I'd best be off, then,' he mumbled.

Dora followed him out of the back door. 'Thanks for helping to look for her,' she said.

'I promised you, didn't I?'

'All the same, it was nice of you.'

'Nice?' His mouth curled. 'That's not a word people use about me too often.'

'Well, I think you're nice.'

'Do you?' He was standing very close to her, looking down at her in the darkness. 'Do you really like me, Dora?'

''Course I do.'

The air crackled with tension. Slowly, as if drawn by a force she couldn't control, she turned her face up to his. She saw his eyes darken and knew he was going to kiss her. She also knew it was what she wanted more than anything in the world.

He lowered his head to meet hers, blocking out the light from the moon. But no sooner had his lips touched hers than Dora felt suffocated, overwhelmed. Memories flooded back, crashing over her like waves, drowning her. Alf Doyle pressing down on her, his kisses hard and wet and tasting of stale beer, his tongue invading her mouth until she couldn't breathe...

'No, stop! Get away from me!' She struggled against Nick, pushing him off. He staggered back, his face blank with shock.

'Sorry,' he said gruffly. 'I thought you wanted me to.' He stepped away from her, his hands dropping to his sides. 'I must have got the wrong idea.'

'I'm sorry,' Dora longed to talk to him, to explain. But the words stuck in her throat.

'No, it's me who's sorry. I didn't mean— I'd never—' He turned away. 'Like I said, I got the wrong idea. It won't happen again.'

'Nick, wait!' she called after him, but he was already stumbling away into the darkness.

Chapter Thirty-Nine

Helen sat in the front pew during Evensong, watching the dust particles dance in the beams of jewel-coloured light from the stained-glass windows, and listened to her father preaching about sin.

She didn't dare meet his eye because she was sure he would know she was the biggest sinner of all. Because she wasn't thinking about how God sent His only son Jesus Christ to die for her; she was wondering how soon she could get back to London to meet Charlie Denton.

She had forgotten when she'd arranged to meet Charlie that she had the whole of Sunday off, and that meant going home to visit her parents. There was no question of getting out of it; her mother would want to know why Helen couldn't come, and ask all sorts of questions, and Helen would end up having to tell her everything because she was such a hopeless liar in the face of Constance's merciless questioning.

It had been hard enough keeping the truth from her all day. Helen had tried to keep as busy as she could: handing out prayer books before the morning service, staying behind to tidy up the church afterwards, and running errands around the parish. Anything to prevent her from having to be alone with her mother.

She was almost too nervous to eat her lunch. She sat at the big mahogany table in the dining room opposite William, ploughing her way steadily through her roast beef and Yorkshire pudding, trying desperately not to make eye contact with anyone. And all the time her thoughts kept straying treacherously to that evening. What should she wear? Where would they go? Would Charlie even turn up? Even though he'd told her how much he was looking forward to it, she still couldn't quite believe he really meant it.

'What on earth are you smiling at, Helen?'

She looked up. Her mother was watching her from the other end of the table.

'Nothing, Mother,' she said quickly.

'You seem rather giddy today. Are you sure you're not sickening for something?' Constance's sharp features creased in a frown. 'You are keep-

381

ing regular, I hope? I wonder if perhaps you need an aperient?'

'I'm quite well, Mother, thank you.' Helen caught William's eye across the table and fought to conceal a smile. Only her mother would think happiness was an ailment that needed to be treated with a laxative.

Now William sat slumped in the pew beside her, his arms folded, eyes closed. Helen nudged him sharply.

'Eh? What? Amen.' He woke up with a start and snatched up his prayer book as it slid off his knee. 'Is it finished?' he mumbled.

'No, and you could at least pretend to listen.' Helen frowned at him. 'What time are you going back to London?'

'As soon as I can decently get away – why?'

'Can I have a lift back with you?'

'I thought you usually caught the later train?'

'I can't this evening. I'm – meeting someone,' Helen replied evasively.

'Oh, yes?' William's eyebrows rose. 'And who is this someone exactly?'

'Shhh!' Before she could reply, her mother shot them a silencing look.

'Never you mind,' Helen whispered. 'Now can I have a lift or can't I?'

William nodded. 'Bessie and I will be glad of your company. Especially if I have to push her all the way up Richmond Hill like last time. Let's try and make ourselves scarce straight after the service, shall we?'

But no such luck. After Evensong, they had to join their parents in greeting the congregation as they filed out of the church.

Helen knew this was the part her mother enjoyed the most, dispensing goodwill to the parishioners who deserved it, and judgment on those who didn't. Very few escaped Constance Tremayne's sharp eye and even sharper tongue.

'Ah, Mrs Ellis, how lovely to see you.' She picked out a harassed-looking, middle-aged woman who was trying to shuffle past, avoiding her eye. 'How are you? And how is young Margaret enjoying married life? Such a pity she couldn't get married in church, but I suppose register offices are quick if nothing else. And under the circumstances speed was rather of the essence, wasn't it?' Constance's voice dripped with sympathy and concern, oblivious to the other woman's blushing face. 'Hopefully once the baby is born we can look forward to arranging a christening?'

As the woman darted off, flustered, Constance turned to Helen. 'Her daughter is a fast piece. Got herself pregnant by a park keeper, can you believe?'

'At least he married her,' Helen said mildly, then flinched as her mother pounced on her remark.

'That makes it acceptable, does it? Not in my book it doesn't. Not in the Lord's book either. A sin is a sin, Helen, no matter how it's dressed up afterwards. Now that girl's poor mother can't hold her head up in her own church any more.' She fixed Helen with such a look, she felt herself wilting with shame. It was all she could do not to fall on her knees and confess her own sin there and then.

Finally she and William managed to get away,

and headed back towards London.

'Who is he then?' her brother asked as soon as they'd pulled out of the sweeping drive of the vicarage.

'I don't know what you're talking about,' Helen said primly.

'Oh, come on, Hels. You've been either as nervous as a cat or grinning like an idiot all day. And I saw the way you blushed when Mother started talking about Mrs Ellis' fast daughter. So who is he? Do I know him?' The colour drained from William's face. 'Please don't tell me it's a medical student? I'm not having my sister being led astray by one of those scoundrels.'

Helen laughed. 'No, it isn't a doctor or a medical student, so you needn't worry about protecting my honour. His name's Charlie.' Even saying it made her smile.

'Charlie, eh? And what does he do, this Charlie?'

'He used to work in a factory. But now he's just started at his uncle's joinery business.' She explained about Charlie's accident, and how they'd met.

'I can see why you didn't want Mother to know about this new boyfriend of yours,' William said, his eyes fixed on the road. 'I don't think she'd approve at all.'

'You won't tell her, will you?' Helen pleaded. 'I mean, he's not even my boyfriend. It's only one date. He probably won't want to see me again after tonight. I just wanted to know what it was like – you know, to go out with someone.'

'Don't worry, Sis, your secret's safe with me.

God knows, you've kept enough of mine over the years.' William reached out and patted her knee. 'Anyway, who's to say it's just one night? You never know, this could be the beginning of a beautiful romance.'

'I doubt it!' Helen said ruefully. But at the same time, she couldn't help wishing that were true.

They made good progress towards the city, and Helen stopped looking at her watch. But just as they reached the outskirts of Putney, the car began to slow ominously.

'Come on, Bessie,' William urged. 'Come on, old girl. Don't let me down now.'

Don't let me down either, Helen prayed silently. But God had obviously decided to pay her back for daydreaming in church, because Bessie began to make an ominous grinding sound.

'I'd better take a look,' William said, pulling over to the side of the road.

Helen sat on the grass verge and watched as he examined the car.

'It's not as bad as I thought,' he said. 'We've got a puncture.'

'And that's not bad news?' Helen asked.

'No, because I can fix it. All we need to do is change the wheel.'

'Is that all?' Helen gave a hollow laugh.

'I'll have it done in a jiffy.' William stripped down to his shirtsleeves. 'Even less if you help me?'

Helen got wearily to her feet. 'I might as well, I suppose. What do I have to do?'

She helped him jack the car up and unscrew the nuts holding the wheel in place. But anxiety made her all thumbs.

'If you're going to keep dropping everything this is going to take even longer,' William snapped, as she dived to retrieve a nut that had rolled under the car. 'Calm down, I'm sure your young man will wait for you.'

'What if he doesn't?' Helen was already convinced Charlie was going to stand her up.

'Hels, he's been waiting for you for three months. Another ten minutes isn't going to make any difference. On second thoughts, make that half an hour,' he sighed, as Helen dropped another wheel nut.

As she helped him lift the heavy wheel into place and held it steady, she said, 'How do you know if someone likes you?'

William grinned. 'Are you asking me for advice? That's a novelty.'

'I won't ask if you're going to make fun of me.'

William paused for a moment to think. Then he said, 'When the evening's over and you're walking away from him, take a look back. If he's looking back at you, too, that means he likes you.'

'Is that it?' Helen laughed.

'That's it.' William tightened the last nut and stood up, brushing down his trousers. 'Come on, we'd better get going. I think you're going to need to get changed before this date of yours.'

Helen looked down at her oil-streaked dress in dismay. 'Oh, no! I won't have time to change.' Tears of frustration pricked her eyes. She'd planned this night so carefully, daydreamed about how Charlie would look at her when he saw her again. And now it was all ruined.

He was sitting on a bench outside the hospital

gates when they pulled up, a sagging bunch of flowers in his hands. Helen lurched forward in her seat, craning her neck to look at him.

'I take it that's your swain?' William was amused. 'He looks as nervous as you are. Probably thinks you've stood him up, poor chap.'

He pulled up alongside Charlie. Helen barely waited for him to stop the car before she tumbled out, tongue-tied and flustered.

'I – I'm so sorry I'm late,' she stammered, fumbling with her shoe, which had got caught in the hem of her dress. 'I know I look an awful mess, but I can explain...'

'It's entirely my fault, I'm afraid.' William got out of the car. 'We got a puncture on our way back from Richmond, and I made my sister help me change the wheel. I can assure you, she usually puts a lot more effort into her appearance.'

'That's all right. I'm just glad you're here.' He handed her the flowers. 'For you,' he said.

'Thank you. They're lovely.'

William stuck out his hand. 'Pleased to meet you. I'm William Tremayne, Helen's brother.'

'Charlie Denton.' Charlie got up slowly, leaning on his stick for support. He looked rather dazed as he shook William's hand. He glanced over his shoulder at Bessie, parked at the kerb. 'Nice motor,' he commented.

'Meet Bessie, my pride and joy. When she's not breaking down and leaving me stranded in the middle of nowhere, that is.'

Helen left the pair of them discussing Bessie's relative merits, and made a dash to the nurses' home.

Millie was in their room, reading an anatomy textbook.

'Can you believe there are so many bones in the human body?' she sighed. 'And why do they all have to have such stupid names?' She looked up at Helen and her mouth fell open. 'Crikey, what happened to you?'

'Don't ask.' Helen frantically unbuttoned her dress. 'I'm supposed to be going out with Charlie tonight, and I've got nothing to wear.' She threw open the wardrobe and stared inside in despair. The few decent dresses she had were all at home in Richmond – her mother had decided very firmly that she would have no need of them while she was training. 'After all, it's not as if you're going gallivanting around London, is it?' she'd sniffed.

'Let me see.' Millie put down her book and stood up to look in Helen's wardrobe. 'You're right, it's not exactly inspiring, is it?'

'I'll just have to wear this one.' Helen pulled out a pea green dress covered in tiny white spots. It was dull but serviceable. 'It'll do, won't it?'

'If you're going off to visit his maiden aunt, I'm sure it will be very suitable.'

Helen blinked back tears. 'You're not helping!'

'Then put that horrid frock back in your wardrobe and leave it to me.' Millie flung open the other wardrobe where she kept her clothes. Dora and Helen shared a cupboard for their meagre assortment of dresses, skirts and blouses, but Millie's lavish wardrobe of designer gowns had its own home.

'What are you doing?' Helen asked.

'Finding something for you to wear.' Millie rifled through the rail, pulling out and rejecting garments. 'My grandmother ordered me far too many clothes when I did the Season, and insisted I brought them all with me when I came here. I knew they'd come in useful one day ... ah, what about this one?'

She pulled out a dress in a deep burnt orange colour. 'I could never wear it because the colour was far too strong for me. But you could carry it off beautifully with your dark colouring. Here, try it on.'

Helen wanted to argue, but she had no time to demur. And besides, she had never seen such a beautiful dress, let alone worn one.

It was even more beautiful when she'd slipped it on. Millie was right, the colour suited her perfectly. It was made from a soft, fluid fabric that flowed sensuously over her slim body in a way she had never thought possible in the stiff cottons and sensible wools her mother always made her wear.

'Are you sure it's quite decent?' she whispered, unable to take her eyes off her reflection.

'Of course it is. My grandmother would never let me wear anything that wasn't the height of modesty,' Millie said primly. 'Now take it off again and go and wash your face. Then I'll put some lipstick and powder on for you – don't worry, I won't make you look like a tart!' She laughed at Helen's fearful expression, and clapped her hands in joy. 'Oh, this is so exciting, isn't it? Cinderella, you shall go to the ball!'

Chapter Forty

When Helen hurried outside ten minutes later, William and Charlie were leaning against the car, chatting like old friends.

'Sorry to keep you waiting.' She rushed up to them, still smoothing down her dress. They both turned to look at her.

'Oh, my.' Her brother let out a long whistle. 'I didn't recognise you, Hels. My sister scrubs up rather well, wouldn't you say, Charlie?'

Helen watched Charlie's face anxiously. She was still worried that she was overdressed, but the admiring look in his eyes told her she'd got it just right.

'I'll say,' he said. He smiled at her. He looked very attractive himself in a suit and tie, his sandy hair neatly brushed back from his broad, handsome face. Helen felt a tingle of anticipation. This was really happening. She was actually going on a proper date with Charlie Denton!

'Right, well, I'll leave you to it.' They both tore their eyes away from each other to look momentarily at William. 'Have a pleasant evening. And see you look after her, Denton, or you'll have me to answer to.'

'I will,' Charlie promised.

'And you,' William whispered to Helen as he got into his car. 'You see you look after him, too. You've got a good one there, Hels. And there aren't too many of them around.'

He drove off, leaving them alone. Suddenly Helen felt rather awkward and self-conscious, standing there in her borrowed dress, all done up with lipstick and powder. Especially as Charlie didn't seem able to take his eyes off her. She touched her nose, wondering if she still had a smudge of oil there.

'You look beautiful,' he said softly.

'Thank you.'

'I wasn't sure if you were going to come. When you were late I thought you might have changed your mind.'

'I thought you'd change your mind and decide not to wait for me,' Helen confessed.

Charlie grinned. 'Never! I've waited three months for this. So where do you want to go?'

'Wherever you like.' Helen shrugged happily.

'Well, I'm not much for dancing at the moment, but we could go to the pictures, or I could treat you to tea?' His blue eyes searched hers anxiously. For the first time it struck Helen that he was as nervous as she was.

'It's a lovely evening. Why don't we just go for a walk in the park?' she suggested. 'If you're up to walking, that is?'

'I reckon the exercise would do me good. But are you sure? I know most girls would expect a fellow to spend a bit of cash on them, show them a good time. I know my Sally...' He stopped. 'Anyway, I don't want you going back to that nurses' home and telling them all I don't know how to treat a girl properly,' he mumbled, blushing.

'I promise I won't,' Helen reassured him. 'It's

391

far too nice to sit in a stuffy old cinema.'

He grinned. 'The park it is, then.' He crooked his arm. 'You'll have to walk this side of me, I'm afraid. I know a gentleman should walk next to the road, but I need that hand for my stick. If you don't mind?'

'Of course I don't mind.' Helen put her hand under his arm and they walked slowly along the street together. He seemed to be managing very well, walking with only a slight limp.

'How are you coping with the prosthetic?' she asked. 'You're not in any pain or anything?'

He sent her a wry sideways look. 'We're not in hospital now, remember, Nurse Tremayne?'

'Sorry,' Helen smiled apologetically. 'Old habits die hard, I suppose.'

'Yes, well, you're my girl now, not my nurse.'

My girl. Helen savoured the words as they crossed the road and strolled through the ornate wrought-iron park gates. It was a fine early summer's evening, and Victoria Park was still full of families enjoying the fresh air. They stopped for a moment to watch the boats on the lake.

'Do you row?' Helen asked.

'I haven't for a long time. When we were first courting, me and Sal–' He stopped himself short. 'I'm sorry,' he said, his face colouring.

'You can talk about her, you know.' Helen squeezed his arm. 'You were engaged to be married. You're bound to mention her name sometimes.' She looked across the water, sparkling in the low evening sunlight. 'I don't think I've ever been in a rowing boat before,' she mused.

'What, never?' Charlie stared at her. Helen

shook her head.

'My mother always said it was too dangerous.'

'Not if you do it properly. I'll take you one day. You'll be safe with me.'

Helen smiled at him. I know I will, she thought. She gazed at his profile as he looked across the water. She hoped he wasn't thinking about Sally.

'In fact,' Charlie said, 'why don't we do it now?'

'What?' Helen said, half laughing. 'Are you serious? The park will be closing soon.'

'Not for another half an hour or so. We've got plenty of time for a quick spin around the lake. What do you say?'

Helen looked down at her dress. 'I'm not really dressed for rowing!'

'Then you can just sit there and look beautiful while I do all the hard work. Unless you really don't care to?' He frowned, suddenly anxious. 'I want you to enjoy tonight. And if you'd rather do something else...'

Helen looked from him to the boats and back again. Tonight was a time for new experiences, she decided. 'Why not?'

'That's my girl!' Charlie grinned.

Helen almost changed her mind once he'd purchased two tickets from the small booth and she was stepping into the rickety little boat. It swayed and rocked under her feet, nearly knocking her off balance.

'Why won't it keep still?' she laughed.

'Wouldn't be much fun if it did!' Charlie put out his hand to steady her. 'Come on, if I can do it with one leg, you can do it with two!'

They were finally seated and set off, Charlie

pulling strongly on the oars until they were gliding over the water. Fine golden hairs glistened on his strong forearms as they pulled the oars back and forth.

Helen took off her glove and let her fingers trail in the water, watching the dark shapes of the fish darting about beneath them. A few curious ducks paddled by to watch them, then swam off again.

'Well? What do you think?' Charlie asked her.

'It's lovely.' Helen lifted her face to the low evening sun, dappling through the trees. 'It's all really lovely.'

She hadn't known what to expect from her date, but this was far better than anything she could have imagined.

'I don't mind being on the water myself,' Charlie said. 'I don't feel as awkward as I do when I'm walking around. No one's looking at me out here.'

Helen regarded him sympathetically. 'Are you still finding it hard to get used to?' she asked.

'I don't know if I'll ever get used to it, to be honest. I have good days and bad days, like you do with anything else. It's helped a lot, my uncle giving me a job at his joinery firm. I've always been good with my hands, and this is my chance to learn a proper skill. Makes me feel a bit less useless when I'm not earning my own living.' He smiled at her. 'Hark at me, going on!'

'I like listening to you.'

He shook his head. 'But you don't want to hear me moaning. I'm trying to impress you, remember?'

'It would impress me more if we didn't keep

going round in circles,' Helen teased.

'Oh, really?' Charlie's brows rose questioningly. 'If Madam is not happy with the service, perhaps she'd like to have a go herself?'

Helen saw the glint of challenge in his eyes. 'Perhaps she would,' she said, reaching for the oars.

It took a bit of practice, much laughter and rocking of the boat before she got the hang of it. Charlie's hands covered hers as he showed her how to pull back and forth with the oars.

'It's hard work on the arms,' he warned her.

'Not when you're used to hauling people in and out of baths!' Helen replied.

She would have liked to stay in the boat forever, with Charlie, the world drifting past, feeling the sun on her face and hearing the pleasant sound of laughter and birdsong. But all too soon the boat keeper was calling them in, telling them the park was going to be closing in ten minutes.

Helen was worried their date was going to end, too, but then Charlie shyly asked if she would like to have something to eat.

'I know a little cafe near here that's open till nine,' he said. 'It's nothing fancy, but the food's nice.'

'It sounds perfect,' Helen said, taking his arm.

And it was. Charlie was right, the cafe was nothing fancy, with its scrubbed tables and tiled floor. But it was quiet, and the egg and chips were delicious, and even if they'd tasted like sawdust it wouldn't have mattered because she was with Charlie.

They talked endlessly. Helen couldn't believe

she'd ever worried that they might sit in awkward silence with nothing to say to each other. They talked and talked, and laughed until their sides ached over the silliest of things. They were still talking and laughing when the proprietor of the cafe, a large Italian man called Antonio with the broadest cockney accent Helen had ever heard, very politely informed them that he wanted to close up and go home.

Charlie walked Helen back to the hospital through the darkened streets of Bethnal Green. 'I'm sorry it wasn't a posh night out,' he said.

'I didn't mind. I enjoyed it.'

'I mind. You're a proper lady, and you deserve the best.' He paused for a moment. 'The truth is, I've been a bit skint since I lost my job. I'm doing better now I'm working again, but I'm not exactly flush just yet.' He turned to look at her, his face shadowed in the silvery lamplight. 'But I will do better next time, if you give me another chance? I might not be able to treat you to tea at The Ritz just yet, but I reckon I'll be able to stretch to a couple of tickets for the pictures?' He looked anxious. 'What do you say? Will you go out with me again?'

She hadn't meant to say yes. This was meant to be their one and only date. But somehow she found herself nodding eagerly. 'Yes, please,' she said.

Helen walked away from him, through the hospital gates and up the broad sweep of driveway that led to the main hospital building. Shaded lights glowed in the ward windows above her. Happiness rose inside her like a bubble in her chest, until she wanted to laugh out loud, just to let it out.

Before she went through the archway in the main building that led into the courtyard beyond, she remembered what William had said. Steeling herself for disappointment, she cautiously looked back over her shoulder.

Charlie was standing at the gates, outlined by the glow of the lamplight, leaning heavily on his stick, watching her.

Chapter Forty-One

'Guess what? I'm getting an award!'

Lucy Lane made the announcement from her usual position at the head of the table in the dining room, her voice rising imperiously over the clatter of knives and forks. No one responded. They were all too used to Lucy's bragging to bother being impressed any more.

'The Board of Trustees is awarding prizes to the top student from each year on Founder's Day,' Lucy went on, oblivious to their lack of interest. 'They're giving it to Patterson in the third year, Tremayne in second year, and me.' She beamed around at them all. A couple of the students nodded politely, the others just went on eating. 'They're giving out the prizes at the Founder's Day party. Our parents are being invited to watch us. I expect my mother will absolutely insist I have a new dress!' She sighed, as if the whole business

397

was simply too exhausting.

'Listen to her, she's off again.' Katie rolled her eyes at Dora. 'I really wish someone would take her down a peg or two.'

Dora didn't reply. For once, Lucy's bragging washed over her. She had far more important things on her mind.

Today her mum and the kids were due home from their holiday in Loughton, and Dora was anxious to visit and find out how Josie was getting on.

She hoped her mum had let her stay on with Auntie Brenda a bit longer. Anything to keep her out of Alf's clutches.

She was certain in her own mind that he had turned his attentions to her sister. She tried not to think about what poor little Josie had gone through. But over the past three weeks her nightmares had started again. Only this time it was her sister's haunted face that woke her up screaming.

Bea was playing out with some other children from their street when Dora arrived in Griffin Street. She heard her little sister's voice before she'd even turned the corner, bossing everyone about. They were taking turns to bowl a hoop made from the metal rim of an old bicycle wheel. But as soon as she saw Dora, Bea abandoned the game and ran up the street to greet her.

'We've got a hoop, look! Although it's mine really,' she added with a warning glare at the children who hovered nearby. 'I found it.'

But Dora wasn't listening. Her attention was fixed on the skinny, dark-haired girl sitting on the kerb, shoulders hunched, her knees drawn up under her chin.

Dora's stomach plummeted. 'Josie?'

Bea glanced over her shoulder. 'No use talking to her. She don't want to play. Just sits there looking miserable. She's hardly said a dickie bird since we left Auntie Brenda's.' She pulled a face, then turned to Dora, her green eyes brightening. 'You'll play with us, won't you?'

'Later on,' Dora said, already heading across the street towards Josie.

Josie didn't see her until Dora said her name. When she looked up, her face seemed thin and drawn, huge fearful dark eyes above jutting cheekbones.

'What are you doing here?' Josie asked, her voice barely above a whisper.

'I was just about to ask you the same question. I thought you were staying at Auntie Brenda's?'

'Auntie Brenda's eldest has gone down with scarlet fever, so Mum thought I'd be safer at home.'

If only she knew, Dora thought. She sat down next to her on the kerb. 'Are you all right, love?' she asked.

'Yes, of course. Why wouldn't I be?' Josie's voice sounded hollow.

'Why did you run away?'

'I was just being daft.' Josie hugged her knees tighter under her chin. Dora noticed how thin her arms were in her cotton summer dress. At fifteen, she was still no more than a child.

'You must have had a reason...?'

'I told you, I was being daft.' Josie met her eye. 'Don't ask me any more,' she pleaded.

'But I'm your sister. I want to help.'

'You can't,' Josie said. 'You wouldn't understand...'

Wouldn't I, Dora thought. 'Try me,' she begged.

Josie shook her head. 'There's nothing to tell,' she insisted stubbornly. But her wretched face told a different story.

'Josie–'

'Leave it, Dora, please. There's nothing you can do. There's nothing anyone can do.'

Dora stared at her sister's profile, and knew she had to say something. She had kept her secret buried in a deep, dark place, somewhere she would never have to look at it or think about it. But now, for her sister's sake, she had to bring her own shame back out into the light.

'Josie,' she began, already hating the words that came out of her mouth. 'There's something I need to tell you–'

But she didn't have a chance to finish before they heard a yell from inside the house. Bea dropped her hoop with a clatter and started running, Dora and Josie on her heels.

They almost collided with their mother coming out of the back door.

'Oh, Dora, thank God you're here!' She clutched her arm. 'Fetch an ambulance, quickly. Your dad's collapsed!'

Chapter Forty-Two

'Appendicitis,' Sister Holmes said.

She looked at the two women sitting opposite her in her office. One, a careworn, middle-aged woman in a blue coat, was trying desperately not to cry, her eyes fixed on her hands. By contrast, Doyle seemed unnaturally calm. Sister Holmes wondered if she'd really taken in the news.

'Mr Dwyer the consultant is operating now,' Sister Holmes went on.

'My Alf will be all right, won't he?' Mrs Doyle looked up at her anxiously.

Sister Holmes glanced at Doyle. She looked unfamiliar in her faded summer dress, her abundant red curls framing her face. 'He's in the best possible hands,' she replied blandly.

Doyle met her gaze steadily. At least she understood how serious the situation was. Sister Holmes hoped she could explain it to her mother more gently.

'When can I see him?' Rose Doyle asked.

'Not for some time, I'm afraid. Your husband will need time to recover after the operation. But we will let you know the outcome as soon as possible.'

Sister Holmes stood up, indicating the meeting was at an end. Delivering bad news always made her feel uncomfortable. She felt so helpless in the face of people's grief. She was far more at home on the ward, where she could make people feel better in a practical way.

As they left, she said quietly to Doyle, 'Go home with your mother. I will find another nurse to cover the rest of your shift.'

'If it's all the same to you, Sister, I would like to come back on duty at five,' Doyle replied.

Sister Holmes frowned. 'Don't you want to be with your family, under the circumstances?'

Doyle shook her head. 'Mum will have my nan and the kids with her, she won't need me. And I'd like to keep myself busy.'

'Of course. I understand.'

As she looked into the girl's calm green eyes, she wondered if Doyle really had taken in the news. Because if she didn't know better, she could almost believe that Dora Doyle really didn't care.

Outside on the front steps of the hospital, Josie was waiting for them. She jumped up as soon as she saw them.

'Is he–?'

Dora shook her head. 'He's still in theatre. We won't know anything for a few hours.'

She saw the flare of disappointment in Josie's face, quickly masked.

'Thank God I was there,' Rose Doyle said. 'When I think about what might have happened if I'd still been away at our Brenda's–' She shuddered. 'Poor Alf. He's been complaining of those pains for weeks. I told him to go the doctor but he wouldn't have it. He's never trusted doctors and hospitals...' she trailed off, choking back a sob. 'What if anything happens to him?'

'Shh, Mum. Don't take on.' Dora put her arm around her mother's shoulders. 'Mr Dwyer is a top surgeon. He'll look after Alf.'

'I just wish there was something I could do...' She fumbled in her coat pocket for a crumpled handkerchief. 'I s'pose all we can do now is pray.'

Dora caught Josie's eye. She knew what her sister would be praying for. She'd prayed for the same thing herself, night after night, since she was fourteen years old.

'You should go home,' she said.

'Oh no, I'm not going anywhere until my Alf is out of surgery and I know he's all right.'

'You heard what Sister Holmes said. It could be hours. You need to get some rest. I can let you know as soon as I hear anything.'

'She's right, Mum,' Josie said. 'We should let the others know what's going on.'

'I suppose you're right.' Rose looked at Dora beseechingly. 'You will let me know, won't you love? Whatever the news is, I'd rather hear it from you.'

After they'd gone, Dora went round to the patch of waste ground behind the nurses' home, where the nurses hid out to smoke. She was glad the other nurses were still on duty and she had it to herself. She needed to be alone to think.

Her hand shook as she held the match to the tip of her cigarette. She couldn't stop thinking of Alf, lying on that operating table. In her mind, she saw the surgeon opening him up and inspecting the damage to the abdominal cavity and peritoneum. If the appendix was intact, even if it was gangrenous, then it would be a relatively simple procedure to remove it. But if it had ruptured, or perforated during the operation, then it would spread poison all through the abdominal cavity which could kill Alf...

She exhaled, narrowing her eyes against the smoke from her cigarette. She felt guilty for even having such a thought. She was a nurse now. She was supposed to save lives, not pray for them to end.

She heard footsteps approaching and swung around to see Nick Riley heading down the narrow, overgrown pathway that led to the waste ground.

He stopped dead when he saw her, his expression darkening.

'Sorry,' he said gruffly. 'I didn't know you were here.'

'Nick, wait–' Dora called out to him, but he turned and immediately started heading off back down the weed-covered track, his head down as if he couldn't wait to get away from her.

She knew why Nick was avoiding her. It was the same reason he'd ignored her every day for the past week. She'd hurt his pride when she'd rejected him that night Josie went missing.

If only he knew how much she regretted what she'd done. She wished she could explain why she'd pushed him away, to make him understand how Alf had destroyed her trust in any man. But she knew she never would. Like Josie, her terrible secret would stay locked inside her forever.

And Nick would just have to go on hating her.

Nick cursed himself silently. He wished he hadn't ignored Dora like that. But every time he saw her he remembered that night outside her house, and the frustration and humiliation boiled up inside him again.

He didn't blame her for rejecting him. He only blamed himself being such a fool, trying to make a move on her when she wasn't interested in him. When he thought about the look on her face that night he'd kissed her, he just wanted to run away and hide forever.

He could understand why she didn't want to know. She was so far out of his league now. She was a nurse in her smart uniform, destined for better things than a lowly porter with a shady past. She deserved far more than him.

But that night... Just for a moment, before he'd kissed her, he could have sworn she'd wanted him as much as he wanted her.

'Aye aye,' Percy Carson grinned when he got back to the Porters' Lodge. 'I hope you're not thinking of lighting up in here? Mr Hopkins will have your guts for garters.'

'Let him try,' Nick growled, clamping a cigarette between his lips. He usually managed to keep on the right side of the Head Porter but he was just in the mood to give Edwin Hopkins or anyone else what for.

'I'll have one too, since you're offering.' Percy Carson helped himself from Nick's packet. 'I s'pose you've heard about your girlfriend?' he said, picking up the box of matches.

'What girlfriend's that, then?'

'You know. That ginger nurse who's always hanging around you?'

Nick froze. 'What about her?'

405

'Her old man got brought in earlier. Appendicitis. I took him down to theatre myself.' Percy paused a moment while he lit his cigarette. 'In a right bad way he was. If you ask me, he's already a goner... Here, where are you going? You're meant to be in Casualty at half past, remember?'

But Nick was already out of the door, letting it crash shut behind him. All he could think of was Dora's face, pale and distraught as she called his name. Why the hell hadn't he stopped to talk to her? He ran straight to the patch of ground behind the nurses' home, but Dora had gone. All that remained was the smouldering tip of a cigarette.

Dora's heart was beating fast under the starched bib of her apron as she walked back to the ward. She forced herself to go slowly, even though her mind was racing.

She wasn't sure what she would find when she got back to Holmes. Alf must be out of theatre by now, she thought. Unless he was dead.

She felt wicked for thinking it, but at the same time she knew she was walking slowly because she wanted to savour the thought for as long as she could.

But as soon as she walked through the doors and saw Millie's bright face she knew her hopes had been dashed.

'There you are!' She hurried up to her. 'Your stepfather is in the recovery room. They're bringing him up to the ward in a minute. I'm so glad you're here. You can be the first to say hello. Won't that be wonderful?'

406

Dora gritted her teeth and forced herself to smile. 'I can't think of anything I'd like more,' she said.

Chapter Forty-Three

The sun shone brilliantly in a cloudless sky on the June day when Lady Sophia Rushton, only daughter of the Duke and Duchess of Claremont, married the Marquess of Trent at St Margaret's, Westminster. People lined the street, kept back by policemen on horseback, all eager to catch a glimpse of the beautiful young bride as she arrived with her father.

'It's just like the Jubilee,' Millie commented as she looked out of the window of the Rolls-Royce. Crammed inside the car with her were three other bridesmaids, while another car followed behind carrying two more and a brace of pageboys dressed as miniature guardsmen. She straightened the spray of cream roses in her hair. It was hot inside the car, and she could feel perspiration breaking out under her arms. She prayed it wouldn't show on her apricot silk dress.

Inside the church, the cream of society waited. Sophia's mother had spared no expense for her daughter's wedding, and the vast, beautiful church was filled with the heavy, sweet scent of roses and gardenias. Millie joined the retinue of nervous bridesmaids, tweaking their flowers and adjusting their dresses as the bride arrived.

Sophia looked stunning in her dress of heavy silk embroidered lavishly with silver thread that sparkled in the sunshine. Her train was so long, it took all six of the bridesmaids to lay it out straight.

'You look beautiful,' Millie whispered. Even through her veil she could see her friend's eyes shining with joy.

'I'm so nervous,' she confessed, as the organ music swelled majestically in Wagner's 'Wedding Chorus'. 'My hands are shaking so much I can't hold my flowers still.'

'No one will notice,' Millie assured her. 'They'll all be too busy looking at me tripping over your train.'

But she didn't. For once she managed to get through the occasion with no trips, slips or stumbles. She saw her grandmother watching her almost with approval as she filed out of the church after the bride, where a Guard of Honour stood waiting on the steps.

The wedding party was held at the Claremonts' London residence, Claremont House, overlooking St James' Park. Here too, the Duchess had spared no expense. The wedding breakfast was a lavish affair, and afterwards everyone danced to a band in the ballroom, which glittered under the light of the magnificent chandeliers. Millie danced with the best man, who showed no interest in her beyond his duty dance. She was much happier to partner her father, who looked very handsome in his morning dress and didn't mind at all that she tripped over her own feet several times.

'You do realise every eligible woman is watching you?' Millie teased him, as they circled elegantly around the dance floor.

'I dare say they're wondering how an old crock like me can remember the steps!' he joked.

'I wonder if Granny is enjoying herself.'

'I don't know if your grandmother ever enjoys herself unless she's running the show.'

Millie glanced over his shoulder to where Lady Rettingham was sitting with her old friend and bitter rival, the Dowager Duchess of Claremont. She could imagine what they were talking about. The other dowager would most certainly not have missed the opportunity to be smug about her granddaughter's successful marriage, while expressing all kinds of sympathy that Millie was not similarly blessed.

Poor Granny. Millie wished she could give her something to crow about.

After several more dances, each less successful than the last, Millie excused herself to watch from the sidelines instead. In the middle of the dance floor, Sophia and her new husband David danced every dance in each other's arms, hardly noticing the party going on around them.

'Don't they look happy?' Seb joined Millie, handing her a glass of champagne.

'Not as happy as your mother.'

'Ah, yes. She does seem rather satisfied with herself.'

'Like the cat that got the cream.'

Lady Claremont was holding court at the far end of the room, while the guests gathered like satellites around her, admiring and praising her.

'And why not?' Seb said. 'She has her only daughter safely married off, and to a Marquess, no less. It must be such a relief for her. Now she only has her sons to worry about.'

'I thought you had high hopes of Miss Farsley?' Millie could already see Georgina out of the corner of her eye, circling them, ready to pounce. 'You've been dancing with her all evening.'

'Miss Farsley has very high hopes of me. Not the other way around, I assure you.'

'She's very beautiful.'

'And even more snobbish than my mother.' Seb shuddered. 'If I were to marry her, I would be paraded endlessly in front of her wealthy American friends whenever they came over to visit. I would become just another tourist attraction, like the Tower of London.'

Millie laughed, but Seb's expression was serious. 'I mean it,' he said. 'I'm nearly twenty-two. After this summer I will be at a loose end. Either I get married or I become a playboy.'

'I can't imagine you as a playboy!'

'Neither can I,' Seb agreed with a heavy sigh. 'I'm far too sensible, I'm afraid.'

'Seriously, what are you going to do when you leave Oxford?' Millie asked.

'I was thinking of becoming a journalist,' he said. 'I've always liked writing, and my father says he'll use his connections to find me a job. Although to be honest I'd rather start somewhere more humble and work my way up. I don't want everyone thinking I've got the job because of who I am.'

Millie understood only too well how he felt. Having a title and a life of privilege was wonderful, but it could make it difficult to make your own way in the world.

'I'm sure you'll make a wonderful journalist, Seb,' she said.

'Do you think so? I can't really think of anything else I'd like to do. And I do so want to be useful.'

'Good for you,' she said warmly.

'You've inspired me,' he told her with a grin. 'You've set an example to every lazy, over-privileged chap, encouraging us all to get off our backsides and make something of ourselves.'

'Heavens, what a responsibility!'

'I mean it,' he said softly. 'You are an inspiration, Millie. A real breath of fresh air.' He surveyed the dancing couples for a moment. 'So what's the story with your Dr Tremayne?' he asked suddenly.

She frowned at him. She'd almost forgotten he and William had met. 'There is no story. I told you, William's just a friend. Why do you ask?'

'I thought he might be rather keen on you.'

'I doubt it,' Millie laughed. 'And even if he is, I'm not keen on him.'

'Aren't you?' Seb's eyes were fixed on her.

'Dr Tremayne has something of a reputation at the Nightingale,' she said, evading the question.

'Ah.' Seb nodded wisely. 'I suppose it's for the best,' he said. 'Can you imagine what your grandmother would say if she found out you were stepping out with an impoverished junior doctor?'

'I think by this stage she would be grateful I was stepping out with anyone,' Millie sighed.

'Perhaps we should get married?' Seb said suddenly.

Millie laughed. 'What?'

'Why not? We've got a lot going for us,' he said, still with his gaze fixed on the dance floor. 'We

411

get along all right together, don't we?'

'Most of the time,' Millie agreed, trying to straighten her features.

'And it would make our respective families very happy, I'm sure.' He glanced her way. 'What do you say?'

'I say that if that's the best marriage proposal you can come up with, then you really should work on your approach before you seriously pop the question to a girl!'

He pulled a face. 'Who says I wasn't serious? Think about it, Mil.'

She looked into his eyes. He looked so earnest that for a moment she almost believed him. But after knowing him for so many years, she knew how believable Seb's practical jokes could be.

'I really don't think I need to,' she replied.

Seb sighed dramatically, the very picture of a scorned lover. 'Oh, well, I suppose it was worth a try. Tell you what, I'll make a deal with you. If neither of us has found someone to marry us by the time we're twenty-five, we'll marry each other. How about that?'

This time Millie had to laugh. 'I'm sure you'll be snapped up by then, Sebastian.'

Right on cue, Georgina Farsley swanned up behind them. She looked radiant in eau-de-nil georgette that perfectly complemented her dramatic dark colouring.

'There you are!' she cried, as if she hadn't been watching Seb's every move for the past half hour. 'I've been looking for you everywhere. Some of the gang are heading off for supper. We're desperate for you to join us. Please say you'll come?' She was

412

already tugging on his arm.

Seb turned to Millie. 'Will you come too?'

Millie saw the sour look that flashed across Georgina's face. 'I'd love to, but I can't. I have a late pass, but I still have to be ready for duty at seven tomorrow morning.'

'Maybe I shouldn't go either. After all, it's bad form to leave your own sister's wedding...'

'You should,' Millie encouraged him. 'The bride and groom will be leaving soon anyway. Besides,' she added in a low voice, 'you need to practise being a playboy, remember?'

Later, up in Sophia's old bedroom, Millie helped the bride take off her heavy wedding dress and change into her going away outfit, a fitted costume in brilliant emerald green.

'I'm so nervous,' she blurted out, as she sat at her dressing table while Millie unpinned her hair.

'Why? The wedding's over, everything went beautifully. What have you got to be nervous about now?'

'You know. The wedding night.' Sophia met her gaze meaningfully in the mirror. 'I just wish I knew what to expect,' she said. 'I tried to talk to Mummy about it, but she wasn't very helpful. She told me I shouldn't refuse my husband, no matter how much I might want to. But refuse him what?'

Millie hid her smile. While she had still never even kissed a man herself, she had learned a lot from listening to Sister Parker and the women on Wren ward. She now considered herself quite worldly wise, in theory at least.

'Do you really want to know?' she said.

Sophia twisted round to look at her. 'What have

you heard?' she said. 'Tell me, please. I need to know what to expect.'

Millie looked at her friend's desperate face. 'Well...' she began, putting down her hairbrush.

By the time she'd finished, they were both giggling like schoolgirls. 'Are you sure?' Sophia said. 'It all sounds so absurd.'

Millie nodded. 'It is rather, isn't it?'

Sophia reached for her hand. 'Thanks for telling me anyway. I'm not nearly so terrified now.' She smiled archly at Millie. 'I expect it'll be your turn soon!'

'Don't,' Millie groaned. 'Everyone's been nagging me about marriage today. Even your brother's been going on about it.'

'Seb? What did he say?'

'He proposed, would you believe?' Millie picked up the hairbrush and started to brush out her friend's long dark hair again. 'Well, not really. He came up with a ridiculous plan for us to get married if no one else would have us. I think he wants to save me from ending up on the shelf. He can be such a joker sometimes.' She smiled fondly to herself, then glanced up and saw Sophia's serious expression in the mirror. 'What?'

'I don't think he was joking, Millie.'

'Of course he was!'

'You really don't know how he feels about you, do you?' Sophia shook her head, marvelling. 'Millie, my brother has been head over heels in love with you for years. But he's always been too shy to do anything about it. Until now, apparently.' She rolled her eyes. 'I can't believe Seb asked you to marry him like that. I suppose he thought if he

414

pretended it was all a big joke he wouldn't feel so bad if you turned him down. As if anyone would ever accept such an appalling proposal!'

Millie was barely listening to her. She was too dazed by the revelation. 'I had no idea,' she said.

'You won't say anything to Seb, will you?' Sophia pleaded. 'He'd be simply mortified if he thought I'd breathed a word. I just thought you ought to know.'

But Millie wasn't sure she did need to know. She wasn't sure how she was going to face Seb again, knowing he had feelings for her. Sophia's revelation had changed everything between them. 'But I don't want to marry anyone,' she protested.

'I realise that, and so does Seb. You know he'd never put any pressure on you, don't you? He truly admires what you're doing. I think he'd wait for ever for you, if you asked him to.' Sophia smiled and Millie tried to smile back, but her lips were frozen. She didn't want him to wait for ever. She didn't want him to wait at all.

Her father's chauffeur Felix drove her back to the Nightingale. Millie sat deep in thought all the way, still shaken by Sophia's revelation. She had genuinely never realised Seb had any feelings for her beyond just friendship. But now she did, she wasn't quite sure how she felt about it.

She liked him. He was fun, clever, and witty without being unkind: gentle, sensitive and kind-hearted without being utterly wet. He could quote poetry and discuss books as well as he could ride a horse or shoot. And he was good-looking, too. A season of dancing with oafs and listening to bragging bores had taught Millie that she could certainly do a lot worse. But even so...

As the Daimler turned the corner, it illuminated a couple embracing in the shadows of the looming hospital walls. They were in each other's arms, kissing passionately, oblivious to everything around them.

Millie looked away, embarrassed, but not before the young man turned his face towards her and she caught a glimpse of his profile. It was William Tremayne.

'Are you all right, my lady?' She hadn't realised she'd cried out until Felix caught her eye in the rear-view mirror.

'Yes ... thank you, Felix.'

Millie resisted the urge to look back over her shoulder until they'd reached the hospital gates. By then, thankfully, the couple had gone.

Chapter Forty-Four

Dora trailed to the ward with a heavy heart to start her duty, already dreading the thought of seeing Alf again.

Even after three weeks, the sight of him in his blue striped pyjamas, his face florid against the starched pillows, turned her stomach.

Her only consolation was that he seemed as unhappy as she did.

'Oh, it's you,' he greeted her unenthusiastically when she arrived to do his TPRs. 'What do you want?'

She ignored him, reaching for the thermometer over his bed. He eyed her warily. 'What are you doing?' he demanded.

'Taking your temperature, what does it look like?' She shook the thermometer with a flick of her wrist.

'Isn't there anyone else who can do it? What about that blonde piece?' Alf craned his neck, looking desperately around.

'She's on her tea break, so I'm afraid we're stuck with each other.' She jammed the thermometer into his mouth before he could reply.

She gingerly picked up his wrist to check his pulse, and felt him recoil. She watched him curiously as she counted the beats. His eyes were fixed on her, but not in the leering, overconfident way he usually looked at her. This time he looked almost...

Fearful.

That was it, she realised with a shock. Alf was actually afraid of her.

She remembered what her mother had said about Alf being terrified of doctors and hospitals. Now, not only was he in hospital, but he was also completely at her mercy. And after everything he had done to her, no wonder he was scared.

'What you smirking at?' Alf watched her, eyes narrowed suspiciously, when she took the thermometer out of his mouth. 'What does it say? Is it bad news?'

She didn't reply as she noted down the figures on his chart and hooked it back on the end of his bed.

'You didn't ought to go around grinning like a

bloody Cheshire cat when there are sick people about,' Alf grumbled.

'And you didn't ought to go around telling nurses what to do,' Dora said, still smiling. 'I could make life very uncomfortable for you, remember.'

She saw him pale, his face suddenly grey against the snowy pillows. That would give him something to think about, she decided.

And it gave her something to think about too. A way to make sure he didn't hurt her sister again.

Helen had never been in love, but she was sure it must feel something like she felt now, sitting in the stalls of the Rialto, holding hands in the dark with Charlie Denton.

She had been nervous when he first suggested a trip to the pictures. She had never been to the cinema with anyone but her parents before, and then only on very rare occasions when it was a film of which her mother approved. She had also heard the other girls talking about what went on in the back row, and she worried that Charlie's hands might start to wander after the lights went down.

But he was the perfect gentleman as he had been every other time they'd been out together, buying her a box of chocolates and insisting on paying for the tickets.

'I hope you don't mind the stalls?' he said anxiously.

'It makes no difference to me where we sit.' Helen would happily have sat on the floor as long as she was with him.

The last six weeks had been the best of her whole life. Every week she and Charlie would meet on a

Saturday or Sunday afternoon. They would go to the park if it was fine, take a bus trip into town or go for tea at the local cafe. Helen knew the other girls would probably laugh at her – they liked to brag about the smart places they'd been with their boyfriends – but she was content just to be with him.

Charlie had even taken her to meet his family. She already knew his mother from her visits to the hospital, and Mrs Denton was delighted to welcome the shy young nurse into her home.

'You've been a tonic to our Charlie, you really have,' she told Helen, embracing her warmly. 'He's a different lad since he met you.' She lowered her voice. 'Don't say anything, but I never really took to that Sally Watkins. Too full of herself by half.'

Helen had been overwhelmed by Charlie's noisy, boisterous family – his younger brothers and sisters and his down-to-earth dad who sold fruit and veg in the market. It was so different from her own quiet home, where her mother would never even hug her own children, let alone a stranger.

Although now Charlie was dropping hints about meeting her family. It was the only thing spoiling Helen's happiness as she sat in the darkness, watching Robert Donat avoiding spies in *The Thirty-nine Steps*.

She hadn't told her mother about Charlie, of course, and shuddered to think what she would do if Constance ever found out about him.

'You're not ashamed of me, are you?' Charlie had joked when she made yet another excuse.

'Of course not,' Helen said. Her mother would

disapprove even if she were stepping out with the Prince of Wales.

She hadn't set out to deceive her parents, but she had never imagined she would get this far with Charlie. She'd thought that after one or two dates he would get bored and drop her. Then everything would go back to normal and her mother would be none the wiser.

She had never imagined that weeks later they would still be seeing each other. And she certainly never imagined she would fall in love with him.

She hadn't realised she was frowning so hard until she caught Charlie looking questioningly at her in the darkness. She smiled and squeezed his hand reassuringly. She knew that one day she would have to do something about the situation, but not yet. Being truly happy was a rare feeling for Helen, and she wanted to enjoy it for as long as she could.

'Did you enjoy the film?' he asked as they stepped out into the brightly lit foyer.

'Oh, yes, it was smashing.'

'Really? Only you looked as if you were a million miles away.'

'Sorry, I was just thinking about something else.' Helen tucked her arm under his. 'But I loved the film. It was terribly exciting, wasn't it? Especially that bit at the end where the memory man gets shot–'

But Charlie wasn't listening to her. He was staring transfixed at a point beyond Helen's shoulder. She turned to look. Descending the sweeping staircase from the circle on the arm of a good-looking young man was Charlie's fiancée, Sally.

Ex-fiancée, Helen reminded herself. But no one could have told it from the expression on Charlie's face. Their eyes met across the room and Helen felt herself fade into the crowd.

Sally made her way over to them. 'Hello, Charlie,' she said. 'Fancy seeing you here.'

'Sal.' His voice was gruff.

'You know Sam, don't you?' The two men nodded to each other. Helen waited for Charlie to introduce her, but he seemed to have forgotten all about her as he stared at Sally.

They made polite small-talk for a minute or two, then she said, 'Well, we'd best be off. It was nice to see you, Charlie. Maybe see you again sometime?'

They walked back to the hospital in moody silence. Helen could tell Charlie was troubled but she was too afraid to ask why. All she knew was that their evening had been ruined. Seeing Sally had changed everything, she could tell.

They were almost back at the hospital when he suddenly said, 'Do you mind if we sit somewhere for a while? I need to talk to you.'

Helen's stomach dropped. Here it comes, she thought.

'Can't it wait?' she said desperately. 'I've got to be back at the hospital by ten, and it's nearly quarter to.'

'I'd rather say it now, if that's all right?'

No, it isn't all right, Helen wanted to scream. She had the sudden urge to run away, never to hear the words that would end her happiness for ever. But it was already over, she realised sadly. It had been over the moment Charlie set eyes on Sally Watkins again.

They sat on a bench across the road from Victoria Park. Helen stared at the tall iron gates and mentally tried to prepare herself for what she was about to hear.

'I'm sorry about Sal,' Charlie said. 'I didn't know she'd be there, otherwise I would never have suggested going to the pictures.'

'You had to see her sooner or later, I suppose.' And once you did, you realised you were still in love with her and it was all over for us, she added silently.

'I know. I've been wondering what I'd feel like when I saw her again. I'd been dreading it, to be honest. I mean, we'd been together since we were kids. We'd planned our future. She was the girl I wanted to spend the rest of my life with.'

Charlie turned to look at her. His face was so wretched, Helen's heart went out to him. 'Real love doesn't just go away, does it?' he said.

'No,' Helen agreed sadly. She took a deep, shaky breath. 'Look, you don't have to explain. I understand,' she said.

'Do you?'

'Of course. I've been expecting it, to be honest.' She looked down at her hands, unable to meet his eye. If she looked at him, she knew she would cry. 'Like you said, you and Sally were together a long time. You're bound to still have feelings for her. And I'm sure in time, once she gets used to the idea, she'll realise she still has feelings for you, too. If you really love each other then it will work out.' She gathered up her bag and stood up. 'Now if you don't mind, I must be getting back.'

'Hang on.' Charlie's hand closed on her arm,

pulling her back. 'What are you on about? Who says I want Sally back?'

'Don't you?'

'Not a chance.' He frowned at her. 'Why would I want her back when I've got you?'

It took a moment for his words to sink in. And even then Helen wasn't sure she'd understood them. 'I don't understand. You just said...'

'I'll admit, I was dreading seeing her again. I wasn't sure how I'd feel about seeing her on the arm of another man. But when I saw her...' He shook his head. 'I felt nothing. Nothing at all. Except glad that I was with you and not her.'

Helen sank back down on to the bench beside him. She wasn't sure her legs would hold her up. 'But you said real love doesn't just disappear.'

'No, it doesn't. That's what made me realise, what I felt for her was never real love. I was infatuated with her, I suppose. She was the prettiest girl in our street, and I was proud to be seen with her. I was even prouder when she said she'd marry me. But it didn't seem real somehow. We always wanted different things. She was one for going out, living the high life, having a good time. She was always pushing me to get on, make something of myself, bring in more money. It used to drive her mad that I was happy to stay working with the lads at that factory.' His mouth twisted. 'Funny thing is, now I'm working with my uncle, learning a trade, which was what she always wanted me to do. But I'm not doing it for her any more. I want to do it to make *you* proud.'

His hand closed over Helen's. 'I'm not one for making speeches,' he said wryly. 'I've been chewing myself up with nerves all the way here, to be honest. But I knew I couldn't let you go without telling you how I feel about you.' He looked up at her, his eyes gleaming in the lamplight. 'I love you, Helen. I know I'm not much of a bargain, and I can't think why you'd be interested in someone like me when you're so clever and beautiful and could have anyone you wanted. But I just wanted you to know...'

He never finished the sentence. Helen knew it was all wrong, and that a young lady was supposed to wait for a man to make the first move, but she couldn't stop herself from kissing him. And, after a second of surprise, he kissed her back.

It was as terrifyingly wonderful as she had always thought it might be. As his lips moved against hers and she felt the warmth of his hands cupping her face, Helen at last realised what all the other girls giggled and gossiped about. Although she also knew she would never ever tell anyone about this moment, not even Millie and Dora. It was just too special. She wanted it to go on for ever.

It almost did. It was only when they were disturbed by a group of jeering drunks that they reluctantly extricated themselves from each other's arms.

'Look at that! Ain't love grand?' one of the men laughed.

Charlie put his arm around Helen, pulling her closer. 'It is, mate,' he agreed good-naturedly.

'I wouldn't know,' another man said mournfully. 'All I'm going to get from my missus is a battering. She told me next time I was in after closing time she was gonna lock the door on me!'

'Closing time!' Helen whipped round to look at Charlie. 'Oh, no, I'm so late!'

By the time they got back to the nurses' home the black front door was firmly closed.

'How are you going to get in?' Charlie asked.

'I don't know.' Helen looked up at the windows in despair. She knew Millie often shinned up the drainpipe to slip through their attic window, but that was only when Helen was there to leave it open for her. Tonight it would be firmly locked.

She suddenly thought about the time Millie had climbed in through the open window on to Hyde Ward. She knew she would never have the nerve to try anything so daring or dangerous.

'We'll think of something.' Charlie took her hand in the darkness. 'Let's look around the back.'

They picked their way carefully over the uneven patch of ground until they found a tiny window left ajar. 'Where does it lead, do you think?' he asked.

'I'm not sure. It's too small to be a bedroom window. With any luck it's a store room or something.' Helen looked around and found an old flower pot. 'Whatever it is, I'm going to have to risk it. I can't stay out here all night.'

She placed the upturned pot outside the window, climbed up and scrambled through the narrow gap.

'Be careful.' Charlie's last words drifted up to her as she disappeared head first through the tiny window.

She ripped her stockings, but at least she didn't break her neck as she landed on a hard tiled floor. She scrambled to her feet, wishing there was a moon as she groped around in the pitch darkness, trying to find the door. The room seemed to be very small, and as she turned around she blundered into something big and cold and hard. She felt around. It felt like ... a bathtub. She turned around, took another step and banged into a toilet.

A bathroom. She put her hand out and found the doorknob, wincing as it creaked when she turned it. But the creaking was soon drowned out by the sound of scampering feet and frantic yapping.

Helen flattened herself against the wall, hardly daring to breathe as claws scratched frantically at the other side of the door. A moment later she heard shuffling footsteps and Sister Sutton's voice, blurred with sleep, calling out, 'What is it, Sparky? Who's there?' The footsteps shuffled closer. Helen closed her eyes and prayed with all her might. Just as they reached the door, she heard Sister Sutton's voice on the other side.

'Come on, back to bed, you silly dog. Listen to you, yapping at nothing.'

The footsteps started to move away. 'Thank you, Lord,' Helen mouthed into the darkness. But as she turned, she knocked into a shelf and a jar of bath salts crashed to the ground, filling the room with the cloying scent of lily of the valley.

The door opened, the light went on, and Helen found herself staring into the face of Sister Sutton, shiny with face cream and circled with a halo of rollers. The Home Sister let out a scream, and so did Helen a moment later as Sparky sank his teeth into her ankle.

Chapter Forty-Five

'Go away,' Alf grunted. 'I don't want you touching me.'

Dora smiled, enjoying every moment. 'Don't be silly, Alf,' she said briskly. 'I need to smarten you up.'

She followed his wary gaze to the trolley, laden with face cloths, towels, soap – and a razor blade.

'I – I want someone else to do it,' he stammered. 'I don't want you near me.'

'Doyle?' Dora turned as Staff Nurse Lund stuck her head through the curtains surrounding the bed. 'Why haven't you finished washing the patients? The consultant will be here soon.'

'Mr Doyle doesn't want me to wash him, Staff.'

Staff Nurse Lund wrinkled her nose fastidiously. 'Really, Mr Doyle, that won't do at all,' she said. 'It's only a quick wash and brush up. You want to look your best for Mr Dwyer, don't you?' Without waiting for his reply, she turned back to Dora and said, 'Carry on, please, Nurse. And be sure you don't take any more nonsense.'

'No, Staff.' Dora waited until she'd gone, then looked back at Alf. 'You heard her,' she said, picking up a flannel.

Alf yelped as she slapped the cold, clammy cloth around his face. 'That water's stone cold. And do you have to be so bloody rough?' he snapped, jerking his head away. 'I'll tell that Sister if you're not careful.'

'Go on, then.' Dora took a step towards the curtains. 'I'll call her for you, shall I?'

'Don't bother,' Alf grunted. 'The old bitch is just as bad as the rest of you.'

His bravado didn't fool her for a moment. He'd been wary of her ever since she'd made her threat.

Seeing him now made Dora wonder how she'd ever been so afraid of him. His ashen, haggard face, roughened by stubble, looked ten years older. He was no longer the monster who had made her afraid of every moving shadow in the night. He was just a trembling, pathetic coward who couldn't even look her in the eye.

His gaze sharpened when she picked up the razor blade.

'What's the matter, Alf?' Dora grinned. 'You look a bit nervous.'

'Never mind me,' he muttered through a chin smothered with soap. 'You just concentrate on what you're doing with that thing.'

'You're right, I could do someone an injury, couldn't I?' She let the shiny blade flash in front of his terrified eyes. 'It's so easily done, isn't it? One slip and I could have your ear off – or worse.' He said nothing, but perspiration glistened on his brow.

'But it's all right, you're quite safe,' she assured him as she brought the blade down the length of his cheek. 'I've had a lot of practice, and I've got quite a steady hand. Unless something upsets me, of course. Then I just start shaking all over the place.'

She wiped soap off the blade, aware of Alf

watching her every move. 'And do you know what really upsets me, Alf?' she said, as she moved the blade towards his chin again. Her face was so close to his she could see the vein throbbing in his temple. 'People who don't keep their filthy hands off my sister.'

He gave a squeak of terror and tried to jerk away, but she clamped his chin in her hand, trapping him. 'No, no, don't start jigging about all over the place or I really will do you an injury,' she warned softly. She tugged his face around to look into her eyes.

'Are you frightened, Alf?' she whispered. She let the blade rasp against his skin. 'You're not such a big man now, are you?' He held himself rigid, but she could see his eyes bulging with fear. 'Do you want me to stop? That's what we wanted too, me and Josie. But you wouldn't, would you? You kept on hurting us.' She smiled, pushing her face closer to his. 'And do you know what? I'm not going to stop either.'

His eyes screwed shut, his whole body tensed, waiting. She could smell the fear coming off him as she lowered the blade, letting its sharp edge rest just below his ear.

I could kill him, she thought. Just one little nick in the right place, and he'd be gone forever.

She lowered the blade. 'D'you know what? You're not worth doing time for.'

He took a deep, shuddering breath. 'You're mad,' he croaked, his hand going to his throat.

'Touch my sister again and you'll see how mad I can be.' He flinched back as she thrust the blade under his nose. 'I'm warning you, Alf Doyle. If you

429

so much as lay a finger on Josie again, I'll come after you. And it'll take more than a surgeon to put you right.'

Kathleen Fox was shocked to see Helen Tremayne, of all people, standing in front of her desk. She was even more shocked when she found out why.

'Let me be clear about this.' She read the notes in front of her again. 'You were discovered hiding in Sister Sutton's bathroom late last night, is that correct?'

'Yes, Sister.' Tremayne's head hung low, her voice was barely above a whisper.

'And may I ask why?'

As Tremayne explained, it was all Kathleen could do not to smile. It was only the young nurse's utter mortification, and the fact that Miss Hanley was standing hatchet-faced beside her, that stopped her.

'I see,' she said, when Helen had finished her stumbling explanation. 'You gave Sister Sutton quite a fright,' she observed.

'Yes, Matron. I'm sorry, Matron.' Helen's eyes were red-rimmed, circled by dark shadows. She looked as if she'd been awake all night.

Kathleen looked down at her notes and bit her lip to stop herself from laughing out loud. 'This is a very serious situation indeed,' she said. 'Who knows what Sister Sutton could have been doing when you fell through her bathroom window? It could have been extremely embarrassing.' She pinched her mouth tight. 'You have an exemplary record of conduct at this hospital, and I am very

430

disappointed that you have let yourself down.'

'And no doubt your mother will be very disappointed too,' Miss Hanley added severely.

Tremayne looked up sharply. 'Please don't tell my mother, Matron!'

The fear in her eyes startled Kathleen. She had never seen a girl look so afraid.

'And why should we not tell her?' Miss Hanley demanded, clearly enjoying the moment.

'Because ... because I'm afraid she will be very vexed,' Tremayne said lamely.

'You should have thought of that before you did it, shouldn't you?' Miss Hanley said sternly.

Matron saw Tremayne's chin quiver with the effort of not crying. She could understand how the poor girl felt. She had seen Mrs Tremayne vexed many times. She had also seen her trailing her daughter around like a pet spaniel, to scold or kick as the mood took her.

'Since Sister Sutton has very generously agreed to say no more about it, and bearing in mind your exemplary record of conduct up until now, I see no reason to involve your mother,' she announced. Ignoring Miss Hanley's gasp of annoyance behind her, she added, 'However, that does not mean you are off the hook by any means. You broke the rules, and you must be punished. You will have your leave cancelled for the next two weeks. And rest assured that if this happens again, we will have to reconsider whether to inform your mother.'

'Yes, Matron. Thank you, Matron.' Relief lit up the nurse's strained face.

After Tremayne had gone, Kathleen steeled

431

herself for the inevitable reprimand from Miss Hanley.

'I must say, Matron, that I'm sure if I were Mrs Tremayne I would like to be informed of my daughter's behaviour,' she said.

I dare say you would, Kathleen thought. And you'd probably punish her just as severely, too.

'May I remind you, Miss Hanley, that we do not make a habit of informing other students' mothers when their daughters misbehave,' she replied. 'Or we would be on the telephone or writing letters all day, don't you think?'

'Yes, but Constance ... Mrs Tremayne ... is different,' Miss Hanley insisted. 'She would want to know.'

'And what good would that do? Nurse Tremayne has already received adequate punishment. After all, I run the nursing staff of this hospital, not Constance Tremayne.'

The maid came in with the tea tray before Miss Hanley could reply. Kathleen quickly changed the subject to the new allocations for the following month. But as she watched her Assistant Matron sipping tea, she had no doubt that Miss Hanley would tell Mrs Tremayne at the first opportunity.

For poor Helen Tremayne's sake, Kathleen would have to try to ensure the opportunity did not present itself.

'Really, Agatha, don't you think you're taking it all too seriously? It was only a prank, after all.'

'Only a prank?' Agatha Sutton's eyes grew beady. 'You may find it amusing, Florence, but I can assure you I do not. In fact, I'm still deeply upset by it. I haven't been able to venture into my bathroom after dark since.' She gave a dramatic shudder that set all her chins wobbling. Florence Parker didn't lift her eyes from her sewing, but Veronica Hanley could see her lips pursed together as she tried to stop herself from smiling.

Miss Hanley herself couldn't see anything funny about it. She didn't believe Agatha Sutton was taking it too seriously, either. If anything, it was Matron who was at fault for not considering the Home Sister's feelings in the matter.

'I agree, it's completely unacceptable,' she said, stabbing her needle into the patchwork. 'Trespass is very serious, and Helen Tremayne should have been punished severely for what she did to poor Agatha.'

'You make it sound as if she lay in wait in that bathroom deliberately to jump out at her,' Florence shook her head. 'Really, the poor girl was simply in the wrong place at the wrong time.' Her blue eyes twinkled. 'It's rather funny when you think about it. I wish I'd seen her face!'

She chuckled to herself. Veronica and Agatha exchanged a look of horror. Florence Parker was an excellent nurse, but she could be very modern at times.

'I really don't think it's funny at all,' Veronica said. 'It could have been very embarrassing for poor Agatha.'

'An invasion of my privacy,' Agatha Sutton put in. 'Poor Sparky hasn't been the same since, either.'

At the sound of his name, the little dog lifted

his head from where he had been snoozing on the rug at their feet, then sank down again.

'You see?' Agatha said. 'He is utterly traumatised, poor lamb.'

'So you think Matron should have dismissed Tremayne because of what she did to your dog, is that it?' Florence's voice was sharp. 'Everyone is allowed to make a mistake, surely? Why, I remember when I was young...' She looked up, saw their expressions and her voice trailed off. 'Well, it doesn't matter,' she said briskly. 'What does matter is that Tremayne is a wonderful nurse and an extremely hard worker. She would be a great loss to this hospital.'

'I agree with you,' Veronica said. 'No one would want to see her dismissed. She is an asset to the Nightingale. I wish there were more like her.' In fact, Helen was usually one of the few students of whom she whole-heartedly approved. 'But don't you see? That is why I feel she should be disciplined. Before she is led astray.'

Agatha Sutton said, 'Her mother should have been informed, at the very least.'

'That busybody!' Florence shook her head. 'She has her nose stuck into our business far too much as it is.'

'This hospital is her business,' Veronica insisted stubbornly. 'And Helen is her daughter. She has a right to know if the girl is in moral danger...'

'Good heavens, Veronica, you make this place sound like Sodom and Gomorrah!' Florence stared at her, her eyes narrowing. 'I hope you're not thinking of informing Mrs Tremayne yourself?'

434

'I think I would want to know, if it were my daughter.'

'And I think such decisions are best left to Matron. Don't you agree, Agatha?'

'I think Veronica must do as her conscience dictates,' the Home Sister said primly, leaning forward with great effort to offer a biscuit to Sparky.

'As long as it is her conscience speaking, and not a desire to score points at Matron's expense? Because such a situation could backfire very badly indeed.'

Veronica was silent, concentrating on her stitching. She could feel Florence's eyes fixed on her, but refused to meet her gaze.

Florence was wrong, she told herself, this had nothing to do with Matron. Helen Tremayne was an excellent nurse with a bright future ahead of her. It was for the girl's sake that she had to speak up.

Mrs Tremayne would expect nothing less from her.

Chapter Forty-Six

Founder's Day dawned bright and clear, as if Mrs Tremayne had organised the weather as well as the event itself. She stood in the centre of the courtyard, dressed in all her finery, greeting the guests as they arrived. Music from a string quartet mingled with the chink of china and muted murmurs of polite conversation.

Millie watched them arrive from the window of Holmes Ward. She was sad to miss the fun but their leave had been cancelled because they were far too busy. They'd had several emergency admissions over the past few days, and there were extra beds arranged down the middle of the ward. On top of it all, their senior had gone down with glandular fever and there was no one to cover for her.

Not that that had stopped Sister Holmes and Staff Nurse Lund from sloping off to join the party. 'I am trusting you and Doyle to look after the ward while we're away,' Sister instructed them. 'You know where we are if there are any emergencies, although hopefully you should be able to manage.' She sent Millie a severe look. 'Please try not to lose any patients while we are away.'

'It's not fair,' Millie complained to Dora when they had gone. 'Now I know how Cinderella felt when she wasn't allowed to go to the ball.'

'No point moaning about it,' Dora shrugged. 'It's your turn to change Mr Abbott's dressing, by the way.'

Millie pulled a face. 'Do I have to?' She was rather afraid of Mr Abbott. He had been admitted the previous day with a mysterious leg wound. Rumour had it he was a notorious East End villain who had been shot by a rival gangster. Rumour also had it that the police were keeping guard outside the hospital to make sure he didn't escape.

Sister Holmes had warned them to ignore the gossip. 'It really should not concern us who or what he is,' she told them firmly. 'As far as we are concerned, he is just another patient who needs our care and attention.'

Mr Abbott, for his part, gave nothing away. He was polite and appreciative of the care he was given. But his craggy, scarred face still gave Millie the shivers.

'I'll swop with you, if you like?' Dora offered. She had been in a very good mood since her stepfather had been discharged a week earlier. It must be the relief that he was fully recovered, Millie thought.

'No, it's all right. I mustn't shirk my responsibilities.'

Be professional, she told herself as she washed her hands and took the sterilised swabs and dressings out of the drum. Remember, he's just another patient.

Mr Abbott was sitting up in bed, reading *Sporting Life*.

'All right, Nurse?' he greeted her cheerfully. 'How's it going?'

'Good afternoon, Mr Abbott.' Millie desperately tried not to make eye contact as she carefully removed the dressing from his wound.

'Quite a to-do outside today. What's that all about, then?'

'It's Founder's Day. They're having a garden party in the courtyard.' She examined the wound. It seemed to be healing nicely.

'Are you not invited, then?'

'I'm afraid not. We're far too busy. Sister and Staff have gone, though.'

'And they've left you and that other young nurse here to hold the fort by yourselves? Shame. That's not right, is it?'

'It's the way of the world for us students, un-

437

fortunately.' Millie worked as quickly as she could, applying the dressing pad and pinning the bandages in place. 'There, that's done. How does it feel?'

'It feels fine, Nurse. You've done a good job there.' As he smiled up at her, Millie tried to drag her gaze away from the faint silvery line running the length of his cheek. 'And you can be sure I'll be having words with that sister of yours about leaving you here on your own,' he said, as Millie pushed back the curtains.

Five minutes later Dora followed her into the sluice room. 'Shall I take those dressings down to the stoke hole for you?' she offered.

She really was in a good mood, Millie decided. Wild horses wouldn't have dragged her down to the basement otherwise.

While Dora was gone, Millie went into the kitchen to prepare the drinks. The box of matches was damp, and she was struggling to light one when a voice behind her said, 'Allow me.'

She turned around. William took a box of matches out of his pocket, struck one and lit the gas.

'What are you doing here?' she asked.

'I've brought you a present.' He handed her a cake, delicately iced in pink. 'I thought if you couldn't go to the party, then the party should come to you.'

'We're not allowed to eat on the ward, remember?' Millie turned away from him to fill the kettle under the tap. 'Anyway, shouldn't you give it to your girlfriend Hollins?'

She hadn't spoken to William properly since

438

the night of Sophia's wedding, when she'd seen him kissing Amy Hollins. But it was common knowledge that they were stepping out together now. Amy hadn't stopped bragging about it in the nurses' home.

He gave her a maddening smile. 'It's not serious between us.'

That's not what she thinks, Millie thought. 'It's of no consequence to me, I'm sure.'

She put the kettle on to boil and set about preparing the drinks, aware all the time of him watching her. Finally, she could stand it no longer.

'Was there something else you wanted?' she asked rudely.

He shrugged. 'Not really.'

'Then why are you still hanging around?'

'Because I can't stay away from you.'

She swung around to face him, ready to give him an angry mouthful. But he wasn't smiling or flirting any more. His dark eyes were desolate.

'I mean it,' he said. 'I know it's wrong of me, and unfair on you and Amy, but I can't help it. I just can't seem to stop thinking about you.'

'William–' She took a step towards him but he backed away.

'Don't,' he said. 'I'm trying to be honourable and do the right thing, but if you come any nearer I don't think I'll be able to stop myself kissing you.'

'Who says I'd want you to stop?'

She took another step towards him, close enough to feel the warmth of his body, just as Dora appeared in the kitchen doorway.

'Sorry to interrupt,' she said. 'But have you seen Mr Abbott?'

Lucy Lane sat in the hospital dining room in her pretty new dress, eating her lunch as fast as she could and trying not to cry. This should have been the best day of her life, and it was turning out to be one of the worst.

Her award lay on the table beside her, a shiny plaque bearing the Nightingale crest, and underneath it her name and the words *1935 Best First Year Student* engraved in curly copperplate.

It had been such a proud moment for her. She had thought of little else for days, imagining the applause ringing in her ears as she stepped forward, as graceful as a debutante, to collect her award from Mr Enright, the Chairman of the Trustees. She thought about how she would turn to face the onlookers and pick out her mother and father, sitting in the front row, watching her with pride. She would meet her father's eye, and he would smile and nod approvingly.

Except it hadn't happened like that. Her father had cancelled at the last minute, saying he had to fly to Paris for an important business meeting.

'I'm sure there will be other prize givings, darling,' he'd said, his rich, deep voice echoing down the telephone line. 'And I'll bring you something special home to make up for it. A gift from Cartier, perhaps?'

Lucy tried to sound enthusiastic, but she found it hard to speak through her utter disappointment. Even worse, when she'd called that morning to make sure her mother was still coming, Hemmings the butler had told her that Mrs Lane was indisposed.

Lucy stared at the plaque, her eyes misting. No prizes for guessing why her mother was unwell. She shuddered to think of the servants putting her to bed and then gossiping downstairs about all the empty bottles in the drawing room.

Katie O'Hara clattered into the dining room with some of the other first years, laughing and chattering together. They stopped dead when they saw Lucy.

'Hello,' Katie greeted her. 'I thought you'd be out celebrating? Wasn't your father supposed to be taking you to The Ritz?'

Lucy stared down at her plate. 'He had to attend an important business meeting.'

'That's strange. I thought you always said he'd drop everything for his precious little girl?'

'He wanted to come but I insisted he had to go to his meeting,' Lucy lied. 'Sometimes work has to come first.'

'So no one was there to see poor Lucy collect her prize.' Katie seemed determined to make her suffer, her mouth turned down in a parody of pity.

'At least I won a prize,' Lucy snapped back.

'I'm surprised you didn't win one for showing off,' Katie retorted.

'I can't help being the best, can I?'

'No, but you can help bragging about it.' Katie O'Hara was usually a mild-mannered kind of girl who seemed to take everything in her stride. But for some reason her Irish temper took over today. 'We're all just about sick of you, do you know that? You seem to think we're all so impressed by who you are and what you've got, but we're not. To tell you the truth, we're tired of hearing about it.'

Lucy stared at her, shocked. She knew she laid it on a bit thick with the other girls sometimes, but she didn't think they resented her for it so much. Seeing the spite in Katie O'Hara's face shook her.

'You give yourself all these airs and graces, but just because you've got this and that and your dad's got a fancy title doesn't make you better than us,' Katie went on.

'I – I didn't say I was,' Lucy stammered.

'Not much, you don't! You never miss a chance to tell us how grand you are, what a great life you have. You're always looking down on us, making out we're all peasants, not fit to clean your boots! What makes *you* so special?'

Lucy thought about her father, who barely remembered she existed, and her mother, too preoccupied with her own misery to spare any thought for her daughter. The last thing she ever felt was special.

'This is pointless,' Dora said, when they'd searched the ward and all the side rooms for the third time. 'He's hardly going to be hiding under a bed, is he? He's probably legged it by now.'

'You're right,' Millie said. 'We should spread out and search the whole building.'

'What about the patients?'

They looked back down the ward. Fortunately none of the men seemed to have noticed that someone had escaped from their midst as they snoozed or read their newspapers.

'You stay and keep an eye on everyone. I'll go and search for Mr Abbott,' Millie said. She

442

already felt guilty enough that it was her fault he was on the loose

'I'll come with you,' said William. 'I'm not having you tackle a desperate criminal by yourself.'

'You don't have to.'

'I want to.'

'Oh, for heaven's sake, just get going, will you?' Dora snapped. 'And make sure you're back before Sister Holmes!'

They hurried along the corridors, checking all the side rooms and store cupboards.

'This wouldn't have happened if you hadn't kept me talking in the kitchen,' Millie accused William as they puffed and panted up a flight of stairs to the roof.

'It wouldn't have happened if you hadn't told Mr Abbott you and Amy were in charge of the ward alone.'

They reached the roof and stopped for breath. 'There's no sign of him up here,' William said, looking around as Millie doubled over, holding her side.

'Where else could he be? We've searched everywhere else.'

'There's one place we haven't looked.'

Millie followed William's gaze down to the garden party below.

'He might be mingling with the guests, waiting for his chance to escape. We're going to have to go down there and look for him.'

'Can't you go on your own?' Millie pleaded. 'If Sister or Staff see me at the party they'll have my guts for garters.'

'That might be a bit difficult, since I have no

443

idea what this Mr Abbott looks like.'

'What will we do if we find him?' Millie asked, as they joined the other party guests. She kept her head down, fearful that she would be spotted by Sister Holmes at any moment. 'We can't very well apprehend him in front of everyone, can we?'

'We'll cross that bridge when we come to it,' William replied. 'You have to find him first.'

Millie spotted Staff Nurse Lund in the crowd, beat a hasty retreat – and crashed straight into Helen, coming the other way with a plate of sandwiches.

'Why are you sneaking around?' She saw William standing behind Millie and her frown deepened. 'Oh, it's you. I might have known you'd be involved.'

'We're looking for someone,' he told her.

'Oh, yes? Who?'

They glanced at each other. 'I suppose we should tell her,' William said. 'You never know, she might be able to help.'

Helen looked from one to the other, her eyes narrowed. 'Tell me what?'

'We've lost a patient,' Millie blurted out.

'A dangerous convict,' William added.

'But he probably won't get far, because he has a gunshot wound in his leg,' Millie said.

Helen's mouth fell open. 'But why haven't you told the police? You must warn them at once.'

She thrust the plate of sandwiches into Millie's hands and started off towards the gate. William held on to her wrist.

'Don't,' he begged. 'We're in enough trouble as it is.'

'You'll be in a lot more trouble if you allow a wanted man to slip past the police.' Helen looked around. 'He could be anywhere!'

'I know,' Millie said miserably. 'You're right, we should tell the police.'

'You'll get fired if you tell them,' William reminded her.

'People could get hurt if we don't,' Millie said.

Helen looked from one to the other. 'Oh, for heaven's sake!' She rolled her eyes. 'Wait here. And don't say a word to anyone until I get back.'

They watched her head off towards the porters' lodge. 'What do you think she's doing?' Millie asked.

William shrugged. 'Maybe she's going to ask Mr Hopkins for help?'

'She's wasting her time then. Mr Hopkins is a miserable old man. He'll report us all to Matron as soon as look at us.'

'Don't you believe it,' said William. 'Old Hopkins has a soft spot for Helen. She's like the daughter he never had.'

Sure enough, a moment later she returned from the porters' lodge. 'It's all sorted,' she said. 'Mr Hopkins has got his porters on red alert, searching the building. If anyone can find him, they can.'

'What about us? What should we do?' Millie asked.

Helen sent her a stern look. 'Go back to the ward and keep your head down, if you know what's good for you,' she advised. 'And for heaven's sake, try to stay calm!'

It wasn't easy. Millie tried to keep her mind on looking after the patients, but she couldn't stop pacing to the window and looking out over the courtyard.

'The party's breaking up,' she said gloomily. Any minute now Sister Holmes would be returning to the ward. Then all hell would break loose.

'I don't know why you're looking so sorry for yourself, I'll be in just as much trouble as you,' Dora reminded her. 'I went off to the stoke hole and left you by yourself, remember?'

Millie chewed her lip. 'How bad do you think it will be?'

Dora stared at her. 'Benedict, we both left the ward and allowed a wanted criminal to escape. You tell me.'

They jumped as the double doors flew open. But instead of Sister Holmes and Staff Nurse Lund, two porters came in, pushing a patient on a trolley. He was covered from head to toe by a thin white sheet.

'Blimey, he doesn't look well,' one of the patients observed, glancing up from his crossword.

'I know Mr Dwyer's a good surgeon, but I didn't think he could raise 'em from the dead,' said another.

'There's been a mistake,' Millie started to say, 'we can't possibly...' Then she saw William bringing up the rear.

'Take him to bed seven,' he instructed.

Millie and Dora followed them to where the screens were still pulled around Mr Abbott's bed. It was only when they were safely concealed that William whisked the sheet off to reveal the craggy-faced criminal sleeping peacefully.

'But I don't understand,' Millie said, as the porters lifted him gently back into bed. 'How...? Where...?'

'Two of the porters found him hiding out in the basement,' William said. 'I had to give him a sedative to get him to come quietly.'

Millie clapped her hands with joy. 'You are brilliant!'

'It's Helen you should thank,' he said. 'If she hadn't mobilised the porters to help, I doubt we would have found him.'

'When you've quite finished, I think I can hear Sister Holmes coming up the corridor,' Dora interrupted them.

They had barely managed to get rid of William and the porters with their trolley when Sister Holmes came through the doors with Staff Nurse Lund at her heels. Her face was grave.

'Benedict. My office, immediately,' she said.

Millie and Dora exchanged anguished looks.

'Do you think she knows?' Millie whispered. Dora could only shrug helplessly in reply.

'Benedict!' Sister Holmes called from her office doorway.

Millie trailed in miserably, already preparing her excuses.

'Sit down, Benedict.' Millie did as she was told, still mystified. Reprimands were usually delivered standing toe to toe, bellowed at a level deafening enough to make your ears ring. But Sister Holmes' voice was softer, almost as if she were talking to a patient.

'Is there something wrong, Sister?' Millie asked.

Sister Holmes sat down opposite her, her eyes

full of compassion.

'It's about your father,' she said. 'There's been an accident...'

Chapter Forty-Seven

It was a miracle Henry Rettingham had survived, the doctors said.

Millie had helped comfort many distraught families on the wards. She had ushered them to a side room, plied them with hot sweet tea while the consultant delivered his bad news, and listened to them weeping behind the screens around their loved one's bed. And yet no matter how desperately sad she felt for them, she had never really understood the depth of their despair until now, when she herself sat with her grandmother in a consultant's office, listening to him tell her she might lose her precious father.

She already knew the details of the accident. Felix had explained it when he'd picked her up from the station an hour earlier. While out riding early that morning, Samson had taken fright at something and thrown her father off. The horse must have kicked him in the head as he galloped off, knocking him out. When Samson galloped back into the yard alone, the stable lad had raised the alarm.

They'd found her father staggering back down the road. He'd seemed fine, if a little groggy. But a few hours later he had complained of a headache, and by the afternoon he had collapsed.

The consultant explained that her father's unconsciousness was due to a build up of pressure in his brain. Cerebral oedema. Millie saw the words swimming in front of her eyes as if they were printed in a textbook. They had never meant anything to her as she'd yawned her way through Sister Parker's lecture. Now they meant life or death.

'Is there any sign of haemorrhage?' she asked.

The consultant's brows lifted. 'How do you know...?'

'I'm training to be a nurse. I would appreciate your being frank with me, Mr Cossard.'

She saw his frown, and understood his irritation. Consultants did not like to be questioned, especially not by silly young girls who thought they understood medical matters just because they'd washed a few bedpans.

But she was not about to be fobbed off either. This was her father, and she intended to keep asking questions, no matter how much it irked Philip Cossard.

Finally, he said, 'Thankfully there is no sign as yet. However, we must be prepared for such an eventuality.'

Millie nodded. 'And in the meantime, all you can do is control the cerebral oedema and intercranial pressure.'

'Indeed.' He looked at her consideringly. 'I do not need to tell you, Lady Amelia, that the next few hours and days are absolutely critical. If we can keep the swelling and pressure controlled and your father regains consciousness, then there is a good chance he will make a full recovery.'

'And if he doesn't, we must prepare ourselves for the worst,' Millie finished for him. She looked at her grandmother, stiff-faced in the chair next to her. She could tell it was taking every ounce of self-control the Dowager Countess had not to weep for her son. 'May we see him?'

'Of course.' The consultant nodded to a nurse, who stood by the door.

Her father was in a small private room off the main ward. Seriously ill patients were often 'specialed', as it was called. Only qualified nurses or the most senior students were allowed to tend to them.

Everything looked familiar to Millie – the drip stands, the metal bed, the overpowering smell of disinfectant, the muted sounds of a busy ward close by. But somehow it felt so very different when it was her own father lying in the bed.

Her grandmother crossed the room to his bedside. 'I don't understand it. There is hardly a scratch on him.' She looked over her shoulder at Millie. 'Do you think they might be mistaken about the severity of his condition? Surely if he was that badly injured there would be a wound...?'

Millie came to her side. She desperately wanted to offer her grandmother the hope she craved. But she also knew how cruel that would be.

'All the damage is inside his skull, Granny,' she said gently. 'The fall and the blow to his head have shaken his brain badly and caused it to swell. The doctors are hoping that by giving him lots of time and rest the pressure will subside.'

'And then he will recover?'

If his brain doesn't start to leak blood, Millie thought. And even if it doesn't, they wouldn't know for a while how the vitality of the medullary centres had been threatened. He might well live, but might not fully recover.

But there was no reason to burden her grandmother with such depressing thoughts. The elderly lady was holding on to the metal bedhead as if she would fall down without its support.

'Yes, Granny. He will recover,' Millie said flatly.

She pulled up a chair for her grandmother and found one for herself. They sat in silence for a long time, both lost in their thoughts. The Dowager Countess held her son's hand in her own thin beringed one.

'Does he know we're here, do you think?' she asked.

'It's hard to say. I hope so.'

A nurse came in, looking crisp and professional in her blue uniform. Millie watched as she checked the patient's temperature, pulse and respiration. She spoke to him while she worked, explaining what she was doing. Millie remembered all the times she'd had to chat away to Mrs Jones' lifeless body while she was training. At the time it had seemed so silly, but now it all made sense. She was treating him like a person, not just a patient. Millie watched the nurse work, and itched to do something practical herself. She had never felt so useless, just sitting there.

They sat with him until the evening turned to night. Millie heard the soft patter of footsteps along the corridor outside as the night staff came on duty.

Beside her, her grandmother's eyelids drooped. 'You should go home, Granny,' Millie said quietly. 'You need to get some rest.'

'I'm afraid you're right, child. It has been a rather long and worrying day.' She rose stiffly to her feet. 'I will ask Felix to bring the car for us.'

'Oh, no, I'm staying here.'

'But you need your rest too.'

'How can I possibly sleep?' Millie looked at her father. 'Besides, I want to be here. Just in case he wakes up.' Or the worst happens, she added silently.

If her grandmother had any inkling of what was in her heart, she didn't let on. 'You might be in the way,' she said anxiously. 'The nurses are bound to be very busy.'

'All the more reason I should stay. I can keep an eye on him during the night. I'm sure, the night staff will appreciate that.' She looked up at her grandmother, her mouth firm with determination. 'Whatever anyone says, I'm staying,' she insisted.

The Dowager Countess sighed. 'I can see that as usual your mind is made up on the matter, regardless of what anyone else thinks,' she said heavily. 'Very well, have it your own way. But I insist you return home first thing in the morning. We must try to maintain normality for the sake of the servants, if nothing else.'

The night nurse was surprised when she came in to turn down the lights and found Millie curled up in a chair, half asleep by her father's bed.

'You really should go home,' she advised. 'Sister would have a fit if she knew anyone was here overnight.'

'Sister won't be back until tomorrow morning. She doesn't have to know, does she?' Millie stretched and yawned.

'I suppose not.' The nurse looked down at her sympathetically. 'You look worn out. Would you like a cup of tea?'

'No, thank you.'

The nurse shaded the light with a green cloth and straightened the sheets. 'I'll be back in an hour,' she said. 'But do call me if you're concerned about anything.'

'Is there anything I can do for him?' Millie asked quickly, before she left. 'I feel so useless.'

The nurse gave her a kindly smile. 'Talk to him,' she advised. 'He may not respond, but a familiar voice might get through to him.'

And so Millie talked. She chatted about nothing, telling him about her life in London, Dora and Helen, the funny things that had happened to her on the wards. It felt strange, making small talk into nothingness. It was as if her father was at the end of a very long tunnel. She couldn't see him, but she knew he was there. All she could do was shout to him and hope he knew she was there too. And that he would find his way back to her.

And so it continued throughout the following day, and the day after that. Millie talked to him, read to him from *The Times* and even tried to do the crossword, although she found it a struggle without her father's help.

She also persuaded Mr Cossard and the ward sister to allow her to take over some of his practical care, such as washing and shaving him and rubbing methylated spirits and powder into his shoulders and back to keep pressure sores at bay. They even found a spare apron and cap for her once they saw how determined she was to help.

By night, she curled up in the chair in his room. After her first uncomfortable night, when it became obvious that nothing would persuade her to go home to her bed, the kindly nurse brought her an armchair from the sister's office during the night, whisking it away again at the first light of dawn.

Her grandmother disapproved of seeing Millie, her sleeves rolled up to the elbows, starched cap covering her fair curls, tending to her father.

'It's hardly fitting behaviour for a young lady,' she scolded. But even she had to admit she found it a comfort, knowing Millie was there with him.

'Should I arrange for the rest of your luggage to be brought down from London?' she asked, as the third day dawned and she watched Millie and another nurse changing the bed.

'That won't be necessary. I can manage with what I've brought with me.'

Lady Rettingham looked at her sharply. 'How long are you planning to stay?'

'I don't know.' Millie gazed down at her father, still unconscious in the bed. As every day passed, her hope dimmed. 'I shan't leave until – we know how Daddy is. Matron has told me to take as much time off as I need.'

Her grandmother was silent. Millie glanced up at her tense face as she gazed out of the window towards the sunny hospital gardens and sensed that all was not well. She finished tucking in the corner of the sheet and straightened up to look at her. 'Is there something wrong, Granny?' she asked.

'I'm just rather surprised, that's all. I assumed you would not be returning to London.'

Millie stared at her uncomprehending. 'But I have to go back. My training...'

'You heard what the consultant said.' Her grandmother turned to her. 'We must prepare ourselves for the worst. What if anything happens to your father? Who will run the estate?'

'The estate manager can look after it, surely?'

'And who is going to give him his orders? Who is going to make the decisions, make sure everything is done properly?'

'Are you suggesting that I should come home and run Billinghurst myself?' The idea was so ridiculous Millie would have laughed if she hadn't been so worn down by worry and exhaustion.

'Until the next heir claims the estate, certainly.' Her grandmother stared at her blankly. 'We have to face facts, Amelia. I know you believed your father would live for ever and you could chase your dreams to your heart's content, but that is not the case. We have to accept that he may die...'

'No!' Millie shouted.

'...and if he does,' her grandmother continued relentlessly, 'then Billinghurst will pass to Cousin Robert and that will be the end of it. But if your father survives, there is a very real possibility he may suffer some kind of mental incapacity that will prevent him from resuming his duties of running the estate. And what do you think will happen then? Are we to allow Billinghurst to crumble into the ground while you indulge yourself in

London? You have a duty, Amelia. Not to some sick strangers in the East End but to us, your family. And the sooner you realise that, the better.'

The Dowager Countess stared out of the window. 'Of course, none of this would have happened if you had married and settled down two years ago. Then we might even have had an heir for Billinghurst by now, instead of facing the prospect of being thrown out of our own home by a stranger.'

Millie stared at her, hot tears stinging her eyes. 'That isn't going to happen,' she said firmly. 'Daddy is going to get better.'

Her grandmother turned weary eyes to meet hers. 'I sincerely hope so, child,' she said. 'For all our sakes.'

Chapter Forty-Eight

Millie left her grandmother sitting by her father's bedside and went back to the house to rest and change her clothes. She was still feeling shaken by their argument but didn't blame her grandmother for her outburst; Lady Rettingham was just as tired and worn out with worry as Millie was.

As they crested the hill above the house, Millie ordered Felix to stop the car so she could get some fresh air. Cooped up inside the hospital, she hadn't realised how much she'd missed the warmth of the sun on her face, or the scent of air untainted by disinfectant.

She gazed down at the house below her. Billing-hurst looked beautiful, its honey-coloured walls burnished gold by the July sunshine. It nestled like a bright jewel on a cushion of rich green velvet, surrounded by fields of crops and orchards heavy with early fruit. Her grandmother was right; Billinghurst needed someone to manage it. She knew her father's estate manager, Jackson, was an experienced man who could be trusted with the day-to-day decisions. But he acted on the instructions of her father when it came to the overall running of the estate. She certainly couldn't imagine him taking orders from her, a twenty-year-old girl with little authority or experience.

And what if her father died? As much as her mind shrank from the prospect, it was one they all had to face. As every day passed, his chances of recovery lessened. If he died, the estate would pass to the legal heir, a distant cousin from North-umberland whom none of them had ever met.

She understood her grandmother's worry and frustration. Once the new Earl of Rettingham took over, there would be no place for either her or Millie. She didn't expect Cousin Robert would see them penniless on the streets, but their circum-stances would be very different. For one thing, Millie would no longer bring with her the Billing-hurst estate or the possibility of an earldom for her son. She finally realised why her grandmother had tried so hard to instil in her a sense of urgency about finding a husband. Like it or not, she had a duty to provide the estate with a suitable heir to inherit her father's title. The stability of so many lives depended on her.

The problem was she had thought her father was immortal. He had always seemed so strong, so indestructible. He was the foundation stone on which she had built her life, the reason she could go off and pursue her selfish dreams. She'd known that one day she would have to come home and settle down, but had somehow imagined that her time was infinite.

Now, too late, she understood how limited it really was.

'Oh, my lady!' Polly greeted her in dismay when she arrived home.

'I know. I look awful, don't I?' Millie said ruefully. 'I feel awful, too. I need a bath and a change of clothes.'

'Yes, my lady.' The way Polly looked her up and down, it was clear she felt it would take more than a new dress to put her right. 'Will you be requiring luncheon?'

'Just bring me a tray to my room, will you?' Millie couldn't face the prospect of sitting alone at the vast dining-room table. She would feel her father's absence even more acutely if there was no one to talk to or laugh with.

It was bliss to sink into the deep tub. Millie submerged herself luxuriously, feeling her muscles relax in the warm, scented water. How different from the bathrooms at the nurses' home, where hot water was as rationed as everything else, and pros had to make do with a few tepid inches after the seniors had used it all up.

After her bath Polly helped her dress, and the kitchen maid brought up a silver tray laden with slices of cold ham and chicken, and delicate slivers of bread and butter. Millie thanked her, but even as she looked at the food she knew she couldn't eat it.

'That will be all, Polly,' Millie dismissed her maid.

'Are you sure, my lady? I could finish curling your hair for you?'

'I can manage, thank you.' Millie couldn't keep the irritation out of her voice. She desperately wanted to be alone, and Polly's insistent fussing was beginning to tear at her already shredded nerves. She knew it wasn't the girl's fault, she was only trying to do her job, but what did it really matter if Millie's hair was perfectly curled or hanging in rats' tails? Her father was dying. Nothing mattered any more.

'We must maintain normality for the sake of the servants, if nothing else.' As grandmother's stern admonishment came into her head, Millie felt a bubble of hysterical laughter rising up inside her.

Then she caught sight of herself in the mirror and realised why poor Polly had been so anxious to attend to her. She looked perfectly dreadful. Her face was drawn and grey-tinged, eyes threaded with spidery red veins and ringed with dark circles like bruises.

She started to laugh, a harsh, spiky sound that echoed around her empty bedroom and made her feel as if she was going quite mad. She tugged a brush carelessly through her curls. Behind her in the mirror, she caught sight of her bed. The pale pink silk coverlet and big feather pillows looked so soft and inviting, she felt herself drawn towards it. Surely it wouldn't hurt to sink into its warm, enveloping depths just for five minutes…?

She hadn't meant to close her eyes, let alone fall asleep.

But the next thing she knew Polly was shaking her awake. 'Sorry to disturb you, my lady, but you have a visitor.'

Millie sat up, groggy with sleep. 'What – what time is it?'

'Just after four o'clock, my lady.'

'What? Why didn't anyone wake me sooner?' She threw back the covers and leapt out of bed so quickly her legs buckled under her. 'I have to get back to the hospital – where are my shoes?' She began searching around desperately.

'But what about your visitor, my lady?'

Millie turned to look at her, uncomprehending. 'What visitor?'

'Lord Sebastian is here, Lady Amelia.'

'Seb's here?' Her brain, still fuzzy with sleep, tried to make sense of it. Why was Seb here? The last she'd heard from him, he was on a shooting party in Scotland with Georgina Farsley's family.

'He is very anxious to see you, my lady.'

Ignoring Polly's protests that she couldn't possibly meet her visitor with her clothes all crumpled and her hair a tangled mess, Millie hurried out of the room.

Looking over the galleried landing, she could see Seb pacing in the hall. He was still dressed in his shooting tweeds, his cap clenched in his hands.

She stopped at the top of the staircase to compose herself. She might look a complete fright, but she didn't want Seb to think she had fallen to pieces entirely.

He swung around as she descended the stairs. 'Millie!' He rushed over to her, holding out his arms, then remembered himself and dropped them to his sides.

'Seb,' she greeted him. 'This is a surprise. I thought you were in Scotland?'

'I was. I drove straight down as soon as I heard.' His eyes searched her face anxiously. 'How is he?'

'My father has not yet regained consciousness.' Millie forced herself to sound calm.

'But he will recover?'

'I – I don't know.' Her voice faltered. 'The doctors say he has a chance. But with every passing day that he remains unconscious...' She stopped herself, pushing away the thought. She could feel her fears start to overcome her, and struggled to keep them at bay.

What would her grandmother do in this situation? she asked herself. She would be calm and gracious at all times, whatever she might be feeling inside.

'You came all the way down from Scotland, you say? You must be very tired.' She forced a smile. 'Please come into the drawing room and rest.' She led the way. 'Would you like something to eat? Yes, of course you would. I'll get Mrs Saunders to send something up...' She reached for the bell to summon the butler, but Seb stopped her.

'For God's sake, Millie, what's wrong with you? I didn't come all this way for a social visit. I came because I was worried about you.' He put his hands on her arms, steadying her. 'You don't have to do this,' he said softly. 'You don't have to make polite conversation, as if we're at a wretched tennis

461

party.' He ducked his head to look into her eyes. 'It's me, Seb. Your friend, remember?'

Millie lifted her gaze to meet his. His grey eyes were so full of kindness and understanding, she felt herself begin to crumble.

'Please don't be nice to me, Seb. I don't think I can bear it,' she said, her chin quivering.

'Oh, Millie.' He opened his arms and she fell into them.

He held her for a long time as she sobbed against his chest, her tears soaking the rough tweed of his jacket. It was such a relief to hold someone, to be close to them. The steady, reassuring beat of his heart calmed her. She no longer felt as if she was alone, stuck in the middle of a terrifying nightmare with no escape.

'I'm sorry,' she mumbled, her face still buried against him. 'This is not very ladylike behaviour. I don't know what my grandmother would say.'

'I couldn't care less what your grandmother thinks.' He guided her gently to the couch and sat down beside her.

'Even so, you should let me arrange something for you to eat.'

'Perhaps later.' He pulled a handkerchief out of his pocket and carefully dried her tears. 'Oh, Millie, I've been so worried about you. All the way down here, I couldn't stop thinking about you, wondering how you were...'

'It was very kind of you to come. I'm sorry if I ruined your shooting.'

'Do you really think I could have stamped around the highlands, pretending to shoot deer, knowing what you were going through?' He

462

laughed harshly. 'I'm sure those poor stags will be most grateful there's one less gun to worry about. Besides, Georgina seemed to be shooting enough for everyone. She has a rather bloodthirsty nature, it turns out.'

Millie smiled in spite of herself. She could just imagine the extremely determined Miss Farsley tracking down her quarry through the heather.

'She always did enjoy the hunt.'

Seb rolled his eyes. 'Don't I know it! I understand exactly how those wretched deer feel.' He touched Millie's chin with one finger, turning her face towards his. 'That's better. I like to see you smile.'

'I must look a complete fright.' Millie touched her stringy curls.

'You look adorable, as always.' Seb's face was close to her, only inches away. Then he seemed to remember himself, and stood up. 'Do you think it would be possible for me to see your father? Is he allowed visitors other than family?'

'I'm sure that would be all right. Anyway, you are Daddy's godson, which makes you practically family.'

Seb nodded. 'I must say, your father has always been very good to me. Far more of a parent than my own dear papa anyway.' He smiled wryly.

Millie thought about the dissolute duke, bed hopping his way through most of high society and once again it struck her how lucky she was in her own father. But for how long? She swallowed hard, determined not to allow herself to cry again. 'Let me arrange something for you to eat, and then we'll go back to the hospital,' she said.

Her grandmother expressed no surprise when Millie walked into her father's room with Seb in tow.

Millie went straight to her father's bedside. 'How is he?'

'Still no change, I'm afraid.' The Dowager Countess squeezed her son's hand. 'The nurses come in and out, but there's nothing anyone can do for him. I know we haven't lost him,' she said with feeling. 'He's in there somewhere. If only there was some way we could rouse him.'

'That's why we have to talk to him,' Millie said firmly. 'If he hears our voices, he can find his way to us.'

She saw the look that passed between Seb and her grandmother. 'It's true,' she insisted. 'He will come back to us, I know he will.'

'Of course he will,' the Dowager Countess said soothingly. 'In the meantime, we must keep our vigil and pray.' She looked up at Seb. 'But perhaps now you're here, Sebastian, you can persuade my granddaughter to rest occasionally?'

'I'll do my best, Lady Rettingham.'

'Good. In that case I will take my leave of you both. You will be staying with us I hope, Sebastian?'

'I would very much like that.'

Millie looked from one to the other, her eyes narrowing. Unexpected visitors always put her grandmother out of sorts, so why was she so calm about Seb's arrival? Unless...

'Did Granny send for you?' she demanded, as soon as they were alone.

464

'Yes and no,' he admitted.

'What does that mean?'

'She sent word informing me of your father's illness. I am his godson, after all. She didn't summon me, but I'm sure she knew I would hardly stay away.'

'I do wish she wouldn't meddle.'

'Grandmothers are made to meddle. Mine is the most atrocious meddler, as I'm sure you know.' He sent her a sidelong look. 'Why? Would you rather I weren't here?'

She turned her head to look at him. 'No,' she admitted with a smile. 'I'm glad you're here, Seb.'

Chapter Forty-Nine

They sat together at her father's bedside all evening. Millie would have stayed there all night too, if Seb hadn't gently persuaded her to go home and rest. 'You'll do your father no good at all if you're exhausted,' he reasoned. 'Do you think he wants to wake up and see you looking like death?'

All through the following day he was there by her side. And the day after that.

'You don't have to stay, you know,' she said, over and over again. But the answer was always the same.

'I know I don't have to. But I want to.'

As they sat there together, Millie opened her heart and confided in him her fears for the estate.

'Granny's right,' she sighed. 'Jackson is a good

465

man, but someone needs to take charge there. There's so much to be done. The hops will be ready for picking soon, and then there's the fruit and all the other crops...'

'Let me help,' Seb said.

'You?'

'Don't sound so surprised,' he laughed. 'I know I might seem like a bumbling fool, but I do know something about running an estate. Who do you think has been looking after Lyford while my brother's been in the army and my father's been – well, doing whatever he does? I would like to help,' he said earnestly. 'I could help keep an eye on everything until your father is well enough to take over the reins again.'

The way he said it touched Millie. It gave her hope that one day everything would be back to normal, even though in the back of her mind she knew it wouldn't.

'Would you?' she said hopefully. 'It would be such a relief to know Billinghurst was in good hands.'

'Of course. You know I'd do anything to help you.' He took her hand and for a moment they stared into each other's eyes. 'Millie–' Seb started to say, but she cut him off.

'I'd better read to Daddy.' She withdrew her hand from his and picked up the folded copy of *The Times* she had brought from home. 'He needs to know what's happening in the world.'

Seb rose to his feet. 'I'll take a stroll, if you don't mind? I need some fresh air.'

Millie watched him out of the window, walking briskly down towards the stream that ran through the hospital grounds. Dear Seb. He was the kindest, most wonderful friend she could ever wish for. But she knew he wanted more than that.

Could she offer him anything other than friendship? She knew she loved being with him, that she needed his strength and his unshakable good humour. He was the only one she could really talk to, and she missed him when he wasn't by her side.

But was that the same as love? He didn't make her heart flutter, or her head spin. But perhaps those kinds of feelings didn't really count? She pushed her troubled thoughts aside, opened up the newspaper and scanned through the stories.

'"Parliament has finally passed the new Government of India Act,"' she read aloud. '"It gives all provinces full representative and elective governments." Just think, thirty million Indians will finally have the vote. I think that's a good thing, don't you, Daddy? Although it says the Viceroy and his governors retain veto powers. I hope they don't use them. That wouldn't be very fair, would it?' She laughed to herself. 'Listen to me! A week ago I wouldn't have given a fig about politics, and now I'm quite au fait with it all. You always said I should take more interest in current affairs, didn't you?'

She stared at her father's waxy, lifeless face, willing him to respond, to be proud of her. But there was only silence.

Choking back tears, she turned hurriedly to the crossword, rustling the pages. As usual, she could only manage a few of the clues before she was completely stumped.

'Twelve across. "Left in the dark". Eight letters. Now what could that be?' She chewed the end of her pencil thoughtfully. 'Electric? That's to do with the dark, isn't it? Although I suppose it's more light than dark. Abandon? No, that's only seven letters. Maybe it's abandons? Although that has nothing to do with dark, has it?'

She gazed at her father. 'I bet you'd know it straight away, wouldn't you? You'd just say the answer as if it were the simplest thing in the world. You always know the answer, don't you, Daddy? You just say it, and it's completely obvious.' She caught her breath on a sob. 'Oh, Daddy, why aren't you here to help me?'

Grief, exhaustion, frustration and every other emotion she had been storing up came pouring out as she sat by his bedside, weeping silently, her shoulders heaving.

'Sinister.'

The whisper was so faint, Millie wasn't sure she'd heard it at first.

She looked up in disbelief. 'Daddy?'

She saw his dry lips move slightly. No words this time, but it was enough. His eyelids fluttered for a second, then closed again.

'Nurse!' Millie screamed. She ran for the door and crashed into the nurse who was hurrying in.

'What is it? What's happened?'

'He's woken up!' It was all Millie could do not to hug her. 'He spoke to me.'

Everything happened very fast after that. The nurse called for Mr Cossard, who finally appeared after what seemed like hours, examined his patient and declared that, yes indeed, there

468

did seem to be signs of life.

'But we must be cautious until we know the extent of any possible damage,' he cautioned.

'He can't be too damaged if he can still do *The Times* crossword, can he?' Millie was too delighted to listen to the warnings. 'I must tell Seb.' She looked out of the window. There was no sign of him in the grounds, but she knew he would be there.

She found him straight away. He was sitting on the bank by the stream, smoking and staring out into the water.

'Seb!' He shot to his feet and tossed his cigarette into the stream when he saw her running towards him, calling his name. Millie saw the flicker of concern on his face as he wondered what news she was bringing.

She launched herself into his arms, overcome by joy and relief. 'He's awake, Seb,' she whispered. 'Daddy's going to be all right.'

'Thank God.' She felt him relax, and his arms went around her, holding her tight. For a moment neither of them moved. Then they slowly pulled apart. Millie looked up into his eyes, finding them dark with desire, and felt herself weaken.

'Millie?' His voice was hoarse, uncertain.

For an answer, she put her hands up to his face and kissed him. It seemed like the most natural thing in the world. Seb's kiss was shy and tentative at first and she could sense him holding back, as if he almost didn't dare believe it was really happening. Then a moment later the floodgates opened and he was kissing her with a ferocity and passion she could hardly have imagined in him.

She went on kissing him for a long time, not wanting to let him go, afraid to break the spell. But finally it was broken and they pulled apart.

'We'd better go back inside.' Millie's gaze slid away from his, unable to meet his eyes.

'Shall I telephone your grandmother and let her know? Or would you prefer me to drive back and fetch her?' Seb asked, as they walked back to the hospital building.

'It might be best if you telephone her. She may need some time to compose herself. Granny hates being caught unawares.'

They were talking like strangers, Millie thought, not like two people who had just shared a moment of intense passion. She began to wonder if she'd imagined it.

Chapter Fifty

'Happy birthday, sweetheart.'

Helen stared in joyful surprise at the parcel Charlie placed into her hands. It was carefully wrapped and tied with pink ribbon.

'You didn't have to get me anything. I really didn't expect it.'

'What kind of a bloke doesn't buy his girl a present on her birthday?' He nodded towards it. 'Go on, then. Open it. I want to see if you like it.'

Helen's fingers trembled as she untied the silky bow. It wasn't even her birthday until the following day, but it was already the best she had ever had. Charlie had arranged for her to have tea with his family, and his mum had prepared a wonderful spread for her, including a big birthday cake she had iced herself. Everyone had joined in a heartfelt but tuneless chorus of 'Happy Birthday To You', then Charlie's younger brothers and sister had crowded round to help her blow out the candles. This was followed by a mad rush as everyone dived in to get the biggest slice.

'Hold it, you lot, there's plenty for everyone!' Mrs Denton laughed, brandishing the cake slice to keep them at bay. 'Anyway, our Helen gets the first piece, as she's the birthday girl.'

Helen beamed. Our Helen. It was the first time anyone had ever called her that.

'I s'pose you'll be having a big party with your family, too?' Mrs Denton had said. Helen had smiled, and made some neutral reply. But she had never had a birthday party in her life. Her mother disapproved of rowdy celebrations. She didn't approve of birthdays in general, feeling it was wrong for anyone to be singled out for special attention. Of course Helen had cards and presents, but Constance always managed to take the edge off her joy by making her give up a favourite toy to the local children's home.

'You must remember those less fortunate than yourself,' she always said. Although Helen hadn't been able to think of anyone less fortunate than her as she'd tearfully parted company with her favourite teddy or most cherished book.

After the tea party, Charlie had taken her aside into the hall to give her his present. 'I didn't want to give it to you in front of everyone else in case

471

you didn't like it,' he confessed shyly.

Now Helen carefully unfastened the bow and peeled back the wrapping paper to reveal a beautiful jewellery box in polished golden wood. Inside it was lined with red velvet, with small compartments for all her trinkets.

'I made it myself at my uncle's works,' Charlie said proudly. 'I know it's not much, but I thought you might like it?'

'Oh, Charlie, it's the nicest present I've ever had!' It didn't even matter that she had no jewellery to put in it. Just the thought that he'd taken the time and the trouble to make something especially for her was enough. Helen threw her arms around his neck. 'Oh, Charlie, I love it. And I love you, too.'

He put his hands up to grasp her wrists, pulling away from her. His blue eyes searched hers. 'Do you mean it?'

'Yes, it's perfect.'

'Not the box. Did you mean what you just said – about loving me?'

She hadn't realised the words had escaped her. She'd been too shy to say them out loud before, even though they sang in her heart constantly.

She nodded. 'Say it again,' Charlie said.

Helen felt a warm blush rising in her face. 'I can't.'

'Go on, say it. Please.'

She raised her eyes to meet his. 'I love you, Charlie Denton,' she whispered.

He walked her back to the hospital, right up to the gates. He would have walked her to the door of the nurses' home if she hadn't stopped him.

'I'm not sure I want to let you go,' he said, his arm tightening around her waist. 'I'm frightened I'll never see you again.'

'Don't be silly! We're going to the pictures next Friday, remember?'

'But that's a whole week away! How am I going to manage until then?'

'You'll manage,' she laughed. 'Now go. I've got to get changed and be back on duty by five.'

'On one condition.'

'What's that?'

'That you say you love me again.'

'I can't!' Helen looked around, embarrassed. 'Not here.'

'Say it again, or I'll stand right here until you do.'

He looked so obstinate, standing there leaning on his stick, that Helen laughed. 'All right, then.' She lowered her voice. 'I love you, Charlie Denton. Is that enough for you?'

He thought about it for a moment. 'I would have preferred you to shout it from the rooftops, but that will do for now, I s'pose.' He bent forward, and kissed her gently on the lips. 'I'll see you next Friday.'

He walked away, limping on his stick. Helen went in through the hospital gates and was crossing the courtyard when she heard his voice, loud and clear as a bell, ringing out over the hospital wall.

'I love you, Nurse Helen Tremayne!'

It seemed to ring out for ever like an echo around the tranquil courtyard. All around her people looked up to see where the sound was coming from. Helen stood rooted to the spot, her whole body flaming with heat, certain everyone must be looking at her. But embarrassed as she felt, she also couldn't stop smiling.

And then she turned around and saw her mother waiting for her outside the black front door of the nurses' home and the smile froze on her face.

A wave of fear crashed over Helen, making her gulp for air. She wanted to run, but her feet were already moving, dragging her towards her mother as if pulled by an invisible thread.

Constance Tremayne stood on the steps, as still as a statue, both hands clutching the strap of her sensible handbag.

'Go inside,' she ordered through tight, unmoving lips.

The nurses' home was closed to families or friends, but as usual the rules did not apply to Constance Tremayne as she led the way into the empty sitting room. The July sun shone through the bay window, throwing a broad patch of light on to the worn, sagging settees. A solitary teacup from the previous night sat in a sticky ring on the table.

Constance stood at the window, back turned to her daughter, staring out across the courtyard. Helen had got used to reading her mother's moods. From the set of her stiff spine to her tightly clenched hands, it was obvious she was furious.

Helen fixed her gaze on the teacup, braced herself, and waited.

'Who is he?' Constance asked finally.

'His name is Charlie.' Her voice came out as a whisper.

'How long has this been going on?'

'Nearly three months.'

Her mother turned around to face her. 'You have been lying to me for that long? I had no idea you could be so deceitful.'

'I haven't lied to you, I just...'

'Be quiet, Helen.'

'But Mother...'

'I will tell you when you can speak.' Constance gazed out of the window again. 'I suppose he is the reason you were caught coming back late?'

Helen's heart sank. It was too much to hope that her mother would not have found out about that. She knew everything.

'Well? What have you to say for yourself?'

She stared down at the box in her hands. 'I'm sorry, Mother.'

Helen felt the chill of her mother's wintry gaze on her. 'I'm afraid sorry is not enough, Helen. I wonder if you realise how deeply disappointed I am in you?' She came to stand before her. 'You have let yourself and your family down. I brought you up to be a decent girl, to have high moral standards. I did not bring you up to stay out all hours and behave like a common tart!'

'I'm not a tart!' Helen protested. 'I just have a boyfriend, that's all. Lots of girls have boyfriends.'

'Not you! You're better than that. I will not have your name tainted with scandal, do you hear me? I will not have people whispering about you behind your back, saying you're no better than you ought to be. I don't think you quite understand, Helen, I have an excellent name in this hospital. I won't have you tainting it with your

475

sordid little liaisons!'

'It's not a sordid liaison,' she protested. 'Charlie's a nice boy. I've even met his family. I'm sure if you got to know him...'

'I have no intention of getting to know him, because you won't be seeing him again,' Constance declared flatly.

'But Mother—'

She held up a hand for silence. 'That's enough, Helen. I don't wish to talk about it any more. I've made my decision and that's the end of it.'

Helen stared at her, shocked. Constance was already gathering up her handbag, as if the matter were settled.

'Y-you can't say that,' she stammered. 'I love Charlie.'

'Love! For heaven's sake, Helen, do you know how utterly ridiculous you sound? Why, you're like one of those simpering fools in *Peg's Paper!*' Her mother gave her a pitying look. 'You have no idea what you're talking about. You're far too young and naive, you don't know the first thing about it.'

Helen watched her adjust her gloves, fastening the buttons at her wrists, fastidious as ever.

'So I'm never going to be allowed to have a boyfriend, is that it?' she asked quietly.

'Of course you can have a boyfriend, Helen. Don't be so melodramatic.' Constance paused to consider the matter. 'When you're older, and you've finished your training, then I'm sure a suitable young man will come along.'

'And I suppose you'll tell me where and when to find him?' The words were out before she could stop herself.

Her mother stared at her. 'Don't be impertinent, Helen.'

'I'm not being impertinent. I just don't understand why I can't have a boyfriend. William has lots of girlfriends, and you don't say anything to him.'

She saw her mother's expression soften. 'William is different. He is a young man, and he doesn't need my guidance so much.'

Really? Helen thought. For a moment she was tempted to tell her mother the real reason for Peggy Gibson's breakdown. But she couldn't betray William and she didn't think her mother would believe her anyway. Constance Tremayne doted on her son.

'You are a young, impressionable girl and you must be protected for your own good,' she went on briskly. 'Which is why I have decided to remove you from this hospital.'

'What?' Helen stared at her in dismay. 'But why?'

'Because I am no longer satisfied that it is a suitable place for you to continue your training.' Constance absently ran one gloved finger along the window ledge and inspected it for dust.

'But I don't want to go. I like it here. I've made friends.'

'And I'm sure you'll make friends elsewhere.' She snapped her handbag shut. 'Now, I must be going. I shall expect you for tea tomorrow, since it is your birthday.'

'You can't do this.'

Her mother was almost at the door before Helen managed to get the words out. Constance stopped and stared at her. 'I beg your pardon?'

Helen couldn't look at her. She fixed her eyes on the jewellery box in her hands instead. It made her think of Charlie, which gave her courage she'd never had before. 'You can't run my life for me like this. You've always decided everything for me, but not any more. You can't take me away from here, and you can't tell me who I can and can't fall in love with.'

'Of course I can, Helen. I am your mother. I have your best interests at heart.'

'No, you don't. All you've ever wanted to do is turn me into a copy of yourself. But I'm not you, and I'm sick of doing everything you say. I want to be allowed to think for myself–'

The slap was hard and sudden, catching her off balance. Helen staggered sideways and the box fell from her hands.

'You see?' Her mother's tight-lipped face swam before her eyes. 'The very fact that you're answering me back shows me how out of control you are. The sooner we remove you from this place, the better.'

She left. Helen heard the front door bang shut and sank to her knees. Her beautiful jewellery box lay in pieces on the rug, its lid broken off. Seeing it there, broken in two, hurt more than any blow her mother could have given her.

She picked up the pieces and tried to fit them back together, but she couldn't see through a hot blur of tears. Finally she gave up as misery overtook her and she started to sob. She heard the sound of the front door again, and knew she should pick herself up and stop crying, but she couldn't. She didn't care if one of the other students saw her, or if Sister Sutton came in. She didn't care about anything any more.

Footsteps passed the sitting room, and then stopped.

'Tremayne?' Dora's voice came from the doorway. 'What is it? What's happened?'

Helen tried to explain, but she couldn't speak for crying.

'Come on, it's all right. We'll sort it out.' She heard the crackle of starched fabric as Dora knelt beside her. 'Come on, love. Don't get upset. Bit of glue and it'll be as right as rain.'

As Dora put her arms around her shaking shoulders, Helen wished she could explain it would take more than a bit of glue to mend her broken heart.

Chapter Fifty-One

'Why, Mrs Tremayne, what a pleasant surprise. I didn't know we had a meeting today?'

Kathleen Fox's smile was strained as she returned from her morning round to find Constance waiting for her in her office.

'We didn't.' Constance quivered like a highly strung racehorse, a sure sign of impending trouble. 'But there's a matter I wish to discuss with you.'

What is it this time? Kathleen wondered. A nurse being allowed off duty five minutes early? Too much coal being used to fire up the stoke hole? She braced herself for the worst.

'It's about my daughter,' Constance said.

Kathleen's heart sank. So Miss Hanley had managed to be the bearer of bad tidings after all.

'Oh, yes?' She took her seat behind her desk.

'I'm removing her from this hospital.'

Kathleen looked up sharply. She'd been expecting a rebuke, possibly even a lecture. But not this. 'I beg your pardon?'

'I am taking Helen away from the Nightingale. I have put my intentions in writing.' She rummaged in her handbag and produced an envelope, which she pushed across the desk to Kathleen. 'As you'll see, I intend to take Helen away as soon as possible—'

'But you can't!' Kathleen stared dumbly at the letter on the desk, still struggling to take in what she was hearing. 'Helen's approaching her final year. Another few months and she'll be taking her State Final.'

'She can finish her studies elsewhere. I have been in contact with St Andrew's in Aberdeen. They are more than happy to accept her, given her record and good character.'

'You're sending her all the way to Scotland?'

Constance Tremayne's mouth tightened. 'St Andrew's has an excellent reputation as a teaching hospital.'

'Yes, but even so...' Then Kathleen saw the spite gleaming in Constance Tremayne's eyes, and it all made perfect sense.

'You're doing this to punish her,' she said flatly.

Outrage flared in Constance's taut face. 'I'm doing what's best for my daughter.'

'Are you? Is that really why you're doing this,

480

Mrs Tremayne?'

They faced each other across the desk, neither of them blinking. Then, finally, Constance said, 'If you must know, I have grave concerns about the way this hospital is being run, and in particular the moral welfare of the young nurses in your care.'

Kathleen could feel her temper rising and held on to it grimly. 'I can assure you, Helen's moral welfare is not in danger,' she said.

'Is that so?' Constance's Tremayne's brows arched. 'And are you aware, Matron, that for the past three months my daughter has been seeing – a man?'

The way she said it made it sound as if Helen had been consorting with white slave traders.

'Lots of the nurses have boyfriends, Mrs Tremayne,' Kathleen said mildly.

'Not my daughter!' Constance Tremayne looked genuinely shocked. 'What is more, she's been seeing this – this person in secret.'

I'm not surprised, Kathleen thought. How else was the girl to have any kind of private life? She thought about poor downtrodden Helen Tremayne, who walked with her head down and never dared stand up for herself even when the other girls provoked and tormented her.

'Helen is an upright, moral girl of excellent character,' Constance continued. 'Or she was, until all this happened.'

'Oh, come along, Mrs Tremayne!' Kathleen couldn't help smiling. 'You can't condemn the girl just for falling in love.'

'In love?' Constance Tremayne went white to

481

her lips, her face rigid with rage and shock. 'My daughter is not *in love*, Matron. She doesn't know the meaning of the word. She's become infatuated, allowed herself to be led astray with all kinds of silly notions she knows nothing about. She should be concentrating on her studies, not filling her head with fanciful nonsense about boys and romance! If this silliness continues she will end up failing her exams.'

'I can't see that happening at all,' Kathleen reasoned. 'Helen is a very conscientious girl. She takes her studies very seriously indeed. I certainly haven't seen any evidence of silliness, as you call it.'

'Really? And what do you call her recent rule-breaking?' Mrs Tremayne pounced triumphantly. 'Helen wouldn't have dreamt of staying out late before she met this person.' Her mouth curled with distaste. 'So you see, it's starting already. And what will happen next, I wonder? What else is this reprobate going to talk her into? I've already seen her defy me because she's so besotted with him. How long before he really leads her astray, takes advantage of her?' Her eyes blazed fiercely bright, and an angry vein pulsed in her temple. 'Helen is a naïve young girl. She could end up disgraced, her life in ruins. I won't have that happen, do you hear? I will not allow that to happen to my daughter!'

Kathleen regarded her carefully. She had never seen Constance Tremayne so furious before. She looked as if she was ready to explode.

Kathleen's next words were spoken in a calm and deliberate manner. 'Have you met this young man, Mrs Tremayne?' she asked mildly.

'Met him? Of course I haven't met him!' Constance Tremayne's voice was shrill. 'I have no intention of doing so. I want to end this nonsense, nip it in the bud before Helen's future is ruined.'

'And you think sending her to Scotland will solve the problem, do you?'

'It will put her out of harm's way.' Constance was quieter now, clutching her handbag in front of her like a shield of righteousness.

'I believe they have young men north of the border too,' Kathleen pointed out. She saw Constance Tremayne bristle with anger again, and quickly tried to calm her. 'I understand you want to protect your daughter, Mrs Tremayne, but you can't shield her for ever.'

'How can you possibly understand?' Constance flashed back. 'You're not a mother.'

'I know, but–'

'Then kindly don't try to tell me how to bring up my own daughter.' Constance Tremayne stood up and straightened her hat. 'Anyway, this is not a matter for discussion,' she said briskly. 'I've made my decision, and that's final.'

'And what does Helen think?'

Constance Tremayne frowned, as if the thought hadn't even occurred to her. 'Helen will do as she's told.'

'For how long?'

'I beg your pardon?'

'I've seen the way you treat her, the way you talk to her.' Kathleen could feel her anger rolling like a rock down a hill, gaining momentum. 'You terrify and bully that poor girl until she doesn't know which way to turn. One day she is going to stand up for herself, and when she does you'll only have yourself to blame!'

The two women faced each other across the desk. Constance's eyes were fixed on Kathleen's face, coldly accusing. 'I have made my decision,' she repeated firmly. 'And you can be sure the Board of Trustees will hear about the way you have spoken to me!'

'It's nothing compared to what I'd like to say,' Kathleen muttered as the door closed. She closed her eyes and sighed heavily. She was sure she hadn't done herself or poor Helen any favours, but she couldn't help flying off the handle. Constance Tremayne was simply insufferable.

Seized by a sudden fit of rage, she picked up a wooden paperweight and hurled it at the door, narrowly missing Miss Hanley as she opened it.

'Don't you ever knock?' Kathleen snapped, for once too angry to be civil. She was tired of tip-toeing around her Assistant Matron while Miss Hanley seemed to do as she pleased.

'Is there something wrong, Matron?'

'You could say that.' Kathleen stared across the desk at her. Miss Hanley stood erect and implacable, her immaculately starched uniform stretched over her broad shoulders, hands folded in front of her. Kathleen suddenly wished she had another paperweight to hurl.

'We've had a visit from Mrs Tremayne,' she said.

'Oh, yes?' The tiniest hint of a smile tugged at the corners of Miss Hanley's thin mouth. No doubt she was relishing the thought of the drubbing Kathleen would have received.

'For once I wasn't the one in trouble.' She kept her voice deliberately light. 'It seems someone has seen fit to inform Mrs Tremayne about her daughter's recent reprimand. I wonder who that could have been?' Miss Hanley's broad face gave nothing away. 'At any rate, the damage is done now. Mrs Tremayne is so appalled by the lack of discipline in this hospital that she intends to take Helen away.'

Kathleen had the small satisfaction of seeing Miss Hanley's jaw drop. 'But she can't!' she burst out. 'Helen is one of the best students we have. The Nightingale needs girls like her.'

'I agree. But apparently St Andrew's in Aberdeen will be having the benefit of her excellent training from now on.'

Kathleen watched a mottled purple hue creep up from under Miss Hanley's starched collar as she took in the news. She was pleased her assistant was so shaken. Perhaps now she could see the damage her meddling had done.

Kathleen only hoped she was proud of herself.

'Are you quite well, Veronica? You're very quiet this evening,' Florence observed as they sat in the small patch of garden beside the nurses' home. It was a warm, sunny evening, far too pleasant to be indoors, so the sisters had brought folding chairs out on to the lawn for their patchwork session.

But Veronica Hanley was barely aware of the warmth of the sun dappling through the chestnut trees, or of the sewing in her lap. Her thoughts were straying elsewhere.

'I must confess, I'm a little dismayed by the

485

news about Tremayne,' she admitted finally.

'Oh, yes. Poor Tremayne.' Sister Parker shook her head. 'Such a bright girl. And such a loss to this hospital.'

'I don't know why you'd say that, after what she did to me.' Agatha Sutton's chins wobbled with indignation.

Florence Parker restrained her smile. 'I wonder how her mother found out?' she mused.

Veronica was aware of Florence's eyes fixed on her. She kept her gaze on her sewing, which had become uneven and ugly through lack of attention. She sighed and began picking the stitches out.

'I must say, I'm surprised at Mrs Tremayne's reaction,' she said.

'Are you? I can't say I am. She's always struck me as a vindictive sort of woman,' Florence said sharply.

'Yes, but given her own background...' Veronica shut her mouth like a trap, biting back the words.

Agatha went on stitching, blithely unaware, but it was too much to hope Florence hadn't noticed. She regarded her keenly.

'You were about to say something else, Veronica?'

She yanked out another stitch, breaking the thread in her agitation. 'I just thought, as a vicar's wife, she might have shown a little more forgiveness,' she muttered.

'She does seem to be judging her poor daughter rather harshly,' Florence remarked.

Doesn't she just? Veronica thought. Her feelings were as tangled as the threads of her patchwork. And try as she might, she couldn't seem to sort them out.

'I suppose you're right,' Agatha agreed with a sigh. 'The wretched girl did almost give me a heart attack, but I suppose no one is perfect, are they?'

'Apart from Constance Tremayne, of course,' Florence reminded her.

Is she? Veronica pursed her mouth over her stitching.

She might seem harsh, but she believed in fairness. And Constance Tremayne really wasn't being fair. Especially given everything Veronica knew about her.

'Are you sure you're quite all right, Veronica? You're being quite merciless with that patchwork. It's practically in shreds,' Florence Parker observed.

'Yes, I know. Forgive me.' Veronica let her sewing fall into her lap. 'I'm not in the mood this evening, I'm afraid. I have a great deal on my mind.'

The two sisters regarded her expectantly, but Veronica said nothing more. There was only one person she could talk to now, and that was Constance Tremayne.

Chapter Fifty-Two

In August, it was time to change wards again. Dora was sorry to say goodbye to Sister Holmes and Male Surgical, especially when she found out she would be going to Gynae. Sister Wren

487

wasn't nearly so interested in training as she was in putting her feet up in her sitting room and flirting with the doctors. As long as Dora did as she was told and kept herself busy, Sister Wren left her to her own devices.

Which might have been a blessing, had it not been for Lettie Pike the ward maid.

She was Sister Wren's eyes and ears on the ward. While Sister Wren relaxed in her sitting room, Lettie would spy on the nurses. Nothing seemed to get past her beady eye, and she took great delight in making sure the students got into trouble as often as possible.

Poor Dora was the special focus of her attention. As she found out when she had to miss her dinner break one day. Light-headed with hunger, she'd risked eating some of the patients' leftovers in the kitchen. It was only a piece of cold cod, but Lettie Pike made sure Sister Wren found out all about it.

'No eating on the wards!' Sister had screamed at her in front of everyone. 'Good heavens, Doyle, no wonder you're so fat!'

Even when Lettie couldn't land Dora into trouble, she singled her out for yet more spite.

'Did you know my Ruby's courting Nick Riley?' she would say almost every day. 'Very keen on her, he is. Ruby thought he might have been sweet on you once, but he says he was never interested.'

Dora did her best to ignore her as she went on counting the dirty towels and sheets for the laundry. It was none of her business who Nick Riley was courting, she told herself firmly. If she'd had any chance with him at all, it was definitely in the past.

But one day Lettie Pike had a new nugget of gossip with which to torment Dora.

'I thought your Josie was going to be a teacher?' she said casually, as she barged Dora out of the way to fill her cleaning bucket in the sluice.

'That's right.'

'Then how come my Ruby saw her sniffing around in Gold's yesterday?'

Dora frowned. 'She's sure it was our Josie?'

'Blimey, girl, we've lived next door long enough to know if it was her or not!' Lettie rolled her eyes. 'I'm telling you, my Ruby saw her. Having a fine old chat with Esther Gold, she was, asking if there were any jobs going.' She raised her voice over the roar of the tap. 'Very surprising, I must say, seeing as how your mum's always boasting about her taking all these exams.'

She turned off the tap and hauled the bucket out of the sink. 'I asked your mum about it, but she just said she didn't know nothing. Made out like I was making trouble, she did. I told her, my Ruby saw her with her own eyes. And my Ruby doesn't tell lies.'

Not much, she doesn't! Dora nearly laughed out loud. Ruby Pike could be a proper little story-teller when she wanted to be. But there was no reason why she'd lie about something like that.

Dora frowned. There had to be something more to it, something even her mother didn't know.

Somewhere inside her, a dark and nameless fear began to uncoil itself again.

Two days later, Dora sent word for Josie to meet her in Victoria Park. It was a hot, sunny Saturday and the park was crowded with families, children playing and young couples strolling hand in hand.

The Josie she knew would have loved a day like this. She would have been in the park with her friends or Bea and Little Alfie, squealing with fun and laughter as she chased them around on the grass.

But sitting on a park bench, Dora scarcely recognised the thin, nervous young girl who approached her, head down, dragging her feet. Seeing her, Dora's heart sank to her shoes.

'All right, Jose?' she greeted her. 'Lovely day, ain't it?'

'S'all right, I s'pose.' Josie stopped a few feet away and eyed her cautiously. 'What do you want?' she asked. Then, before she could reply, she said, 'I suppose Mum told you to talk to me about Gold's? Well, you're wasting your time. I've made up my mind and I'm not going to change it.' Her chin lifted defiantly.

'So it's true, then? You want to leave school?' Dora shaded her eyes with her hand and squinted up at her. 'Why, Josie? I thought you loved school? What about your certificates?'

'I don't need any certificates.'

'You'll need them if you want to be a teacher, surely?'

'I don't want to be a teacher,' Josie said flatly. 'I just want to leave school and start earning some money, so I can–'

She didn't finish the sentence, but she didn't have to. Dora understood why she wanted to leave school. It was to escape Alf.

Hadn't she done the same thing herself? Part of

490

her reason for becoming a nurse was so she wouldn't have to live under the same roof as him. But if she'd known that by leaving she would be condemning her sister to the same living hell, she would never have done it.

'What is it, Josie?' she whispered. 'You can tell me.'

She looked at Josie's dark, wretched eyes and remembered the bright little child she had been. Was this really the same girl who always had her head in a book? Who ran to school every morning and stayed behind every afternoon, and helped the younger kids with their reading and sums?

Alf Doyle had taken away more than her sister's innocence. He had taken away her hopes and her dreams, too.

And in spite of her warning, he was still doing it.

She stood up. Suddenly her legs seemed to be as fragile as pipe cleaners, barely able to support her.

'Josie, I need to know,' she said hoarsely. 'Is it Alf?'

Josie's head shot back and Dora saw shock spark in her eyes. Then she turned on her heel abruptly and began walking away.

'Josie, please!' Dora watched her go, hurrying along the path, shouldering her way through the couples and the families as if she couldn't get away fast enough. She was disappearing, slipping away from her. Another second and it would be too late...

'It happened to me too, Josie!' she called out.

The words seemed to echo around inside her head. A few people turned to look at her curiously, a dumpy red-headed girl standing in the middle of the path, shouting nonsense into the air.

Dora stood and waited, straining her eyes to catch a glimpse of her sister. But Josie had already gone, lost in the crowd.

Lost for ever.

Defeated, she turned away to go, just as a small voice behind her called her name.

Dora swung round. There, on the path, stood Josie. She looked so small and lost, tears streaming down her face.

'Is it ... is it true?' she asked. 'It's not just me?'

Dora rushed to her, and a moment later they were clinging to each other, not even caring who might be watching them. Josie was crying, sobbing so much her slender body shook. Dora wanted to cry too as she clung to her, stroking her hair.

'We need to talk,' she whispered. 'No more secrets, all right? It's the only way, Jose.'

They walked. Round and round Victoria Park, until their legs ached. Then they sat on a bench and watched the ducks swimming on the lake. Josie's hand felt small and trusting in Dora's, just as it had when they were young and she had brought her here to feed the ducks.

Dora kept her eyes fixed on a fat brown duck, bobbing under the water for fish, as her sister talked. Dora could hear the fear in her voice as she falteringly told how Alf started sneaking into her room at night, how she'd tried to fight him off but he was too strong for her. How she was too consumed with terror and shame to tell her mother what had happened.

It was all so depressingly familiar. And yet it

was so much worse that it had happened to Josie. Dora could almost forgive Alf doing it to her, she was nothing special after all. But not Josie…

'He made it seem as if it was my fault, as if I'd made him do it. As if I'd w-wanted it to happen…' Josie turned anguished eyes to Dora. 'But I didn't want it to happen. It was so horrible…'

'I know, love.' Dora let go of her sister's hand and slid her arm along the back of the bench to hug her narrow shoulders. 'And that's why you ran away?'

Josie nodded. 'I just wanted it to stop,' she said. 'And then when he went into hospital… I know this sounds wicked, but I prayed for him to die.'

'You're not the only one,' Dora said grimly.

'It was better after he came home. For a while, anyway,' Josie said, gulping back her tears. 'I thought it was all going to be all right again. But then a couple of weeks ago, he started coming back into my room…'

She looked around at Dora. 'I don't know what else to do. I feel like it's my fault.'

That's what he relies on, Dora thought. 'It wasn't you, Josie. It was him.'

She picked up a stone and aimed it into the lake. She'd thought she hated Alf before, but it was nothing like the white hot hatred she felt for him now. Touching her was one thing, but laying his dirty hands on Josie was something far, far worse.

And after she'd warned him, too.

'You don't have to worry about this any more,' she said. 'I'll make it stop. For good, this time.'

'How?' Josie whipped round to face her, panic in her eyes. 'You won't tell Mum, will you? Please don't tell her, Dor. I couldn't stand it if anyone else knew...'

'It's all right, Jose.' Dora hugged her close. 'Don't you fret. I told you I'll look after you, didn't I? And I will.'

'How?' Josie said. 'How will you make everything all right?'

Dora threw another stone into the surface of the lake, shattering the stillness like glass.

I'll kill him if I have to, she thought.

Chapter Fifty-Three

Dora made sure she called round to Griffin Street in the middle of the day, when she knew her mother would be out delivering mending back to the laundry, and Nanna Winnie had taken the kids to the market. She also knew Alf was working the late shift, so he was bound to be home.

He came stomping down the stairs as she let herself in, dressed in his vest and doing up the buckle on his belt.

'Oh, it's you.' He shouldered past her to sit himself down in his favourite armchair. 'You might as well stick the kettle on, seeing as you're here,' he said, picking up the newspaper to peruse the racing results.

Dora bit back the retort that sprang to her lips and went into the scullery without a word. She had to bide her time.

She stood in the scullery, trying to calm herself

494

down. Through the net curtains, she could see Danny Riley perched on top of the coal cellar as usual. She waved distractedly to him as she warmed the pot and made the tea.

'To what do we owe this pleasure, anyway?' Alf asked sarcastically as she plonked his mug of tea down in front of him.

'You know very well.' She stood over him. 'I warned you, didn't I? I told you to leave Josie alone.'

He shot her a quick, guarded look. Then slowly, a sneer spread across his face. 'And what are you going to do about it?' he mocked. 'Cut my throat with a razor blade again?' He shook his head pityingly. 'Sorry, love, you should have done it while you had the chance. 'Cos your little tricks won't work in this house. You might have had the upper hand in that hospital of yours, but out here what I say goes.'

Dora watched him as he picked up his mug. 'And what if I tell Mum?'

'You won't.' He slurped his tea. 'And I'll tell you why, shall I? Because it will ruin her life. And you wouldn't want to do that to your poor mum, would you? Not after everything she's been through.'

'It couldn't be worse than living with a monster like you.'

'Is that right? Maybe you can tell her that when she's living in the workhouse with the rest of the family.'

She watched him, supremely confident as ever. A tingle of hatred spread upwards from her toes.

He looked up and caught her staring. 'What

495

you looking at?'

'You.'

'Well, don't.' He frowned irritably. 'You get on my nerves. I've a good mind to tell Rose I don't want you round here any more.'

'She'd never do that.'

'I reckon I could make her do anything I wanted,' he smirked. 'Just like I can make you and your sister do anything, too.'

Helplessness washed over her. Alf was right. She was powerless to hurt him any more. Not without hurting the rest of her family too.

All she could do was try to appeal to his better nature. If he'd ever had one.

'Leave Josie alone,' she begged. 'She's just a kid, she doesn't deserve to be treated like this.'

Alf tipped the last of his tea into his gaping mouth. 'You know what I think?' he said. 'I reckon you're jealous of that little sister of yours.'

Dora gripped her hands together to stop herself lunging at him.

'That's it, isn't it? You're jealous because she's got me now and you haven't.'

Dora stared at him. He really believed it, she thought. He was deluded enough to actually think that she and Josie wanted him.

In that moment a plan came into her mind. 'You're right,' she said flatly. 'I am jealous.' She forced herself to move towards him, her legs as stiff as a puppet's, her smile fixed. 'Get rid of her, Alf. Then it can be just you and me again. Just like old times.'

His eyes narrowed for a moment, as if he couldn't quite trust what he was hearing. Then he leered, showing dirty yellow teeth.

'I knew it,' he said. 'I knew you wanted me for yourself.'

Dora held herself rigid as he stood up and came towards her. She could smell the sweat on him, see the wiry greying hair of his chest curling above his stained vest. His hands gripped her arms, pinning them to her sides as he forced himself against her, his mouth clamped on hers. As his tongue invaded her mouth, Dora forced her mind to go blank.

Do it for Josie, she told herself over and over again. Do it to protect your sister...

And then suddenly, abruptly, he released her, throwing her across the room with such force that she landed against the back door with a crash.

'No thanks,' he said gruffly. 'Why would I want an ugly little cow like you in my bed when I could have a pretty little thing like Josie?' He looked down on her, pityingly. 'Shall I tell you something?' he said. 'I really had to force myself to do it to you sometimes. God, if I hadn't been desperate...'

He broke off at the sound of Nanna's voice in the back yard.

'All right, Danny love? You guarding that coal hole again? No danger of anyone getting their hands on our coal with you around, is there, mate?'

Dora barely had time to scramble to her feet before her grandmother came in through the back door, laden down with shopping.

'I'm telling you, that market isn't what it was,' she said, shaking her head. 'Time was when you could – oh, hello,' she stopped when she saw Dora. 'This is a nice surprise. D'you want a cup of tea?'

'I–'

'She's on her way out,' Alf interrupted Dora before she had a chance to speak.

Nick knew something was wrong the minute he walked in through the door. Danny was huddled in a corner, his head buried in his arms. He'd been picking at the ends of his bony fingers until they bled, a sure sign he was anxious.

'All right, mate?' Nick shrugged off his coat and went over to him. 'What's the matter? Has Mum had a go at you again?' He would swing for her if she'd hit him again. You only had to raise your hand to Danny to send him into hysterics.

As Danny lifted his face to look at him, Nick saw his red-rimmed eyes and the rivulets streaming from his nose. He looked as if he'd been crying for hours.

'What's happened?' He crouched down until his face was level with his brother's, forcing his voice to stay calm even though anger pulsed through him. 'Who did this to you?' Whoever it was, he was going to tear them limb from limb. Slowly.

Danny wiped his nose clumsily on his frayed sleeve. 'Alf h-hit Dora,' he managed to stammer.

Nick went cold. 'You what?'

'I s-saw him,' Danny's lip wobbled. 'He g-grabbed her, then he th-threw her like this–' he pushed with his arms, nearly knocking his brother off balance.

Nick frowned. 'Why would he do something like that, Danny? It doesn't sound like Alf.' It couldn't

498

be true, he told himself. Although he knew his brother wasn't capable of telling a lie, sometimes he got confused.

'I saw it!' Danny insisted. 'I was sitting out th-there.' He pointed towards the back yard. 'I saw Dora going in, and th-then I heard her telling Alf to l-leave Josie alone. She s-said she'd tell their m-mum but he just laughed at her. And then he ... he hit her.'

He started to cry again, weeping noisy tears into his shirt sleeve. Nick automatically fished a handkerchief out of his pocket and thrust it at him, his thoughts elsewhere.

That dirty, filthy bastard. He felt himself begin to shake with anger. Suddenly it all made sense. Why Josie had run away, why Dora had been so worried about her.

Had he touched Dora too? He didn't want to think about it, but remembering how she'd shrunk from him when he'd tried to kiss her...

He shot to his feet, propelled by a rage so white hot it would have sent him hammering Alf Doyle's door down if Danny hadn't whimpered with fear.

'N-Nick, please,' he begged. 'D-don't look like that. I don't like it when you l-look like that.'

Nick looked at his brother, barely seeing him through a mist of fury as red as blood. Then, slowly, he forced himself to take a deep, steadying breath. He unclenched his fists, stretching his fingers until the knuckles cracked.

Alf Doyle could wait, he decided.

'It's all right, Danny,' he soothed his agitated brother. 'See? I've calmed down. I'm not going to do anything, mate. You ain't got nothing to fear. Now let's see if there's anything in the house for tea, eh?'

Chapter Fifty-Four

Henry Rettingham was well enough to return home. He walked slowly into the house, supported by Seb and Felix the chauffeur on either side. Millie and her grandmother gathered in the drawing room to greet him, waiting patiently as he lowered himself agonisingly slowly into his leather chair.

The doctors had warned that his recovery would be lengthy, but Millie hadn't realised how difficult it would be for him until she watched him try to lift the tea Patchett the butler brought in for him.

As his cup rattled on the saucer, she sprang forward to help.

'Here, let me—'

Her father waved her away. 'No, Amelia, I – I have to learn to do these things for ... myself,' he insisted. His voice was slurred, each word dragged out of him with effort. It hurt Millie to hear him struggle so much.

She glanced at Seb for guidance. He smiled and gave her a reassuring nod. It was such a relief having him there, she thought. Somehow she didn't feel quite so alone.

He had been wonderful, helping to run the estate while her father was recovering. 'Not that it needs much running,' he told Millie. 'Between them, your father and Jackson have got the place going like clockwork.'

They had slipped into a comfortable domestic routine. Once Millie was reassured that her father was getting better, she'd allowed herself to take time away from his bedside at the hospital. She was surprised by how fully occupied her days were. If she wasn't running the house, discussing dinner plans and laundry lists with the housekeeper Mrs Saunders, she was riding out with Seb to visit the tenants or meeting the estate manager. As August progressed, the itinerant hop pickers began to arrive in vanloads from London for the annual harvest. Millie helped organise them into their teams, and sorted out temporary accommodation for them. With her training in mind, she even brought in the St Francis Mission to set up a mobile medical centre in one of the old barns. She helped out there sometimes, bandaging strained ligaments, bathing sore eyes and administering medicine. It felt good to be busy and useful all day, and to feel the sun on her face as she worked, instead of being stuck in the gloomy wards.

She kept promising herself she would return to London. But as time wore on, she wondered if London was really where she wanted to be.

'I wonder if I should stay here?' she mused to Seb one evening at dinner. 'I've missed so much of my training, I might not be able to catch up. And with Daddy still being so ill...'

'Your father is making progress,' Seb reminded her. 'And you know he would be absolutely livid with you if you didn't go back to London.'

'Would he?' Millie wasn't so sure.

In the end it was Henry himself who gave her the answer. She had been sitting with him, going through the accounts, when he suddenly said, 'You and Sebastian have done an ... excellent job. I'm sure we shall all miss you when you return to L-London.'

She lifted the ledgers from his lap and placed them carefully on the rug at his feet. 'Who says I'm going back?'

He frowned at her. 'I may have had a blow to the ... head, but I have not forgotten you have your ... training to finish.'

'Don't you want me at Billinghurst?' she asked lightly.

'Of course I do. Nothing would make me ... happier.' His face twisted with the effort of speaking. 'But only after you finish your ... training.' He put out a shaky hand to her. 'Nursing is your dream, Millie. Finish your training, and then...'

And then what? she thought. He was right, nursing was her dream. But his illness had made her realise that she had other responsibilities, too.

But her father wouldn't hear of her staying. And so, with a heavy heart, and a great deal of remonstration from her grandmother, she caught the train back to London.

The Dowager Countess was so beside herself with outrage, she took herself off to the Dower House and refused to speak to Millie at all before she left.

'She'll get over it,' Seb laughed as he drove her to the station.

'You don't know Granny.' Millie turned to him,

her face anxious. 'You do think I'm doing the right thing, don't you? Or am I just being selfish?'

'We've been through all this,' he said wisely. 'You don't need to worry about your father. I'll stay and keep an eye on him, make sure he doesn't do too much. Although the way he's going, he won't need me for much longer. I can tell he's itching to be rid of me!'

'Nonsense, he loves having you at Billinghurst. You're like the son he never had.' Millie sent Seb a sidelong look. 'I'm very grateful for your help.'

'Grateful?' He laughed. 'I'd sort of hoped you'd feel more for me than that by now.'

She stared ahead of her at the winding country lane. Neither of them had referred to their kiss since it had happened, although she knew it was playing on his mind as much as it was on hers.

Millie still felt wretchedly confused. She knew she had relied on him too much, gone far beyond the bounds of friendship. He had every right to think their relationship had changed. But was she ready for that?

'You don't have to stay until the train comes,' she said as Seb helped her on to the platform with her luggage.

'Why do you keep trying to send me away when all I want is to be with you?' Their eyes met. 'I'm sorry,' he said. 'I shouldn't say these things to you. I know it's not what you want to hear.' He smiled bracingly. 'We're just friends, that's all. I know that, and I've accepted it. I mean, it would be idiotic of me to say I wasn't bitterly disappointed, but I'm sure in time I'll learn to–' He pulled a wry face. 'Do you think I should shut up now?'

'I think that would be a good idea.'

There were a few other people on the platform. Further down, a young couple not much older than them were saying a passionate goodbye. Millie tried hard not to stare as they clung to each other fiercely, neither of them wanting to let go. What did it feel like to be that much in love? she wondered.

She glanced at Seb from under the brim of her hat. He was watching the couple too, his face envious.

Darling Seb. When she'd told him she was grateful, she'd meant so much more than that. She simply couldn't have got through the past couple of weeks without him. The relief when she saw him that day, standing in the hall, dressed in his shooting tweeds, having driven all the way down from Scotland just to be with her. From that moment she'd felt as if she could breathe again, as if everything'd be all right simply because he was with her.

And he had been with her ever since. His reassuring presence was always at her side as she sat with her father. He had held her when she'd cried tears of despair during the darkest moments, and he was the one who made her laugh when she'd desperately needed cheering up. Somehow he always knew what she was thinking, and the right thing to say to make it better.

She looked across at his finely drawn profile as he gazed down the line, waiting for the train, committing to memory the long, straight line of his nose, the curve of his lips and the sharp angle of his chin. As if he knew he was being observed, he turned to look at her with a puzzled smile, his fair brows drawn over warm grey eyes.

She suddenly realised how much she'd miss that smile, miss him. That was the real reason she had been so reluctant to go back to London. It wasn't the thought of saying goodbye to Billinghurst that upset her, or even of leaving her father. It was the thought of going through a whole day without seeing Seb.

'What is it?' he said.

'Nothing, I just–' Millie struggled to find the right words. Oh, God, why had she left it until now to realise how she felt? It was so typical of her, always the last to catch on, as Dora would say.

And now she'd left it too late. The train was approaching, the tracks rumbling. All along the platform the passengers were starting to galvanise themselves.

'Seb,' she started to say, but he was already gathering up her cases.

'What will you do when you get to London?' he asked. 'You will take a taxi, won't you? You can't possibly struggle on the bus with all this luggage.'

'Seb–'

'Do you think you'll be able to telephone when you get back to the hospital? I know your father will be worried about you, even if he says he isn't.'

'Seb, listen...' Her words were drowned out by the hiss of the train's brakes as it rumbled to a halt. People were starting to move, doors opening and banging shut, porters busy with luggage. Seb loaded her cases on to the train, not looking at her, as if he were determined to keep himself busy and detached.

'Seb!' Everything suddenly seemed to go very

quiet as Millie screamed out his name.

He turned to face her. 'Yes?'

'Would you mind awfully doing something for me?'

'What's that?' He smiled at her, his kind, handsome face squinting in the sun.

'Shut up and kiss me,' she said.

Chapter Fifty-Five

Veronica Hanley marched up the worn stone steps to St Oswald's Church Vicarage and rapped smartly on the door with far more confidence than she was feeling. For all she had travelled the world with her father's regiment, she was never really at ease outside the familiar surroundings of the Nightingale Hospital. She felt uncomfortable out of uniform, too, in her squashed hat and old coat that smelt of mothballs.

For tuppence she would have turned around and got straight back on the bus to Bethnal Green. But she'd come all this way and now she had to see it through. Show some backbone, as her father used to say.

She hoped Mrs Tremayne would forgive the intrusion. She hoped even more she would forgive what Veronica had to say.

The housekeeper showed her into the drawing room, a beautiful sunny room with French windows that opened out on to the garden. Veronica stood for a moment, admiring the beautifully manicured lawn, trimmed by immaculate borders, not a flower out of place. It was exactly the kind of garden she herself would have designed, appealing to her sense of order.

'Miss Hanley?' Constance Tremayne greeted her from the doorway. She looked rather put out to see her. 'This is most unexpected,' she said in a cool voice. 'You're lucky to have caught me, I'm due at a charity committee meeting in an hour.'

'I won't keep you, Mrs Tremayne. I'm sure you're very busy.' Veronica's throat suddenly felt very dry. She would have appreciated a cup of tea, but Mrs Tremayne didn't look as if she was about to offer her one. 'I've come about Helen. You're not really thinking of sending her to Scotland, are you?'

'Not thinking about it, Miss Hanley. I'm going to do it. As soon as it can be arranged, in fact.' Mrs Tremayne advanced into the room. She looked neat as ever in her sage green twinset and tweed skirt, her hair immaculately knotted at the nape of her neck. She was such a tiny, delicate creature, Veronica felt like a clodhopper next to her.

Constance Tremayne bestowed a smile on her. 'Actually, Miss Hanley, I've been meaning to thank you. If you hadn't alerted me to what was going on, I might never have found out what my daughter was up to. And then, heaven knows what would have happened.' Her shoulders shuddered delicately. 'Thanks to you, I have managed to step in and stop Helen from making a grave mistake, one which could have blighted her whole future.'

'That's just it,' Veronica said. 'I think you are the one making the mistake. You shouldn't take Helen away from the Nightingale.' She noticed Constance Tremayne's darkening expression, but blundered on, 'She's an excellent student, and an asset to the hospital. And what's more I believe she is happy and settled there. It'd be so unfair to uproot her and move her all the way to Scotland. Who knows what effect it'll have on her studies.'

'Miss Hanley, please.' Constance held up one hand to silence her. 'I have no wish to offend you, but as I explained to Matron, neither you nor she has any idea what it's like to bring up a daughter. Helen is young and naïve. She doesn't know her own mind. She must be protected from her own base desires...'

Veronica Hanley stared at her in frustration. She wished she understood delicacy and tact, because she needed them for what she had to say next. For a moment she almost wished she had Matron's facility with words. She might not approve of Kathleen Fox's methods, or indeed anything much about her, but she had to admit Matron had a way of talking that seemed to get through to people. Unlike Veronica, who just seemed to blunder about, trampling over everything like the big, clumsy thing she was.

A bull in a china shop, her mother had always called her. That was exactly what she felt like now.

'Well, Miss Hanley,' Constance was already dismissing her. 'Thank you for coming all this way, but I do have another appointment...'

'Wait.' Veronica rummaged in her ancient handbag. It had been her mother's and had lain unused at the back of her wardrobe for such a long time the leather was cracked and dry. 'I have a

508

photograph I would like to show you. I think it's in here somewhere...'

Constance tutted. 'Can't it wait, Miss Hanley? Only I am in rather a hurry.'

'Please, it won't take a moment ... ah, here it is.' She pulled the photograph out of her bag. The sepia image had yellowed with age. 'I think you might find it interesting.'

Constance Tremayne took the photograph with a heavy sigh. 'Really, Miss Hanley, I don't have time to...' She stopped dead as her gaze fixed on the figures in the photograph.

Veronica had seen the colour drain from people's faces when they were given bad news about a loved one. And here it was, happening to Constance Tremayne. Her skin turned the colour of putty.

'I don't understand,' she said faintly. 'How did you get this?'

'Before I began my training at the Nightingale, I was a cadet nurse at a hospital on the south coast. St Anthony's in Whitstable. That's a photograph of all the staff, taken one Christmas.' She pointed over Mrs Tremayne's shoulder at the chubby girl standing head and shoulders above her neighours in the middle of a row. 'That's me. I was a big galumphing thing even then.' She moved her finger up to the back row of the photograph. 'Those are the sisters, and those,' she traced some more of the faces, 'are the staff nurses. I can still remember their names, all these years later. Porter, Casey ... and there's Nurse Brown. She was on the TB ward. Very efficient. I must confess, I always wanted to be like her.'

'Fascinating, I'm sure.' Constance recovered her composure as she handed the photograph back.

'But something happened to Staff Nurse Brown. Something rather shocking, I'm afraid.' Miss Hanley gazed at the photograph for a moment longer. 'I've never had anything to do with gossip. Even as a cadet, I kept myself to myself and never joined in when the other girls gleefully spread rumours about each other. I think it's rather ghoulish to derive enjoyment from other people's misfortune, don't you? But even with my head in a book, I still heard stories. And the one about Staff Nurse Brown was just too difficult to ignore. Everywhere I went in the hospital, people seemed to be talking about it.'

She put the photograph back in her bag and snapped the clasp shut. It echoed around the silence of the room like shotgun fire.

'You see, this unfortunate young woman fell in love with a doctor. A much older man, and married, too. Anyone with any sense could see straight away that he was just toying with her – apparently this man was notorious in the hospital as a seducer of innocent young nurses. But the poor, besotted girl truly believed that he loved her as she loved him, and that one day he would leave his wife and they would be together.

'Eventually, of course, their affair was discovered, and there was a huge scandal,' Veronica continued. 'Suddenly this poor young woman's folly was exposed in front of everyone. But she still didn't care, because she genuinely believed that her lover would rescue her. But he didn't. He avoided the scandal, kept his wife and his position at the hospital, and this girl was left to face the music alone. A dreadful business.'

Colour swept Constance's taut cheekbones, but she said nothing.

'Of course, she was sent away in disgrace,' Veronica said. 'She'd lost everything, including her good name. She had no choice but to leave the town where she'd grown up and move somewhere else. Start all over again, if you like.' She shook her head. 'I sometimes wonder what happened to her. I like to think she was able to start again, become the respectable, upstanding person she was always supposed to be, and find someone who was worthy of her love. I also like to think that her experience might have given her some kind of compassion and understanding. Especially where her own children are concerned.'

'It might just as easily have made her want to protect those she loved from suffering the same fate.'

'I'm sure you're right,' Veronica agreed. 'But hopefully she would also be wise enough to see that crushing the spirit out of them could only make them more determined to rebel against her. It might even drive them to make the same mistakes she did.'

She gazed at Constance who was now staring fixedly out of the window, as still as a statue. Only the convulsive movement of her throat showed she hadn't been turned to stone.

'I think Staff Nurse Brown would bring up her children to know right from wrong,' Veronica continued. 'I also think she would trust them to make the right decisions when the time came.'

There was a long, heavy silence. Veronica held her breath as Constance Tremayne turned to face her. Her face was a carefully blank mask.

'It's a very nice story,' she said pleasantly. 'But if you've quite finished, I do have my committee meeting?'

'Of course. I won't take up any more of your time.'

Miss Hanley heard the front door close behind her but didn't look back until she reached the end of the drive. She'd half expected Mrs Tremayne to be standing at the window, watching her go, but she was nowhere in sight.

She cursed herself for coming. She didn't know if she'd made it better or worse for Helen Tremayne by trying to talk to her mother. And there was so much more she wished she'd said, too. She wanted to assure Mrs Tremayne that she would never tell her story again, not to another living soul. She wanted to tell her how much she respected and admired her, how she looked up to her.

Just as she'd once looked up to poor Constance Brown.

Chapter Fifty-Six

'I'm so sorry,' Helen said.

She had never felt more wretched in her life than she did at that moment, sitting across the table from Charlie in the brightly lit cafe where

512

they'd shared so many happier times. They had been sitting there all evening, and Antonio the proprietor was wiping tables, ready to close up.

But neither of them wanted to leave, because they knew it was the last time they were going to be together.

'I don't understand,' Charlie said again, his voice choked. 'I thought you loved me?'

'I do, more than anything.' Helen had only begun to realise how much now she knew she was going to lose him.

'Then why can't we be together?'

Helen sighed. They'd talked about it endlessly, going round and round in agonising circles, both of them getting more and more upset and frustrated.

'How can we stay together when I'm going to be in Scotland? I couldn't expect you to wait for me.'

'You know I'd wait for ever for you.'

Helen shook her head. 'It wouldn't be fair on you. You deserve to be free, to find someone else.'

'How many more times do I have to tell you? I don't want anyone but you!' Charlie ran his hand through his hair, exasperated.

'We have to make a clean break. It's for the best,' Helen said firmly.

In her heart she desperately wanted to ask him to wait for her. But she knew she couldn't. Whatever Charlie might say, he was bound to find someone else while she was away. And painful as it might be now, she knew it would be a lot worse to have to find out in six months, or a year's time that he'd stopped loving her.

Charlie stared down into his empty teacup. 'It's not fair,' he said. 'Why does it have to be Scotland? Why can't your mum just let you carry on your training here?'

Because she wants to punish me, Helen thought bleakly. 'She thinks it would be best.'

'Is it because of me?' he asked.

Helen looked into his blue eyes, so sad and desperate for reassurance. 'It's my fault,' she said. 'I shouldn't have started seeing you behind her back. I should have known she'd find out, and that she'd be angry with me for lying to her.'

'You hardly lied to her, did you?' Charlie reasoned. 'Not telling her something isn't the same as telling her a downright lie.'

'Not as far as my mother is concerned. She likes to know everything about my life.'

Charlie thought for a moment. 'What if I was to talk to her?' he said suddenly. 'Perhaps if I was to meet her, let her see I was a decent sort of bloke, she'd change her mind and let you stay?'

'You don't know my mother.' Helen shook her head. 'She never changes her mind about anything. Once she's decided something, that's it.'

She wondered what her mother would make of Charlie anyway. To Helen, he was the most handsome, wonderful, loving man in the world. But no one would ever meet Constance Tremayne's impossibly high standards.

'It sounds as if you've already given up?' he said. 'Don't you want us to be together?'

'You know I do.'

'Then fight!' he urged, gripping her hand. 'Helen, I'm ready to try anything, do anything, it takes to keep you. And all you're doing is sighing and shaking your head and telling me it's all useless, that it won't work. Why don't you stand up to your mother, tell her you won't be pushed around any more?' He sent her a hurt look. 'Unless you really don't care about me?'

'That's not fair!' she protested. 'Of course I care about you. I love you.'

'But not enough to stand up to your mother?'

Helen swallowed hard. Charlie was right, she was being a coward.

Millie had told her much the same thing the day before.

'You don't really want to leave, do you?' she had said, her big blue eyes swimming with tears.

'Of course I don't.' A year ago, Helen might not have cared what happened to her. But over the past months she had made good friends at Nightingale's, and now she knew she would be heartbroken to say goodbye.

'Then tell her you're not going,' Millie shrugged, as if it was the easiest thing in the world. 'She can't make you do anything you don't want to do.'

'You don't know my mother.'

'I know that if I really wanted something, I wouldn't let anyone stand in my way,' Millie had said firmly.

It was easy for her, Helen thought. She hadn't been brought up under an iron rule. The idea of making her own decisions was so strange to Helen, she wasn't sure she would even be able to do so without Constance Tremayne's approval.

They were both silent, lost in their own thoughts. Helen glanced up at the clock on the wall, ticking away the minutes treacherously. Soon she would have to be getting back to the hospital.

'I'm sorry.' Charlie threaded his fingers through hers. 'I shouldn't have got angry at you. We haven't got that much time left together, I don't want to spend it arguing.'

'I do love you,' Helen said unhappily. 'And if I had my way, we'd be together every minute of the day, but...'

'Then let me come with you,' Charlie cut across her words, his fingers tightening around hers. 'If you have to go to Scotland, then so will I.'

Helen stared at him. 'I couldn't ask you to do that.'

'You're not asking me, I'm offering. I could move up to Scotland, find digs near your hospital.' His face was eager. 'Then we could see each other all the time, and no one would be able to say anything about it.'

'But my mother–'

'What would she know about it? She'd be miles away. Don't you think it's a good idea? It's so simple, I don't know why I haven't thought of it before!'

He laughed in delight, but Helen was hesitant. 'How would you live?'

'I'd get a job, of course. I know I might not be able to run around like I used to, but there's bound to be some kind of work I can do.' He grinned. 'I could be a haggis-maker. Or a sporran-hunter. Or – I don't know – Scotland's only one-legged bagpipe player. I could do something, anyway.'

His good humour was so infectious, Helen

smiled in spite of herself. But deep down she was still wary. 'What about your family? You wouldn't be able to see them as much as you do now.' She knew how close Charlie was to his parents and brothers and sisters, and how much it would hurt him not to be with them.

'So what? I'd be with you, and that's what's really important.' He beamed at her. 'What do you think?'

Helen chewed her lip. She desperately wanted to say yes, but she knew that would just be selfish. 'You're a Londoner, you'd be lost in Scotland.'

'I'd be lost without you.'

Antonio, a big man in a greasy apron, began cleaning their table. 'Haven't you two got homes to go to?' he said irritably.

'I'm sorry.' Helen instantly started to get up, but Charlie held on to her hand, pulling her back down into her seat. 'I can't let you go,' he said quietly.

'I can't let you go, either.' Her heart was already aching at the thought of never seeing him again.

'Then marry me.'

Everything seemed to stop dead in that moment. Even Antonio stopped wiping their table and looked up.

'What did you say?' Helen frowned.

'Marry me.' Charlie's eyes shone, full of hope. 'I dunno why I didn't think of it before. It's obvious, isn't it? We could get wed, and then we could live in Scotland as man and wife, and there'd be nothing your mum or anyone else could do about it.'

'She could try to stop the wedding.'

'Not if we eloped.' He grinned at her. 'Where is

it couples run off to? Gretna something?'

'Green,' Helen said faintly. 'Gretna Green.'

'That's in Scotland, isn't it? We could get wed on the way, and then turn up as a married couple.'

'But I couldn't!' Helen whispered, shocked. 'My mother…'

'Your mother wouldn't know a thing about it. And by the time she found out, it would be too late.' Charlie grinned. 'Come on, what do you say?'

'I – I don't know what to say.' Helen gaped at him, then at Antonio, who was staring openly now. She was too overwhelmed by the idea that someone actually loved her enough to want to marry her to think of anything else.

'Then say yes.'

Helen opened and closed her mouth, but no sound came out. In the end it was Antonio who spoke up.

'Blimey, mate, if you want the young lady to accept your proposal then you're going to have to come up with a better one than that!' he laughed.

Charlie glanced at her. Then, with a great effort and hanging on to the back of the chair for support, he slowly lowered himself on to his good knee.

Helen felt as if she were in a strange dream as he took her hand in his.

'Helen Tremayne,' his voice was solemn, but his eyes sparkled with mirth as they met hers, 'will you please do me the great honour of agreeing to run away with me and be my wife?'

Helen looked down at him. All kinds of thoughts went through her head. This was impossible, impulsive, complete madness and they would never get away with it. She could almost see her mother, face pinched with disapproval, dismissing the idea on her behalf.

'Yes, please,' she said.

Chapter Fifty-Seven

She ran all the way back to the nurses' home, her mind in a whirl. Had she really just accepted Charlie's proposal? She could scarcely believe it. She'd never done anything impulsive in her life.

As she lined up with the others for her turn in the bathroom, she could barely stop herself from laughing out loud. She had no idea what she had let herself in for. She'd left Charlie promising to borrow a car to get them to Gretna Green. All she had to do was to pack and be ready to leave at teatime the following day.

But tomorrow was also the day she was due to meet her mother to go through the arrangements for her move to St Andrew's.

One way or another, I'm going to Scotland, she thought, smiling at herself in the bathroom mirror as she brushed her teeth.

Millie had, as usual, ignored the ten o'clock curfew, to meet her aunt for dinner, but Dora was already in bed when Helen crept back into their room just as Sister Sutton was calling for lights out.

She undressed quickly in the dark and changed

into her flannel nightdress, shivering in the cold. It was a warm summer's night, but their attic bedroom was freezing as usual.

Moving quietly so as not to disturb Dora, Helen eased open her wardrobe doors and groped in the dark for her few items of clothes. There wasn't much to pack, at any rate. She carefully pulled her suitcase out from under her bed, and had just opened it when Dora's voice came sleepily out of the darkness.

'What are you doing?'

Helen looked up sharply. She could see Dora lying on her side, her eyes glinting in the gloom, watching her.

'I thought you were asleep.'

'I guessed that.' Dora sat up, pulling the blanket around her chin. 'Are you going somewhere?'

'I – just thought I'd get ready for Scotland.' At least it wasn't a lie, she told herself.

Dora faced Helen in the darkness. 'I thought you weren't leaving for a few days yet?'

'I'm not.'

'So why have you started packing in the middle of the night?' Helen heard the shrewd tone of Dora's voice. There was no fooling her. She had far too much East End cunning for that.

'You're up to something, aren't you?' she said. 'It's all right, you don't have to tell me. Not if you don't want to.'

Helen hesitated. She knew she could trust Dora. She seemed like the kind who would be good at keeping secrets. She scrambled into bed, shivering as her bare feet touched the icy starched linen sheets.

'I'm running away,' she said.

Dora listened carefully as Helen explained her plan to elope with Charlie to Gretna Green.

'It all sounds very romantic,' she said finally.

'It's the only way we can be together,' Helen said.

'And what will you do when you're married? Have you thought about that?'

'I–' Helen faltered.

'You won't be able to continue your training. Not up in Scotland, or down here, or anywhere else.'

'That doesn't matter,' Helen said bravely. 'As long as I'm with Charlie.'

'You might say that now, but how will you feel in a few years' time? You'd be giving up an awful lot to be with him, remember?'

'It would be worth it.'

'I hope you're right. I hope your Charlie is worth burning all your bridges for, because that's what you'll be doing, make no mistake about that.'

Helen heard the bedsprings creak as Dora lay down again. She lay on her back too, staring up at the ceiling in the darkness. She could feel some of her confidence ebbing away. Dora was right. Once she married Charlie her life would change completely. She would not just be giving up nursing, she'd be giving up everything. Her mother would never speak to her again, and she'd make sure the rest of her family didn't either. Much as Helen loved Charlie, was she ready to throw in her lot with a young man she had known a matter of months?

'I'll tell you something else, too,' Dora said. 'If you do a flit now, you'll be proving your mum right, won't you? You'll be proving that Charlie is a bad influence and that you can't be trusted to think for yourself.'

Helen watched the shadows deepening on the sloped eaves. Dora was right again, she thought miserably.

'So what can I do?' she whispered.

Dora rolled over on to her side to face her in the darkness. 'Talk to your mum. I know you think you can't do it, but you can,' she urged, as Helen opened her mouth to argue. 'What's the worst she could do to you? Rant and rave a bit, perhaps. Give you a good hiding. But whatever she does, it can't be that bad. All you've got to do is stand up to her.'

Stand up to her? Helen's heart beat faster at the thought. 'I'm not sure I can,' she whispered.

'It's either that or lose Charlie,' Dora said. 'It's up to you which you think you can bear.'

After a sleepless night of tossing and turning, Helen made up her mind. She had arranged to meet her mother during her afternoon break, after dinner. But late in the morning there had been an emergency on the ward, and Helen had been kept on to help deal with it. She had missed dinner but was still five minutes late as she hurried to the courtyard to meet her mother. Her stomach began to flutter when she saw Constance sitting on the bench under the trees.

She seemed so lost in thought she didn't notice Helen until she had walked right up to her.

'Mother?'

Constance looked up. 'Oh, Helen. There you are.' She had braced herself for the inevitable telling off for being late, so her mother's wavering smile caught her completely off balance.

'I – I'm sorry I'm late,' she stammered. 'There was an emergency.'

'It doesn't matter. These things happen in a hospital, don't they?' her mother dismissed it. 'Have you had anything to eat?'

Helen shook her head. 'There wasn't time.'

'Then you must have something.' Constance stood up, picked up her handbag and hooked it over her arm. 'Come along.'

She led the way out on to the main road, striding purposefully ahead, with Helen trailing behind. 'Now,' she said. 'Where would you like to go?'

Helen stared at her, dumbfounded by the question. Her mother never asked her opinion about anything. 'I – I don't mind,' she managed finally.

'Then I suggest we find somewhere close by since I think it might rain.' Her mother held her hand out and squinted up at the sky.

Helen looked up into the grubby clouds overhead. This wasn't right. There was something very strange going on, she could feel it. And it was nothing to do with the weather, either.

As they approached the cafe, Helen realised with panic that it was the same place she and Charlie had been the previous night.

'Should we go somewhere else?' she suggested quickly.

Her mother frowned at her. 'I didn't think you

had any preference?'

'I – I don't, but there's another place on the other side of the park which I've heard is very nice,' she invented hastily.

'Nonsense, we're here now.' Constance was already opening the door. The bell over the door jangled, making Helen jump. She prayed the proprietor wasn't around. She let out a sigh of relief as the curtains at the back of the cafe parted and a young girl appeared, carrying a tray laden with pots of tea.

As luck would have it, her mother chose exactly the same table in the window where Helen and Charlie had sat the day before. Helen picked up the menu and perused it listlessly, waiting for her mother to order.

The waitress came over, her pad poised. Helen listened as her mother went through her usual tiresome routine, questioning the girl closely about the freshness of the sandwiches and the quality of the tea: 'Is it Indian? Do you warm the pot first? So many places don't, and I can always tell, you know.'

Helen tuned out, gazing through the window at the street. Rain had started to spatter down on the pavements, sending people running for cover into doorways and under trees.

She wondered what Charlie was doing now. Had he kept his promise to find a car in which to make their escape? She smiled at the thought of what he was prepared to do to make sure they stayed together. With all the effort he was making, the least she could do was talk to her mother. And if her plan worked, they might not have to leave

London at all.

'Helen?' Her mother's sharp voice brought her back to reality. She looked up. Constance and the waitress were looking at her expectantly.

'What do you want to order? The waitress doesn't have all day, you know.'

Helen looked back at the menu in a panic. Her mother had never asked her what she wanted before, she'd always chosen her food just as she chose everything else.

'Just a pot of tea and a toasted teacake, please,' she said finally.

'That's hardly adequate, is it?' her mother commented disapprovingly, her mouth tightening as the waitress went back to the kitchen with their order. 'You'll be fainting later on the ward.'

But she didn't summon the waitress back, or change Helen's order. Helen stared at her.

'Are you all right, Mother?' she asked worriedly.

'Yes, of course. Why shouldn't I be?' But Constance was fidgety and ill-at-ease as she fiddled with the buttons on her gloves. She didn't seem quite as sure of herself as usual.

The bell jangled, and Helen felt an icy chill run down her spine when she heard the cheery Italian cockney lilt of Antonio the proprietor's voice.

'It's raining cats and dogs out there,' he announced to the customers sitting at the tables. 'You're in the best place, I reckon.'

Helen didn't dare lift her head to look at him as he bustled past, his arms full of cardboard boxes. She prayed he wouldn't see her.

'Now,' her mother said. 'About St Andrew's.'

Helen felt her palms turn clammy with fear. It

was now or never. Panic and nerves made her forget the speech she'd spent all night carefully preparing. Suddenly it felt as if her tongue had swelled up in her mouth, making words impossible.

'Mother, I've been thinking,' she started to say. But at that moment, Antonio appeared from behind the curtain again. He caught Helen's eye, and grinned broadly.

'Hello there,' he greeted her. 'Back already, I see. Here, Jenny,' he called back through the curtain to the waitress. 'Here's that girl I was telling you about. The one whose boyfriend proposed last night.'

The deathly silence that followed seemed to suck all the air out of the room. Helen stared down at the wooden table, not daring to meet her mother's eye.

'Proposed?' Constance said coldly.

'I can explain,' Helen said, and then realised she couldn't.

'I think you'd better.' Her mother waited expectantly, her face taut with suppressed emotion.

But before she could begin to speak, the bell over the door jangled again and in walked Charlie, leaning heavily on his stick, his hair dripping from the rain.

'And here's the fella who proposed!' Antonio called out in delight from behind the counter. 'Hurry up, Jenny, you're missing all the fun here!'

Everyone in the cafe fell silent, watching them, as Charlie made his way over to their table. Helen held her breath.

'What are you doing here?' she whispered.

'How did you know where we were?'

'I followed you from the hospital.' He turned to Constance, who was sitting as rigid as a statue opposite them. 'Hello, Mrs Tremayne. My name is Charlie Denton. I'm pleased to meet you.'

He held out his hand. Mrs Tremayne stared at it with contempt, as if he'd tried to present her with a dead fish.

'I wish I could say the same about you,' she said tightly.

Charlie's hand fell limply back to his side, but he refused to be intimidated. 'I'm sorry to interrupt, Mrs Tremayne, but I have something to say to Helen,' he continued bravely.

'Can't it wait?' she pleaded, glancing nervously around the busy cafe.

'No, it can't.' Charlie took a deep breath. 'I've changed my mind,' he said. 'I've decided I don't want to marry you.'

'What?' Helen and her mother chorused in shock.

'Jenny!' Antonio bellowed through the curtain. 'Put that bread down and get out here now!'

'I mean, I do want to marry you, one day. But not now. Not like this.' He turned back to Mrs Tremayne. 'Do you mind if I sit down?' he asked. 'I can't stand for very long on this leg of mine.'

Helen's mother gave a nod and Charlie drew up a chair and lowered himself heavily into it. He turned to Helen again. His face was haggard, with purple shadows under his blue eyes. Helen guessed he'd had a sleepless night too. 'I've been thinking about it,' he said. 'I love you, Helen. Too much to want to run away and elope.'

'Elope?' she heard her mother say faintly.

'When I marry you, I want it to be because we both want to,' Charlie went on, 'not because it's the only way we can be together. And I want all our families to be there, too, to see us make our vows to each other. Even you, Mrs T.' He smiled at Constance. 'I want the whole world to see how much I love you. And I want you to finish your training first,' he added. 'Because I reckon you're a wonderful nurse, Helen, and you deserve to do it.'

There was a long silence. Someone sighed on the other side of the cafe. Out of the corner of her eye, Helen could see Antonio wiping away a tear with his grubby apron.

She and Charlie both turned to look at her mother. Mrs Tremayne sat ramrod-straight. Helen saw the icy look in her eyes and realised with a feeling of creeping dread that she was going to put Charlie firmly in his place.

'We've heard a great deal about what you want, young man,' she said in a clipped voice. 'Have you considered asking my daughter what she might want?' She turned to Helen. 'What do you have to say about this?'

Helen looked from Charlie's beseeching face to her mother's stony expression. She could feel him silently urging her on, willing her to speak her mind.

She swallowed the dry lump of fear that clogged her throat. 'I don't want to go to Scotland,' she managed finally. 'I want to stay at the Nightingale and finish my training.'

She steeled herself to look at her mother, waiting for the thunderclap of rage to crash over her head. Constance's face remained impassive.

'Very well,' she said.

Helen and Charlie looked at each other. 'Do you really mean it?' Helen whispered. She was sure it couldn't be that easy.

'Of course. Surely you didn't think I was going to frog march you off to Aberdeen without your agreement, did you?' Constance looked incredulous. 'If you would rather stay at the Nightingale, then I will speak to Matron and arrange it. I'm sure she will have something to say about the matter, but no doubt we will come to some sort of understanding.' Her lips thinned. 'But I expect you to work very hard during your final year. And if I hear anything to suggest otherwise,' she sent Charlie a stern look, 'I will be forced to reconsider.'

'Yes, Mother.' Helen could feel happiness bubbling up inside her. She wanted to hug her, but didn't think Constance would welcome such a public display.

Or perhaps she would. Five minutes ago she would have been certain that her mother was going to send Charlie packing and probably banish Helen to a convent for even daring to think about elopement. But here she was, calmly accepting it all.

Helen reached for Charlie's hand under the table and held on to it tightly. She couldn't imagine what might have brought about her mother's change of heart, but she was grateful for it. The waitress brought over their tray, and set down the tea in front of them. Constance put her hand against the side of the pot, testing it.

'You haven't warmed this pot, have you?' she snapped. 'I told you, I can always tell. Take it away at once.'

Helen smiled to herself. It was good to see her mother hadn't changed completely.

Chapter Fifty-Eight

'The drinks are on me!'

Alf Doyle looked around the public bar of the Rose & Crown, feeling like the Pearly King of Bethnal Green. He'd had a big win on the horses, he had money in his pocket and everyone in the pub was his friend.

'You're a lucky man, all right Alf,' Len Pike raised his pint to him. 'First the gee-gees and then that lovely missus to go home to. I'm telling you, if I had a smashing looking woman like that waiting for me at home, I wouldn't be wasting my time drinking beer with us ugly mugs!' He grimaced. 'As it goes, I have to get sozzled before I can go home and face my old woman!'

Alf laughed, but he wasn't thinking about Rose. Granted, she was still a nice looking woman, and she looked after him a treat. But she had turned forty, there was grey in her hair and she just didn't do it for him any more.

Not like Josie... He smiled and wetted his lips with the tip of his tongue at the thought of her.

He downed his pint, bade goodbye to his friends

and stepped out of the pub into the cool evening air. He weaved his way slowly home past the docks, nipping down the shadowy little alley the locals called Cutthroat Lane. The name didn't bother him. He often staggered home that way, and he'd never had any trouble. He could take care of himself, anyway. He was a big bloke, and not many men were brave enough to tackle him.

He was trying to make up his mind whether to treat himself to some jellied eels when the fist came out of nowhere, knocking him flat on his back. Alf felt the trickle of blood from his nose as he lay winded on the cobbles, gasping for breath. Suddenly he knew he'd been a fool to flash the cash around the pub. Now his luck had run out.

He groped in his pocket for his wallet, pulled it out and tossed it across towards the shadows.

'Here's my money,' he stammered. 'Take it. Whatever you want.'

'I don't want your money.'

A moment later a figure stepped out of the shadows into the greenish lamplight, and Alf found himself squinting up in confusion at the familiar face towering over him.

'Hello, Alf,' said Nick Riley. 'I'd like a little chat, if you've got a minute?'

The news that Alf Doyle had done a runner spread around Griffin Street like wildfire. And it wasn't long before rumours started to fly. Some people reckoned he had a woman on the Isle of Dogs, others claimed he'd done a bunk up north to escape big gambling debts. The only thing they could agree on was that Alf Doyle had been a quiet one, and that the quiet ones were the worst.

Through it all, Rose Doyle maintained a dignified silence. She went on working every day, taking in mending, cleaning her house and looking after her children, always ready with a kind word and a smile for the neighbours, even though she knew they were gossiping behind her back. But in private Dora could see she was devastated.

'I don't understand it,' she would say over and over again. 'I thought we were so happy? Why would he just walk out like that?'

Sometimes she would convince herself that something dreadful had happened to him. 'My Alf wouldn't just up sticks and leave his family. No one's seen him at work, either. Something's happened to him, I know it has. He could be lying murdered somewhere. Or else he's topped himself.'

'People don't pack up their bags if they're planning to do themselves in, Rose,' Nanna Winnie pointed out. 'Face it, girl, none of us knew Alf as well as we thought we did.'

Josie and Dora exchanged looks but said nothing. They couldn't understand it either, although Dora knew her sister was as grateful as she was for his mysterious disappearance.

'Do you think he'll come back?' Josie asked her fearfully, just after he vanished.

'I don't know, Jose. I wish I did.'

'Why did he go, I wonder?'

Dora shrugged. 'Maybe he realised what he'd done and decided he couldn't live with himself?' Although that didn't seem very likely from the way he'd treated her.

'Well, I hope he's dead,' Josie said with feeling. 'I hope he's lying at the bottom of the Thames.'

'Shh, don't let Mum hear you talk like that,' Dora warned. She felt desperately sorry for her mother. No matter how badly Alf had treated them, she hated to see Rose Doyle suffer. It was so cruel of Alf just to walk out on her.

She felt even worse when she heard the neighbours gossiping.

'Well, who'd have thought it?' Lettie Pike could barely contain her glee. 'Looks like the Doyles have come down in the world. Poor Rose, how's she going to cope with no man to keep her?'

'Same way you manage, I dare say,' Nanna Winnie had replied sharply. 'I don't see your Len putting himself out to keep you. Why else do you have to go out scrubbing hospital floors?'

The only one who showed her mother any sympathy was June Riley. 'I know what it's like to have your husband run off,' she reminded them. 'My Reg did the very same thing, remember? Went off without a by-your-leave, he did.'

Dora thought about Reg Riley, disappearing off in the night. It was just like Alf, in a way. Except everyone knew Nick was the one who'd driven him out.

It made her wonder if Nick had had anything to do with Alf's disappearance. But why would he? It wasn't as if Alf had done anything to Nick. Not like his bullying father.

But all the same, the idea unsettled her.

'You don't know where Alf went, do you?' she asked him one evening as he sat in the back yard, smoking a cigarette.

He stared back at her, his blue eyes unreadable. 'Why should I?'

'No reason.' She was silly for even thinking it, she decided.

Before he could say any more, Ruby came out into the yard, dressed up to the nines as usual in a dress of emerald green and a matching hat fastened to her blonde curls with pearl-tipped pins.

'There you are,' she said, her scarlet-painted lips stretching into a broad smile. Dora watched her sashay over to Nick and thread her arm possessively through his. 'Have you seen the time? We should be going soon.'

He stubbed out his cigarette and got to his feet. 'Ready when you are.'

'Going somewhere nice?' Dora asked lightly.

'Nick's taking me out dancing.' Ruby couldn't keep the delighted grin off her face. 'There's a new show band on at the Palais.'

Dora looked at him. 'I didn't know you liked dancing?'

'He's never tried it, have you, Nicky? It'll be a new experience for you. The first of many, I hope.' She winked at Dora.

Nick sent her one last look before he followed Ruby out of the back gate. Dora thought she saw a flash of longing in his eyes, but that was probably wishful thinking. She sat down on an upturned bucket and stared up at the sky. Damn you, Alf Doyle, she cursed silently. He might have been out of her life, but he would never be out of her head.

It was a long time since Kathleen had seen Amelia Benedict in her office. The young student had thrown herself into her studies since returning to the Nightingale a month before. And according to the ward reports, her nursing skills were improving too. So it was with great disappointment that she heard the news that Benedict had to tell her.

'You're engaged? Does this mean you will be leaving the Nightingale?'

'Oh, no, Matron. Not at all. Seb – Sebastian, my fiancé – and I have discussed it, and we're planning a long engagement. We're not even going to think about getting married until after I've finished my training here.'

'I see.' Kathleen considered this for a moment. 'I must say, Benedict, it is a great pity you will not be a nurse here at the Nightingale. We had high hopes for you.'

'Did you, Matron?' Benedict seemed genuinely surprised.

'Of course. But we'll never know now, will we?' Kathleen fixed her with a steady look. 'I do hope that you will not allow your wedding plans to distract you from your studies?'

'Oh, no, Matron.'

'We shall see about that,' Kathleen murmured, when she had dismissed Benedict. 'I'm rather worried she'll get caught up with wedding dresses and so forth and forget all about what she is supposed to be doing,' she confided in Miss Hanley.

'It might be a good thing if she does,' the Assistant Matron said irritably. 'I've never heard of such a ridiculous idea! What on earth is the point of wasting all that time and effort training the girl if she is not going to join the profession and use her skills?'

'I agree,' Kathleen said. 'It seems a huge waste, doesn't it? But Benedict has another two years of training ahead of her. Who knows what will happen in that time? People change their minds, don't they?'

Just look at Constance Tremayne, she thought. Two weeks ago she would never have imagined her changing her mind about anything. And yet she had. Kathleen still wasn't sure what had made her decide to allow Helen to remain at the Nightingale, but it was a blessed relief when she had.

Come to think of it, she hadn't seen much of Mrs Tremayne since she'd made her decision. And Miss Hanley had started to look slightly pained whenever her name was mentioned. Kathleen wondered if they'd had some kind of falling out. Disagreeable though it might be, she could only hope they had, as it made for a far more peaceful life when they weren't joined in an unholy alliance against her.

There was a soft tap on the door and the maid came in, carrying a tea tray. Kathleen turned to her assistant. 'Imagine that, Miss Hanley. We are actually agreed on something.' She smiled, and picked up the teapot. 'There may be hope for us yet,' she said.

Helen was getting changed at the nurses' home when Millie came rushing in.

'Sorry I'm late,' she said breathlessly, throwing off her red-lined cloak and reaching up to unpin her cap. 'Sister Willis was absolutely beastly and refused to let me go off duty. And then I had to come the long way back because Sister Holmes

536

and Sister Wren were talking on the stairs.' She wrenched out the last pin and shook her fair curls free. 'There, that's better.'

Helen smiled as Millie flopped backwards on her bed, arms outstretched. 'How did your meeting with Matron go?'

'Not too badly, all things considered. I really wasn't sure how she'd take it. I half expected her to tell me never to darken Nightingale's doors again, but she was actually quite sweet about it. Not sure if old Manly Hanley was too thrilled, though.'

'She's probably worried you won't have your mind on your studies now you're engaged,' Helen observed, hanging up her uniform carefully.

'Well, that's just silly. I wouldn't be here if I didn't want to pass my exams. Seb and I agreed, we wouldn't even think about getting married until I qualified. I wouldn't have told anyone, but Granny went ahead and put that announcement in *The Times*. I'm sure she only did it so I wouldn't back out and change my mind.'

'You wouldn't want to change your mind, would you?'

'Of course not. Why would I?'

Why indeed? Helen thought. Millie's engagement had been so typically sudden and impulsive, Helen wondered if she'd really thought it through. But she seemed happy, and her fiancé was obviously a nice chap with a sensible head on his shoulders. Perhaps he'd be just what Millie needed to curb her wild impulses?

Unlike her brother. Helen felt a pang, remembering William's expression when she'd broken the news of Millie's engagement to him.

'Well, that's marvellous. I'm delighted for her.' He'd smiled bracingly. But Helen had seen the flash of pain in his eyes and knew him too well to be fooled.

Just for a moment she wondered if she'd made a mistake, trying to keep them apart. She'd been so sure his attraction to Millie was just a passing fancy, but his feelings for her seemed to run a lot deeper than that. Had Helen somehow managed to keep him from the love of his life? She truly hoped not. William deserved to find someone who made him as happy as she was with Charlie.

'Talking of backing out ... I hope you haven't changed your mind about this afternoon?' Millie rolled over on the bed and propped her chin in her hand to look at Helen.

She swallowed hard. 'Of course not.'

'Good. Because the appointment is in–' she checked her watch '–half an hour.'

'I'm looking forward to it.' It was a lie, of course. Helen had been awake half the night, wondering if she was doing the right thing. 'Is Doyle still coming with us?'

'I've arranged to meet her there.' Millie rolled off the bed. 'I'd better get my skates on, hadn't I?' she said, unbuttoning her collar. 'Don't want to keep Madame Daphne waiting, do we?'

As usual, Millie took ages getting ready, and Dora was already waiting for them when they hurried up the street just after three.

'I thought you'd changed your mind?' she grinned.

'Honestly, why does everyone think I'm going

to change my mind?' Helen huffed.

Dora and Millie looked at each other. 'You changed your mind last week,' Millie reminded her.

'Well, I'm not going to change it now.' Helen took a deep breath and pushed through the door ahead of them.

She didn't think she'd ever seen so many shades of pink as there were in Madame Daphne's hair salon. The air was perfumed with the smell of lavender mingled with peroxide and hair lacquer. Helen had never been inside such a place before. It seemed terribly frivolous. Madame Daphne greeted them effusively. She was a small, round woman in a pink smock that perfectly matched her lipstick. For a woman who claimed to be French, she had the broadest East-End accent Helen had ever heard.

'I've never seen such a lovely head of hair,' she said admiringly as she brushed Helen's long dark tresses. 'It's nearly down to your waist. And so shiny, too. Seems a pity to cut it all off.'

'Is it?' Helen gulped at her reflection in the mirror. Maybe she was right? Maybe this was all a big mistake? It had been Millie's idea, and look how rash she was...

'Although short hair is all the fashion these days,' Madame Daphne assured her hastily, seeing Helen's look of panic. 'Look at mine.'

Helen looked. Madame Daphne's halo of stiff, teased curls didn't reassure her.

'You can change your mind if you want?' Millie whispered.

'No, she can't,' Dora put in. 'I haven't taken a

day off just so I can watch her having the heebie-jeebies. Besides, she knows she wants it cut. She's been on about it for ages. Cut it off,' she instructed the hairdresser.

Madame Daphne smiled at Helen in the mirror, scissors poised. 'Shall I?'

Helen hesitated. Dora was right, she'd been wanting to cut her hair for ages. And Charlie was all for it, too.

'You'd still be beautiful to me if you had your head shaved and wore a hat made of bananas,' he'd assured her.

Helen smiled, thinking about him. She could hardly believe that a year ago she'd been so lonely. Now she had a boyfriend who adored her, and friends who cared about her. Even her mother was making more of an effort to understand her. Although Helen wasn't sure how she would feel about her getting her hair cut. Constance Tremayne had always had very strong opinions about Helen's appearance, and was bound to be furious that she hadn't consulted her about it. Helen could almost see her face in the mirror, her expression pinched with disapproval.

'Short hair is fast, Helen.'

Yes, Mother, she replied in her head. But it's my hair, and my life.

She met Madame Daphne's eye as she stood over her, scissors snapping expectantly a few inches from her ear.

'Do it,' she said.

Acknowledgements

First of all, a big thank you to my agent Caroline Sheldon and my editor Rosie de Courcy for taking a chance on me and letting me loose on the Nightingale Girls. I hope I've justified your faith in me!

I'm also grateful to the Royal College of Nursing Archives and to Graham Thurgood for allowing me to plunder his PhD research at Huddersfield University. And to all the real life nurses who have come forward to tell me their stories. I'd particularly like to thank Lucy Staples, and Alison Heath and her friends for a wonderful afternoon of tea and reminiscences. I look forward to another meeting!

Finally, I'd like to thank my husband Ken and my daughter Harriet for putting up with the despair and tantrums, my friends for not minding when I couldn't come out to play for months, and the team at *Your Local Link* magazine in York for knowing when not to ask how the book was coming along.

The publishers hope that this book has given you enjoyable reading. Large Print Books are especially designed to be as easy to see and hold as possible. If you wish a complete list of our books please ask at your local library or write directly to:

Magna Large Print Books
Magna House, Long Preston,
Skipton, North Yorkshire.
BD23 4ND

This Large Print Book for the partially sighted, who cannot read normal print, is published under the auspices of

THE ULVERSCROFT FOUNDATION